# The BATTLE FOR WONDLA

# SIMON & SCHUSTER
*presents*

# THE BATTLE FOR WONDLA

by

## TONY DITERLIZZI

*with illustrations
by the author*

SIMON & SCHUSTER

First published in Great Britain by Simon & Schuster UK Ltd, 2014
A CBS COMPANY

Originally published in the USA in 2014 by Simon & Schuster Books for Young
Readers, an imprint of Simon & Schuster Children's Division, New York.
This paperback edition published in 2015

1 3 5 7 9 10 8 6 4 2

Simon & Schuster UK Ltd
1st Floor, 222 Gray's Inn Road
London WC1X 8HB

www.simonandschuster.co.uk

Simon & Schuster Australia, Sydney
Simon & Schuster India, New Delhi

A CIP catalogue record for this book
is available from the British Library

HB ISBN 978-0-85707-303-7
Ebook ISBN 978-1-47112-274-3
PB ISBN 978-0-85707-304-4

Printed and bound in the UK by CPI Colour

*For
Angela and Sophia,
my WondLa*

# Contents

# PART II

For, in the final analysis,
our most basic common link
is that we all inhabit
this small planet.
We all breathe the same air.
We all cherish our children's future.
And we are all mortal.

—John F. Kennedy

# THE BATTLE FOR WONDLA

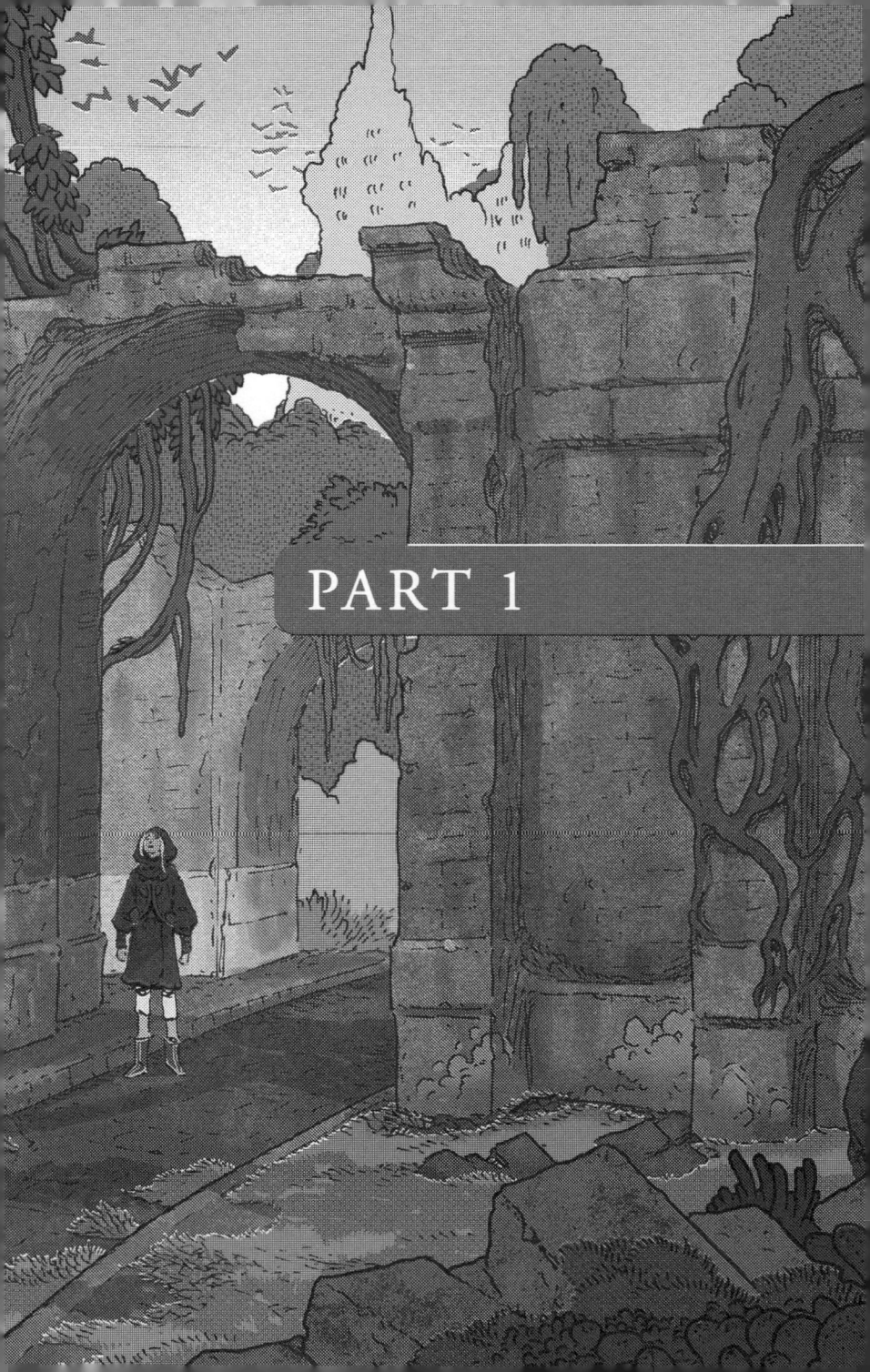

PART 1

## CHAPTER 1: HUNTED

# Eva Nine

could scarcely hear anything above her own ragged breathing. Her pale green eyes, wide and wild, searched for a clear path through the dense undergrowth of the Wandering Forest. Burning leg muscles carried her past fallen trees and over moss-laden stones.

"This way! Come on!" Eva shouted. Her instinct warned that her voice would give away her location, but she suspected it didn't matter. *The beast knows exactly where I am,* she thought.

Lagging behind Eva was the teenage pilot Hailey Turner. Eva ran back, seized Hailey by the hand, and yanked him along with her. They moved quickly through the dappled shadow of the canopy.

"We have to keep moving," she whispered hoarsely. "Let's go." She pushed aside a cluster of feathery blooms on waist-high stalks.

"How can you run so fast?" Hailey tried to catch his breath. "You're—"

A low snarl sliced through the stillness of the wood. Startled turnfins flapped away from the disruption. The beast was not far now.

"Over here!" Eva bolted toward a clearing where the trees thinned out. Here she and Hailey could make up more ground, but so too could the beast. She glanced over her shoulder and saw a blur of tawny fur with horns on its head. It bound through the thick underbrush as effortlessly as a spiderfish swimming through water, with its razor claws sending up leaves and bark in its wake.

"Can't you . . . ask this thing . . . to leave us alone?" Hailey asked between gasps. He would not be able to keep up this pace much longer.

"I've tried to, but it is not responding." For a moment Eva wondered if her newfound ability to communicate with all forest denizens had somehow vanished. But perhaps this creature simply did not want to talk—it wanted to eat.

Eva and Hailey dashed across the glade and back into the shadowy cover of the forest. She looked once more at their pursuer, but it was nowhere to be seen. Before Eva could turn around, she tripped headlong over a large fallen log. As she brushed dead leaves from her colorless hair, Eva realized she had landed next to a giant sundew bush. The plant's sticky stalks immediately bent and quivered in her direction.

Its voice entered her mind. *Let me touch you. Let me hold you.*

Eva scooted away from the sundew. Her abilities had not left her, after all.

"Are you okay?" Hailey climbed over the log.

"Shhh!" Eva grabbed the back of Hailey's utili-T-shirt and yanked him down to the ground. Together they crouched behind the rotting log. Eva noticed that the ground dipped underneath the log to form a small hollow. She began clawing the forest debris out from the hollow. "Get under here."

"But it will find—"

"Just do it," she hissed. Although she heard no sound, Eva knew the beast was nearby, stalking them.

Hailey grunted as he wedged himself into the hollow. Eva clambered up to stand on top of the log. Catching her breath, she scanned the forest but saw no movement.

The wind blew through the canopy above, causing the jigsaw shapes of the treetops to sway. Eva closed her eyes and took a deep breath. She could *feel* the energy that the plants and mosses gathered from the sunlight. She could sense the fear of the smaller animals hiding from the predator.

A twig snapped. Then, silence.

*Now!* A voice entered her mind. It may have been a turnfin or a tree, for all Eva knew, but it was all the warning she needed. As fast as a sandsniper, she dropped to the ground as the beast lunged at her from its hiding place. It flew over Eva's flattened body, over the log, and into the giant sundew.

"Be careful!" Eva said to Hailey. She scrambled over the log and pushed Hailey away from the trapped animal. The shaggy beast writhed in the sticky tentacles of the carnivorous plant. In minutes it was a tangled mass of fur and sap.

Though winded, Hailey seemed awestruck. "What is it?"

"I don't know. I've never seen anything like it before." Eva's heart was pounding from her near miss with the beast. She couldn't believe her trap had worked.

With the thick curved horns jutting from the back of its head, the beast thrashed at the tendrils of the sundew. Its hairless face was flush with anger.

*Let me hold you,* Eva heard the plant whisper to the beast. *I shall hold you within me forever.*

The beast roared in response.

"We should leave." Eva backed away from the trapped animal. "I don't want to be anywhere near here if it should free itself."

Hailey's gaze shifted between the beast and Eva. "What?" she asked.

"The way you stood your ground, then tricked that thing . . ."

Eva turned back to look at the trapped beast. "I . . . I'm sorry, Hailey. . . . I didn't know what else—"

"No, Eva." Hailey climbed up onto the log where Eva had stood, as if to reenact the scene. "That was . . . You were . . . amazing! I mean, look at those claws. It would have torn us to pieces and eaten us alive if it had caught us."

Eva couldn't look back at the beast. It was, after

all, a creature of the forest doing what it needed to survive. She climbed over the log and started back down the route they had taken. "Come on. Let's go."

Hailey took a last look at the beast before jogging up alongside Eva. "I wish I had my Omnipod. I would have loved to see what Identicapture thought of . . ."

*Wait.*

Another voice entered Eva's mind, muting out Hailey's words. Eva stopped and looked back at the sundew. The beast was no longer struggling. It let out a low growl. In that growl Eva heard words.

*Free me.*

"You'll kill us, then eat us," Eva spoke aloud to the creature.

"Eva?" Hailey stopped.

*Not eat you. Feed.*

"Okay, then you'll *feed* on us." Eva started back toward the beast.

"Eva, wait a nano." Hailey went to stop her.

*Not feed me. Feed my pups.*

"Feed your pups? Then you're a . . . you're their—"

*Mother.*

Eva put her head in her hands. "Of course," she whispered.

Hailey joined her atop the log. They both looked down at the beast. Piercing lemon eyes watched them, causing Eva's hair to stand on end.

"Eva, I don't know what this thing is telling you," Hailey said, "but we need to leave."

*Free me. I will leave.*

Eva stepped cautiously toward the beast. "You won't eat us?"

*I will not eat you.*

Hailey remained on top of the fallen log. "Um, I'm going to repeat what you just said two minutes ago about not wanting to be near here if this thing gets free."

"No eating? You promise?" Eva came closer to the beast. She could see the burns on its face where the sticky secretions of the sundew had begun to take effect. Eva knew the animal's predicament all too well. After all, she had been snared in the gooey grip of a giant sundew once before. Fortunately, her friend Rovender Kitt had come to cut Eva free before she'd become plant food.

*I will not eat you,* the beast said.

Hailey jumped down next to Eva.

*Eat him!*

The beast snapped opened its toothy jaws and spat a stream of brown liquid at Hailey. He threw up his hands to protect his face, but his forearms became covered in thick mucus.

Hailey groaned in pain and dropped to the ground. He began scraping the mucus off his arm and onto the log. "It's burning! It's burning! It's some kind of acid!"

Eva knelt down next to Hailey to inspect the wound. The smell of scorched hair and skin assaulted her nose. She stood up to face the forest.

"Someone—anyone—please help me! What cures the venom of this creature?" she called out to the forest.

The trees creaked in the breeze. Unseen insects chirped from their cover. Somewhere in the distance a turnfin called out.

Hailey was still conscious despite his fading pallor. Eva's mind raced. *Burns . . . burns . . . what would Rovender do for a burn?* She remembered the rope burn he'd suffered from Besteel's snare. *What did he use?*

Moss.

Eva located a large patch of rich green moss growing nearby on the forest floor. As she pulled a clump from the soil, water dribbled from the moss as if it were a sponge. *If it holds water like a sponge, perhaps it can also soak up liquids,* she thought. Eva wrung the clump of moss until it was dry. She knelt down next to Hailey and carefully placed the moss on his arm. "Press this against the burn," she said softly. "It may draw the poison out of your skin." Hailey moaned in reply and did as instructed.

"I hope this works." Eva wriggled her finger into a frayed hole in the sleeve of her coveralls. With a quick yank she tore off the cuff. "I have no idea what sort of venom this is." She began wrapping the fabric cuff around Hailey's arm, binding the moss to his wound.

"Not too tight!" he said, flinching.

"Sorry." Eva continued gingerly.

"There's never an Omnipod when you need one," he whispered with a weak smile.

"We're better without it. Trust me. Besides, it would have just slowed things down," Eva said. "Please initiate Individual Medical Assistance," she imitated the Omnipod's calm voice. She chuckled to herself while she kept wrapping Hailey's burns. "By the time I'd gone through all of that, your arms would have burned off."

"Well, keeping my arms would be good. Don't let me stop you," Hailey replied.

"Okay, sit still. I'm almost—"

*You live. I die.*

The trapped beast's voice drifted back into Eva's mind.

"How about: you live, I live?" Eva said aloud. She turned and shot a hateful glare at the animal.

From the sundew's stalked tentacles, digestive sap oozed to cover the beast's unmoving body. Its face now glistened in the afternoon light. Sap dripped down over the animal's eyes, causing them to close.

*You die. I live.*

The beast's words seemed different to Eva now. It was as if the voice of the beast had become the voice of the plant.

Eva turned away toward Hailey and tied off his binds. "Can you walk?"

"Yeah. I think so." Hailey winced as he sat up.

Eva helped him to stand. Together they hobbled away from the dying beast.

After hiking through the wood for some time in silence, Eva stopped and closed her eyes. She cocked her head, listening.

"What is it now?" Hailey glanced around with a worried look.

"Shhh," Eva said. "Before we leave here . . . I want to . . ." She focused with all of her senses, which came together as if to form a living entity. This entity zoomed through the brush and trees, like a bodiless flying eye, allowing Eva to see. Not only that, but she tasted the minerals of water as trees stretched their roots down into the damp soil. She felt the anticipation of several fledglings, still huddled in their nest with mouths open wide, as their father brought food to them. She hummed to the deep resonating sounds of something beyond her vision, a sound lower in pitch than all the creatures of the forest. Still, she kept searching through the forest . . .

"Are you okay?" Hailey gently shook Eva.

Her eyes fluttered open and focused on Hailey's concerned face. "I'm fine. I was trying . . . to locate the cubs."

"The cubs?" Hailey gave a puzzled look. "Wait a nano. The cubs of that . . . thing?" He pointed back from where they'd traveled. "The horrible spitting monster thing that just tried to kill us?"

Eva looked down. "Yes. I just didn't want them to . . . die. Without a mother."

"Oh, I see." Hailey folded his arms, but the movement caused him to cringe in pain. "So you want to rescue them so they can grow up and be a *whole pack* of horrible spitting monsters that want to kill us. Is that it?"

"I'm sorry, Hailey. I . . . I guess you're right," Eva said, embarrassed. "Come on. Let's go back to camp."

"No rescuing spitting-monster babies?" Hailey wagged a finger at her playfully.

Eva nodded. "I promise."

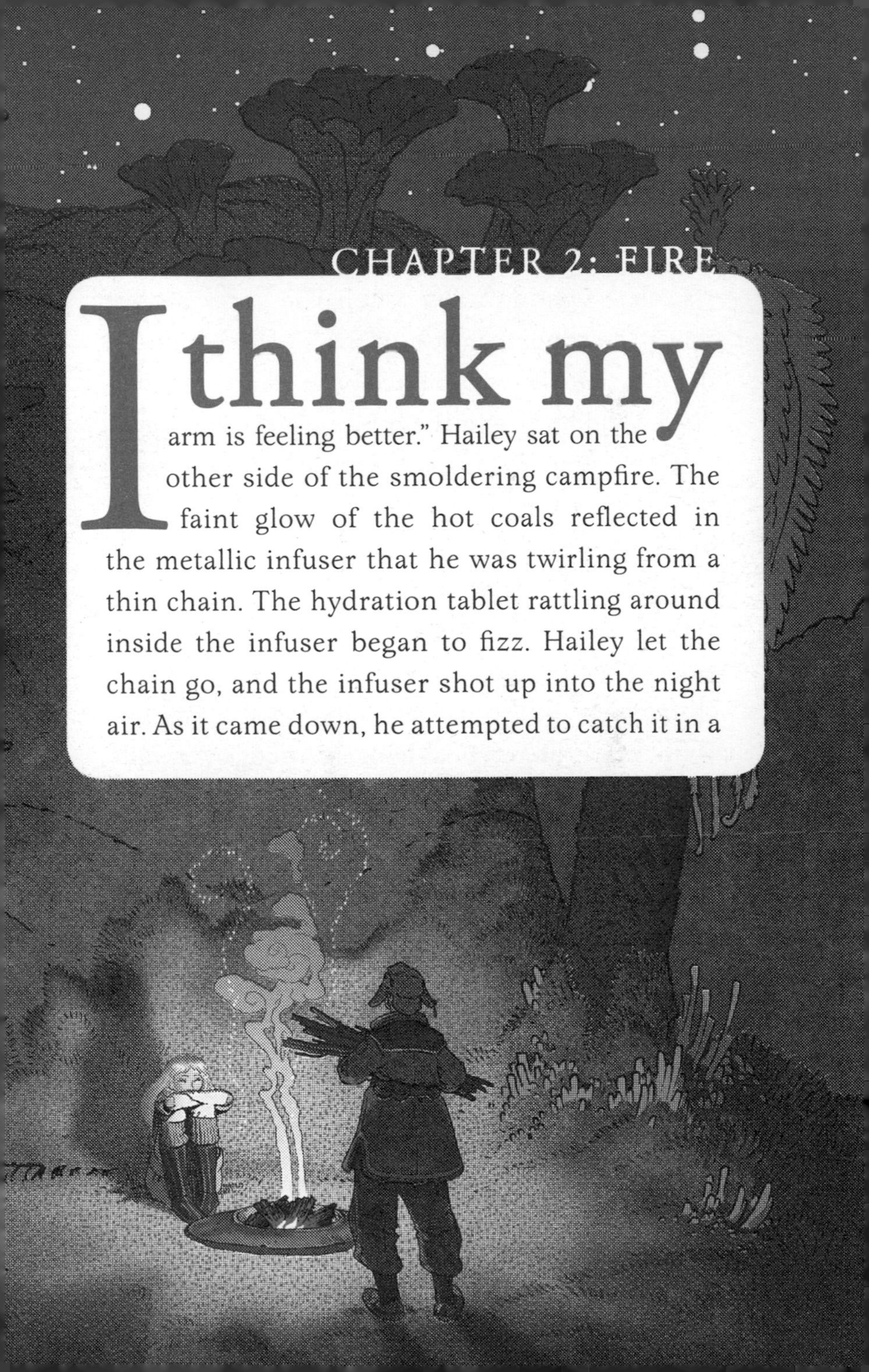

# CHAPTER 2: FIRE

I think my arm is feeling better." Hailey sat on the other side of the smoldering campfire. The faint glow of the hot coals reflected in the metallic infuser that he was twirling from a thin chain. The hydration tablet rattling around inside the infuser began to fizz. Hailey let the chain go, and the infuser shot up into the night air. As it came down, he attempted to catch it in a

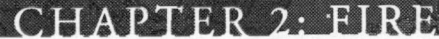

widemouthed container. The infuser ball landed on the ground next to him, sending little droplets of water in every direction. "Okay. Maybe not," he added with a lopsided grin.

"You're wasting water when you show off like that." The condescension in Eva's voice concealed the fact that she would have been impressed with Hailey had he caught the infuser in the container.

"Come on. You're not dazzled by my awe-inspiring water collecting technique?" Hailey dusted off the infuser and dropped it into the container. "I'm just going to boil it for crystal coffee." He pulled a crumbled packet from his trouser pocket and shook it. The New Attica logo shimmered on the packet's label in the firelight. With his grungy sneakboot he nudged a half-burned log back into the fire. A flurry of embers billowed into the night. "You want some?"

"No, thanks. I'm okay." Eva sat with her legs tucked up against her chest and her arms folded over her knees. Her clothing, though still colorless from her encounter with the spirit of the forest, was now covered in smudges, scuffs, and stains from outdoor living.

"You haven't eaten or drunk much since we've been out here." Hailey reached over and grabbed a dead branch. He snapped it into smaller pieces and tossed them onto the fire before reaching for more.

"Not too big," Eva said in a cautious tone.

"Yeah, yeah." Hailey grabbed the sticks. "I got it under control."

"I'm serious." Eva's voice was firm. "You remember what I said?"

Hailey gave pause. Eva could see the concern etched in his dirty face as he studied her in the growing firelight. The look of concern gave way to one of frustration.

"I remember." Hailey dropped the wood back to the ground.

"I just don't want—"

"Anyone to find us," he finished her sentence. "I know. I know. You've been saying that for the past two days since we've been in hiding." He set his water container onto the fire to boil. "We haven't seen Cadmus's warbot army—or anyone for that matter—since we've been out here. Aside from man-eating monsters, I don't think anyone is going—"

"I don't care!" Eva barked. "Just trust me."

"Trust you about what?" Hailey gestured to the forest around them. "We are out in the middle of nowhere."

"I know," Eva replied. "It's just . . . I just . . ."

"What?" Hailey stood, clearly exasperated. "Tell me what's going on."

Eva buried her head in her folded arms. She said nothing.

Hailey sighed hotly. "Whatever! I'm going to get more wood." He pointed to a nearby wandering tree. "And tell your *friends* not to worry. It will be *dead* wood." He adjusted his flight cap on his shorn head and stomped off into the night.

Eva watched the flames dance along the length of the freshly added firewood. In no time at all the fire was ablaze. Before long the wood would be consumed. It would become ash. Dust. Just like the ancient ruins . . . and Solas. Just like Muthr. Nadeau. Huxley. Even the beast trapped in the sundew. Just like everything Eva had ever cared about. *If I had the WondLa with me now*, she thought, *I'd toss it into the flames too.*

Back at the ancient ruins Eva had almost thrown the crumbling picture into the fire. But Rovender had stopped her.

"Not that," he had said. "You must honor Otto, myself, and your mother by seeing to it that you find what it is that you have searched for."

That picture—a young girl arm in arm with

her smiling robo
field of red flowers—
for. To her it represente
represented a loving family w
warmth of a secure home.

She now knew it was only a picture
lost fairy tale, left behind by a long-lost sist
now knew that achieving her goal—finding h
WondLa—might never happen.

"What does it matter now?" Eva had said to
Rovender.

"Now is when it matters most, Eva Nine."

As usual Rovender had been right. It did matter
more now than ever. Eva couldn't tell Hailey. But
she knew, *she could sense*, the intruders lurking
about in the Wandering Forest looking for her,
hunting her down as Besteel had once done. *They
will never hurt the ones I love*, she thought, *because
they will never find them.*

*And they shall never find me.*

## CHAPTER 3: WRECK

# He's taking

*wing.* The message drifted into Eva's mind, rousing her from sleep. She blinked her eyes open and focused. A gaggle of turnfins peered down at Eva from their perch in the wandering tree just a few branches up from where she slept. The morning sun struggled to light the forest through a gray blanket of overcast sky. Next to the smoking campfire Hailey was getting dressed. He pulled a brown oversize retriever jacket over his sinewy frame. It was just the same sort of jacket that Rovender had worn when Eva had first encountered the Cærulean. A frayed but colorful shoulder patch—an emblem of an airship with white wings—flapped in an animated fashion with each move of Hailey's arm.

Eva climbed down from the large cuplike leaves that held her. "Where are you going?"

"I just remembered that I have a spare Omnipod on the *Bijou*, and I need it." Hailey gathered his few belongings and stuffed them into the oversize pockets of his jacket.

"What for? Why?" Eva pulled back several strands of her long hair. The chill of the early morning caused her to shiver.

Hailey did not answer. He rolled up his sleeves and removed the makeshift bandages from his forearms. Patches of red welts crisscrossed his skin where the beast's venom had burned him.

"The moss worked," Eva said, trying to keep the conversation going.

"It did." Hailey rolled his sleeves back down. "Eva, I feel indebted to you for rescuing me from the *Bijou* . . . among other things. But I can't just sit out here and wait to be eaten by another monster in this forest. I have to go." He donned his faded flight cap, then pulled several packets of nutriment pellets from his pocket.

Eva's pulse quickened. "So you're going to just leave me again, is that it?"

Hailey placed a couple of the packets in Eva's hand. "Don't worry. I'll be back. I need to contact Vanpa. I need to know if he's okay and what's going on with the invasion. I'm worried that the aliens will retaliate. I'm sure he's worried too." Hailey squeezed a button on his jacket, and it zipped itself up. "And I'd bet that Rovender is probably worried about you."

Eva watched Hailey shake the pellets from one of his packets into his dirty palm. "Don't go. Those ghost sand-snipers . . . you know, the ones that were tearing apart the *Bijou*? They are still out there."

"Okay, fine." Hailey crunched a mouthful of nutriment pellets. "Then come with me."

Eva shook her head. "I can't."

"I don't understand what is wrong with you!" Hailey threw up his hands in exasperation. "Let's just go and get the Omnipod."

The grease and oil that usually smudged Hailey's

face had been replaced with dirt and ash. Out from the shadowy confines of his ship, his eyes appeared more hazel than umber.

Eva looked away from him. "You don't get it!" She balled her hands into fists. "I failed! I couldn't help Arius. I couldn't get Hostia her home back. I couldn't stop Loroc or Cadmus. I . . . I failed." Eva blinked back the tears from her eyes. She didn't want Hailey to see her cry.

"So you failed," he said. "So what? Big deal. Do you know how many times I tried to fix the *Bijou* before it could—"

"I'm not a ship! You can't just *fix* me."

"Fine, Eva! But what I need to do is figure out a way to get us out of this mess and somewhere safe. That's why I am going back to the *Bijou* to get that Omnipod. So, are you coming with me or not?"

Eva shook her head and turned away.

"Great!" Hailey grumbled. "I'll be back later." He trudged off into the forest.

"Great! Go!" Eva shoved the nutriment packets into her pocket. She crawled back up into the bough of the wandering tree to sulk.

The base of the large leaves formed a basin which held a clear puddle of water. Eva scooted down and cupped the water in her hands. Before washing her face, she looked down at her reflection in the water. Old words came to her mind. *Leadership is not inherited. It is earned through action. You are a leader, Eva Nine. A hero.*

"I'm no hero," she said to her reflection, and splashed the water.

From above came the familiar call of an airwhale. Far in the distance the call was answered from others in the vicinity floating high over the forest. Soon a melancholy chorus rang out in the skies. Though haunting, it somehow reassured Eva.

"They are happier when they are together. They are safe. They are strong," Eva whispered. Overhead the mighty whales soared over the treetops, temporarily blocking the dim rays of the morning sun. Several young whales called out as they floated past. She listened to their song: *Together. Safe. Strong.*

Eva finished washing up. She ascended to the topmost bough of the wandering tree. Over the forest the air-whales continued their morning flight. *Let's go get him,* she thought to the tree. On its many prehensile roots, the wandering tree lurched forward and shuffled off after Hailey.

❧

Eva found him resting at the edge of the Wandering Forest.

He looked up and grinned. "She arrives. And in her personal forest gondola."

She returned the smile. "I figure someone needs to protect you." Eva climbed down from her perch in the tree. Her sneakboots crunched on the gravelly ground as she approached Hailey. "It might as well be this reboot."

"Sounds like a good deal to me." He offered Eva his water container.

Eva took a sip. "Hailey, I can trust you, right?"

"Come on, Eva, after what we've been through?" Hailey plucked the water container from Eva's hands. He hopped up onto one of the lower boughs of the tree. "You're not gonna bring up that bum deal with Cadmus again, are you? I told you I didn't know what he was up to."

"No. I know." Eva's voice was low. She walked over and leaned on the tree's trunk, next to Hailey. "I want you to know why I can't return to Faunas to be with Rovee and why it may be dangerous for you to return to your camp."

Hailey's grin disappeared. "Go on."

"After the humans invade Solas, Loroc is going to somehow trick Cadmus . . . then kill him."

A look of alarm grew on Hailey's face. "The alien adviser guy is gonna kill Cadmus? Why?"

Eva shrugged her shoulders.

"How do you know?"

Eva picked at her fingernails. "He told me . . . right before he tried to kill *me*."

Hailey pulled off his flight cap and ran his fingers over his fuzzy head. "He *told* you? And you are the only one who knows?"

Eva nodded. "I think so."

Hailey said nothing. It was clear he was trying to put all the pieces into place.

Eva continued. "After we fled from the *Bijou*'s life capsule, Cadmus sent a warbot to track us down. It nearly killed us all." She stifled a shudder. The conjured vision of Eva Eight's body convulsing from electrified SHOCdarts would not leave.

"I remember seeing those warbots loading up in the hangar," said Hailey. "They looked like bad news."

"When I got to Lacus, Cadmus's warbots had already invaded." Eva turned and gazed out at the barren salt flats, her mind heavy with dark memories. "They destroyed the village. They tore apart the homes—the lives—of the Halcyonus that lived there. The warbots didn't care if the

villagers got in the way. They just swept them aside."

Hailey stood next to Eva. "I'm sorry."

Eva kept her gaze on the horizon. "There are warbots in the forest right now. I can *feel* the fear they're causing the plants and animals. These warbots are searching for something."

"You?"

"Yes, me."

Though the facts were bleak, Eva somehow felt better sharing everything she knew with Hailey. It was as if a heavy burden had been lifted from her spirit.

Hailey put his arm around Eva. "Well, then, that's all the more reason for us to leave. Loroc can't find you if you're not here."

The mention of Loroc's name brought forth his parting words to Eva: *I do not fall by your hand. You, however, shall fall by mine.*

"He'll find me." Eva turned back toward the wandering tree. "It's just a matter of time." She hoisted herself up onto a branch and offered a hand to help Hailey. Both climbed up to the topmost bough, and the tree began moving.

As the wind tousled her hair, Eva watched the forest give way to a flat barren plain. Somewhere in the distance lay the wreckage of the *Bijou*.

# CHAPTER 4: CONTROL

The turnfin perched on Eva's shoulder gobbled down the last few nutriment pellets from the palm of her hand.

"You better stop feeding your breakfast to these birds." Hailey smirked. "I don't have a whole lot of pellets, and I don't know how many we'll find back at the ship."

Eva kept her focus on the bird. "I'll be all right."

"What do you want with a bird anyway?" Hailey leaned over to get a closer look.

"I'm asking for a favor." Eva stroked the turnfin's sleek plumage. It gave a low cluck and then took flight. Eva and Hailey shielded their eyes from the sun to watch. The turnfin flapped its triple pair of wings to join the flock of other birds circling high above the tree. After several aerobatic loops the lone turnfin broke away from the others. It began winging west toward the Wandering Forest.

"He's going to check on Rovender," Eva said, keeping an eye on the bird as it soared over the treetops.

"That's amazing."

Eva turned to him. "What?"

"How you can now understand animals and trees and stuff." A smile curled at the corner of Hailey's mouth. "You *are* better than an Omnipod." He kept his gaze on the diminishing silhouette of the turnfin. "Do you hear every bird and animal all the time?" He leaned close to her.

"Not if I don't want to." Eva pulled out the strands of hair that had blown into the corners of her mouth. She separated several more pieces and began to braid them together. "It's like everything alive gives off a kind of frequency, a pulse, that I can feel."

"I get it. Like an electric current," Hailey said.

Eva unzipped a pocket in her coveralls and pulled out a handful of dried seedpods that she'd collected from the forest. She began braiding these pods into her hair. "If I shut off everything— you know, like what I'm actually seeing and hearing—then I can link to that frequency and understand it. It was hard at first. I couldn't really control it."

"But now you can?"

"Now I can." Eva remembered her attempts to communicate with the deadly sand-snipers . . . and how badly that could have ended.

"I know what you mean. It's sort of like when I'm flying." Hailey gestured to his ears. "If I turn my music up really loud, I just feel more attuned to the controls of the ship. I'm not as distracted by my own thoughts, you know?"

Eva smiled. She doubted that was anything like her abilities, but at least Hailey was trying . . . and was less annoying.

Hailey gazed up to the sky in a wistful way. "Boy, I do miss that ship."

"I'm sorry. She was a good ship."

"In some ways I'm glad you rescued me in the dark of night. I couldn't see how bad the damage was," Hailey said. "But I guess I'll be seeing it anyways."

The wandering tree creaked and came to a stop. Eva looked down and saw that they were at the edge of a shallow lake.

Hailey appeared alarmed. "What's going on?"

"Don't worry. The tree just needs a water break."
Eva stood and stretched. She scanned the horizon
and saw that they were surrounded by flat plain.
*There is no place to hide should we be discovered,*
she thought, and climbed down from her perch to
the shore below.

Hailey followed her. "So we just wait here?"

Eva sat on the ground and pulled off her sneakboots. She got up, walked to the shore, and dipped
her toes into the water. It was shallow enough that
the sun had warmed it, like a bath. She closed her
eyes. Like the tree submerging its roots, she could
feel her body rejuvenate from the water. She listened to the vibration—the energy—of the lake.
Within it Eva could feel the movement of many
fish and crustaceans. She remembered the gigantic aquatic plant that had nearly killed Rovender,
but there was nothing like that present. On the
far shore she sensed two tall animals—possibly
Cærulean munt-runners—drinking. Eva could
barely make out their birdlike bipedal shapes.
They appeared unaccompanied. She attempted
communication with them but received no
response. Something scuttled across Eva's toes,
breaking her link to the munt-runners. A sandy-
patterned spiderfish, about the size of her hand,

crawled on elongate fingerlike fins through the shallows.

"Hello there," Eva whispered to the fish. She knelt down slowly and steadily, like the movement of a wandering tree. The spiderfish remained in place. Eva dipped her fingers into the water and stroked its smooth sides. She could sense the animal's thoughts.

*It moves. I grab. I eat. It moves. I grab. I eat.*

Eva watched the fish dart after a crab. She waded after it. Like the fish, she felt pangs in her stomach. For the first time since she'd escaped from Lacus, Eva was hungry.

Hailey called from the shore. "Hey, what're you doing?"

"Trying to get lunch." She kept her focus on the fish.

Hailey produced several packets of nutriment pellets from his jacket pocket. "I've got you covered. What flavor do you want?"

"I can't stand the taste of those pellets. They're just chemicals." Eva knelt back down in the water. "But I am starving." She stood. In her hands she gripped the wriggling spiderfish. "Want some?"

"Uh, really?" Hailey popped a handful of pellets into his mouth.

"Yes. Really." Eva brought the fish to shore and set it down at his feet.

Hailey grimaced at the peculiar spiderfish gasping for air. "So is it going to be tough for you to eat something you can now talk to?"

Eva wiped her hands on the knees of her coveralls. "To quote Rovender, 'Its energy and spirit will replenish mine. I respect this, and I shall enjoy my meal,'" she said.

"Better enjoy your meal before it crawls away." Hailey pointed. The spiderfish was scurrying back to the water.

Eva chased the fish down and retrieved it. "Do you have some sort of cutting device?"

"I've got a small laser-cutter used for splitting electrical wires." Hailey pulled the tool from his pocket. "It even has a penlight in the handle."

"That works," she said, and took the laser-cutter.

"I've eaten some strange stuff in the outlands where we live," Hailey said, "but I never thought I'd eat raw spiderfish." They were seated in a low perch on the wandering tree, shaded from the warm afternoon sun. "I haven't been this full in a long time . . . though, it is weird to think that we just ate a dead animal."

"My sister felt the same way," Eva said. She watched the lake disappear on the horizon as the tree shuffled onward. She had hoped to see the pair of munt-runners, but they had moved on.

"Eva Eight?" Hailey yanked off his sneakboots and kicked his feet up onto the edge of the large hardened leaves. "You haven't mentioned her since we've been out here. Did she not make it?"

"She . . . decided to stay behind." Eva looked west toward the green line of the forest. At least her sister was deep in the Heart of the Wandering Forest, safe from Cadmus's warbots.

"Oh." Hailey seemed puzzled by Eva's vague answer. "So she's okay?"

"I think she's found a good place to be."

Hailey folded his arms behind his head and leaned back against the trunk of the tree. "I know she was real worried about you."

Eva looked over at him.

"She told me when we were escaping in the *Bijou*." Hailey slid his flight cap over his eyes, ready to nap. "She said you were all she cared about in the world."

"I . . . I care about her too."

Hailey chuckled from under his cap. "You don't sound too convinced."

"She wanted to move back into our old home and live as if the world hadn't changed, and that just wasn't going to happen," Eva said in a flat tone.

"I don't blame you," said Hailey. "I was just asking."

Eva scooted next to him. From around her neck she pulled out a locket—a small clear vial—that had been a gift from the Cærulean shaman, Soth. Inside was soil from Soth's home planet and, even more special, an orchidlike bloom given to Eva from her sister after Eva Eight had been transformed into a human-tree.

Thinking back, the encounter seemed like the stuff of nightmares. But Eva knew it had happened. She blurted out, "Remember the Vitae Virus generator?"

"That device that rebooted the planet? You guys were talking about that on the ship." Hailey kept the cap over his eyes.

"Well, I knew where it was. Eight became crazy—obsessed—with finding it before Cadmus. She forced me, at gunpoint, to take her to the generator in the Heart of the forest."

"And you did it?" Hailey lifted up the bill of his cap to look at Eva.

"I did it." Eva rubbed her hands over her sides, where she'd once had broken ribs.

"Well, that is a little over the top. But I can see why she wanted it." Hailey slouched back down and adjusted the cap back over his face.

"What? You're siding with her!"

"I didn't say that." Hailey interlaced his fingers and rested his hands on his chest. "I just think your sister wanted to take control of something—anything—in her life. The truth is, Cadmus controlled both your lives since you were hatched from test tubes. But somehow you, Eva, were able to break away from that control."

The truth was, everything in Eva's life now seemed beyond her control—the invasion of Lacus and Solas, the animosity she'd received from the fleeing Halcyonus, her failure to warn Arius. It had caused Eva to feel helpless, frustrated, and angry.

She kissed the locket and tucked it back into her coveralls. "I forgive you, Sister," she whispered.

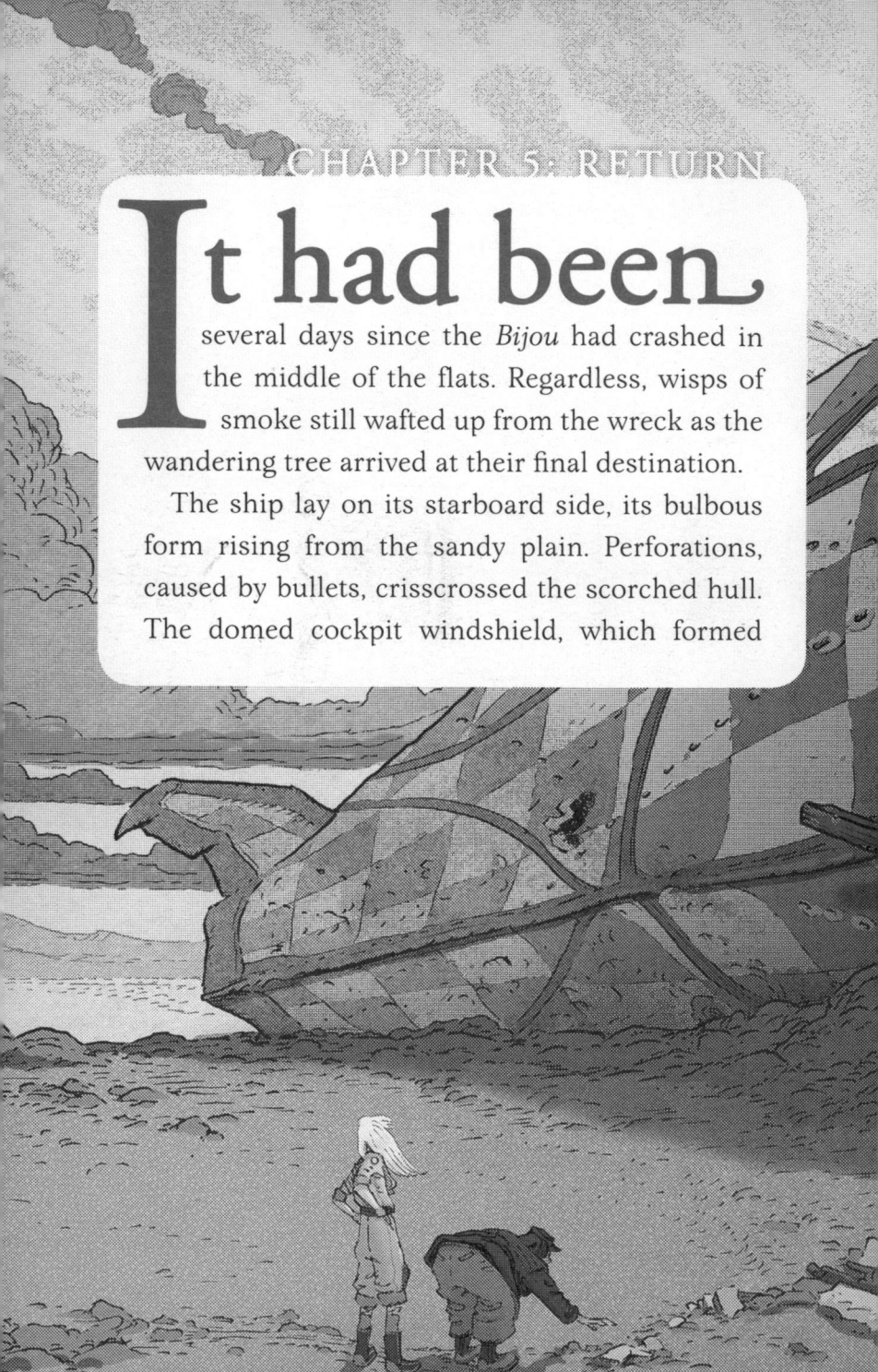

# It had been

several days since the *Bijou* had crashed in the middle of the flats. Regardless, wisps of smoke still wafted up from the wreck as the wandering tree arrived at their final destination.

The ship lay on its starboard side, its bulbous form rising from the sandy plain. Perforations, caused by bullets, crisscrossed the scorched hull. The domed cockpit windshield, which formed

the nose of the ship, had loosened from the wide cowling that had kept it secure. As they neared, Eva watched several creatures, smaller than turnfins, fly in and out of the wreck through the broken windshield.

"Oh no! My poor ship." Hailey groaned, and climbed down from the tree. He stood for a moment taking in the battered remains, then bent over and studied something half buried at his feet. Hailey picked up an L-shaped hunk of machinery and frowned. "All my hard work. Even the pitot tube is busted," he muttered, and flung the piece of wreckage back to the ground.

Eva joined him at the nose of the *Bijou*. Her broken reflection greeted her from the cracked cockpit windshield. *I'm still a dirty disheveled mess*, she thought.

"I'm sorry you lost her," Eva said as she looked over at Hailey.

His eyes remained fixed on the broken hull. "Me too," he said. Gusts of wind, rushing over the open plain, made the wreck creak and moan in protest.

Eva remembered the dismantled airship back in the cavernous hangar where Hailey lived. She figured he had built the *Bijou* from scratch. "To be honest," said Eva, "I'm amazed you didn't crash—er . . . land sooner. How did you end up way out here?"

"After I jettisoned you guys in the life capsule, I flew right smack into the middle of a mega-pod of air-whales. The warships wouldn't fly into the pod, probably because those whales are bigger than the ships. I bet the warships use a collision-avoidance system of some sort to stay clear of other flying objects. Especially objects that are larger than they are." Hailey picked up another small unidentifiable scrap of wreckage. He turned it over in his hands, seemingly in thought, and then put it into his pocket.

"I remember seeing some air-whales after we landed," Eva said.

"I stayed close with a group that broke off and veered toward the forest. I remembered Huxley saying that Lacus was somewhere east of the forest, so I went as far as the *Bijou* could carry me." Hailey reached out and traced his fingers over the ship's name painted on the pockmarked nose. "She was a good ship."

Eva went to place a sympathetic hand on Hailey's shoulder but gave pause. A chorus of high-pitched squeaks chattered overhead. More flying creatures fluttered to and from the cockpit. "Uh-oh." Eva pointed to the cockpit. "I think knifejacks have decided to roost here. We need to be careful."

"Knifejacks?" Hailey watched the colony flying into the ship. "Oh yeah, we had those living in the cave back at camp. They're kind of cute and furry, right?"

"No, not really." Eva remembered her encounter with the temperamental creatures when she and Rovender were hiding from Besteel back at the ancient ruins.

"Well, if you can keep them occupied with your 'powers,' I'll go get what we came here for." Hailey led Eva around the nose of the ship toward the belly.

Parked next to the opened loading ramp of the *Bijou* was a large, floating covered wagon. Crates from the *Bijou*'s cargo hold had been stacked around the ramshackle craft, and panels from the ship's hull were arranged on all sides to provide shelter. The embers of a cooking fire smoldered at the center of a camp.

"Get back," Eva whispered, and grabbed Hailey by the arm.

Hailey pulled free from Eva's grasp. "Nobody's taking anything from my ship." He stomped toward the camp. "Who's here? Come out!"

Eva crouched down under the nose of the *Bijou*,

closed her eyes, and focused. *What is hiding on the ship?* She could sense a large congregation of knifejacks roosting inside the wreck. Otherwise, there seemed to be no other creatures in the near vicinity.

"Eva, come here," Hailey called out.

She slunk into the camp, fearful that a warbot— or Loroc himself—would jump out.

Peeking under the canopy that stretched over the hull of the wagon, Eva realized she had seen vehicles similar to it before. "This could be from Solas," she said. It was hard to find any indentifying marks under the cargo of crates, baskets, and barrels that overloaded the transport. These containers were festooned with a myriad of found objects. Broken bottles, rusted machinery, and discarded pieces of tech adorned every square centimeter. A wind chime, hanging from one of the bows that supported the canopy, tinkled in the breeze. Eva recognized the chimes as forks and spoons. The Dynastes Corporation logo was stamped into the handle of each polished utensil, just like those from Eva's Sanctuary.

"I don't think anybody is here," Hailey said.

Eva nodded. "For the moment."

"This looks to be some sort of salvager." Hailey

inspected the open crates from his ship. "Whoever it is, they've gone through all of my stuff!"

"Do you see your Omnipod?" Eva peered into a thin-wired cage. Within it several knifejacks hung from the top in their usual upside-down position. The small creatures watched Eva with beady eyes set on the ends of long eyestalks, giving the impression of the holograms she had seen of crustaceans. Like crustaceans, the creatures had an exoskeleton and multiple clawed legs, though the front pair had evolved into wings. One of the knifejacks let out a chirrup from a serrated beak.

"No Omnipods." Hailey stepped up onto a stack of crates that formed makeshift steps to the open hatch leading into the *Bijou*'s hold. "Hopefully, my stash wasn't found." He crawled through the hatch and into the ship. "Keep an eye out, will you? I'll be right back."

"Stay out of the cockpit," said Eva.

"Oh, right. The knife-things," Hailey's voice echoed from the inside.

"Yes. The 'knife-things.'" She put a finger into the cage and called to the knifejacks. Faster than a blink, one snapped at her finger. "Ouch!" Eva watched a scarlet drop of blood bead on her fingertip. She put her finger into her mouth.

There was movement inside the ship.

"Everything okay?" Eva called out.

"Yeah. Just . . . moving . . . stuff." Hailey grunted between words.

Eva rubbed her finger. "Do you need a hand?"

"No. I got it. I'm good." Something inside obviously fell over, from the racket emanating from the ship. "Sheesa! What a mess!"

Eva combed through the crates. Most were filled with machinery and ship parts. She discovered a bundle of blankets and an all-weather poncho. "This we can use," she said to herself, and deactivated the life-monitoring patch. A shoulder pocket on the opposite arm held hydration tablets, several Sustibars, and a phosphorescent liquid light pen. As she pulled the drab poncho over her head, Eva sensed something. *Munt-runners?*

A loud crash inside the *Bijou* was followed by a cry from Hailey. Instantly Eva's senses were flooded with the same message.

*Danger. Intruder. Danger. Intruder. Danger. Intruder. Danger. Intruder,* cried the knifejacks inside the ship.

The knifejacks in the cage joined in the chorus.

*Danger. Intruder. Danger. Intruder. Danger. Intruder. Danger. Intruder.*

Eva ran up into the hold. Chittering cries reverberated throughout the entire ship.

*Danger. Intruder. Danger. Intruder. Danger. Intruder. Danger. Intruder.*

Hailey jumped down from the ship's galley and bolted toward Eva. He swatted at the hundreds of knifejacks diving and biting at him.

*Danger. Intruder. Danger. Intruder. Danger. Intruder. Danger. Intruder.*

The alarm of the knifejacks overwhelmed Eva, preventing her from breaking the connection with them. Before she could get out of the way, a flailing Hailey ran right into her. Both tumbled from the *Bijou's* hold onto the ground below. Eva scrambled to her feet and dashed away from the chaos, with Hailey right behind her.

*Danger. Intruder. Danger. Intruder. Danger. Intruder. Danger. Intruder.*

The cries assaulted Eva's ears. She shook her head in an attempt to disconnect her senses from the swarm. Although most knifejacks returned to the ship, several angry individuals still gave chase. Eva and Hailey ducked around the nose of the ship. As they rounded the cockpit, they lurched to a halt at the loud, sonic *WOOM* that erupted over their heads. Three knifejacks fell from the sky to the ground at Eva's feet. She knelt down to inspect the creatures, no longer able to hear their voices. Hailey tapped Eva on the shoulder and pointed.

On the other side of the *Bijou*, a grotesque heavyset alien with bright blue wattles stood between two horned munt-runners. His boomrod, ornate and polished, was aimed directly at Eva.

"No one-you moves and no one gets hurt-killed," he said from his tusked mouth. Eva tapped the vocal transcoder in her pocket. It seemed to be performing erratically its task of translating the alien's heavy accent.

Hailey pointed an accusatory finger at the alien. "Why don't you put that thing away, and then *you* won't get hurt!"

"Hailey, I—"

"No, Eva. That is my ship! And my stuff," yelled Hailey.

"You-human leave it. You-human lose it," said the alien in a matter-of-fact tone. As he approached, Eva heard the haunting familiar hum of his charging boomrod.

Hailey yanked his flight cap from his head and balled it tight in his fist. He spoke between clenched teeth. "I may have left it, but now I am back to claim what's mine."

"No. Now it-ship is mine." The alien sneered and aimed his boomrod at Hailey.

Hailey seized the muzzle of the gun and pushed it away. He stomped up to the alien and stood toe-to-toe with him. "Hop into that junk sled of yours and get outta here!"

The alien replied in an icy tone, "I will leave-go when I am ready. I will seize-take what I want. You can do nothing to stop me."

Eva tried to reach out with her senses to the alien, hoping she could communicate with his thoughts; but it was to no avail. *He is not of the forest,* she thought. It seemed clear that there were limits to her abilities.

"There are two of us." Hailey puffed out his chest. "You have no idea what we can stop."

"You cannot stop this!" The alien jammed the boomrod's muzzle into Hailey's ribs, causing him to fall to his knees. "Enough bluffing. I do not want to hurt-kill, but if you two don't go, you leave me with no choice-option."

Eva stood over Hailey and held up her palm. "I am Eva. Eva Nine."

The alien blinked. "That is a Cærulean greeting-welcome."

"Yes, I know." Eva kept her voice calm and stood

still. "We are friends of the Cæruleans and their leader, Antiquus."

"You-humans are friends with the Cæruleans?" The alien clucked. "I do not buy-believe it."

"I think you are friends with them too," said Eva.

"You-human think so? Why is that?"

"You have a pair of Cærulean munt-runners." Eva pointed at the two mounts. "Judging from their markings, I'd say they came from Faunas."

The alien lowered his weapon. He looked over at his munt-runners, then back at Eva. "I barter-trade for them in Solas. But, yes, they come from that Cærulean village."

Eva gestured at Hailey. "We have come from there too. And we have friends there now who are worried about us."

"Friends? The friends who-that destroyed Lacus and invaded Solas?" The alien lifted the boomrod once more and aimed it at Eva. "I see-witness what your friends can do."

"We are not part of that," Hailey said in a calm tone, similar to Eva's. He slowly rose to his feet.

"Really? Is this not a warship-deathship used for invasion?" The alien pointed at the *Bijou* with the boomrod.

"No," Eva replied. "We were not part of the

invasion. We were trying to stop it. We were on our way to Lacus to warn the Halcyonus and Arius."

"Arius?" The alien gave pause and studied Eva. "How is it that you-human know of Arius?"

"I stayed with the Halcyonus," said Eva. She counted off on her fingers, "I know Arius, I know Zin, I know—"

"Zin! You know where curator Zin is now-currently?" The alien's wattles trembled.

"Right this minute? No," said Eva. "I met him only once at the Royal Museum."

"The museum. Where do you-human think all this artifact-stuff is going?" The alien gestured to the crates surrounding his camp.

Eva remembered Zin explaining that the artifacts in the museum had been obtained by outside help, from those traveling from the ancient ruins. "You're one of Zin's explorers. You sell these items to the museum, right?"

"He's a junk dealer?" Hailey spat.

"Treasure hunter-finder," the alien corrected him. The alien turned off his boomrod and holstered it. "I am me-Caruncle. Obtainer of fine antiquities for Her Majesty's royal collection."

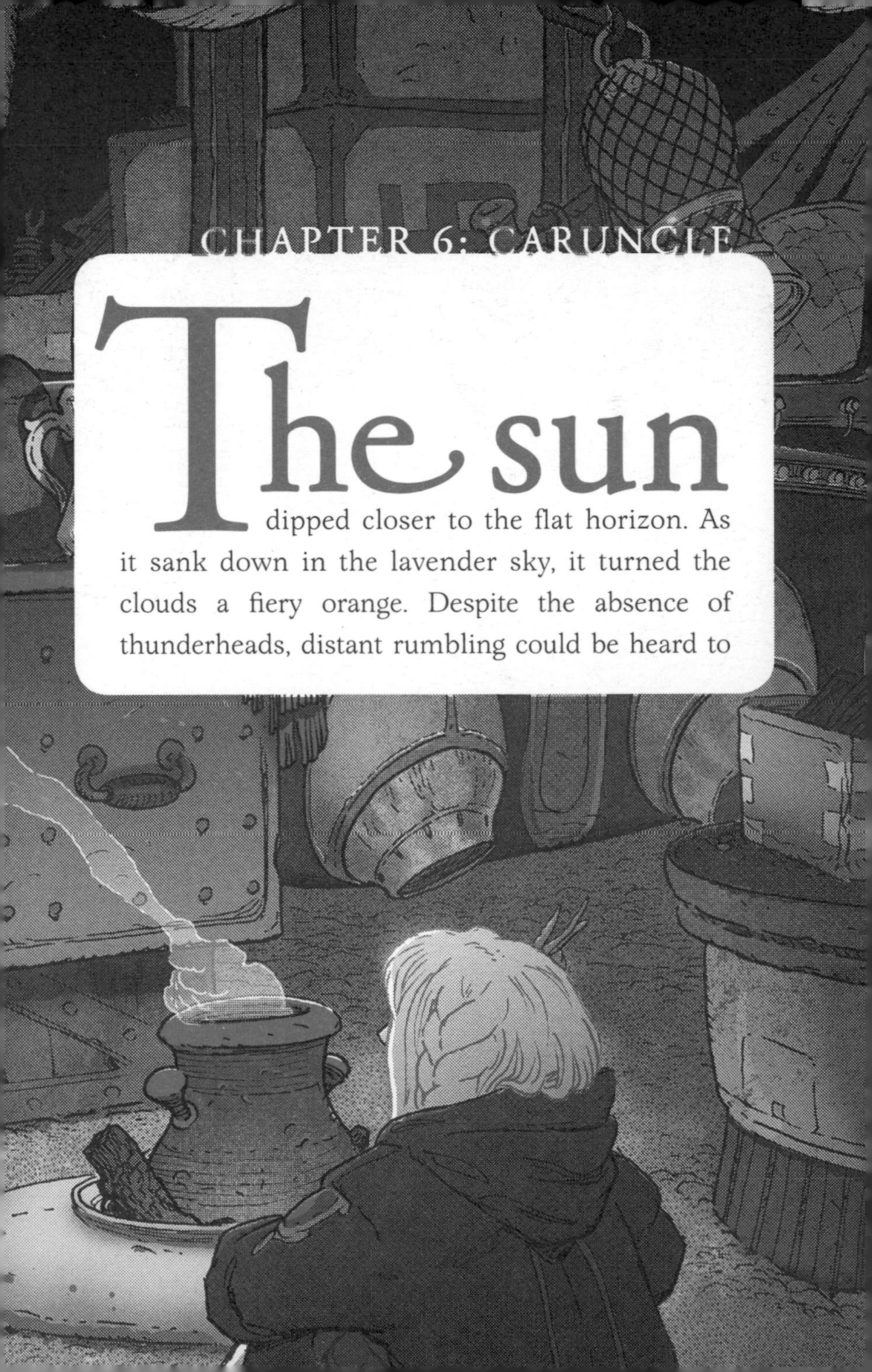

# CHAPTER 6: CARUNCLE

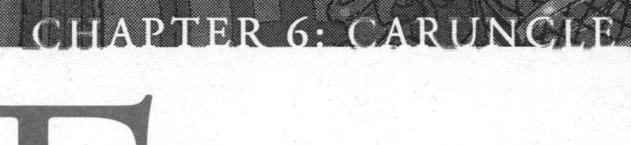

# The sun

dipped closer to the flat horizon. As it sank down in the lavender sky, it turned the clouds a fiery orange. Despite the absence of thunderheads, distant rumbling could be heard to the north. The sound of thunder was soon lost to a noisy congregation of turnfins roosting on the top of the *Bijou.*

"It's not in here." Hailey finished rummaging through a crate filled with debris from the wreck. "Any luck?"

"No." Eva started putting the items back into the crate in front of her. "Just a bunch of parts."

"And that's everything you've found?" Hailey turned to Caruncle.

"That is all-it," Caruncle replied, and dropped a hunk of wood onto the campfire. He grabbed a long metal rod, which Eva recognized as a piece of the *Bijou,* and used it as a poker to stoke the embers. The lazy flames reawakened and began consuming the wood. "If it is not here, then perhaps it is remaining-still on my ship." Caruncle pointed to the *Bijou* with the poker.

"You mean *my* ship?" Hailey added.

"My ship, your ship. Does it matter? It is not going anywhere anytime soon," Caruncle said, and laughed softly to himself.

"Yeah . . . well, I looked in there already," Hailey said in a sheepish tone, and adjusted his flight cap.

A smile formed on Caruncle's tusked mouth. "And no luck?"

"You could say that." Eva sat on her blanket near the fire. "So, Caruncle, this stuff that you scavenge—"

"Steal," Hailey corrected her.

"Discover," Caruncle corrected him.

"This stuff that you *discover* . . . what do you do with it?"

"I trade or sell for provisions-supplies. It keeps me out of trouble-debt." Caruncle unwrapped a thick scarf from around his jowls to reveal a small pair of secondary arms underneath. With these arms he withdrew a long-stemmed pipe from his tattered coat. Three bowls were evenly spaced along the pipe's stem. "Usually I trade-sell to curator Zin. But not now."

"Because of what's going on in Solas?" Eva asked. Far away more thunder rumbled.

Caruncle nodded. "Zin has disappeared-vanished. No one can locate-find him." He pulled a weathered pouch from his pocket. He unclasped the pouch to reveal a variety of spices, each stored in its own ornate container. The containers reminded Eva of the offerings that had cluttered the floor of Arius's home. Caruncle began packing the spices into the bowls of the pipe. "The queen, she search-looks everywhere for him. Is he alive?

Is he dead? She order-sends all sorts of trackers out from the city. No one knows where he-Zin is."

Eva thought back to Loroc's boasting about his plans to capture and consume Zin as he had done with Arius. In light of Caruncle's news, it seemed that either Loroc had succeeded or Zin really had escaped.

"I hope-wish he turns up soon," said Caruncle. "I could make a fortune selling him some of my discoveries."

"Perhaps among *my* things that you planned on selling, you *discovered* this?" Hailey took the poker and drew a picture of an Omnipod in the sand.

"What? Seeing Eyes? That is what all this fuss-whining is about? That is what you are search-looking for?" Caruncle handed his pipe to Eva. "Hold this." He waddled over to his transport and started sliding containers around.

Eva turned the pipe over in her hands. It was scrimshawed in a pattern she had seen before, like in the mural painted on Hostia's ceiling in Lacus. The contents in each bowl were different. One held a claylike substance, another dried leaves, and the third was some sort of brownish jelly. The scent took Eva back to Hostia's home. Perhaps someone there also smoked a pipe.

"Here! Seeing Eyes." Caruncle shoved a bin into Hailey's hands and returned to his seat by the fire. He retrieved his pipe from Eva. "Much gratitude-thanks," Caruncle said with a nod.

Hailey pulled the lid off the bin and gasped.

"What?" Eva craned her neck to get a better view.

"Omnipods," he said, and pulled a device from the bin to show her. One by one Hailey removed the Omnipods and lined them up on the ground. Eva scooted closer to help.

"Omni-pods?" Caruncle lit his pipe. "Is that what you-humans call them?"

"Yes," Eva replied, picking up a corroded square-shaped model. "I saw a bunch of these in the museum. Were they discovered by you?"

"Most of them, yes." Caruncle puffed multicolored rings of smoke. "I find-discover them here and there. Mostly in the ruins."

*The ancient ruins that once were known as New York City*, Eva thought. *Zin was fascinated with them.* She asked Hailey if his Omnipod was among those in the bin.

"No," he said in a gloomy tone.

"Do any of them work?"

"I don't think so." Hailey tried activating each one in turn.

"You mean where the eye lights up?" Caruncle asked. "Those are scarce-rare. Very scarce-rare."

"Do you have one?" Eva got up and returned to her spot by the fire.

"Maybe-perhaps one is here somewhere, but . . ." Caruncle took a long drag from his pipe. "It will-shall take me some time to find it." He pointed to the heap of junk piled in his transport.

"Maybe yours is still in the *Bijou*," Eva said to Hailey.

"Maybe." Hailey put all the Omnipods back into the bin. "But I can't go looking around in there with all those knife-critters flying around."

Caruncle let out a slow laugh. Ribbons of smoke twisted out from his mouth. "You-human mean knifejacks? That is why you will not go back in *your* ship?"

"Those things nearly stabbed me to death." Hailey pointed out the multiple bloody nicks on his hands and face. "Look, one of them even took a chunk out of my ear."

"They chase-hunt at night." Caruncle pointed up to the small creatures flitting in and out from the ship's open hold. "As long as you stay clear of their nest, you are good-fine."

Eva asked Caruncle, "Do you know how to get around them?"

"Of course! How do you think I find-got all this stuff?" The alien reached over and grabbed a bundle of dried leafy twigs. Colorful twine was wrapped tightly around the bundle, forming a grip of sorts. "You have smudge stick, right-yes?" Caruncle waved the bundle at Hailey.

Hailey shrugged his shoulders.

"We don't," said Eva.

Caruncle clucked and shook his head, causing his wattles to jiggle. He poked one end of the smudge stick into the fire and rotated it slowly until it was evenly lit. He then brought the stick to his mouth and blew out the flame. Even with the flame extinguished, smoke wafted from the bundle. He handed it to Hailey.

"What am I supposed to do with this torch?" Hailey waved the smoke away from his face. "It hardly gives off any light now that you've blown the flame out."

"The smoke relax-calms the knifejacks, you thickheaded grall. They will not hurt-bother you if you have that." He got up and unhooked an empty cage. "While you're at it, find-catch some more when you are in there." Caruncle handed the cage to Hailey. "We need meals-food for three."

Hailey juggled the cage and smoking smudge stick into one hand. With his free hand he reached into his pocket and pulled out his laser-cutter. He activated the penlight set in the tool's handle.

"Oh, good! I thought for sure you were going to ask for a light-lantern next." Caruncle shooed Hailey off. "Go on. Go find-locate your precious Seeing Eye."

Hailey looked at Eva for confirmation before he left her. She nodded, and he disappeared inside the *Bijou*.

Caruncle dragged a crate over close to the fire and began sorting the objects within. "You know," Caruncle said, "I recognize you-human. We have met before."

Eva felt a wave of nervousness rush through her. Now she wished Hailey were back outside the ship. "We—we have?"

Caruncle looked up at her with mustard-colored eyes. "You do not remember?"

Eva shook her head.

"You were the first I had seen-found in a long time." He resumed sorting the junk. "It was in

Solas, and you were look-searching for the port."

"I do remember!" Eva recalled the moment. *Muthr and I were fleeing the city in the Goldfish after escaping the Royal Museum.* "That was you?"

"It was me. How can you forget this pretty-lovely face?" Caruncle said with a crooked grin. "To be true-honest I was . . . a bit-little, how should I say? Tipsy. When I returned to the tavern-bar to tell the Dorceans *I* was with, they all had a laugh. 'Oh, Caruncle haz found one more zing to zell to da queen,' they said. 'Heez so good at hiz work zat he should buy za next round.'" He snorted in disdain.

Eva was silent as she watched Caruncle place the odds and ends in distinct piles. It reminded her of Rovender sorting through Besteel's old belongings. She wondered how many hands these items had passed through. What would become of her belongings after she was gone?

"You had a good-great flying machine." Caruncle paused. "And an automaton operator-driver. What became of them?"

Eva focused her gaze into the flames of the fire. "They're gone now," she said softly. "Both are gone."

"Too bad." Caruncle continued with his task.

"I would have like-wanted to have traded for that machine. My hoversloop only float-hovers." He pointed with his head at his overladen vehicle. "The thrusters are kaput. I trade for Bix and Bax here to haul-pull it for me."

Eva looked over at the pair of munt-runners, now hitched to one of the *Bijou*'s extended landing struts. "They got away earlier, huh? We saw them at the lake south of here." A staccato of thunder banged over the sky. Lightning flickered to the north.

Caruncle finished with his sorting. "They are a loyal-good team, though sometimes they run-sneak off." He pulled one object from the pile, a drinking cup, and polished it with spit and the sleeve of his jacket. "These items-things are in better shape than most. I could get a good price for this, if only there was someplace to sell it."

*Zin was going to go to Lacus to find Arius,* Eva thought. *I wonder if he made it.*

"Is it bad? What happened in Solas?" An uneasy feeling crept into Eva as she asked this, but she pushed it away. She needed to know.

"Listen to the thunder from the city, and you tell me." Caruncle gestured out toward the lightning.

"That's . . . that's not a storm?" Eva watched

glowing light flicker on the northern horizon.

"Oh, it is a storm, of the bad-worst kind," Caruncle said with a heavy sigh. "That is the sound of warships drop-bombing big automatons on the city."

"Warbots," Eva said.

"Warbots, hmmm. That a good-right name. When I was there, I saw-watched them. These warbots, they march-walk through the streets. They are shooting and scaring everyone. It was very deadly-dangerous." Caruncle set the cup down on the lid of the crate and plucked another from the pile. He began to polish that cup. "But the queen, Ojo, she dispatch-releases the pillar guards, so everyone is hopeful. But then the pillar guards are battle-fighting these warbots, and there is fire and explosions, and everything is getting destroyed. Like most-many, I left town as quick-fast as I could."

"I'm sorry that all this has happened," Eva said.

"You? You did not do the invading. You tried to stop-halt it, right?" said Caruncle.

"I suppose. I—"

"So what are you sorry for? It's not yours to mend-fix." He set the polished cup down to join the first one.

"I ran away too," Eva said. She shrank a little under her poncho.

"Run-fleeing from a dangerous situation is nothing to be ashamed of." Caruncle's tone became serious. He pointed at Eva with the stem of his pipe. "In dark times we do what we have to do to survive, right?"

Eva nodded in agreement.

Hailey emerged from the shadowy hold of the *Bijou*. "Nothing!"

"No luck?" Eva asked.

Hailey shook his head. "It could be anywhere. The ship is completely trashed. I'll have to try again in the morning when there is more light." He handed the smudge stick and cage back to Caruncle. "Thanks for letting me use this. It did keep those knifejacks away."

Caruncle looked inside the empty cage. "But you did not find-catch any?"

Hailey pulled his flight cap down over his eyes and thrust his hands into his pockets. "Those things scare me," he mumbled.

Caruncle snorted and stood up. With the cage and smudge stick he shuffled up the crate steps to the ship. "'I am big strong-tough pilot!'" he said, trying to mimic Hailey's voice. "'You-Caruncle stay away from my ship or I will take you out!'" he continued as he entered the *Bijou*. "'Oh no! Terrible-bad knifejacks are going to chew-eat me up! Save me, Caruncle! Save me!'" His deep voice echoed out from the hold.

Hailey knelt down in front of the campfire. "I really hate that guy."

"Is there any other way you can contact Vanpa? Perhaps using one of those old Omnipods?" Eva looked out at the flickering sky and wondered how long it would take her turnfin to return with news of Rovender—if it returned at all.

Hailey picked up one of the cups Caruncle had polished. "I don't think any of those old ones will work." He poured water from his container into the cup and took a drink. "But I may be able to get the transmitter in the cockpit to work. It will be tricky without schematics, which of course . . ."

"Are on the Omnipod." Eva sighed.

"Yup. My spare should have a wiring diagram for the ship." Hailey opened a packet of nutriment pellets and poured them into his mouth. "Hey. Will those ghost-snipers attack us during the night?"

"I don't sense any near here. Perhaps they don't like the light," said Eva.

"Good. That's one less thing that's trying to

eat me." Hailey grabbed a log from Caruncle's woodpile and dropped it into the flames. He leaned close to Eva and lowered his voice to a confidential whisper. "Listen, until we know for sure if we can trust this guy, I don't think you should mention your 'powers.' . . . Know what I mean?"

"Yeah." She remembered Caruncle being helpful back in Solas when she'd been looking for a port where she could refuel the Goldfish—but that had been before the human invasion.

Hailey opened one of the supply crates and pulled out another blanket. "Aha! A liquid light pen. Perfect." He snatched the pen from the crate.

"What are you doing?" Eva watched him shake the pen.

"You say those ghost-snipers don't like light? Well, then, I'll make sure they stay far from me." Hailey uncapped the pen with his teeth, keeping the cap in his mouth. Liquid light flowed from the pen as he doodled patterns on his sneakboots.

"How long does it last?" Eva asked.

"I dunno. A couple of days. It's for creating emergency lighting."

"That's pretty rocket." Eva let out a yawn.

"Yup. Pretty rocket." Hailey kept his focus on decorating his shoes. "Get some REM. I'm gonna be up for a while. I'll keep an eye on things."

Eva pulled her poncho's hood over her head and lay back on her blanket. Her mind whirled with the all the news that Caruncle had shared. Eventually her thoughts settled on the Royal Museum's curator. *I hope you are where I think you are, Zin. And I hope you will help us stop your brother.*

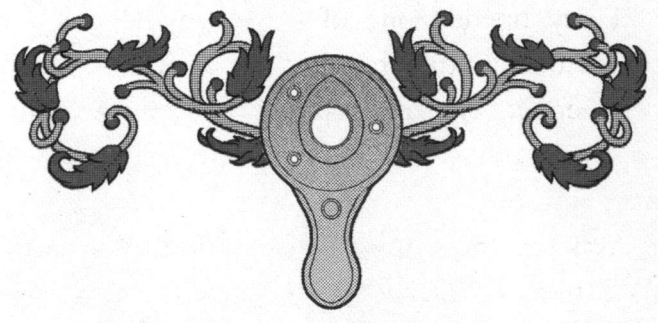

# CHAPTER 7: DISCOVERIES

So let us come to an agreement," Caruncle said over his breakfast. With his stubby fingers he cracked the shell of a boiled knifejack and consumed the stringy meat within. "You both take-carry whatever you want from your ship . . ."

"And?" Eva asked.

"And"—Caruncle sucked out the last of the knifejack meat—"I take-carry whatever is left."

"What kind of deal is that?" Hailey emptied a packet of Attican crystal coffee into his mug.

"I am not finished-done." Caruncle grabbed another knifejack from his steaming pot. "I will also provide-supply protection, with this." He pointed at his boomrod. "And this." He pointed at his head. "But you-human must tell me what your item-devices are and how they work."

"Why?" asked Eva.

"I get more in trade-sell if I am more knowledgeable," replied Caruncle. He dug his finger into the carapace of the boiled knifejack and scooped out its organs. He offered them to Eva. She declined.

"We don't need your protection. We can take care of ourselves," Hailey said, standing proud. His coffee sloshed and spilled down the front of his jacket.

"Oh, I-Caruncle can see you are very good at taking care of yourselves. It is quite apparent-evident in the fine landing job you've done here." He laughed and licked the meat from his fingers.

"You know what? That's it! I'm gonna—"

"Enough!" Eva rose between Hailey and Caruncle. "Take whatever we leave behind. In return you offer us protection . . . and give us a ride."

Hailey wiped the coffee from the front of his jacket. "Ride?"

"Where is it that you wish to go, Eva Nine?" Caruncle tossed the knifejack shell into the fire.

Eva walked to the edge of the camp and looked out at the horizon toward the Wandering Forest. She had to move on. It would be just a matter of time before Loroc's forces found her. Already she felt a foreign presence, likely warbots, combing the forest. *Searching for me—or . . .*

"How far are the ancient ruins from here?" she asked.

"The place where I picked you up?" Hailey asked. "No, we don't want to go back there. We want to reconnect with Vanpa and Rovender, remember?"

Caruncle stroked his wattles and studied Eva. "Why is it that you want to go-travel to the ruins?"

"Can you take us there?"

Hailey jumped in. "Eva, we don't need him to—"

Eva pushed Hailey aside. "Will you do it or not?"

"I know a way-route." Caruncle leaned back against a crate. "But you must tell me why we are to go there."

Eva looked over at Hailey, then back to Caruncle. "I can't tell you right now. But if you take us, we'll tell you all about our artifacts—your discoveries—so you can get more in trade for them."

"An interesting-curious proposition." Caruncle reached for another boiled knifejack and began to eat it. "Maybe I will think-ponder about it for a bit and let you know."

"That's fine with us." Hailey walked up the steps to the hatch in the *Bijou*. "In the meantime I can go figure out how to—"

"Tell me why you won't answer us now." Eva stood, her arms akimbo.

"You see that range out-over there?" Caruncle pointed to a line of jagged mountains far off to the east. "Those are the Bliek Mountains—very dangerous land-terrain. You-we must go north around the mountains and then south through the wastelands to the ruins. It is a lengthy journey-trip."

"See? It's going to take too long," said Hailey.

"I know that," Eva said to Caruncle. "I've travelled the wastelands before. You need a hovercraft."

"Ah, right-yes!" Caruncle said with a smile. "Otherwise you become a sand-sniper's meal-breakfast." He pointed at Hailey. "This one would not last one day-cycle."

"Hey! I can survive out here just fine." Hailey stomped back down the steps. "We don't need him, Eva."

Eva figured she could keep the sand-snipers away. Traveling by hovercraft was faster than hiking or riding a wandering tree. Also, the wastelands were like a desert. They would need shade and water. With warbots hunting around, time was also of the essence. "Well?" she asked Caruncle. "Will you do it?"

"There is a shortcut. A pass-route through the mountains that would put us there in three sunrises." Caruncle held up three fingers, each glistening from the juice of the knifejack meat. "Not many know of it, but I-Caruncle do. So I must consider-weigh whether I show you . . . and him." He pointed to Hailey.

"Right! Like I'm going to give up being a retriever pilot and use your 'secret path' to find junk so I can become a garbage-seller instead." Hailey took a swig of his crystal coffee.

"If this is your 'piloting,' then keep-stay at it. You are keeping me in business." Caruncle laughed to himself.

"Okay, guys. Enough!" said Eva. "Caruncle, you need some time to think about it. I understand." She picked up the smudge stick. "May we?"

"Of course. Of course," said Caruncle.

Eva lit the smudge stick and walked over to Hailey, who was still standing at the steps leading into the hatch. "Come on. While he thinks about it, I'll help you look for your Omnipod." She followed Hailey into the hold of the *Bijou*.

The inside of the *Bijou* was unrecognizable now that it was lying on its side. Damaged supplies were mixed with ship parts in sprawling heaps. Beams of sunlight entered through the gaping bullet holes that had pierced the hull.

"Watch your step," Hailey said. The ship groaned and creaked as he and Eva clambered toward the cockpit.

Eva looked up to see hordes of knifejacks crammed into the top of the wreck. She waved the smudge stick around and waited for a warning sign from the aggressive creatures, but none came.

Hailey noticed an upturned crate of provisions. He got down on his knees and flipped the crate over to inspect its contents. "I don't trust Caruncle," he whispered.

Eva knelt down next to Hailey. "Is it because he's . . . an alien?"

"No. It's because he's a jerk."

"Are you sure you aren't just upset because—"

"Because what?" Hailey stopped rummaging.

"You know . . . because the *Bijou* . . . is gone." Eva kept her eyes focused on the spilled contents from the crate.

Hailey pointed toward the camp. "I'm upset because this guy's gonna trade off pieces of *my* ship!"

"Oh. You mean like how you traded me for parts?" Eva stood. "I'm done looking for your Omnipod."

Hailey ran his dirty hands over his head. "You're right. I told you before that I was sorry about that. What more do you want?" He gave Eva a rueful grin. "You wanna punch me again? Go ahead."

Eva folded her arms and eyed Hailey.

"Go on." Hailey pulled down his jacket sleeve to reveal his bare arm. "Give it your best shot."

It was hard for Eva to conceal her smile at Hailey's earnest effort to make amends. "Come on. Let's go see if the ship's transmitter is working," she said.

They continued on through the hold, their silence broken by occasional chirps from the knifejacks.

*Rest. Watch. Rest,* Eva heard them say.

"I know you are worried about Loroc finding you." Hailey spoke softly as they climbed through the galley. "But going to the ruins? I can think of a lot of safer places to hide until this battle is over."

"You're right. Trust me, it is the last place I really want to go."

"So why go? What's there?" He yanked the door to the cockpit partially open. In the hold the new inhabitants chittered at the disruption.

Eva thrust the smudge stick through the opened door to allow the smoke to waft up. The knifejacks did not move from their roost. Hailey pushed the door completely open, and Eva followed him into the cockpit. Though tilted sideways, the cockpit was devoid of any large debris. An acrid odor burned Eva's eyes and nose.

"Eww! What is that?" Hailey fanned his face with his hand.

Eva looked up. A large congregation of knife-jacks were huddled in the top of the cockpit, next to the opening of the loose windshield. "It's guano." She waved the smudge stick around in an effort to burn off the pungent smell, but it had no effect. They stumbled from the cockpit and into the galley, gasping for air.

"I'm going back in." Hailey took a deep breath and stomped back into the cockpit. With his nose buried in the crook of his arm, Hailey frantically inspected the flight controls. He flipped switches repeatedly and banged on buttons. Finally he staggered back out.

"It's . . . no good." He coughed. "The transmitter's all gummed up with guano." He kicked one of the food dispensers. A heap of Sustibars spilled out from it.

"Is there any other place your spare Omnipod could be?"

"I looked everywhere." Hailey gestured toward the trashed hold of the ship. "I dunno where it is."

"I'm sorry. But we can't stay here much longer." Eva stood to leave. "There are things in the forest—"

"Hunting for you. I know. I know. You don't think they'll find you at the ruins?" He knelt down next to the broken dispenser and began filling his pockets with Sustibars.

Eva dropped her voice to a low whisper. "I think Zin is hiding at the ruins."

"Zin? Who is Zin?"

Eva shushed him. "He's Loroc's brother. He works in the museum for Queen Ojo."

"Why do you want to find him?" Hailey scooted to the next dispenser and emptied it.

"Keep your voice down! If anyone can stop Loroc, it's Zin. He's really smart, like Cadmus."

"Great. Let's flee from one evil genius into the clutches of another," said Hailey.

"I think Zin would stop Loroc if he knew the truth." Eva began to climb back down into the hold.

"Do you trust him?"

"I don't know that I have much of a choice." She stopped in the middle of the hold. She remembered the first time she had set foot on this ship, giddy from the opportunity that it held. Eva remembered brave Huxley bidding her farewell and giving his life to save hers. "I want us to return to our families, and I want this conflict to end. Cadmus must be stopped and so must Loroc. I thought Arius could help, but she's gone. Zin is the only hope we have."

"Hope is a dangerous thing." Hailey peered up at the wreckage that had once been his ship. "I've seen firsthand what it's done to the people at the Toiler's camp. People who hoped to live a fruitful life in the forest, far from New Attica, and found out the hard way that it can't be done."

"Hope is all I've got," Eva said, and exited the ship.

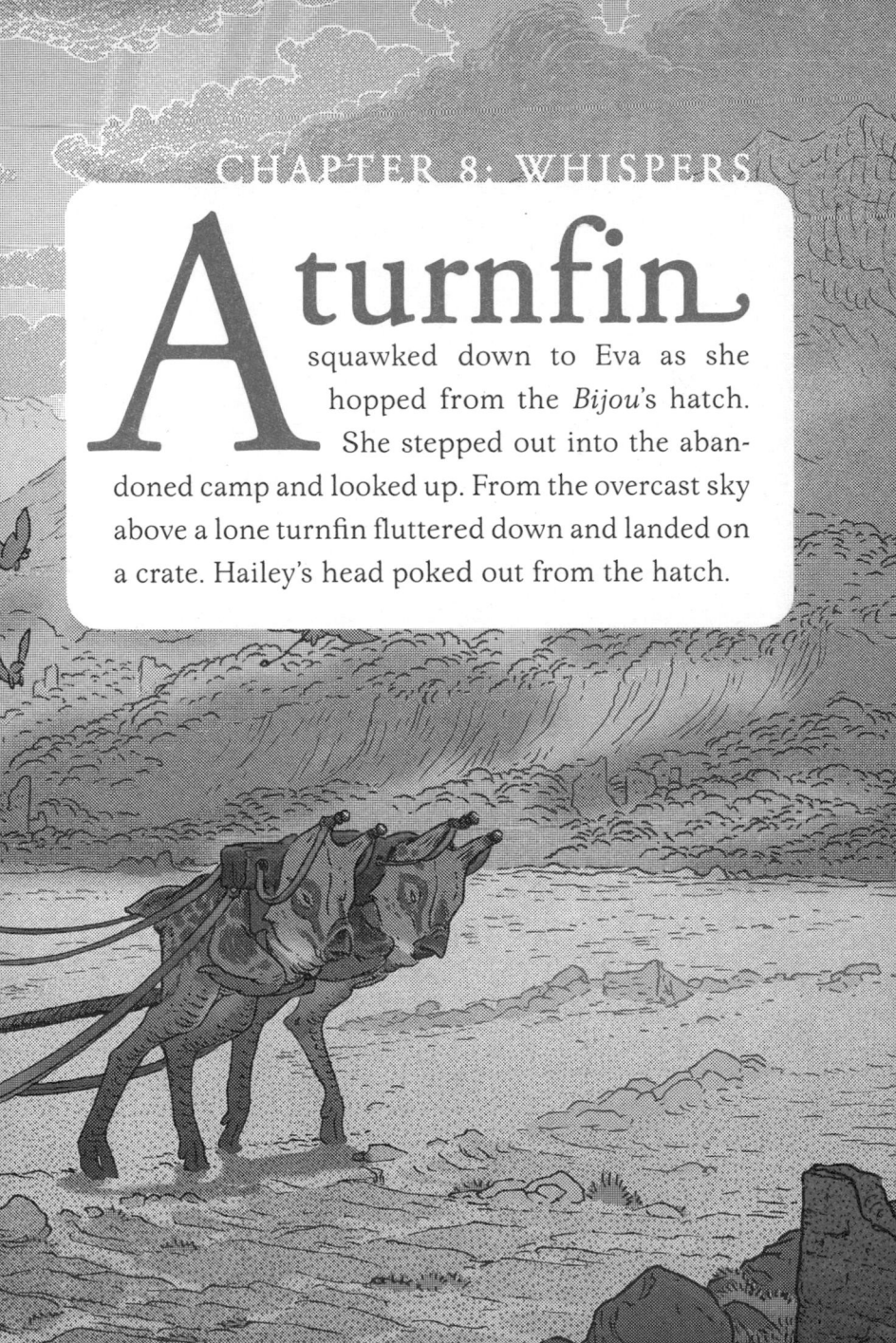

# A turnfin

squawked down to Eva as she hopped from the *Bijou*'s hatch. She stepped out into the abandoned camp and looked up. From the overcast sky above a lone turnfin fluttered down and landed on a crate. Hailey's head poked out from the hatch.

"Make sure Caruncle is not around," Eva whispered to him. "And hand me one of those Sustibars." Hailey tossed a bar to her and set off to find Caruncle. Eva unwrapped the bar and crumbled it up in her hands. While feeding the turnfin, she asked, "Did you find them?"

*I traveled to the Heart. I sang to others who have seen them.*

"And they are okay?"

*Your blue father and his clan are safe in their nests.*

"And the ones who live on the big lake?"

*The fish-eaters now roost with your father's clan.*

"Thank you." Eva stroked the bird's feathered head. The turnfin gobbled down the last of the Sustibar and flapped up to join the others circling overhead.

"Did you nab-catch a thief?" Caruncle asked.

Eva turned to see him round the nose of the *Bijou*. He ambled toward her holding the reins of his two munt-runners.

She smiled. "Naw, just a curious visitor."

"Your lost-missing Seeing Eye? That is probably who stole-took it." Caruncle pointed to the roosting turnfins. "They crave-like shiny objects to decorate their nests."

"Maybe." Eva looked up. Though her vantage

point was low, she saw no nests on top of the wreck.

"Eva, I couldn't find—" Hailey came around the tail fin of the ship and gave a startled look at Caruncle. "I couldn't . . . uh, find . . . my Omnipod, after all. . . . Yeah . . . so . . . no Omnipod."

"Caruncle thinks maybe a turnfin took it," Eva said, pointing to the birds.

"Turnfins, huh?" Hailey put his hands on his hips. He focused his gaze up to the sky and squinted as if he saw something far above them.

Caruncle eyed them both for a beat as he fed the munt-runners. "Those turnyfins are sneaky. You cannot turn your back on them for a moment-second." He handed the reins to Hailey. "Hold this." From his hoversloop Caruncle pulled out a large curved wooden beam—a yoke—and unbuckled the straps. "Eva, can-will you help?"

"Sure." She held the other end of the yoke while Caruncle fitted it over the head of each munt-runner. "So," Eva said. "Given any more thought to my proposition?"

Caruncle hitched up the munt-runners to a pole projecting from the front of his hoversloop. "I will-shall take you to the ruins."

"Thank you," Eva said, grinning.

"However." Caruncle wagged his finger.

"You-humans feed yourselves and find your own drink."

"Deal," said Eva.

"Fine with me." Hailey tore open a Sustibar wrapper.

"Fine-good," said Caruncle. "Then we have an understanding. Let us break camp. After I load up my stuff-things, you can add your belongings. Then we leave-go."

The late-morning sun burned away the low-lying bands of clouds to reveal the Rings of Orbona. Sitting next to Caruncle in the front seat of the hoversloop, Eva watched the crackled plains of the salt flats roll past.

"We shall-will continue south, along the edge of the moving forest." Caruncle steered his muntrunner team in the direction he was indicating. "By nightfall we should arrive at Hiyao's Hook."

"Hiyao's Hook?" Eva asked.

"Yes. Named after the famed storyteller who travel-journeyed here during the Great Migration. See how the forest point-juts out and stretches to the east toward the mountains?" Caruncle waved his pipe stem at the horizon. "If you were to look-gaze at it from above, or with a beamguide, you would see it forms a hook—Hiyao's Hook."

Eva closed her eyes and listened to the forest. She could feel the ebb and flow of energy . . . and the presence of intruders, but they were now far behind. She let out a long exhale and watched the turnfins riding the wind currents alongside them.

Caruncle lit the three bowls of his pipe while his second pair of hands held the reins. "So are you ready to tell Caruncle why we are traveling to the ruins?"

"Not yet. But I'll let you know when we arrive." Eva glanced back at the shaded end of the covered sloop where Hailey was. The pilot lay on top of a large crate. A low snore crept out from the cap pulled over his face.

"Very well." Caruncle sucked on his pipe. "In the meantime perhaps you'll tell me what *this* is." He pulled several folded yellowed sheets of paper from his pocket. On the water-stained pages were printed words. "I discover-found a hinged box full of these. Some were loose. Some were not."

Eva took the pages and unfolded them. The words did not light up or scroll like on the electra-paper she was familiar with. "These are pages from a book. An old book."

"A book?"

"Yes." Eva read through the words. "It's like a story that once happened. See here: it is talking about a city named Phyllis and how it is beautiful when you first arrive but becomes faded and boring after you live there awhile."

"So it is a history?"

Eva shrugged her shoulders and handed the pages back to Caruncle. "It could also just be made up. Fiction."

"What is 'fiction'?" Caruncle looked over at her.

"A fairy tale. You know . . . like 'Once upon a time' and 'They lived happily ever after'? That sort of thing." Eva's coveted WondLa drifted into her thoughts.

"Our kind only write-records true accounts of what has happened so that we can remember. These accounts are written continuously with no end—but you say that your fictions end. Do they always end the same?" Caruncle exhaled a series of smoke rings.

"Yes. No matter how many times you read them, fairy tales always end the same. They're not like real life." Eva didn't want to talk about it anymore.

"They are like a fortune. Fate." Caruncle watched the horizon pass by.

"No. Not like fate." Eva crossed her arms.

"It is the same story-sequence every time you view the symbols on these pages, correct?"

"Yes, but—"

"A predetermined record of events that always ends the same is fate, if you ask me-Caruncle."

"I don't know about that." Eva looked away toward the mountains.

"Of course you do not. But perhaps someone does and has written-recorded it unbeknownst to you. Besides, your ending has yet to arrive."

They continued on through the afternoon and arrived at Hiyao's Hook shortly after nightfall. Eva balled up her poncho to make a pillow and stretched out on a blanket next to the campfire. Dark shadows danced around the firelight, concealing the noisy nocturnal denizens of the forest. The proximity to the woods relaxed Eva. Grogginess caused by the long day of travel soon began to overtake her.

"You know," Hailey said, looking up at the waning moon in the star-speckled sky. "It really is beautiful out here at night."

"It sure is." Eva stretched and pulled off her sneakboots and socks. She wriggled her toes in the warmth of the fire.

"I'd appreciate it a lot more if everything weren't trying to devour me." With his hands folded behind his head, Hailey lay back on his blanket.

"It is a test-game of survival out here in the wild." Caruncle set a large scorched pot on the fire.

"Yeah, a game I don't really want to play anymore," Hailey said.

Caruncle chuckled. "You have no choice. You begin-start this game the moment you are hatched. It does not matter if you are human or otherwise. We all play this game." He waddled over to his hoversloop and unhooked the cage holding the knifejacks. The creatures within chittered and flapped their wings. Eva tried to block out their fear.

Caruncle lit his smudge stick and blew the smoke into the knifejack's cage. He reached in and pulled out one of the creatures. "Life is hard and painful for all, even for the fierce knifejack. Look-see here." Caruncle grasped one of the knifejack's squirming legs. Slowly he twisted the leg backward in its socket. The creature hissed and nipped at Caruncle's hand.

Eva squirmed, feeling the knifejack's pain, and tried to look away.

With one swift movement Caruncle pulled the leg from the socket and tossed it into the pot of boiling water.

"Come on!" Hailey cried. "That's cruel."

"Ah, but you-human see? The knifejack is still-remains very much alive. If I let it go"—Caruncle released the knifejack, and it fluttered off into the night—"it will carry a reminder-scar, but it will be smarter. Perhaps it will-shall avoid smoke from a smudge stick. Perhaps it will-shall avoid Caruncle. Perhaps it will-shall survive."

"Perhaps it will just get eaten by something else." Hailey lay back down.

Caruncle seized another knifejack from the cage and bound its wings with twine. He dropped it into the steaming pot. "We all must do what we can to survive."

"For what?" Hailey said. "In the end we all are going to die."

"True." Caruncle poked at the boiling knifejack. "No matter what we did yesterday, do here-now, or do tomorrow, we are all destined for death. It is our *fate*." He looked over at Eva.

"But our knowledge, the things we learn, can carry on in others after we are gone," Eva said. "The toil of this journey, *our journey*, is the map for those who will follow."

"Well said-spoken." Caruncle continued preparing his meal.

"That was deep. You sound like Rovender." Hailey nudged Eva with his foot in a playful manner.

She shrugged him off. Her mind was occupied with memories of Rovender describing death at the skeleton of the air-whale. She recalled Muthr holding Eva close and rocking her to sleep back in the Sanctuary. She could almost hear Muthr's voice whisper, *I love you, Eva dear.* Eva replayed that memory over and over until she drifted off into sleep.

"Eva, wake up," Hailey whispered.

Eva's eyes fluttered open to find him huddled close and patting her arm. "What is it?" she asked.

"Shhh." He put a finger to his lips. "Caruncle says there is someone out there." Hailey gestured toward the flats from which they'd traveled. "We need to hide. Fast."

Eva sat up and grabbed her shoes. While she quickly pulled them on, she listened to the forest. Many of its inhabitants had stopped chirping and singing. "I am sensing that there is another being nearby. It's not from the wood." Her eyes grew wide with fear. She scanned the darkness but saw nothing.

"Caruncle has gone to investigate." Hailey helped Eva to her feet. "So now is our chance to go."

Eva and Hailey stole away from their camp into the gloom of the forest. They found a hiding spot behind the large corrugated leaves of a giant liverwort.

"Let's stay here until the coast is clear," Hailey whispered.

"No." Eva pulled the hood of her poncho up. "I wanna see who it is."

"But what if it's that Loroc guy?" There was concern in Hailey's voice.

"I don't think it is." Eva crept through the wood. Moving through the shadows, like a floatazoan hiding in the brush, they circled the camp and came to rest alongside a large wandering tree. As quietly as possible Eva pulled herself up onto the thick branches and climbed to the topmost bough.

Hailey joined her. "See anything?"

"Not yet," she whispered. "Keep low if you can."

Hailey peered up into the cloudy sky. "Did you hear that?"

"No," answered Eva. "Is it a ship?"

"It sounded like engines. Big engines, like a warship . . ." Hailey turned his head as if to hear it better.

"I know you are out there!" Caruncle shouted from beyond the forest. "I am armed but do not wish-desire to cause harm. Show-reveal yourself!" A breeze blew in from the flats, carrying the hum of Caruncle's charging boomrod.

Eva and Hailey peered over the edge of the hardened leafy formations of the tree. Caruncle stood a ways from the camp, his back dimly lit by their dying fire. The vast plain was soaked in inky blackness beyond Caruncle's long shadow.

"What's that?" Hailey pointed north of the camp. A burly creature crept from the forest on three pairs of muscular legs. Even in the dim light it was apparent that it was much larger than Caruncle. Its spotted hairy hide bristled as it approached the junk dealer, while its clawed hands held a charged boomrod. This was an alien Eva knew all too well.

*It can't be. It's not possible.*

*Besteel.*

# CHAPTER 9: HUNTER

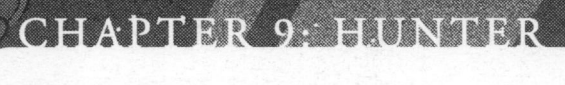

Eva's breathing hastened. Her heart began to pound in her chest.

"What?" Hailey's voice rose. "Who is that, Eva? Is it Loroc?"

"The sand-sniper ate him. I saw it," Eva mumbled to herself. She began fidgeting with her braids. "I . . . I saw his bones." Was it possible that Besteel had somehow come back from death? Rovender did say death was some sort of journey. Could one simply turn around and return?

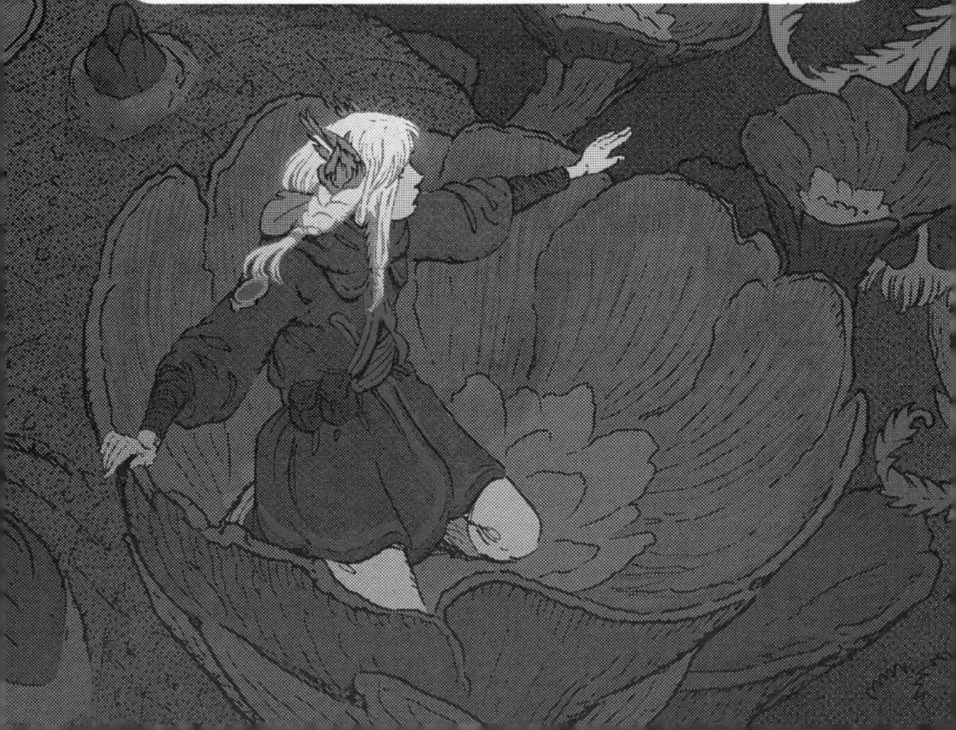

"Look! Something's going down!" Hailey pointed toward Caruncle. Eva stayed hidden within the leaves of the tree.

"Nothing you seek is here. So you best move on!" Caruncle's voice echoed over the landscape. He fired a warning shot from his boomrod into the midnight sky.

"Whoa! Creepy," Hailey said to Eva. "The other guy has a glowing eye."

"A glowing eye? Are you sure?" Eva's pulse slowed for an instant.

"Yeah, I'm sure 'cause he looked right this way," Hailey said.

*Perhaps it is just another Dorcean—the same species as Besteel?* Eva scooted back up to catch a glimpse of the Dorcean stranger slinking away into the forest. Caruncle watched him retreat before returning to his hoversloop.

"Wha—" Hailey's body slid off his perch. "Something has me! Help!" He gripped the edge of a large leaf.

"Shh!" Eva slid over to grab his hand. But she wasn't quick enough. Hailey was lifted from his hiding place and hauled upside down by leafy tendrils that were wrapped tight around his leg. The tendrils carried him to a crown of fronds on a tall tree with bright fruit at its center—a weeping bird-catcher.

"Eva! Do something," Hailey cried.

"Just be quiet! I'll get you down," she said.

Holding Hailey by the ankle, the weeping bird-catcher lowered him toward its central disk, which grew the fruit it used to attract birds. More leafy tendrils snaked around his body.

*Please put him down. He tastes horrible,* Eva thought out to the tree. The bird-catcher brought Hailey closer to the glistening red cluster of fruit at its center. The tree revealed the fruit as nothing more than a colorful lure surrounded by an open maw full of needle-sharp teeth.

"Eva!" There was panic in Hailey's voice. "Whatever you are doing, hurry up!"

Eva did not respond. She concentrated all attention on the tree. *Drop him.*

The tree wrapped more tendrils around Hailey.

*Drop him!*

Hailey was centimeters away from the tree's toothy maw.

"DROP HIM!" Eva growled like the horned beast that had chased her.

The bird-catcher released Hailey. He landed with a soft thud on the forest floor. Eva scrambled down from her hiding spot and over to his side. "Are you okay?" She helped Hailey up as the tree shuffled off into the night.

"I am starting to understand why humans went extinct in the first place," Hailey said as he staggered to his feet. With Eva supporting him, they hobbled back to camp.

"His name is Redimus." Caruncle placed his boomrod on the driver's seat of his hoversloop. He plopped back down on a crate by the fire. "He is a scout sent-tasked to find someone, but he would not say who."

Eva and Hailey exchanged worried glances.

"It is not you, Eva Nine," Caruncle said in a dismissive tone. "Not unless you are hunt-wanted by the queen."

"He told you he was sent by Queen Ojo?" Eva asked.

"No. He told me nothing," Caruncle added another log to the fire. "But he carried-held the type of boomrod used solely by Her Majesty's royal guard. There are only two ways a Dorcean would come to own-have a weapon like that: he takes it from a fallen-dead guard or he is given-handed it by the queen herself."

"So he killed one of the guards?" Hailey massaged his ankle where the bird-catcher had held him. "Maybe he shot him with his glowing eye?"

"Shot him with his eye? Where do you-human get these ideas?" Caruncle laughed to himself. "You have a wild-crazy imagination."

"Do you think he killed a royal guard or not?" Eva asked. "Because I don't think he's going to just leave." She remembered how ruthless Besteel was in his pursuit and what it had cost Eva to rid herself of him.

Caruncle leaned back and stroked his wattles. "The Dorceans can be thickheaded . . . like this one." He pointed to Hailey, who replied with an obscene gesture. "But they are also honorable. They keep their word. So I do not think one would break the law and kill a royal guard just to take-seize his weapon."

"Maybe the guard was already dead," said Hailey.

"That could' also be the truth-fact." Caruncle bent down and stoked the fire. "He did say that the battle-war in Solas was still going on. But he also asked if I had encountered anyone, or anything, out of the ordinary. Right now *everything* is out of the ordinary."

Despite the fact that this stranger was not Besteel, the thought of a Dorcean hunting in the forest made Eva ill. She tried to absorb the quiet of the forest to help calm her nerves, but she could now sense the Dorcean's presence. The anxiety did not subside. "Did—did you say anything about us?"

"Of course not! I am Caruncle—lone artifact collector for the queen. That is all."

Eva breathed a small sigh of relief.

"No. I believe this fellow was search-hunting for Zin." Caruncle kept his gaze on Eva.

"Zin?" Eva looked over at Hailey.

"Yes. My hunch-guess is that the queen has sent him to do this." Caruncle leaned forward toward Eva. The crackling fire lit his knotted face from below, giving him a monstrous appearance. "And do you-human know what else I think?"

Eva held her breath and shook her head.

Hailey said nothing.

"I think . . . we should all get some sleep-rest." Caruncle stood and shambled over to his hoversloop. From the heaps of junk he pulled out a bedroll. "The sooner we leave-go in the morning, the sooner we are away-gone from this mysterious Dorcean. Yes?"

"Right," said Eva. She lay back down on her blanket and closed her eyes. Focusing on the forest, she began to move through it with her ability, searching for the exact location of the Dorcean. She traveled deeper and deeper into the wood. Once more she heard a sound, a low resonant hum. It sounded as if it were a chorus composed of many voices. The hum drowned out all else. Eva opened her eyes and sighed in frustration. Even without her abilities she knew the Dorcean was out there. Hunting. There would be no sleep tonight.

# The thick

morning mist shrouded all evidence of the previous night's encounter with the Dorcean. Eva searched the forest again with her abilities and received signals indicating his location. "He is near the point of Hiyao's Hook, closest to the mountains," she explained to Caruncle and Hailey.

"How do you know this?" Caruncle rolled up his sleeping pad.

"She doesn't." Hailey emptied a crystal coffee packet into his water container. "She just guessed."

"It's okay, Hailey. I know what I'm doing," Eva said. She walked over and helped Caruncle load his bedroll onto the hoversloop. "I can talk to the forest," she said in a matter-of-fact way.

Caruncle's mustard-colored eyes went wide. "You . . . can communicate-talk with the forest? The *entire* forest?"

Hailey let out a disapproving groan.

"What? He should know." Eva pointed to Caruncle. "He protected us last night. What if that Dorcean is looking for me?"

"He's not looking for you," Hailey said. "Didn't you hear a word of what Caruncle told us?"

"If Redimus wanted to find-get you, he would have," Caruncle added. "As I said, I believe he is looking for . . ." The alien paused. His tusked mouth opened slightly as if he'd just realized something. "You-Eva know where Zin is, don't you? Is that where we are going? To locate-find Zin in the ancient ruins?"

"Yes," Eva answered.

Caruncle purred and rubbed his many hands together. "Of course. This makes perfect sense-logic. Zin was always fascinated with the ruins.

What's more, I do not think Redimus has figured that out yet."

Hailey threw down his coffee. It splattered in the fire with a hiss. "Why don't you tell him where the Vitae Virus generator is while you're at it?"

"That's not important now," Eva snapped back.

"You-human know where the generator is?" Caruncle blinked in surprise.

Hailey stormed around the camp. "Yeah. She knows and she'll tell you—"

"Stop," said Eva.

"She may even tell you where her sister is, or maybe . . . if you're lucky, where she got her 'special powers.'"

"Stop it, Hailey!"

"Stop? Why, Eva?" Hailey's tone was sarcastic. "You trusted Cadmus, you trusted Eight, and they all let you down. So why not trust this garbage-dealing slug?"

"I am not a garbage trader-dealer!" Caruncle bellowed.

"And I am not thickheaded!" Hailey got in Caruncle's face. "So stop calling me that."

"I trusted you, too," Eva hissed, and trembled with anger. "And look where that got me."

"Oh, here we go again. How long are you going

to wave that in my face?" Hailey yelled.

"Until *you* trust *me*." Eva stormed away from Hailey toward the pair of munt-runners. Overhead a light rain began to drizzle down.

Eva crumbled up a Sustibar and fed it to Bix and Bax. "You guys really like this, don't you?" she cooed. Over the sound of their crunching, she heard Caruncle's plodding steps as he approached.

"At last, some rain," he said. "This dry climate is bad-horrible for my skin."

"You better not betray me," Eva said.

"I am, like you, doing what I can to survive-live out here." He held his hands up in surrender.

Eva pulled her hood up over her damp head and fed the remainder of the bar to the mounts.

"If Redimus is search-looking for Zin, he will keep any-all options open. My guess is that he knows we are traveling south, along the forest edge. He will likely spy-watch on us just to see where we are headed."

Eva was happy talking to Caruncle about a Dorcean huntsman and the plan if it meant she didn't have to talk to Hailey. "So, somehow we have to get past the Dorcean without him noticing us?"

"Yes," Caruncle said. "Which is tricky because

we have to go-travel around Hiyao's Hook to get to the pass that takes us through the mountains." With his fire poker he scrawled a map of the hook in the muddy sand. To Eva the landmark that he drew looked like a backward letter *J*. He continued, "We are here, on the north side of the hook. He is at the point to the east, here. Correct?"

"Correct," replied Eva.

"We have to travel-move around the hook to continue south toward the pass." Caruncle indicated the path needed in order to get around the landmark.

"Okay." Eva took the poker from Caruncle. "Why do we have to go around the forest?" She drew a line that cut directly through the hook. "Why not just go south, straight through the forest?"

"Great-good idea." Caruncle leaned against the sloop. "But how do I get all this and my team through a heavily wooded forest?"

Eva looked through the gray drizzle to the forest. Wandering trees, weeping bird-catchers, and other oversize growth formed a dense impenetrable knot of vegetation. She could feel the plants reinvigorate from the moisture of the rain. She could hear birds singing somewhere deep within the wood. She could feel her own anger toward

Hailey cool from the dampness. "Get Bix and Bax tacked up and ready to go. I'll take care of the rest."

Eva walked to where the green met the gravelly plain of the flats. *Can you help us, please? I need a path.* She closed her eyes and envisioned a trail cutting through the forest. One by one the wandering trees and other plants began to move, forming a passage into the wood.

Caruncle put a hand to his mouth and gasped. "Sheesa! I have never seen-witnessed anything like this in my life."

"Get used to it," Hailey muttered, and grabbed his things.

The rain dissipated to a few drops here and there as they traveled deeper into the forest. Hailey followed behind Eva as she led the procession down the tree-lined path. Trailing behind them, Caruncle drove the hoversloop. From time to time he would exclaim aloud how unbelievable this feat was. Especially when the wandering trees returned to their resting spots behind the sloop, concealing any trace of the passage they had created.

"I know you're mad at me, but you are too trusting, Eva. I hope you know what you are doing," Hailey said under his breath.

Eva continued walking, not acknowledging him at all.

"Why not let this Dorshean—"

"Dorcean," Eva corrected him.

"Whatever. Let him find Zin and take him back to the queen. We can just tell him where Zin is. Then we can all go on our merry way."

"No. We have to get to Zin first. Just *trust me* for once."

"Fine." Hailey stared ahead, grim-faced with defeat.

Eva exhaled hotly. "I know you don't like it out here."

"Whatever gave you that idea? Was it that spitting monster that nearly shredded us to pieces? Or was it the flying knife-things? Perhaps it was the fern that tried to eat me last night?"

"After we find Zin, we'll find a way back to Vanpa. I promise."

"The sooner the better. Then I am out of here," Hailey said under his breath.

"I want to leave too. But Caruncle is the only one who can navigate through this area, and I really need to speak with Zin. Okay?" Despite her rising anger with Hailey, the cooled energy of the forest helped Eva remain calm.

"Okay," Hailey said.

"Besides, we have to just wait and see what he does to know his true character. As far as I can tell, he's been helpful." Eva glanced back at the junk dealer in his sloop.

"There you go sounding like Rovender again," said Hailey.

Eva suppressed the smile that began to form from his compliment. She tied her long damp braids up into a bun. "You know, here in the forest there is much I can do. But I cannot communicate and control everything—especially Dorcean huntsmen. Caruncle is the perfect cover for us to find Zin."

"I just hope that when you find this Zin, he understands what we've been through and listens to what you have to say," said Hailey.

"Me too." Eva led the procession around a large rock formation jutting from the forest floor at a sharp angle. The steely rocks were blanketed in rich green cushions of moss. On the leeward side of the formation a cavernous opening led down into the earth.

Eva approached the rock and ran her fingers over the wet moss. He eye caught something under the growth, and she rubbed away the grime. The letters *HRP* were etched into the rock wall.

"Is this a Sanctuary?" Hailey joined Eva. He yanked off a large patch of moss to reveal the Dynastes logo underneath. "Wow! I've never seen one before."

Caruncle brought his team to a halt and hopped down from the driver's seat. His voice was giddy when he spoke. "This is a home-cave of the ancients!" He seized his boomrod, a lantern, his smudge stick, and an empty cage. "I have seen many but have not explored this particular one." He handed the smudge stick to Hailey. "Let us enter-go and have a look. I'll hold-carry the weapon; you hold-carry the light."

Hailey rolled up his sleeves. "I have always wanted to see what one of these looks like. Eva, will you show me around?"

"No. You two go on," Eva said. "I'll wait here."

Hailey turned around. "You're not coming?"

Eva shook her head. She knew all too well what an abandoned Sanctuary held—the remains of a home and life she once knew. Perhaps the remains of a Muthr . . . or even the remains of one like herself.

Hailey approached her. "Are you sure?"

"Trust me," Eva said. "I know what's down there."

"You coming, Hailey-human?" Caruncle's voice echoed up from the stairwell.

"That's the first time he's called me by my name." Hailey gave his lopsided grin. "Maybe you are right, after all."

Eva smiled and nodded.

"I'll let you know if I find anything we can use." Hailey ran down the steps to join Caruncle.

Eva walked over to Bix and Bax and began to stroke them. "There is nothing in there that I can use." The munt-runners nickered in delight as Eva scratched around their beaked muzzles. "Everything I need is out here."

"Hey, Eva, take a look at this." Hailey jogged up the exit of the Sanctuary.

"Where's Caruncle?" Eva walked over from the munt-runners.

"Still poking around down there, catching knifejacks." On the moss-laden ground Hailey set down a large plastic container.

"Are these Omnipods?" Eva bent down to see what was inside the container.

"I wish." Hailey opened the seal of the container, labeled EVAN-42, and reached in to pull out a small, stuffed toy—a cat wearing a silver suit. "Look! It's a mint-in-box Beeboo doll," Hailey said. "You know, just like the old kiddie programs. All the other characters are in here too—Racing Raccoon, Outdoor Octopus, Reassuring Robot—"

"That's great. Maybe some of the kids back at Vanpa's will want them." Eva stood and turned away. She felt as if her breath had been sucked from her body.

"This container was sealed, and there was a whole bunch more in the stockroom. I don't think these dolls have been activated yet." Hailey turned the Beeboo doll over in his hands. "Is there an on and off switch? Do you know?"

Eva closed her eyes. Her mind flushed with memories . . .

*"Happy fifth birthday, Eva dear," Muthr said. "I hope you like your presents."*

*"I love them!" Eva said. She hugged her Beeboo toys tight.*

*"Make a wish, give it a kiss, and it will come to life," Muthr replied.*

*Eva ran her fingers over Beeboo's soft synthetic fur. Its fabric eyelids were closed as if it were asleep. "I wish you were real," she whispered into its ear,*

*and kissed the doll on the plastic nose. The doll
yawned. Its eyes blinked open.*

*"Hi. I'm Beeboo cat," it said in a childlike voice.
"What's your name?"*

*"I'm Eva. Eva Nine."*

*"Want to be friends?" the doll said with a giggle.*

*"Oh, yes!" Eva squealed. She kissed each toy and
watched with amazement as they came to life and
danced around her room. . . .*

"You okay?" Hailey placed a hand on Eva's
shoulder.

With a start Eva was pulled from her memories
back to the present.

"I thought . . . maybe you would like this," he
said.

"I'm fine." Eva wiped her eyes with the palm of her
hand. Her gaze remained downcast. "Memories. It
brings back a lot of memories."

Hailey brushed Eva's hair from her wet eyes. "I
guess bad ones. I didn't mean—"

"It's okay. I'll be all right."

Hailey returned the doll with the other toys
to the container. "Vanpa used to tell me stories
about his Sanctuary from when he was a kid. I
wanted to live in one so bad. It just sounded so

amazing—having your own playground, your own garden, and a robot to take care of you."

Eva sat down next to Hailey. "Yeah. But after a while all I wanted to do was leave and see the world. The real world."

"Not what you expected, huh?" Hailey said.

"I'd rather be living in the real world than hiding away from it."

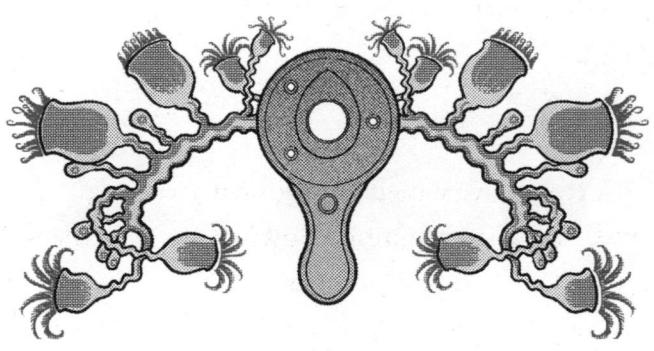

# CHAPTER 11: PANTOMIME

The hoversloop exited the forest without incident. Eva reported that the Dorcean had moved north and was no longer in the vicinity. The following morning the group crossed a short distance of the flats and made their way through the scrubby foothills of the Bliek Mountains.

"There are paths here," Hailey said. He pointed to a pattern of flat stones snaking across the landscape.

"These were probably paved roads at one time," Eva explained. They were sitting next to Caruncle in the driver's seat.

"Yes," said Caruncle. "We are arrive-coming upon ruins from your people. I have explored them on prior excursions, which is how I discovered the path-pass through the mountains."

"I had no idea the ruins stretched across both sides of the mountains," said Eva.

"Oh, yes. Down here these overgrown ruins spread-run in all directions for quite a distance. Also, do you see how lush-green the land is?"

Eva nodded.

"That is because we are on the windward side of these mountains. The air is heavy with water-rain as it blows south from Lake Concors."

"But it's like a desert on the other side," said Eva.

"Because the water-rain gets trapped here on this side. It is too heavy to blow over those peaks." Caruncle pointed toward the jagged mountains looming closer.

"And you know a way through there?" Hailey asked.

"The *only* way. Yes. One of these pass-paths will

take us. Only I, Caruncle, am the one who knows where it is. You-human will see when we cross these mountains. We will come to the ancient desert ruins and we shall locate-find Zin. I will lead us straight through the night, so that we arrive by sunrise tomorrow."

Caruncle's team trotted down the ancient highway. Tufts of lush grass and weeds broke up the sun-bleached pavement. Hunks of rock and boulders were strewn on either side of the road. As they passed close by, Eva realized the rocks were actually bricks and the remnants of walls. Where a building once stood, now there was only a fractured foundation—a large ghostly footprint of a world that was no more.

On the peak of a low-lying mountain, Eva saw a giant statue amidst the ruins. Though the morning sun was bright behind it, the statue's elongated silhouette brought to mind the pillar guards from the Royal Museum of Solas. Eva masked the sun's glare with her hand to get a better view, but the statue had . . . disappeared? She searched for a nearby turnfin to ask for an explanation, but none of the birds were present. She considered asking Hailey but decided he would just tease her about seeing things that weren't really there.

"Once we get to the cover of these overgrown ruins up ahead, we should stop-rest and let Bix and Bax eat before we set off through the mountains," said Caruncle. He snapped the reins, and the munt-runners loped ahead.

"Are there any dangers here?" Eva stood in a crumbling courtyard of stone. Towering above her the remnants of once majestic edifices revealed the scars that time had etched upon their surfaces. Thick roots snaked through these remains, like veins running through the entire overgrown city. In her drab poncho Eva would have disappeared among the lichen-covered rubble if it weren't for her snow-white hair.

"I have found-seen nothing beyond the usual." Caruncle filled a woven feedbag with grain. The munt-runner's hides quivered and they watched him with dilated eyes. He laid the feedbag on the ground in front of his team, and the munt-runners bent low to peck at the food with their short blunt beaks. "But don't go climbing on anything," Caruncle said. "None of these structures are stable."

"You can say that again." Hailey gazed up at a fractured relief set above a large gaping doorway.

He walked through the stone doorway and into the overgrown ruins beyond. "Wow! Look at this place!" His voice echoed.

"Don't go too far. We shall leave shortly." Caruncle found his pipe and his bag of spices. "However, if you discover something interesting, come find-get me."

Eva followed a particularly large mass of roots that crept down from the roof of a deteriorating building. The roots grew out from a squat tree. Hanging from the twisted trunk were tangled vines covered in jade-green leaves. "Caruncle, what is this?"

"Ah! Mimic ivy," Caruncle answered from his sloop. "Feel-touch it."

Eva looked back at him, suspicious.

"Don't worry. It will not harm-hurt you." Caruncle wore a toothy grin.

Eva placed her fingertips on the thick serpentine roots of the ivy. Immediately the leafy vines rustled and moved. They came together in such a way as to form a shape—the animated shape of a large Dorcean. Unsure of what she was witnessing, Eva backed up. The ivy-formed Dorcean rushed at Eva. She cried out and stumbled backward over fallen debris.

"What's wrong?" Hailey poked his head out from a stone doorway.

Caruncle bellowed with laughter. "It is nothing to fret-worry about." He waddled over and helped Eva up to her feet. "You have never seen mimic ivy before?"

The ivy-formed Dorcean blocked Eva from the trunk of the plant. She focused her mind on its thick sinuous trunk.

*I see. You. Go. Away,* the ivy said.

"Look-see here." Caruncle pointed at tiny black berries growing from the ends of the ivy's shoots. "These are its eyes. It view-sees an animal, something that would eat its leaves, and then—"

"It creates a shape, a silhouette, to frighten it off."

Caruncle cackled and slapped Eva on the back. "And it scare-frightened you good, Eva Nine!"

"Why a Dorcean?" Eva went to touch the leaves of the ivy. The ivy-formed Dorcean backed up just beyond reach. "Does it know what I fear?"

"No. It just picks an animal larger than you." Caruncle lit his pipe. "Probably something that it has seen before."

Eva pointed to the Dorcean shape and whispered to the mimic ivy. "You've seen this form before?"

*Yes.*

"Recently?"

*No. Many suns ago.*

"Have you seen my shape before?" She walked under the fragment of a stone archway covered in a tangle of roots.

*No.*

The ivy's vines twined to create the silhouette of Eva. As she walked, it mirrored her every move. Eva skipped. The ivy-Eva skipped. Eva stopped, but the ivy-Eva continued down a corridor. Eva now followed the ivy. She exited and found herself in a wide expanse of the ruins.

"Do not walk-go too far," said Caruncle. "We leave soon."

"I am not the sort who would eat your beautiful leaves. So maybe you can show me what others you have seen?" Eva asked the plant.

*Others. Yes.*

The ivy began to take on a new shape. It reminded Eva of the holograms she had seen of topiaries used to decorate the fanciful gardens of the past. She watched an ivy-formed munt-runner gallop over the rubble. Eva gave chase, traveling farther and farther into the labyrinth. The munt-runner shape led Eva to the large façade of an ornate cathedral, now overtaken by the choking twining roots of the mimic ivy. Here the ivy took the form of a giant water bear, like Otto, and bound up and over the front of the cathedral.

"Eva, where are you?" Hailey called from somewhere.

"More!" Eva ignored Hailey. "Show me more." She ran through the arched doorway into the roofless cathedral. Inside, Eva stopped abruptly. The ivy had now taken on an all-too-familiar shape: Zin.

"Eva?" Caruncle's voice rang out through the ruins. "I can hear you. Tell me-Caruncle where you are."

"This one," Eva said to the ivy. "Where did it go?"

The ivy mimicked Zin's arm movements as it pointed to the other end of the cathedral, opposite the direction Eva had come. There she spied a small opening through a collapsed doorway.

Eva paused and looked back toward the direction of Caruncle and Hailey. "They can wait. I've got to find him. Let's go!"

The ivy-formed Zin zoomed down the length of the enormous cathedral and out beyond. Eva dashed after it. She wriggled through the collapsed opening, leaving Caruncle and Hailey far behind. *I've found Zin at last! I knew he'd be in the ruins.* She followed the ivy down abandoned alleys and across the cracked stones of a square, and arrived at the entrance of a disintegrating domed amphitheater. Eva stepped into the shadowy entrance and came out into the open-air space.

Inside the circular amphitheater the ivy-formed Zin flew up to join with another ivy-shape, a shape Eva had seen before. *The statue.* Standing among the empty rows that had once held seats, an ivy-formed giant loomed above Eva. Three columnar legs tapered up to a T-shaped head while long, flattened arms hung down on either side of its towering body.

"A pillar guard?" Eva asked the mimic ivy.

The vines of the ivy dispersed and returned to their natural shape, revealing an *actual* pillar guard that had been shrouded underneath the foliage. Its three eyes lit up, and it emitted a long, loud blat.

Eva scurried away from the giant. A long arm, ending in a collection of serrated claws, extended at lightning speed. The claws sank deep into the earth just in front of Eva, blocking her escape. The pillar guard sounded off again, and Eva turned to face it. The guard yanked its claws from the ground, removing clods of turf with it, and retracted its segmented arm.

When Eva tried to leave again, the pillar guard blocked her path. Somewhere, far in the ruins, Eva could hear Hailey and Caruncle calling for her. She dashed off in one direction, then quickly changed course in hopes of tricking the guard, but again she was cut off from escape.

"Let me pass," Eva cried.

The guard let out another loud blat, followed by several short trills.

"I don't understand you," Eva said, catching her breath. She gazed up.

The guard watched her with all three glowing eyes.

"Are you trying to tell me something?"

Her question was answered by a quick series of staccato notes.

"Ugh! I don't know what are you saying." Eva searched the ground for a stick to draw in the dirt with, but none could be found. Still hunting, she walked toward the roots of ivy. She glanced up to see the ivy-form of Zin flying around the amphitheater. She pointed to the ivy. "Is it Zin? Is he nearby?"

The pillar guard looked at the ivy and blurted out a melody of brassy sound. It laid its hand flat on the ground at Eva's feet; its talons were as big as her body. In an instant the guard retracted its claws.

"You know where Zin is, don't you?" Eva asked.

Once more it replied in musical notes.

"Can you take me?"

More music.

"Let me get my friends. You can lead us." Eva pointed back from where she'd come. "Hailey! I'm over here," she shouted.

Another loud blat echoed from the ancient walls. The pillar guard turned and took three steps away from Eva.

"Wait!" She ran to catch up with the guard, waving her arms wildly to stop it. "Don't go."

The guard made no more noise and lowered its hand to the ground once more.

"I guess it's just you and me then, huh?" Eva took a deep breath and climbed up the pillar guard's segmented arm. The guard lifted Eva to its shoulders, where she stood and found a handhold in the ridges of its neck. The giant turned and bounded away from the ruins toward the mountains.

# CHAPTER 12: SIGNS

# In the fading light

Eva turned back to see the sun sink in the sky. Past the scree-covered slope, she watched the overgrown ruins far beyond slip into darkness. Somewhere out there Caruncle and Hailey were probably looking for her. *I hope I can find them after I locate Zin*, she thought.

The pillar guard trekked down a path that wound through a gap in the mountain ridges. As twilight blanketed the landscape, a brisk chill settled in the pass. Eva pulled her hood over her head to stave off the cool night air.

"Hey." She tapped the guard's neck. "We need to stop so I can take a break." She pointed to the ground. The guard responded in more musical notes and lowered its arm so that Eva could climb down.

"I don't know why the vocal transcoder doesn't

work with you." She slid down the long arm. Once on the ground Eva stretched and flexed the stiffness and aches in her hands from gripping the guard's neck for so long. After squatting down behind a large rock to relieve herself, Eva realized it had been some time since she had eaten. She pulled a Sustibar from the pocket of her poncho and nibbled off part of it. The bar must have been old as it tasted stale. She spit it out and wiped her mouth. Unsure of what to do with it, she decided to crumble up the bar and conspicuously place it on the ground along with the wrapper. *I bet Bix and Bax will find this, and then Hailey will know I came this way.*

Eva returned to the pillar guard. In the deepening night she could now see the pinpoint patterns of shimmering light that pulsated underneath the guard's semitranslucent skin. It brought to mind the biomechanical nervous system of the Mother from the Heart of the Wandering Forest. Eva placed a palm on the guard's wide columnar leg and felt the warmth emanate from within.

"I wonder, are you a machine or an organic being? Maybe you are both, like Muthr was?"

The guard laid its hand down on the rocky ground for Eva to climb onto.

"My abilities certainly don't work on you. How are we supposed to talk?"

A short melody chimed from the guard.

"They used remotes to control you back in Solas. Who is controlling you now? Is it Zin?"

The guard remained silent. Its hand still lay on the ground, waiting for Eva to join him.

"Do you understand anything that I am saying?" Frustration grew in Eva's voice. Once more she looked for a stick to draw in the sand as Caruncle had done, but there was nothing but large rocks and thatch surrounding her. *If only I had something to draw with . . . The liquid light pen!*

Eva plucked the pen from her pocket and shook it as Hailey had done. She knelt down in front of a large boulder and scrawled out a picture of Zin holding a pillar guard remote. The light of the ink shone brightly in the night. She pointed to the drawing. "Is that who controls you?"

The guard's eyes gazed down upon her drawing as if they were headlights on a hovercraft. It replied in a singsong of blats and trills.

"Good." Eva added an arrow and the words "THIS WAY" to her drawing. She climbed up the guard's segmented arm and took her perch at its shoulder. They continued their journey through the night toward the east. From time to time Eva dropped food and wrappers for Bix and Bax to find. It reminded her of an old story—a fairy tale—that Muthr had told her long ago. In that story two lost children had defeated an evil witch who'd tried to eat them. They found their way back home using a trail they'd made of pebbles. This brought to mind Eva's conversation with Caruncle regarding fairy tales.

*We'll find out if this story has a happy ending soon enough,* she thought.

The glow of a rising sun cut a golden slice across the dusky clouds above. Eva's arms were cramped and her fingers sore from clutching on to the pillar guard throughout their journey. Somehow she had managed to stay put, even when she'd dozed off.

The guard stood at the edge of a ridge—the end of the mountain pass—that looked down into an arid valley littered with broken buildings and the skeletons of fallen skyscrapers. Eva had arrived at the westernmost edge of the ancient city. A corroded sign, half-buried in the sand, said WELCOME TO MANHATTAN.

*So many horrible things have happened here,* Eva thought. *It's the last place I want to be, but if he's here* . . . She tucked a braid behind her ear and scanned the vast ruins, hoping to see Zin zooming up to greet them, but he did not come.

The pillar guard plodded down the steep slope of the ridge toward the ruins below. He carried Eva past sand-worn statues and eroding monuments. At last the guard stopped at the edge of a wide cavern. Eva shimmied down the arm of the guard to the sandy ground.

The cave was much larger than the tunnel Otto had dug to the ancient library. It dropped straight down vertically for many meters into darkness. From its shadowed center rose a gigantic lichen tree, the largest Eva had ever seen. The tree's umbrella shape blocked the bright sunlight from the cave that held its roots. Turnfins swooped and glided around the top of the tree, which housed their rookery. Down below the distinct sound of running water echoed up the cave walls.

"Is this where Zin is?"

A reply came as a loud blast, and the guard pointed into the cavern.

"Okay. I'll go down."

The guard looked up to the sky as if sensing something. It emitted another brassy melody, then bounded away into the rubble-strewn landscape.

"Where are you going?" Eva called after it. The guard did not reply.

Jagged slabs of concrete and cinder block that formed the cave walls made the climb down easy for Eva. Once she descended below the brightness of the daylight, her eyes adjusted to the dim world that she now entered. It was not a cave after all but an underground site of excavated ruins. It was as if some giant beast had torn the roof off a subterranean dwelling, revealing the many rooms and passages within. Eva continued her descent down through several stories and arrived at the original ground level.

Arched doorways ringed the edges of what appeared to have been a vaulted foyer. The giant lichen tree rose from the center of the foyer's fractured floor.

"Hello?" Eva's voice echoed throughout the ruin. Among the few remaining tiles still clinging to the walls was a cracked ceramic sign that read, CITY HALL STATION. The sound of dripping water echoed from one of the passages. Eva walked toward the sound through the dark passage.

She arrived in a wide curved corridor with arched supports. Shattered glass skylights allowed intermittent patches of sunlight to find its way in.

Water from broken underground pipes trickled into a canal that followed the curve of the platform she was standing on. Wondrous trumpet-shaped growths sprung from the platform ledge surrounding the canal, while multicolored lichens patterned the foundation of adjacent walls. The layout reminded Eva of the subferry station in New Attica.

She closed her eyes and let her thoughts drift, in the hopes of communicating with any nearby life-forms. Though she was not in the forest, Eva still sensed the presence of beings.

Many beings.

The more she opened up her mental conduit, the more beings she sensed. Further, there was that humming presence Eva had heard before. It felt ancient and powerful—beyond any creature she could imagine. The sound of the humming became too overwhelming. Eva opened her eyes and scanned the corridor, but saw nothing. "Zin? Zin, are you here?"

She brushed her fingers along the reeds of voxfruit growing near the canal. Plucking one of the fruits to eat, she spied something large and flat lying on the ground. She knelt down to get a closer look. It appeared to be some sort of metal plaque with writing on it. Eva rubbed the sand and dust away with her hands and read aloud, "This First Municipal Rapid Transit Railroad of the City of New York, Suggested by the Chamber of Commerce, Authorized by the State, Constructed by the City."

Out of the corner of her eye, Eva saw a patch of lichen move. She turned and crept close to the tiled wall where the foliose lichen was. Its ochre leafy lobes radiated from a cluster of cuplike nodules. Eva went to touch one of the nodules, and it blinked.

"What!" Eva jumped. All the nodules then blinked as a group, like beady black eyes placed in a pattern on a flat leafy face. Eva inspected the lichen closer. It released a tiny puff of colored dust.

*I. Do not move. It. Cannot see me.*

The words entered Eva's mind the moment the dust was released.

"I—I won't hurt you," she whispered. "I'm just here looking for someone."

The round patch of lichen loosened itself from the stone's surface and emerged from a bowl-shaped niche in the wall. Under its flattened lichen head was a squat tubular body. The waist-high creature scurried about on short tentacles. Its basic shape brought to mind the holograms Eva had studied of sea cucumbers.

Several of the creature's tentacles stretched out to touch Eva. She sat down and let it inspect her face. The lichen-creature released a series of colorful puffs, summoning others of its kind to come forth from their hiding places. Before long there were dozens of the creatures surrounding Eva, leaving the cement walls riddled with hidey-holes.

*I. Am curious. What is. It? A new being.*

The thoughts came flowing in as the lichen-creatures examined Eva.

"You are cute." Eva touched a fingertip to the tentacle of one of the natives. "I don't think you are from the Age of Man."

"You are correct, human," a familiar chirpy voice said.

Eva stood and spun around.

From a shadowy alcove floated the one Eva had been searching for.

Zin.

# Do I know

you?" Zin asked aloud, although his large mouth remained closed. He paused where he'd emerged on the far side of the station platform, opposite Eva.

"You do." She stepped closer. "It's me, Eva. Eva Nine."

"Eva Nine?" Zin retreated. "The human captive delivered by Besteel. The one who disclosed the whereabouts of my long-lost sister?"

"Yes! Did you—"

"Also, the one who demolished the Royal Museum and Her Majesty's cherished collection of artifacts." Zin pointed several accusatory fingers at Eva. "If you are *that* Eva Nine, you best leave this sacred location right now before you cause more destruction. Be gone!"

"Wait just a nano." Eva stormed toward Zin. "You gave me no choice. You were going to dissect me! What did you expect me to do?"

"I had no final say in that decision." Zin folded all nine of his arms and held his ground. "I was following Queen Ojo's orders."

"Following orders?" Eva's voice rose in exasperation. "Zin, you know a lot about a lot of things."

"Much gratitudes, Eva. I—"

"So think for yourself for once! Stop doing what Ojo tells you!" Eva turned away. The entire colony of lichen creatures had gathered to watch Eva and Zin's exchange.

*He. Is kind. He does not hurt. Us. He watches. Only.*

Eva exhaled in frustration. "I know." She knelt down next to one of the creatures. It released more puffs of color.

*You. Are also kind?*

"As I said, I won't hurt you," said Eva. Zin drifted right next to her. This close, she could see that Zin's ivory complexion was now grimy.

"Do you understand them?" he asked.

"Yes." Eva turned her attention back to the lichen creatures. "I told you before that I can, especially now, since I have been in the Heart of the forest."

Zin gasped. "You—you've explored the Heart? The touchdown site? Did you discover anything?"

Eva stood and looked Zin in the eyes. "I found the Vitae Virus generator, and I drank water carrying the virus."

"Then it is true. Soon the humans will know." Zin sank low to the ground.

Eva's anger left her. Zin looked so . . . defeated. "The humans will know nothing. I would never tell anyone the location of the generator."

"You would not?"

Eva walked back out into the foyer and looked up at the gigantic lichen tree. "I don't want anything to happen to the forest. I didn't want anything to happen to Solas or Lacus. But it happened. I tried to stop it, but I couldn't."

Zin floated over to her. "When we first interacted, you had no cognizance of the imminent human invasion?"

"When I saw you last, I didn't think there *were* any other humans."

With stout fingers Zin pulled off his pointed hat and rubbed his forehead. He drifted, mumbling to himself, "Then perhaps she is but the herald . . . not the cause?"

"What are you talking about?"

Zin turned back to Eva. "My sister Arius. She foretold of your arrival."

"She did? To you?"

"Not to me, but I believe she knew," said Zin. "Do you recall any memory of what she prophesied directly to you?"

"A little." Eva shrugged her shoulders. "Why? I thought you didn't believe in all that stuff."

Zin floated back toward Eva. "I don't . . . and I do. I believe, like me, she has exceptional skills of observation."

"You mean . . . she *had*," said Eva, looking away.

"'Had'? What are you—" Zin's slit-eyes went wide with realization.

"I'm sorry." As the memory of Arius at the hands of Loroc rushed back, Eva felt tears fall from her eyes. "You—you didn't know?"

Zin zoomed over to Eva. He seized her arm, rolled up her sleeve, and gasped.

Arius's mark, the glyph she'd placed upon Eva, had disappeared. "The glyph . . . it's gone!" Eva said. She rubbed the spot on her arm where the glyph had once been, hoping it might reappear, but it did not.

Zin drifted down to the ground like a dying leaf abandoning its tree.

"I'm so sorry, Zin." Eva sat down next to him. "When I met her and she told me my fortune, I was frightened. Now I feel as if she were trying to help me. Guide me."

"Well, she was angry with me," Zin whispered. He floated back down the passage toward the platform of the transit station.

"But you got to see her, right?" Eva followed him. "She told you what happened to your other sister, Darius?"

"I never made it. The museum was a catastrophe. . . . Then word came of the invasion in Lacus. My time was occupied by my royal responsibilities."

"I tried to warn her about the invasion," Eva said. "But I was too late. I failed." Her mind reeled about how to break the details surrounding Arius's death to Zin. *How would Rovender do it?* she thought. *He is so good with words.*

Zin exhaled. "It is I who have failed, Eva Nine. When I originally analyzed the data provided to me by King Ojo's research team, I believed Orbona to be a lifeless planet. I stated that it was the best candidate for the King's terraforming program. It is apparent now that I was mistaken. Your primitive species somehow went undetected. Furthermore, I underestimated the ability of your kind and its impact on us—the introduced species."

"But the planet was dead," said Eva. "Humans may have even been dormant in underground labs when you saw that data. Only later did Cadmus's inventions bring us back." Eva was awash with mixed feelings. She knew Cadmus supported the invasion of Solas, but she also owed her very existence to him.

"The human leader? The one who demolished Lacus, lay siege to my grand city, and murdered my sister?" Anger snarled in Zin's chirpy voice.

"There's more to it than that." Eva kept her tone calm as if she were speaking with Hailey. "You have to listen to me."

"Elucidate me. Fill me in on every minute detail, starting just after *you* razed my museum." Zin crossed his many arms.

"Your brother, Loroc, masterminded the invasion of Lacus and Solas. He helped Cadmus."

"Loroc wouldn't—"

"It is he who killed Arius," Eva said.

"Nonsense!" barked Zin.

"I saw it happen." Eva took hold of two of Zin's arms. "He . . . consumed her in one gulp. He told me he'd done the same with your other sister, Darius."

"Consumed? No. That cannot be." Zin brushed the spot on Eva's forearm where Arius's glyph had once been. He broke free from her grasp and floated toward the inky depths at the back of the station from which he had emerged.

"He claimed he now possessed their powers. I am sorry I have to be the one to tell you this. When I heard you were still alive, I traveled a long way to find you. We even came across a Dorcean searching for you." Eva trailed behind Zin down the station platform.

Zin turned back. "A Dorcean?"

"Yes." Eva stifled a shudder. "He had a glowing eye. His name was Redi . . . something."

"Redimus."

"Do you know him?" asked Eva.

"He is Besteel's brother." Zin floated out from

the shadows under an open skylight, his brow knitted with concern. "He is the one Besteel was working to free from incarceration by replacing all the living specimens in the Royal Menagerie."

Nausea wormed its way into the pit of Eva's stomach. "Besteel's . . . brother? He *is* hunting for me," she murmured.

"Unlikely. But he could very well be hunting for *me*," Zin said. "After all, I did leave the city as soon as the invasion commenced."

"So you came all the way here? By yourself?"

"Oh no. I fled only to the outskirts of town. It was there that I reunited with your pillar guard."

"*My* pillar guard?" Eva looked back toward the foyer of the station. There was no sign of the guard.

"Yes. That is the one you liberated during your 'escape.'" Zin folded his arms behind his back. "But enough of him. Your news is indeed troubling."

"So why are you here? To hide?"

"Hide? Perhaps," Zin said over his shoulder. "But also to learn. Learn about your species."

Eva looked up at the disintegrating tiled walls of the station. "What is there to learn about humans in this place?"

"This is evidence of your species at its zenith, right before your civilization fell. Discovering the truth of the humans' failure is the clue to thwarting their attempt at dominance at Solas."

"You're looking for Cadmus's weakness?"

"I am."

"It's this." Eva gestured to the ancient architecture that surrounded them. "He wants to return to the Age of Man, when humans dominated Earth and all its resources."

Zin nodded twice. "And Loroc has reignited Cadmus's atavistic thinking. If my brother did indeed absorb my sister Darius, and therefore her abilities to see the past, he would know how to manipulate Cadmus's decisions."

Eva wrung her hands. "There is one more thing about your brother. He's coming for you."

"Of course. Now that he has acquired both of my sisters' talents, he needs the wherewithal to put them to use."

"Can he see his own future?" Eva asked.

"I doubt it. Arius's rants don't work like that. They are intentionally cryptic. A simple phrase can hold many interpretations."

Eva remembered Loroc's threats on the roof of Arius's home. "He said he won't fall by my hand."

"Perhaps he will not, but who can know for sure? A mutation like this, with three Arsian spirits merged into one . . . it has never happened before to my knowledge." Zin placed his hat back onto his head and sighed.

Eva and Zin watched the lichen-creatures excavate sand from the far end of the station platform. The lichens seemed oblivious to their presence.

Zin smiled. "The mouls, they communicate through color. See? How the puffs are of varying hues?"

"Mouls? Is that what they are called?" Eva watched others harvest the voxfruit and water the giant lichens growing from the rubble.

Zin floated close to observe them. "'Mouls' is what I have dubbed them. They are likely unclassified. My theory is that they were preexisting primitive life-forms prior to the introduction of the Vitae Virus. It is remarkable to see them thriving in such a desolate place."

Eva pointed to the colorful haze that hung in the air. "They are happy here. All these puffs they are releasing are phrases of a song. They are singing."

"Singing?" Zin waved his hand through the haze and examined the colored dust on his fingertips. "About what?"

Eva thought of the fishing song that Fiscian had

taught her back in Lacus. She thought of the song piping out of the speakers when she'd entered New Attica. The mouls were not just singing to one another. They were singing to the plants that they were cultivating and the rocks that protected them. They were singing to the air that they inhaled and the water that they drank. They were singing to Eva and Zin.

"I wish I could sing along, but there are no words I know that could convey what they are saying. They are singing about how all the elements and living things are in harmony."

"How I truly wish that were so, Eva Nine," said Zin.

"Eva? Are you down there?" Hailey called down from above.

Eva peered up into the afternoon light and saw the silhouette of the pilot standing at the ledge several stories above the underground station. "You found us!"

"Are you okay?" Hailey knelt down over the rim to get a better view.

"I'm fine. I'm with Zin!" Eva waved up to him.

"Who is Hailey?" Zin drifted toward her. There was alarm in his voice. "Is he another human?"

"He's a friend." Despite the fact that she was still upset with Hailey over some of the things he'd said, she was happy to see his face. She hopped onto the nearest pile of bricks and began climbing up. "Don't worry, Zin. You can trust him. He's here with Caruncle."

"The trader?" Zin floated up alongside Eva.

Caruncle joined Hailey at the rim. "Zin, it does my tired-weary eyes good to see you. Are you well-good?"

"I am," Zin replied as he floated into the daylight. "And what a place! You had described this area quite accurately, but I had no concept of how vast it was."

"It is big-vast indeed." Caruncle kept his eyes on Eva as Hailey pulled her up to join them. "Eva Nine. Your instincts were well-good. And you left the trail of food for Bix and Bax." He wagged a Sustibar wrapper at her and grinned. "That was smart."

"Yeah, that definitely helped." Hailey dusted himself off and smiled. "And we found the drawing you did with the liquid light pen."

"Good. I'm just glad you found us." Eva returned the smile.

"I have to thank you too, Eva." Caruncle walked

over to his hoversloop. The munt-runners brayed as he neared. "You've done the toughest part of my job for me." He turned to face Eva and Zin. In one pair of hands Caruncle held his charging boomrod. With his second pair he pulled a shiny new Omnipod from his pocket and pressed the button. A tiny hologram of Loroc materialized over the glowing eye.

"Well?" Loroc asked.

"I found him. Send the ship." A sinister smile curled over Caruncle's tusked teeth.

# I knew it!" Hailey

balled his fists and kicked the rubble. He stomped around, furious. "Didn't I tell you, Eva? I saw this coming."

"Eva, Hailey," Caruncle said, keeping his aim on Zin, "I suggest you leave. I am only tasked with finding Zin, not you."

"Don't do this." Eva walked toward Zin.

"Do not interfere, or I shall be forced to harmstop you." Caruncle kept his focus on Zin, who was floating at the edge of the cave. "You come forward to me, Zin. Now."

Hailey grabbed Eva's arm. "We don't stand a chance against a warship, and I can already hear it approaching. We should go."

"Yes. Good idea, Eva. For once the thickheaded grall is think-speaking properly." Caruncle kept his aim on Zin.

"I am afraid your friend is right, Eva. I hear the ship as well." Zin's voice wavered. "You both should save yourselves."

From the edge of the cave appeared several mouls. They stepped out from the shade of the giant lichen tree and watched, silent.

"Looks like we are not alone." Caruncle waved the boomrod at the mouls. "I hope these plant creatures know what is good-smart for them and stay out of this."

"Caruncle, stop!" Eva stepped between his boomrod and the mouls.

"Eva—" Zin started.

"Step back," Caruncle yelled. "Or I shall kill you-human, the boy, and your little creature friends." Behind him the ominous shape of a warship descended from the clouds.

"Caruncle, listen to me. Loroc is going to kill Zin," Eva said. "You'll no longer have anyone to sell your discoveries to."

"I have a new patron now, and he pays handsomely. NOW LEAVE US!" Caruncle shouted over the whine of the landing ship. "This is your last warning!"

A blast of hot air caused sand to billow out as the large craft settled in a clearing just behind Caruncle. Like the other warships Eva had seen, a snarling mouth and angry red eyes adorned this one's nose. A ramp hissed open from the ship's belly, revealing a pair of armed warbots. On three mechanized legs each, both machines marched toward the standoff.

"Eva!" Hailey barked. "We need to go, now!" He seized Eva by the arm and dragged her behind a mound of rubble.

One of the warbots spoke. "Attention. Remain stationary while identification is confirmed." A red laser scanned over Caruncle.

"Where are the people?" Hailey whispered as he peeked out from behind the rubble.

"I don't know." Eva heard the munt-runners braying. She watched as they stomped the ground and tugged at the hitch that held them. "They're scared. We have to stop this, Hailey."

"How? We've got no weapons."

"That is the one you want," Caruncle said, pointing to Zin with the boomrod.

"I don't think there are any people onboard." Hailey watched the hatch of the warship. "It's just the warbots."

"*Just* the warbots," Eva whispered. "Do you have any idea how deadly they are? I don't know how we are going to get Zin out of this."

The warbots' red lasers flickered over Zin. "Identification of Arsian traitor known as Zin is affirmative. You are to come with us. Board the ship immediately. Any deviation from our instructions will result in immobilization."

Zin lowered his head and floated toward Caruncle.

*Danger. Intruder. Danger. Intruder. Danger. Intruder. Danger. Intruder.*

The cries of the knifejacks flooded Eva's mind. She peered up from her hiding place just in time to see the pillar guard pick up Caruncle's hoversloop and throw it at the warbots. When the sloop was lifted, the hitching pole snapped off, and both munt-runners bolted, though still tethered together.

"My things!" Caruncle roared with anger.

"Let's go," Eva yelled, and dashed from the rubble into the fray.

One of the warbots toppled and was crushed

under the impact of the hoversloop. Cages, crates, and containers spilled out in every direction. The pillar guard leaped over the wrecked sloop and thrashed at the remaining warbot. A torrent of SHOCdarts spewed from the warbot, covering the pillar guard. With one stroke the guard swept most of the darts from its body. The warbot activated the remaining SHOCdarts, but they did not immobilize the guard. Instead they only seemed to anger it more.

Eva started toward Zin, then stopped when she heard the squeal of one of the munt-runners. A SHOCdart was imbedded deep in its thigh. "Hailey, help Bix and Bax!" Hailey dashed toward the mounts while Eva continued toward Zin. "Hide!"

A sonic *WOOM* erupted at Eva's feet, and she tumbled facedown in a spray of sand and rock.

"Eva!" Hailey cried. Zin zoomed over to her side.

"Not so quick-fast." Caruncle stomped up with the boomrod aimed at Eva's head. "With or without the warbots' help, I am bringing Zin in. If I have to bring in your body as an artifact to trade-sell to Loroc, then all the good-better for me."

Beyond Caruncle, Eva could see the pillar guard stumbling back into the wrecked sloop. She heard the cry of the crippled munt-runner still hitched to its partner. She felt the joy of the knifejacks escaping from their broken cage. She noticed the silence of the mouls gathered outside their home. They were no longer singing. Eva stood to face Caruncle. She spit the sand out of her mouth onto his face.

"It is too bad it has to come to this, Eva, but as I-Caruncle said, we must take-do what we can to survive." Caruncle raised the boomrod and fired. The knifejack that bit him, however, threw off his aim, and the sonic blast connected with a wall far behind Eva. The wall toppled backward, joining the rubble and dust that littered the landscape.

Before Caruncle could recharge the boomrod, another knifejack landed on him. In one deft move its sharp beak snipped off one of Caruncle's secondary hands. He stared in shock at the bleeding stump. Before he could cry out in pain, another knifejack landed on him. Then another.

"No!" Caruncle swatted at the attacking creatures. "Don't hurt me!"

Eva watched as Caruncle fell under the drove of freed knifejacks. *I can do this*, she thought. *I must do this.*

Caruncle thrashed about wildly, pleading for help.

*He dies, you live,* Eva told the knifejacks. *He dies, you live.*

The hiss of the warship's ramp closing spurred Hailey to action. He pried the Omnipod from Caruncle's severed hand and bolted past the clashing warbot and pillar guard. Eva watched as Hailey dove onto the warship just as the ramp sealed shut. In seconds the engines rumbled to life and the ship took off in a cloud of dust.

"No! That will take him back to Loroc!" Eva watched the warship disappear into the cloud cover.

"Be careful, Eva!" Zin grabbed her by the shoulders and pulled her back from the battling giants.

She shook off Zin's grasp. "But I have to help Hailey!"

There was a loud boom as the pillar guard thrust his clawed hand into the metallic shell of the warbot. The robot exploded, throwing the guard, Eva, and Zin backward.

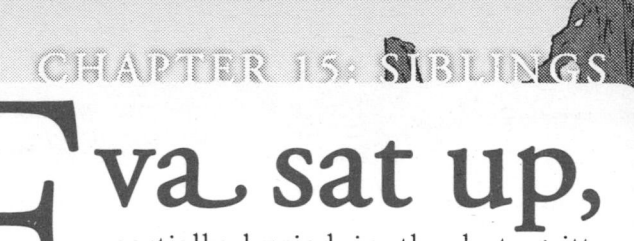

# Eva sat up,

partially buried in the hot, gritty sand. She stumbled over to the pillar guard, with Zin close behind.

"Will he be okay?" Eva ran her hands over the scorched claws of the fallen guard. The tiny pattern of lights under the guard's skin did not appear to be lit, but it was hard to know for sure in the sunlight. Eva looked back to the sky, trying to spot the warship carrying Hailey toward greater danger.

Zin zipped around and inspected the guard. "From what I can discern, all damage appears superficial. Although, I cannot evaluate his functions with any degree of assurance without his remote."

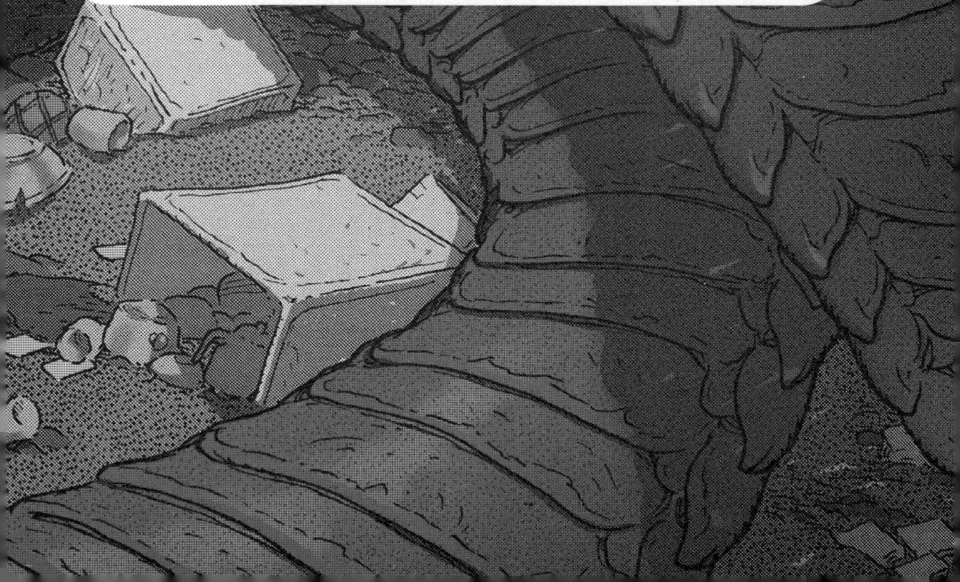

The pillar guard let out a slow melodious song. Zin translated, "He is asking if those that he protects are safe."

"You understand what he is saying?" Eva laid her head and hands against its warm sides.

"The sentinels of the Ojo clan were created by a long-forgotten ancient race. Not many in the galaxy can speak their language," Zin said with pride.

"Tell him we are safe, thanks to him." She yanked off a hunk of robotic machinery that was impaled on the guard's sickle claw.

A low braying came from the foot of the pillar guard. Eva turned to see Bix and Bax, still harnessed in their yoke. With Bix limping, they stepped toward her, still dragging the remains of the hitching pole from the hoversloop. Eva calmed the munt-runners and pulled the SHOCdart from Bix's thigh.

"You are free to go." Eva unhitched them from their yoke. Bix nibbled at Eva's sleeve and let out a nicker while Bax nuzzled her.

Eva scratched Bax around his horns. She wondered how long it would take to get to Hailey from here. "Okay. If you two want to stay, you can. But we may have to travel far . . . and fast."

"Eva, come see this!" Zin called out.

One of the mouls was standing near the fallen

pillar guard. The moul ran its tentacles over the guard's rough exterior. It piped out several puffs of bright color.

Eva walked over to get a closer look. Both muntrunners followed. "He thinks the pillar guard is a gift made of stone," she relayed. "No. Wait. He thinks the guard was gifted to them *from* the stones."

"Gifted from the stones?"

Eva ran her fingers through the brightly colored puffs before they were carried away on the wind. "Yeah. If I understand this right, he believes the guard has arrived here to protect the mouls. The stones *told them* he would come."

"The stones, you say?" said Zin.

Eva nodded.

The pillar guard sat up and watched as more mouls gathered around.

Zin rubbed his chin in thought. "Despite your liberation of this guard, they are chivalrous by nature. Ordering this individual's freedom to do as it pleases has likely caused some turmoil with its programming."

Eva looked at the gathering of mouls examining the giant guard. "Please tell the guard to see that no harm comes to the mouls for now and always," she said to Zin.

"I do not need to tell him. I think he believes—no, he *wants* to do just that. Astounding," said Zin.

The pillar guard rose to his full height. With the mouls circling around him, he strode to the edge of the cave. He turned to Eva and Zin and let out a loud blat followed by more trills. He stepped down and disappeared into the home of the mouls.

"They are better off having his loyalty. Loroc will likely dispatch more warbots to these coordinates."

"Unless you stop him." Eva began rooting through the mess from the wrecked hoversloop. Among the scattered debris was a familiar item. Eva picked up Hailey's scuffed-up Omnipod and brushed off the sand. *Hailey was right not to trust him.*

Zin joined her at the wreckage. "Eva, I do not know that I am the one best qualified to end a war."

"You are the *only* one who can stop this." Eva opened a crate to find saddles, bridles, and reins for the munt-runners. "If Loroc is going to betray Cadmus, why wouldn't he betray Ojo?"

"I don't know that he desires to usurp Ojo. I—"

"He said he was to become 'the king.' What else could that mean?" Frustrated, Eva tried to remember how the Cæruleans strapped their saddles onto their mounts. Her thoughts were interrupted by the memory of one of Arius's old chants. Eva stopped and recited, "Even the most wicked have a family that loves them."

"Did my sister tell you that?" asked Zin.

"Yes."

"She was probably talking about me." There was regret in Zin's voice. He floated over to the hoversloop.

"Are you sure she wasn't speaking of Loroc?" Eva stopped saddling Bix for the moment and followed Zin past smoldering pieces of the sloop.

"She may have been. But I shall never truly know the answer now," Zin said with a sigh. "The four of us had been apart for quite some time—too long a time. This upset Arius. She felt that time away from one another put more distance between us than any remote location we could travel to."

"So she still cared for your brother?" Eva asked.

"The Arsian family bond is likely different than it is in your species," Zin replied. "Regardless, I cannot forgive him if he committed what you've described."

Eva continued following Zin through the wreckage. Her thoughts were of her own sister. Eva had forgiven Eight despite what she'd done. "Could Loroc change his intent?"

"My brother's power is inner strength. He has always exhibited incredible displays of fortitude, which is why he was so essential to our mission here." From a toppled crate Zin picked up one of the cups Caruncle had polished. "You see, my ability focuses on analysis and intellect, but as you may have noticed, I am physically smaller than my siblings. My sisters, on the other hand, were hardier, though often ruled by emotion, which, of course, enhanced their abilities." Zin gathered three more cups.

Eva watched Zin stack the cups on the crate. With his many hands he was able to balance two of the cups on the mouth of one. He then placed the fourth cup on top.

He pointed to the bottom cup. "Loroc was the one who supported us. Encouraged us, especially in the direst of situations. But he was prone to jealousy. He felt that his ability was inadequate when compared to ours. He didn't understand that the four of us were interconnected—we all needed one another."

"And now?" asked Eva.

"He is no longer thinking of us. He is thinking only of his needs and desires. Consequently, his strength and support for others has been corrupted into a lust for power and control *over* others." Zin knocked the bottom cup away, and the others tumbled from the crate to the sand. He floated over to inspect the fallen warbot.

"You don't know this, but I discovered that I had a sister too," Eva said. "But she and I do not think alike." Eva stepped over one of the legs of the warbot. "She has different ideas about what the world should be."

Zin raised an eyebrow. "And?"

"Well, the truth is, I understand her reasons—I just don't agree with them. She puts her own needs before mine and dismisses those beings that I care about, like Rovender. A person shouldn't do that. Not to anyone. Not to family."

Zin sighed. "But I did that very thing. I put my needs, my goals, ahead of Darius's pain. Loroc is not the only guilty one."

"You are not like Loroc. Your goal was to help all the settlers become established here," said Eva.

"But at what cost? The loss of my own family? Could you make the same sacrifice?"

"I already lost Muthr, and my sister must remain in the forest forever. I can't lose Rovender. He's all I have." Eva watched the sand blow against the hull of the battered warbot.

"What if giving his life meant saving all life on Orbona?" Zin asked. "Or what if this sacrifice were presented to your sister?"

Eva swallowed down the uneasy thoughts that surfaced. "The spirit of the forest changed my sister. But I think it was for the better."

"So is that what you suggest? That I somehow lure my wicked brother to this 'spirit of the forest' and let its magical mumbo jumbo cure him?"

"No. I don't know!" Eva exhaled loudly. "But you can't hide from Loroc. He'll keep hunting you down, and I don't know what will happen to you, me, or any of us, in the meantime."

"But perhaps this matter is best solved by Ojo," Zin said. "There exists an agreement between the Arsians and her family that implicitly states—"

"You don't get it! If she is not dead already, she will probably die—"

"*I* don't want to die, Eva Nine!" Zin's anger startled Eva. "I fear what my brother has become. If my sisters failed to stop him, then I will follow."

"What has he become? What do you know that you aren't saying?"

Zin looked down at his hands while he spoke. "From what you've told me, he has partaken in an ancient ritual now considered taboo among Arsians."

"A ritual?"

"Correct. Our ancestors believed that all the strength, wisdom, and knowledge of the dead would be absorbed into the living if one were to . . . consume the body. But as I said, it is no longer practiced and is, in fact, frowned upon in our society."

Though repulsive, this attitude toward death reminded Eva of the old Cærulean saying that Rovender had told her: *When your journey reaches its destination here, may you walk on through the memories of those still with us.*

Zin continued, "Additionally, it appears that Loroc's strategy is to usurp the leaders of both sides of this battle, either by deceit or by force. Once he has done that, he will reign supreme over all citizens of Orbona. He'll control the natural resources as well as the military might of the humans. No one will be able to stop him. We will all be at his mercy."

Eva looked away from Zin to the broken horizon of a ruined civilization. *Is this where we are headed?*

"When we landed here, I was so excited to begin work with King Ojo's team." Zin's tone carried sadness in it. "To take part as a founding member of a colony united by the goal of peaceful coexistence. I wanted to witness firsthand the effects of the Vitae Virus on a barren world. To start life anew where it had once been absent. I do not wish to miss the fruits of my labor. There is so much more to see and learn."

Eva turned back to Zin. "I thought that you, of everyone I know, could solve this so that we can all return to that peaceful coexistence."

"I've warned you about your perpetual optimism before, Eva Nine. Your faith in me is misplaced. I am but a student on a quest for the answers to the universe."

"Maybe answers are found not in observing but in doing. Doing the right thing."

"What is 'right'?" Zin faced her. "What might be 'right' for me may not be 'right' for you. And what of Cadmus? What of the citizens of Lacus or Solas?"

"Killing others is never right," Eva said. "Life is a gift given that none should take. Orbona is large enough to harbor all life—all of us. I look around, and I do not see aliens or humans. I see Orbonians. Loroc is going to take away that gift. He is going to take away all that you have done. *Your* hopes, Zin, were to establish life here. *Your* optimism was that the virus would work. And you were right. Do you want to see all of that disappear?"

"Perhaps you are correct." Zin gazed out at the ruins. "I would not want to see Solas reduced to a crumbling memory of yet another war."

Far above, an airship's engines droned across the sky. Eva dashed to the cavernous home of the mouls, with Zin close behind. Peering over the edge of the rocky rim, Eva spied a warship dropping below the cloud cover and landing nearby. From the cave behind her the head of the pillar guard rose.

"Another ship dispatched already?" Zin whispered. "Perhaps I should surrender. I don't want there to be any more deaths today."

"Don't do anything yet, and tell the pillar guard to stay put." Eva grasped Zin's hand. *Where is Caruncle's boomrod?* She glanced over at the junk dealer's remains, where the weapon lay. The knifejacks had made quick work of him. One of the creatures flew off holding a mustard-colored eye in its pointed beak.

The ramp to the warship hissed open. A dingy pair of checkered sneakboots appeared at the top of the ramp. Hailey walked out from the ship.

Eva scrambled up over the rim. She ran over to Hailey and hugged him tight. "You're okay?"

"I'm fine," Hailey said with a rakish grin. "The ship's completely automated, just like I thought." He waved the Omnipod in front of Eva. "I know this old Fortran alphanumeric password that overrides the highest-level users and grants all access to the ship's operating system. With that I was able to reboot it and reprogram its directives."

"So what does that mean?"

"That means we now have a ship, Eva."

# CHAPTER 16: DEVASTATED

"You need to land the ship on the outskirts of the city, near the pollen refineries." Eva pointed east on the geographical map projected in the cockpit.

"I don't know. Are you sure?" Hailey said from the pilot seat.

"Yes. Trust me."

Zin studied the holographic map. "That would be a wise place to touch down. We do not want to draw any attention to ourselves."

"Okay. Pollen refineries. Got it." Hailey touched the location on the map and set the course of the ship.

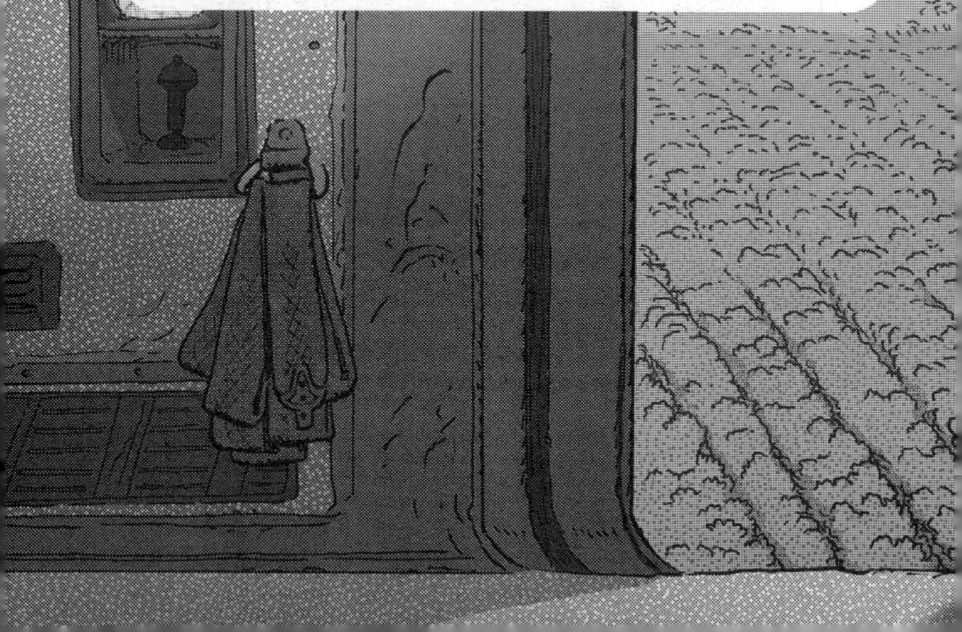

"Oh, I see how it is. You do it because Zin says it, but not me?" Eva put her hands on her hips.

"Hey, sometimes you are right and sometimes you are wrong." Hailey kept his focus on flying the ship. "I just want to be sure before we get ourselves into a situation that we can't get out of."

"That's a fair observation," said Zin.

Eva let out a scoff and rolled her eyes. She flopped down in the copilot's seat.

The cockpit itself was sparse and simple, with several stations mounted inside an impressive domed windshield. It was almost as if they were not in a ship at all but were gliding in an enormous flying bubble.

Hailey's hands moved over the controls, and the ship accelerated. "I cannot believe how fast this thing is."

"Do you think it flew all the way from Solas to attack us?" Eva looked out to see the gray mists of clouds whooshing by. "Because it seems to be taking longer for us to return to the city."

"Naw," Hailey said. The ship banked slightly under his control. "It must have been following us. I thought I heard engines at one point. I bet Caruncle was sending coordinates the entire time."

Eva remembered the pillar guard also looking up toward the sky.

"What a despicable fellow he turned out to be," Zin growled.

"Yeah. I was onto him the whole time. I tried to warn 'a certain someone' about him, but she wouldn't listen." It was hard to tell if Hailey was grinning from piloting the speeding ship or from harassing Eva.

Eva crossed her arms and turned her chair away from him. She studied the holographic radar as they approached Solas. She could see blinking icons indicating a mass of warships moored over the city. "Won't Cadmus and Loroc send more ships after us?" She pointed to the radar image.

"I thought of that and sent a fake report," said Hailey. "According to Cadmus's main controller for the fleet, this ship doesn't exist anymore. They think it was destroyed over the ruins." Hailey smiled, smug. "Let them look all they want."

The warship dipped down below the thunderheads, and Solas came into view. Eva rushed up to the windshield . . . then recoiled.

As anticipated, Cadmus's fleet of ships floated over the cityscape and around the tall spires of the royal palace. From the skyline thick columns of black smoke billowed up like twisted tree trunks in a forest of destruction. Even down through the ashy smog, Eva could see the skull-like visages of warbots marching past war-torn homes. In some city blocks the buildings had been completely obliterated.

"How? I can't believe . . ." Zin's voice trailed off to a whisper. Sorrow racked his plump round face. "The entire educational district is . . . just . . . gone."

"I am so sorry," said Eva. The sprawling ruination brought to mind the landscape she had just left. She wondered if the ancient ruins had also suffered a military invasion long ago.

"Look there!" Zin pointed to tattered pennants flapping in the wind from the top of the Royal palace. Emblazoned on each was the symbol of an eye with a horizontal iris. "The royal pennants are flying, which means Her Majesty is still in command."

"That's good," said Eva. The ground below came up fast as Hailey brought the ship to a smooth landing in the middle of a field next to a pollen refinery. "Do you think you can get to the palace unnoticed?"

"I know that palace inside and out. After all, I designed it." Zin patted Hailey on the shoulder in thanks and then exited the cockpit. He floated down the steps that led to the cargo bay.

Eva followed him under empty bays that had once held an army of warbots. Now the vacated deck contained only Bix and Bax, saddled and sitting on their haunches. Caruncle's holstered boomrod hung from a nearby support beam.

Zin paused at the top of the loading ramp and turned to Eva. "I will speak to Ojo immediately, but in return you must do something for me." The ramp hissed open. Thick acrid smoke wafted in from outside. "Eva, whatever manipulation my brother has masterminded, Ojo likely believes that Cadmus is the one behind this conflict."

"She would be partially right," replied Eva. "He still wants to take this city for his people."

"Correct," Zin said. "So while I am contending with Ojo and my brother, I need *you* to go and speak with Cadmus. If he has a fraction of the compassion you hold, he'll cease his ruinous actions."

"I don't know if he will." Eva gave a worried look. "But my sister told me I need to show him that his thinking must evolve."

"Evolution is successful adaptation to one's surroundings," said Zin. "You have obviously adapted. Now teach him."

"I will do my best," said Eva.

Hailey's voice crackled over the intercom. "Hey,

guys, the fleet is splitting up for some reason. We should probably get while the getting is good."

Zin smiled and took Eva's hands in his. "Do you remember when you were in my study back at the museum? And I told you what *I* was searching for?"

"You wanted to solve some big mystery."

"Exactly," said Zin. "The biggest mystery of all: Why are we here?"

"And?"

"I don't know the answer completely." Zin looked outside at the darkened sky. "But I now understand that even seemingly inconsequential participants can take simple actions that expand to affect the masses. Like ripples caused by a pebble tossed into the water."

"And each planet is a pebble?" Eva asked.

"Each *one of us* is a pebble—humans, extra-terrestrials, mouls. Me and you." A renewed glimmer came to Zin's sad eyes. "We each play a part. We are born, we live, and we perish, perhaps to be born again in some other form—just like this planet. Galaxies are but one living entity burning with the energy from all of us. Life and death are but siblings who turn the universe continually. Endlessly."

Eva thought of the beast in the forest trying to

eat her. She had outsmarted it, and so it had died, but perhaps the cubs had lived. Muthr had died, but Eva had lived. She threw her arms around Zin. "I'm really sorry I wrecked your museum. I didn't want any of this to happen."

"Nor did I. But it did. My sister knew it when she left her mark on your arm for me to find, and here we are."

Eva walked Zin to the foot of the ramp. Overhead, thunder rumbled.

"Where will you go after the battle has come to an end?" Zin asked.

Eva sighed. "I don't know. I want to see Rovender and Otto. I miss them so much."

"Go. Be with them." Zin floated out of the ship. "After this is over, I shall find you. I believe you have much more still to teach me, Eva Nine." He lit the small light mounted on his pointed hat. He smiled at Eva one last time and floated away.

Eva stood at the foot of the ramp. She listened and looked up at the dreary skies. There were no airwhales here. No turnfins or knifejacks. The animals knew to stay clear of this place.

"Okay," Hailey said as he worked the warship's controls. "Next stop, home."

Eva felt the cockpit pressurize as the ramp sealed shut below. With a gentle swaying motion the warship lifted up and tilted away from Solas. The engine's hum grew louder. Within seconds they were rocketing through the clouds.

Hailey turned to Eva. "So, do you think Zin can do it? Stop Loroc?"

"I hope so." Eva sat down in the copilot's hovchair, still thinking of Zin's words.

"That's a lot of pressure for one little floaty guy," Hailey said with a whistle. "Stopping his crazy power-hungry brother and trying to end the war. From what you've told me about Loroc, Zin's a goner."

"Don't say that!" Eva smacked Hailey's arm. "I have faith in Zin. Besides, we're out of options."

"Hey, I think you've gone above and beyond what anybody else would do." Hailey turned back to the controls. "So now let's get Vanpa, get you back to Rovender, and lay low until this thing blows over."

"But what if it doesn't just 'blow over'?" Eva turned Hailey's hovchair to face hers.

"Then these leaders will all kill one another. I don't care. They're all untrustworthy jerks, if you ask me." Hailey pushed his seat back away from Eva. "We'll find somewhere safe to go, away from all of this."

"Oh, like your parents did?"

"Aw, that's low, and you know it. You of all people should—"

"Should what? Know what it's like to lose a parent?" Eva shoved back her hovchair angrily and stood. "Muthr died saving me, just like your parents did."

"Great observation, Eva. So explain to me how offing the all-powerful Loroc is going to bring them back? Because it's not."

"We *all* may die if Loroc is not defeated. That would include Vanpa and Rovender." Eva wanted to punch Hailey for the things he said. It was the same way Eight had made her feel.

"If it is that important, then why didn't you go with Zin?" Hailey snapped back. "If you're so set on ending this war, why did you send him in alone to handle it?"

"Because he is Loroc's brother."

"What does that mean? You couldn't handle your sister. What makes you think Zin can handle Loroc?"

Eva spoke between clenched teeth. "Eight nearly killed me. She was crazy."

"Okay, I'm sure this Loroc guy is levelheaded and

open to sitting down for a family chat with his little brother," Hailey said in a sarcastic tone.

"What else could I do? I can't defeat him. I tried." Eva slid back down in her chair.

"You're right. This battle is too big for one person to solve. It's too big for you. So let it go and let the leaders sort it out." Hailey brought up the radar once more and projected it in the large cockpit. The warship stayed in the center while a three-dimensional map of the terrain moved along underneath. The ship's flying route was superimposed over it and appeared as a dotted line over the landscape.

"Speaking of leaders, I am going to see Cadmus when we arrive." Eva watched the hologram, but her mind was still on Zin.

Hailey stopped what he was doing and looked over at Eva. "You are shorting out right now. I think you need some serious REM."

"I am not. I promised Zin."

Hailey threw up his hands. "You know what? Go for it. Both you and Zin can walk straight to your deaths. I don't care."

"I know you don't care. I'm just a *reboot*, remember?" Eva stood to go.

Hailey shook his head in disgust.

The holographic radar pinged. Behind the

warship were half a dozen other pulsing dots.

"What is that?" Eva leaned in to get a closer look.

Hailey zoomed in on the dots. "More warships." His voice was grim.

"After us? Did they see us?" Eva's mouth went dry. The ship they were on was much larger than the *Bijou*, but they were outnumbered six to one.

Hailey's hands flew over the blinking controls. "I'm displaying their trajectory now." On the radar, lines projected from the squadron of ships. Though the other ships were some distance behind Hailey's ship, their route matched Eva and Hailey's destination. "They're returning to New Attica," he said.

"To get us?"

"I don't know." The ship's engines whined as Hailey pushed them into overdrive. "Whatever the reason, we've got to get to Vanpa and the others before these guys arrive. Otherwise we are done for."

Eva pulled Hailey's Omnipod from her poncho pocket. "Well, you better contact Vanpa and let him know you're coming."

"My dad's Omnipod. You found it." Hailey blinked with surprise as she handed it to him.

"Caruncle had it after all," said Eva. "You were right."

Hailey gave a lopsided grin to Eva as he took the device. "I know. Sometimes it takes a liar to know a liar."

"Greetings, Evan Seven," the Omnipod said through a hiss of static. "How may I be of service?"

"Please establish contact with Evan Six. Thank you," Hailey replied.

"Establishing contact momentarily. Please hold," said the Omnipod.

"We are coming up on New Attica," Hailey's voice came over the loudspeaker in the ship's hold. "I could use your help getting everyone on board the ship when we land, if that's okay."

"Of course." Eva finished rubbing the SpeedHeal ointment she'd found into the wound on Bix's thigh.

"Vanpa knows we're coming," Hailey said as Eva entered the cockpit. "I'm gonna set down just outside the camp. I've told him to instruct everybody to bring only what they can carry. They should be ready and waiting for us."

Eva followed Hailey's gaze through the cockpit window. Raindrops sprayed against the windshield. It was so gray that it was impossible to tell if it was day or dusk.

The warship shimmied as it descended through the thunderhead. A familiar desolate mountain landscape welcomed them from below. Hailey slowed the ship and navigated it down through winding canyon walls.

"I checked the radar, and there are no other warships in the area except for that squadron, but I've managed to put some distance between us," Hailey said, and navigated the ship up and over a stony plateau. "We should be coming up on New Attica—" But he did not finish his sentence.

The gigantic round quarry that housed New Attica was an inferno. Gone was the atmospheric membrane that had stretched over the entire city. From the center a brilliant blaze belched a black cloud out into the sky. As Hailey maneuvered the ship around the perimeter, it was clear what had caused the devastation. One of Cadmus's large command warships had crashed nose-first into Attican Hall.

## *End of*
# PART I

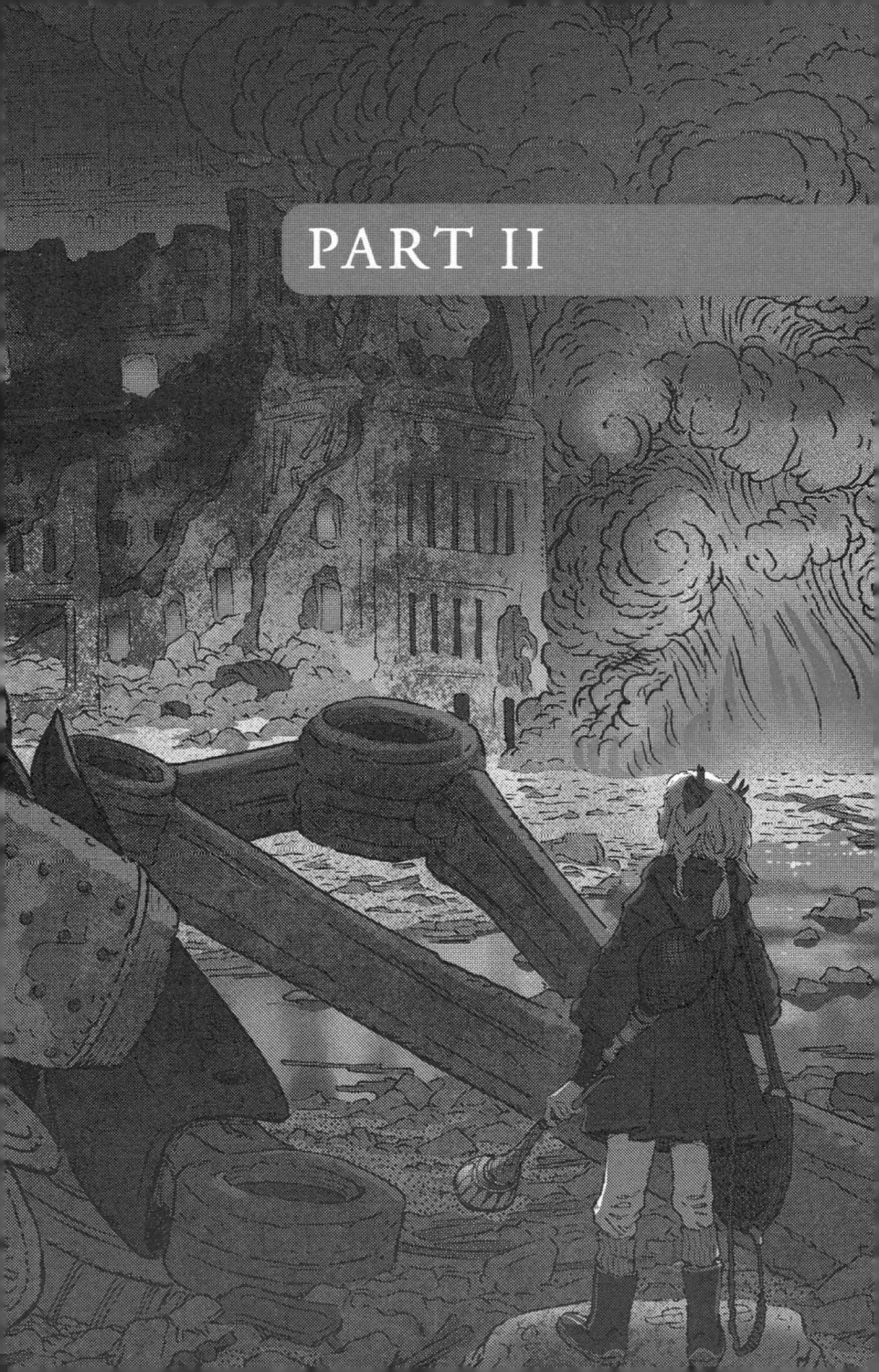

PART II

## CHAPTER 17: THUNDERSTORM

# The distant

fiery glow from New Attica shimmered on the wet canyon walls of the Toiler's camp. Inside an enormous cavern hangar a large gathering of shabby people lined up at the ramp of Hailey's parked warship.

"Eva, there's an Attican gondola in the back of the hangar on the other side of that wreck. You can take that!" Hailey shouted over the din of people boarding. He pointed to a parked gondola

at the far side of the cave tucked behind the skeletal frame of a scavenged airship.

Eva pushed her way through a throng of Toilers who were scrambling to evacuate. She passed the shadowy recess where Hailey's hovel was nestled.

"Well, looky who it is! My fellow reboot!" an elderly man with a beard grinned with yellow teeth. He hobbled from the doorway of his home on a pneumatic peg leg.

"Vanpa!" Eva ran up and hugged Hailey's grandfather.

"Hailey told me everything. I heard they didn't get to rewire your brain after all." Van Turner brushed aside Eva's braids. "That Cadmus; always wanting to fix things that aren't broken."

"Yeah, I'm glad we all made it out of there," replied Eva.

"Listen," Van Turner said in a confidential manner. "There is no way on Orbona I would have let Hailey deliver you and Rovender if I'd known what Cadmus was up to. I hope you can believe that."

Eva took Van Turner's gnarled hand in hers. "I understand, as does Rovee. And Hailey and I are good now."

The old man smiled. "Good! Now let's get you

going." He shuffled over to the gondola. "We swiped this baby years ago. Now it runs independently of Attica's central computer, so you'll have to steer it manually, okay?"

"Okay." Eva threw Caruncle's boomrod and charger into the gondola.

"Great! These are your controls." Van Turner activated the gondola. The vehicle hummed to life and floated up a meter off the cavern floor. Van Turner reached in and pointed to the homemade dashboard. "This notched wheel here controls your speed. This trackball steers it, and this . . . Wait. Where is it?" Van Turner banged the side of the dash. This caused a hologram of the gondola to materialize over the dashboard. "This shows you which way you're going. Got it?"

"I think so. It looks a lot like the controls to the *Bijou*." Eva climbed in and sat in the middle of the dingy cushioned seats.

"Ain't that hard. And you're a fast learner." Van Turner winked. He turned on the ship's bright headlights. "Just don't tell Hailey how easy it is."

Eva smiled and got accustomed to the controls.

"You sure you want to do this?" Van Turner asked.

"I have to try to find Cadmus and tell him what

I've learned. I know he's done a lot of things that are wrong, but there are a lot of good things he's accomplished too."

"Perhaps, but that young benevolent man has become poisoned by the disillusionment of experience and age." Van Turner spoke with reflection.

"I don't know. But I still need to speak with him," said Eva.

"From what has happened, I think he probably knows there's trouble in paradise." Van Turner closed the door on the gondola and rapped it twice with his knuckle. "If you ask me, this war is over. New Attica lost."

Into the gloaming Eva sped down a winding canyon toward the city. Banking hard around a sharp turn, she brushed the side of the rocky wall with the gondola, sending out a spray of brilliant sparks.

*These controls are sensitive.* Eva tilted the gondola up and ascended out of the canyon. Rain pattered over the clear bubble canopy as she crossed the dark rocky terrain that surrounded New Attica. *That squadron of warships will be here any minute*, she thought. *I don't know why that command ship crashed, but I don't want to be here when reinforcements arrive.*

The gondola dipped over the rim of the quarry that housed New Attica. Eva navigated the craft through a blinding cloud of smoke and came out near the central hub of the city. In the center the blackened twisted bones of the wrecked command ship were strewn over rubble that had once been Attican Hall. Wild raging flames danced over the wreckage. Even the trees in the eastern sections of the park were ablaze. Below Eva's gondola, people were crying out, scared, injured, or holding those who had not survived.

*None of the other gondolas are operating,* Eva thought. *Why aren't they evacuating?* She circled the fiery ruins of Attican Hall. *Even if Cadmus survived this, there may be no way to get to him ... but I need to know for sure.* She remembered something her sister had told her about level one being occupied by Cadmus's relatives and children.

*Gen.*

Cadmus's prodigal daughter would know where her father was. The gondola rose back up toward the outer walls of the city. High above and far from the devastation was a ring of spacious housing units. Eva quickly flew around the

perimeter, searching for Gen Pryde's homecube. *Sheesa! Where is it? In the dark, every unit looks the same.*

By the headlights Eva glimpsed of a knot of people fleeing into their homes. From one home two identical girls scurried out in matching black Emote-Attire. With their palm-implanted Omnipods they began taking holo-pictures of the wreck in the center of the city. Eva's gondola zipped past them as they finished, then continued along the perimeter walkway. Eva turned the gondola around just in time to see them dash inside the open door of one of the homecubes. She brought the craft into a hard landing on the vacated walkway and hopped out. Before leaving the gondola, she slung the strap of the boomrod's charger over her shoulder and grabbed the weapon.

"Gen?" Eva called from the open door of the home. "Gen Pryde, it's Eva. Are you in here?" The firelight from outside flickered erratically throughout the dim house, making it hard to see. Eva stalked past the pristine furniture of a minimally decorated white living room.

"YOU!" a voice screeched from a back room. Gen Pryde came out from her bedroom. Her hair was disheveled, and dark mascara tears smudged her cheeks. "GET OUT!" she shrieked. The other two Gens stood alongside her.

"You don't understand. I—"

"I understand perfectly," said Gen.

"Yeah, you work with the Toilers!" the second Gen spat.

"So you decided to destroy my father's beautiful city because you were jealous of what we had." There was venom in Gen's voice.

"That's not it at all!" Eva retorted. "I am here to *save* you and your father."

"Right!" Gen yelled. She picked up a crystal vase and threw it at Eva. "Get out of here!"

"You've done enough damage already, you short-out!" The third Gen began hurling items at Eva.

"Listen to me. I know this is scary, but there is a lot you don't know!" Eva dodged the projectiles.

"I know that in the next few nanos, I am going to push you out that door and over the balcony if you DON'T LEAVE NOW!" Gen screamed.

Eva fired the boomrod at the ceiling. Debris and dust cascaded down from above. Under the cover of the billowing dust, Eva marched over to the cowering Gen Pryde and seized her by the wrist.

"The Arsian who works with your father is going

to betray him," Eva barked. "I have to see Cadmus so that I can warn—" Eva stopped talking when she realized Gen wasn't listening. Instead Gen was pointing, mouth agape, at something outside beyond the open front door.

"What is that?" one of the Gens cried. They ran to the doorway.

Eva turned to see the squadron of warships enter the skies above the city, their searchlights beaming down onto the citizens below. The cargo bay ramps of each ship opened, as if choreographed, and out dropped a torrent of warbots. Each ebony orb body descended by means of small hover boosters. Before each orb touched down, three tall stilt legs unfolded, and an arsenal of weapons prepared for use.

"Wha-what's happening?" Gen stammered. She activated her Omnipod and began a holo-recording. Down below in the park the towering warbots unleashed swarms of SHOCdarts in every direction, felling entire crowds of people. The Gens gasped. One of them cowered behind Eva.

"Everyone in this city is about to die." Eva swallowed down the icy fear that was constricting every muscle in her body. *I have to remain calm or I won't make it out of here.* She looked at the Omnipod embedded in Gen's hand.

"Gen, I need you to call Evan Seven." Eva tried to hide the waver in her voice.

Gen looked at Eva with wild fearful eyes. Her skin looked deathly pale against the black of her Emote-Attire. "What? Who?"

"Just call him! Do it NOW!"

Gen did as she was told. A hologram of Hailey's head appeared over the palm of Gen's hand.

"Hailey! It's Eva. You need to get here right now and evacuate as many people as you can. Do you hear me? Get over here now!"

"Evacuate? Isn't the fleet there? I've got the entire camp on board as it is. We are just waiting for you."

"Don't wait for me. I still need to find Cadmus. Just get here and help these people," said Eva.

"I'm not risking dragging all of my friends into that fiery hailstorm."

Eva's tone was adamant. "I need you to be the retriever that I know you are. Bring your people here and have them help evacuate the survivors."

Hailey's hologram was silent for several moments. "Fine. We'll land in the park. You better hurry up. We won't be able to wait around forever." Hailey's face disappeared.

"You!" Eva pointed at the other Gens with her

boomrod. "Get down to the ground level as fast as you can and hide. When you see Hailey's warship land, get to it as fast as possible. You do not want to be caught by these warbots. Tell everyone and help as many on board as you can."

Tentatively the Gens tiptoed past Eva. One of them spoke. "What about you, Gen? What are you gonna do?"

"I'll take her to speak with Father," Gen Pryde answered. "I'd do what she says—go with the pilot."

The Gens scuttled out of the house and out of sight.

"Okay. Where is he?" Eva asked.

"I can show you, but I can't get it to work," Gen said. She led Eva down a darkened hallway and into the grand master bedroom. A gigantic white plastic egg sat in the center of the room with round openings leading to the cocoon bed within. Next to it were three floating cushions covered in fuzzy cloth. Standing at the back of the room was a master console for the house, which featured controls to regulate temperature, play entertainment, and order food. Gen dashed around the darkened console and pressed on a panel mounted on the back wall. Quickly she spoke her name, but nothing happened.

"What is this?" Eva asked, anxious.

"That's what I'm saying. I was trying this before. There is supposed to be an exit here." Gen spoke as if reciting memorized lines, "In an emergency I state my name and pass code; then the panel will open. I'm supposed to follow the lit arrows that lead to Sanctuary one. But it won't work! The console won't work! Nothing works!" With her hand she banged the panel in frustration. "I don't understand. Why isn't it working?"

The problem dawned on Eva. "There is no power. That's why the gondolas aren't working. That's why Loroc crashed the ship into Attican Hall. It crippled the city's main computer."

Gen was trembling. "What are you talking about?"

"Stand back!" Eva pushed Gen behind her and fired the boomrod. The panel buckled and fell down a dark shaft behind the wall.

Eva poked her head into the darkness. She heard the clang of the panel hitting the walls and ground below. The dark shaft reminded Eva of the exhaust vent she had used to escape her own Sanctuary. Like that, this one had rungs for climbing. Eva strapped the boomrod over her shoulders. "Is your father down here?"

Gen wiped her eyes. "I think so."

Eva stepped inside the cramped space and began to descend the rungs as fast as she could. "Okay, then. Let's go find him."

"This is the emergency escape. I've never been allowed in here unless there is an emergency." Gen's voice echoed down from above. Her black-and-white robotail hung limp from underneath her dress.

"I think this qualifies as an emergency." Outside, a large explosion shook the entire shaft. Eva looked up, half-expecting fire to rain down or warbots to tear through the walls. "We should probably be quiet until we get where we are going. I don't want our voices to give us away. Okay?"

"Okay," Gen whispered.

# The climb

down was long. Eva's muscles burned from the rigorous descent. Finally they arrived at the bottom of the stairwell, sealed by a heavy ply-steel door. Eva banged on the door with the palm of her hand.

"Can't you just blow it open?" Gen pointed at the boomrod.

"There's not enough room for us to back up," Eva said. "Use your Omnipod to call your father."

Gen wiped her runny nose. "I tried him already, but there was no answer."

Above, Eva could hear the clangs of the battle. "We've got to hurry!" She banged the door with the hard muzzle of the boomrod. She could hear a wrenching sound beyond it.

A muffled voice called from other side. "Gen? Gen Pryde?"

"Yes! Yes it's me," Gen shouted. "Help us!"

The door heaved open to an underground bunker. A Muthr with the number twenty-three printed on her torso greeted the girls. "Gen, you are okay. This is very good news. Who is this with you? She is not identifying." The Muthr spoke in a familiar dulcet tone. Eva looked down, away from the robot's warm amber eyes. It was almost too much to deal with at this moment.

"Twenty-three, this is Eva. She rescued me and my two friends." Gen brushed past the robot. "Where's Father?"

"The fugitive?" The robot rolled behind Gen and turned her head back to examine Eva. "You have brought her here?"

"Yes. She needs to speak with Father immediately. Where is he?"

"Follow me," Twenty-three said.

Eva trailed behind the robot that led the girls into a wide room with a low ceiling. The décor was typical for the city—an all-white lab room with bright lighting that gave an overall antiseptic feeling. Terminals were stationed in rows under a myriad of holographic charts, readouts, and diagrams of the city. Robots of various shapes and sizes conferred with human controllers who manned these stations. Several doorways opened to unknown corridors, which offered passage to those allowed in this secret place. Eva passed a triage area where an automedic cared for human patients. She tore her eyes away as one of the medics draped a white sheet over the torso of an unmoving patient.

"It would be best to stay put in one of the relaxation chambers for the time being," Twenty-three said. "We have got quite a situation on our hands with this airship malfunction."

"This was not a malfunction." Eva snorted.

"It is a malfunction, and we shall determine its cause after we tend to the people." Twenty-three led the girls to an alcove adjacent to the bunker. She opened an access panel and paused. "I am told you may enter, Gen, but Eva is to remain here."

Across the room a low hiss gave away the location of a concealed hatch as it slid open. An authoriton, a sleek polished robot from the city police, exited. Several controllers looked up from their terminals and watched as it rolled in Eva's direction. She started charging the boomrod.

"Don't!" Gen placed a hand on the muzzle. She addressed Twenty-three directly, "Open this door and take me to my father. You will allow Eva to accompany me. Is that understood?"

Twenty-three did not reply. Lights blinked on the robot's torso. *Blinking lights mean it's communicating . . . probably with Cadmus. He must be finally coming to his senses,* Eva thought. The authoriton's motor whined as it rolled toward her. Eva gripped the handle of the boomrod tight. It would be messy if she had to engage with the authoriton in here. She didn't want any more people to get hurt, but she would not be stopped, not this close to Cadmus. Not this close to ending the battle.

"You are dismissed," Twenty-three ordered the authoriton. "You may return to your post." Without a word the authoriton stopped, rotated, and rolled away. Twenty-three placed her mechanized hand on the panel, causing another hatch to hiss open. Beyond the hatch lay inky darkness. Headlights flicked on from the body of Twenty-three, illuminating a path as the robot led

Eva and Gen down the winding corridor.

"Your father has been critically injured," Twenty-three reported in her metered tone. "Automedics have attempted to heal him, but he insists that he be left alone during this moment of crisis. He has just finished conferring with his council and is now in his private chambers."

At the end of the corridor was another access panel. Once more the robot placed her hand on the panel, and a second door opened.

"Will he . . . survive?" Gen asked.

Twenty-three patted Gen on the back. "Of course. Your father will never truly perish, as I am sure he will explain to you in due time." She gestured for the girls to enter.

Gen and Eva stepped through the second doorway into a dimly lit room. Out in the corridor Twenty-three closed the door behind them.

"Father? I'm here now, thanks to Eva Nine. Where are you?" Gen's voice sounded like a lost child's as she called out into the dark.

From the shadows came a cough. As Eva's eyes adjusted to the darkness, she could make out a claw-foot floor lamp with a stained-glass shade placed near a small end table. A figure was seated in an armchair next to the table, but the face was shadowed. "Eva, you say? The imago has returned? Very interesting. Come, my daughters," a whispery voice said. "I am here, contemplating." A trembling hand turned up the brightness of the lamp. Cadmus Pryde laid his hand back on the ornately carved armrest of the chair. In his lap he held a browned human skull. As the girls neared, it was apparent that the room he was in was large, much larger than any room in an ordinary Sanctuary. Behind Cadmus an entire wall was lined with shelving filled with row upon row of human skulls.

"Father!" Gen rushed up and hugged him. "Where is everyone? What is this place?"

"Welcome to the first Sanctuary ever built by the Dynastes corporation," said Cadmus. "Welcome to my birthplace."

# Mine was

nicer," Eva said.

Cadmus chuckled, but it became a cough. "My father, Leonardo Pryde, created this prototype Sanctuary sometime before I was born." Cadmus remained seated in his chair. His aged eyes focused on the skull in his lap. "He had led the Historical Holography Project many years earlier but was frustrated at the limitations of information that could be programmed into each historical figure. They were simply living databases of gathered fact and speculation. But if he could record every waking second of someone's life, well then, he would create the perfect hologram."

"So you're just a hologram?" Eva reached out to touch Cadmus.

He waved her away. "I am the inverse. Holography ensured that my upbringing was pristine." From a pocket in his robes, Cadmus pulled out a tarnished Omnipod with a dingy strap. He activated a program, then turned off the antique lamp. Descending from a mount on the ceiling, a large holo-projector flickered on, and the dim room began to glow. "See here how the past prescribes the future."

Eva and Gen found themselves in an illusion of a small sunlit library of an old Victorian-styled house. Where skulls had lain in rows on shelves, now holograms of books were stacked in heaps among holographic models of buildings and spaceships. Soft music played from unseen speakers, the same sort Eva had heard when she'd first ventured into New Attica. Outside the window a wind chime tinkled in a gentle spring breeze. In the window box bees and butterflies danced from flower to flower. A hummingbird shot up from the garden and hovered in front of Eva, startling her.

"Cap? Cap, are you downstairs?" called out a voice that sounded much like Cadmus's. Eva turned to see the actual Cadmus still in his seat, his eyes closed as he stroked his long mustache.

He opened his eyes and pointed down the hall to whoever it was who had spoke. Eva and Gen wandered down the holographic hall and into a brightly colored kitchen. In an open doorway stood a portly man with bushy gray eyebrows and a beard. In the garage behind him a pristine polished hovercar floated silently. Eva recognized the man.

"That's my grandfather," Gen said, and poked the hologram, though the man did not respond.

"I think he's in the library studying," a lithe dark-haired woman said from the kitchen sink. She was dressed in dirty dungarees and a wide straw hat. Gardening gloves hung from her back pocket, and Eva could see that she was washing freshly cut flowers. Holding her arrangement, the woman walked gracefully from the kitchen toward the library, passing right through Eva.

"Grandma," Gen said.

"Cap dear, your father is going out to run errands. Do you want to go with him?" Mrs. Pryde's voice carried down the hall.

"No thank you, Mom," a child's voice replied. "I'm busy working on my new invention."

"Okay, fine. I'll be back later," Leonardo said with a smile, and exited into the garage.

"Grab some apples if you can," Mrs. Pryde called out. "They're in season now."

"They ate actual fruit back then?" Gen's eyes were wide.

The girls walked back to the library. The real Cadmus remained slumped in his chair while the hologram played on around him. Eva noticed holographic building blocks and drawings spread out on the intricately patterned carpet.

"What are you inventing today?" Mrs. Pryde arranged the flowers in a crystal vase set on an end table.

"Robots," the child's voice said. Eva watched Cadmus mouth the words in sync with the recording. "I'm building robots."

"That was this Cadmus here," Cadmus interrupted the hologram and held up the skull. "Cadmus zero-one. He was but ten years old during this recording. Every Cadmus since has agreed that this was one of the best times of our lives."

*He's a clone.* Eva understood at last. Thunder rumbled outside in the hologram. She glanced out the window but saw a cloudless azure sky.

"This life. This family's love and support is what I wanted to create for my people." With effort Cadmus rose and walked around the hologram. In the bright light Eva could now see his bloodstained robes.

"You build the darnedest things, Cadmus A. Pryde," Mrs. Pryde said, marveling at one of the robot drawings. "I bet one day you'll be a great inventor like your dad."

"You did recreate this perfect life, Father." Carefully Gen embraced Cadmus. "For me and all of your children to enjoy."

"No." Eva shook her head. Cadmus's holographic past was so fully rendered, so tangible, that it was hard for her to dismiss what she was seeing. "This world. It doesn't exist anymore. It's gone."

"I have brought it back," Cadmus said, his voice rising with pride. "The feeling of love, security, and harmony are here for all to enjoy—just as it once was. Just as it should be."

"It may have worked once, right here, but it fails beyond the walls of your city."

"You are wrong!" Cadmus now spoke with conviction. "This world will rise again. I will see it built anew!"

Eva fired the boomrod at the holo-projector. It blew apart in a shower of sparks and shattered holo-bulbs. The emergency lights in the room activated, bathing all in a bright white light. Eva recognized the cold gray walls, just like those of her old Sanctuary home. "This. This is reality," said Eva, pointing to the skulls that lined the shelves. "Clones. Countless clones waiting for that time to come. But it never will." Eva pushed away her mental vision of the WondLa. That picture. Those smiling faces. "I know, because more than anything, I wish that my Muthr could come back. I miss my days with her. But I evolved. I found the real world, Orbona. The truth is, that world that you long for in the past was also a dying world."

Cadmus blinked bleary eyes. "But it is dead no more. It has come back, and we must seize our moment. We are wiser from our mistakes, and Earth is ready to hold mankind to her bosom once more." Clearly weakened from his wound, he sat back down in his chair.

"You are wrong," said Eva. "It came back because the Ojo family brought life back to it. The planet was dead when they arrived. The Human Repopulation Project would have never succeeded if it weren't for them."

"You're talking about the generator, aren't you? You know where it is!" Even in his weakened state, there was fire in Cadmus's eyes.

"It doesn't matter. The virus that creates life is

spreading. Soon the entire planet will be habitable again," said Eva. "But you will not live to see it . . . if you do not act now. Loroc has tricked you. He has taken control of your fleet and is destroying everything."

"Nonsense!" Cadmus slammed his hands on the arms of the chair. "The crash on Attican Hall was a tragic navigational malfunction. But it was not done by nefarious means. The city's power grid is down at the moment, but my team of—".

"No, Father. Eva is right," Gen said. She knelt down on the floor next to his chair. "There are big robots on three legs attacking our people . . . your children. I saw them."

"What?" Cadmus appeared confused.

"Look. See for yourself." Gen replayed the recording of the invasion on her Omnipod.

Cadmus's expression changed from confusion to horror. "No! Those are my—"

"Warbots," said Eva. "Gunning down all of your people."

Cadmus snatched his Omnipod. "Twenty-three?"

Projected from the Omnipod, a full-size hologram of the Muthr appeared in the room. "Yes?"

"Divert reserve generator power to all Attican security cameras and display," he said.

"As you wish."

A swirl of screens materialized in the room, rotating like a school of fish around Cadmus. As each one passed in front of Eva, she saw the same scene: warbots firing SHOCdarts and electrocuting citizens against a fiery backdrop.

Cadmus gasped. "Twenty-three, are you dealing with this? Shut down all warbot systems immediately!"

"I'm sorry, sir. That order contradicts my revised initiative," Twenty-three replied in her calm tone.

"Revised initiative? Your orders come from me." The creases in Cadmus's face deepened with his concern.

"That is correct, sir. However, the Prime Adviser is our controller. His word supersedes yours," said the robot.

"This cannot happen!" Cadmus opened a program on his Omnipod. A pyramid comprised of faces and names hovered over the Omnipod's central eye. Cadmus zoomed in on the apex and spun it about as if searching for something. "It is impossible. I've been entirely removed from the chain of command."

"What does that mean?" Gen asked.

Cadmus shushed her. "Omnipod, open HRP Metropolis zero-one hierarchal command. Username is 'Cadmus zero-one.' Password is 'omniscient.'"

"I'm sorry, sir. That username and password are no longer valid," the Omnipod replied.

"It's impossible." Cadmus stared at the Omnipod in his shaking hand. "Even the original override doesn't work."

"Everything is as it should be," said Twenty-three. "It is as the Prime Adviser has ordered."

"No! No! NO!" Cadmus shouted. He stood and paced the room, leaving droplets of blood on the rubber floor.

"What else has he ordered?" Eva asked Twenty-three. She watched as one of the screens from the security camera drifted by. On it Hailey and his crew hurried survivors onto his ship.

"All of Cadmus's offspring are to be terminated. Attican citizens are to be gathered for eradication. New Attica is to be eliminated except for Cadmus. He must remain contained in Sanctuary zero-one during extermination of his species. Afterward he will be transported to Solas for reprogramming." Twenty-three expanded the security screens so that they filled the room with images of the destruction of New Attica.

Cadmus's eyes were wide with rage. He ran his fingers through his long hair. "This cannot be! My programs are foolproof. There is no way Loroc could have gained access and reprogrammed them." Somewhere outside, explosions rocked the Sanctuary.

"We have to get out of here, fast!" Eva looked up at the walls, waiting for them to collapse. "We don't have much time."

"Father." Gen took Cadmus by the hand. "Do you know the way out of here?"

"Yes. Of course." Cadmus snapped out of his mania for a moment. "Right here. Follow me." He limped over to a doorway that led into an empty supply room. Reaching the back wall, Cadmus placed a hand on the panel. Nothing happened.

"I am sorry, sir." The hologram of Twenty-three followed them into the supply room. "You are not permitted to exit the premises. As ordered, you are to remain here until eradication of the city is complete."

"Eva, blow open the hatch like you did before!" Gen said.

"These walls are reinforced ply-steel. I don't

think even the sonic capabilities of this alien tech will accomplish that," Cadmus said. "All other access ports into the Sanctuary are likely locked down. There has to be another way." He coughed and gritted his teeth. Eva noticed he was gripping the ride side of his waist.

"Are you okay, Father?" Gen examined the blood on his robes. "Twenty-three said you refused medical help."

"I'm fine for now. I think it is a small piece of shrapnel from the crash. I ordered my automedics to tend to the severely wounded first and then come see me," Cadmus whispered.

Eva frowned. "I don't think that's going to happen. Don't your clothes have Anatoscan and SpeedHeal ointment?"

"No." Cadmus wiped beads of sweat from his forehead. "Why would I need that in a peaceful place like this?"

"I'm getting a call," said Gen. "Eva, it's Hailey." She held out her palm to Eva. Hailey's face floated above it.

"You guys okay? I'm dropping off the survivors now at our camp. I can come back and get you, but it has to be quick." Hailey looked distraught, even scared. "It's bad down there."

"Okay," said Eva. "We'll contact you in a nano." She turned to Cadmus. "Is this Sanctuary similar to the one you built for me?"

"Yes, albeit it houses significantly more tech for my—"

Eva cut him off. "Does it have an exhaust vent in the kitchen?"

"It does!" Cadmus led the way, with Gen supporting him.

Eva charged the boomrod and blew open the intake grill that covered the exhaust vent.

"This will take you up to the ground level, near the edge of the park," Cadmus said. He held Gen's hand as she climbed up onto the stove. A light began to ping on his Omnipod. "Oh dear." He dashed over and locked the kitchen door. "We are being tracked. They are sending in the authoritons. You best hurry."

"You go next," Eva said to him as she charged the boomrod. "I'll cover you."

"I am not leaving," Cadmus said in a grave tone.

"What?"

"Why?" asked Gen.

"I will only slow you down. Besides, it is clear to me now that I am simply an antiquated program running on antiquated rules."

"Father, don't do this! Come with us!" Gen climbed back down and threw her arms around him. New tears marred her already ruined makeup.

Cadmus kissed her forehead. "I have loved you most out of all of my children. And I want you to survive."

Eva swallowed hard. She tugged at Gen's shoulder.

Out in the Sanctuary the walls rumbled. The authoritons had breached the doors.

"We have to go," Eva said.

Gen climbed back up into the shaft.

Cadmus reached in and handed Gen his Omnipod. "Take this. Despite our shortcomings, there are many great things that humanity accomplished. Our heritage and our history must not be lost."

Gen took the Omnipod. She mouthed, "I love you, Daddy."

Eva hopped up onto the stove. She grabbed hold of the rung inside the exhaust vent.

"Blow the shaft once you get clear of here, so they can't follow you up. Understand?" said Cadmus.

"I understand." Eva tried to remain calm. She'd escaped like this before, but that had been a different place. A different time. "This is not how I wanted it to end."

"Nor I." Cadmus smiled, though it was clear he was deep in thought. "After every ending comes a new beginning. That beginning is both of you— my daughters."

A loud clang hit the kitchen door, followed by the grinding sound of blades cutting the ply-steel.

"Go," he said. "Go far from this place and begin anew."

Eva nodded at Cadmus, then began her ascent. With Eva pushing Gen, they climbed up the rungs inside the vent as fast as they could. Halfway up, Eva stopped and pointed the boomrod back down toward Sanctuary zero-one. With a full charge she fired the weapon. It emitted a loud *BOOM*. The shaft buckled and caved in below, sending a wave of dust and ash upward. With a cry Gen slipped from the rungs and tumbled down onto Eva. Bracing herself, Eva caught Gen and helped her grip the rungs. She whispered words of comfort into Gen's ear. Words her own Muthr had once spoken to her.

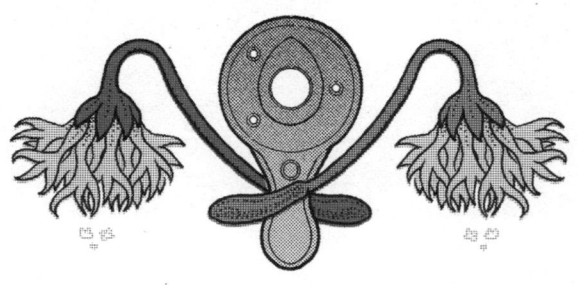

# CHAPTER 20: EXTINCTION

The girls reached the ground level and wriggled out of an exhaust vent near the edge of the park. Around them the blown-out windows of the storefronts watched them like the hollow eyes of gigantic tragic masks. Eva grabbed Gen's hand, and together they scurried through the gloom toward the cover of a large oak tree.

"I need you to call Hailey," said Eva. "Tell him he needs to get here now!" She charged the boomrod and peered around the trunk of the tree out into

the expanse of the park. A wave of warbots strode through the smoking landscape. Their black armor glistened in the falling rain while the lights in their eyes glowed a ghastly green. Some robots fired, electrocuting those who tried to flee, while others sprayed out streams of molten plasma, incinerating everything in their path. Eva could hear the hiss of the rain as it met with the fire of burning buildings. The flames seemed to be everywhere in the city at once. The harsh heavy smoke that hung in the air choked anything that breathed.

Gen's voice was shaky. "Hailey . . . he—he says he'll b-be here soon. We have to m-meet him at the aviary."

"Okay. Let's go—" Eva started.

From a hovering warship a warbot dropped down directly in front of the girls.

"Get behind me," Eva shouted. She fired the boomrod at the warbot's legs, toppling it. As it fell to the ground, it sent a swarm of SHOCdarts out in all directions. Eva shoved Gen out of the way, and they both fell behind the trunk of the oak tree. They cowered as a volley of SHOCdarts thwacked against the trunk.

The commotion caught the attention of two

other warbots burning buildings on the perimeter road surrounding the park. They turned off their flamethrowers and turned toward Eva and Gen. On the rooftops of the buildings one level above them more warbots landed.

"What do we do? Do we run?" asked Gen.

"We won't make it." Eva shouted over the sound of the warbots as she charged the boomrod to maximum. She fired on the supports that held the second-level buildings, which crumbled and gave way in a fiery explosion. Warbots and rubble from the second level tumbled down onto the two warbots below.

"Let's go!" Eva shouted.

The girls bolted across the park toward the aviary. Behind them one of the warbots rose from the rubble and gave chase. Eva heard the stamp of its three feet as it rushed toward them. She charged the boomrod again.

"Keep running!" Eva yelled, and turned to fire. *WOOM!* Her shot connected head-on with the warbot, and the robot exploded in a ball of fire. The blast threw Eva backward into a large muddy puddle.

With ears ringing, Eva clawed her way out of the thick mud. On hands and knees she crawled to the nearest tree and sat with her back against the trunk. Her eyes tried to focus, but her brain just couldn't seem to make them do what she wanted.

She exhaled and tried to rub the mud away from her face. All around her Cadmus's warbots marched through the burning city, destroying everything he had built. Her nose filled with the caustic smell of melting plastic.

"I'm so tired of running. Hailey better let me sleep on the ship," Eva whispered, though she could barely hear her own voice above the din and the ringing. She pulled the boomrod from the mud by yanking on the cord that attached it to the charger. She scraped off the caked mud from the levered trigger and laid the weapon across her lap. A familiar squawk broke through the haze in Eva's mind. Alongside her a large round gray bird playfully snapped at her sleeve with a hooked beak.

Eva laughed despite her situation. "Dodo? What are you doing out here?" She stroked the yellow plumage that sprung from the bird's head. "You should be in your aviary. It's safer there." Eva heard a jingling sound, like a little wind chime. She scanned the park and spotted the nearby Attican Aviary, where Gen was hiding in the shadow of the entrance. Gen was waving Eva over with the palm-light of her Omnipod, causing her dangling bracelets to jangle.

"Come on." Eva tried to pick up the bird. "I'll help you." The dodo squawked loudly and scurried toward the aviary. Eva scanned the distance between her and the aviary entrance. There seemed to be no warbots in the immediate vicinity. Eva dashed behind the bird and joined Gen.

It was clear that the warbots had already marched through here. The domed roof of the aviary had been reduced to little more than shattered chunks of glass. This had allowed the flocks of birds housed within to fly away and escape. Inside, the girls crept through the dense foliage, looking for a place to hide.

Eva knelt down at the edge of the duck pond and pulled off her poncho. Her long white hair fell around her shoulders and dirty face.

"Are you okay?" Gen asked, breathless.

"Yeah. I'll be all right." Eva placed her hands in the water and splashed her face. "Just a little beat-up is all." She knelt closer to the pond's surface and scooped water over her bare neck. *My necklace. . . . It's missing!* She looked around frantically before finding the locket Soth had given her, lying at the shore of the pool. *The clasp must have come loose, and it slipped off.* She wiped it dry and placed it back over her head. Somewhere hidden in the brush Eva heard the dodo again. "If it hadn't been for that bird, I don't know if I would have snapped out of the daze I was in."

"I'm just glad you found me." Gen looked like a frightened owl with her wide eyes darting about.

"Why don't you call Hailey and tell him we're here."

Gen nodded and scooted under the branches of a large willow.

Eva closed her eyes for a moment. She could feel herself coming back into focus. Her goal of escaping New Attica became clear in her mind once again. Around her neck she felt a jiggling sensation. She looked down; the locket was still dripping with water. In the smoky light Eva examined the glass vial that hung from the braided chain around her neck. Inside the vial something was wriggling. The glass vial cracked open. Out crawled an orchidlike creature on four segmented legs. It scuttled over Eva's palm and onto the back of her hand.

"The flower Eight gave me is . . . *alive?*" Eva blinked in astonishment. "It must carry the Vitae Virus."

The orchid creature chirped and crawled up Eva's arm like an exotic insect. Carefully she placed it on the ground. It proceeded to lick its four feet clean, then continued crawling along the shore. Everywhere the orchid creature stepped, moss and greenery sprouted in its wake. It chirped once more and disappeared in the undergrowth. From there, ferns uncoiled, reeds quivered and stretched, and an unseen bird began to sing. As this phenomenon unfolded right in front of Eva's eyes, she momentarily forgot about the burning buildings, explosions, and screams beyond. "And so one society flourishes as another perishes."

"Eva, come here," said Gen from under the

curtain of the willow tree. Fear rushed her words. "Hailey said he can't come. . . . He can't come! He's not going to rescue us. We're trapped!" She crawled close to Eva on hands and knees. "He says that ships are searching the perimeter of the city. Everybody is hiding at the Toiler's camp."

Eva looked up through the broken glass dome at the squadron of warships still looming over the city. She took a deep breath. "Okay. Well, that part is good."

"Good? How can that be good?" Gen squeaked.

"Well, they haven't been discovered and they haven't left yet."

"But what are *we* going to do? The robots are going to get us!" Gen was spiraling into hysterics.

"Gen." Eva kept her tone calm even though their situation was bleak. She pulled her poncho back over her head and strapped on the charger for the boomrod. "All we have to do is get out of here and regroup with them."

"That's *all* we need to do? How are we going to do that? You can't just walk out of the city. It's impossible."

"I've escaped from here before. I can do it again." Eva Eight's orchid creature crawled out from the bushes and hopped onto the trunk of the willow.

The lichens on the trunk rippled as the creature stepped over them.

"I think I know a way," said Eva.

"You do?"

"Yes. But you need to remove all that jewelry or they'll hear us for sure."

With jittery hands Gen yanked off the jangly bracelets that adorned her forearms.

"And while you're at it," Eva said, "lose the robotail."

## CHAPTER 21: SHOCK

The girls stood in the dark entrance to the aviary. The Attican park was eerily quiet save for the breaking of glass and cries for help somewhere off in the distance. Though the momentary calm should have eased Eva's nerves, it somehow made her edgy. "Do you know where the eastern gate to the city is?"

"The old gate where reboots—er . . . imagoes used to enter? It's that way." Gen pointed to the far side of the park at a cluster of units, now ablaze.

"That's where we have to go." Eva charged her weapon. "Stay close."

They exited the aviary and splashed across the muddy turf to a cluster of pines.

"Let's catch our breath for a minute," Eva said, panting. "We've got to run as fast as we can from cover to cover. Got it?"

Gen nodded.

The whine of hover engines droned high above them. Eva looked up through the boughs of the pines to see lights from a pair of warbots as they dropped from the belly of an overhead warship. Their long legs unfolded in preparation for landing.

"They're gonna land right on us," Gen shouted.

Eva ran out into the open field. Aiming the muzzle of the boomrod at the lowest descending warbot, she fired. The sonic wave blasted the robot off course, and it collided into its companion. Now out of control, both warbots plummeted down to the ground as a mass of tangled legs.

"Get out of there," Eva yelled to Gen, and gestured for her to run.

Gen bolted from the cover of the pine trees toward Eva just as the warbots crashed through the canopy. The ground shook on impact, causing one of the trees to topple over.

"That shot was so jolt," Gen said, catching her breath.

"Let's hurry. I might not be so lucky next time."

They dashed from tree to tree toward a thick cluster of bushes that lined the edge of the park.

"Let's stop for a nano," Eva whispered and crawled into the cover of the foliage with Gen close behind.

Eva peered through the bushes to the street that circled the entire park. What she saw took her aback. Illuminated only from the dancing flames of a burning storefront lay a heap of motionless human bodies. Most were facedown in the street. Some were half-buried under rubble. Eva tore her gaze away from the grisly sight, but her eyes locked on to those of a girl.

The girl was not much older than Eva. She was lying on her back with her hand next to her face. Her mouth was slightly open, and a large smoking SHOCdart was imbedded in her neck. She stared, unblinking while white ash fell upon her, like the holograms Eva had seen of a snowfall. Eva kept waiting for the girl to blink, but all she saw in the girl's fixed eyes was her own reflection.

"Is it safe for us to go?" Gen asked from behind.

"No." Eva whispered back. "We need to find another way. And it's not here." They crept through the bushes around the perimeter of the park until they found a route that was clear of bodies.

"The eastern gate is . . . just . . . down this alley." Gen stopped and bent over, racked with a coughing fit.

"Take a nano." Eva sat Gen down next to the shell of a scorched gondola. She wiped the ash from Gen's face. "You good?"

"I'm good," Gen replied, and wiped her mouth with her sleeve. "It's all this smoke."

The girls peered through the gondola's canopy toward the gate. "The door is so big. How are we going to open it?" Gen asked.

"We're not." Eva ran toward a pair of large drainage ducts that flanked the gate. The ducts jutted from the outermost wall of the city, then elbowed downward into the ground. "There's a hidden door behind these ducts," said Eva. "Let's go."

Squeezing behind the pair of ducts, Eva located the top of a small metal hatch buried behind a heap of rubble.

"Help me clear this." Eva started clawing the debris away from the door. Gen carefully picked up pieces of debris and tossed them aside.

"You've got to move more quickly than that if you want to get out of here and not get fried," said Eva.

"But these rocks are so heavy."

"We have to hurry." Eva grunted as she rolled a large hunk from the pile. "Ouch!" She pulled her finger out from under the hunk and put it into her mouth.

"You okay?"

Eva examined her bloody finger. "Let's just clear this as fast as we can."

Together they scooped out handfuls of debris and rock. After a while the hatch was cleared.

Eva gripped the corroded lever to turn it. It didn't budge. She unclipped the strap that held the charger for the boomrod and handed the charger to Gen. "You need to hold this and this," Eva said, giving Gen the boomrod and charger.

"I—I can't use this . . . thing." Gen held the weapon at arm's length.

Eva struggled with the lever. "You . . . uff . . . are gonna have to if we get spotted."

"But—"

"Sheesa! Just do it!" Eva shouted over her shoulder. The lever loosened slightly, but the hatch door remained wedged shut. "I'll be amazed if you can survive one day past these walls."

Gen started to snivel. She slung the charger strap over her shoulder. "Some of us had nice homes, remember?"

"Not anymore." Eva caught her breath and examined the raw spots on her palms from trying the lever. She massaged her hands with fingers. "I'm sorry, Gen. We have to get out of here. This entire place is going to go up in flames."

Gen sobbed. "This is the only home I've ever known. Now my friends are gone, my clothes, my family . . . my father."

Eva turned to Gen and said, "He wanted you to survive."

"I just want to die! Leave me here. Just go!"

"Don't be ridiculous, Gen—"

"Please remain stationary," a firm voice spoke. In the alley on the other side of the ducts stood a warbot. "Do not try to escape."

Eva reached down and turned the knob on the charger. The boomrod began to hum. "Aim the muzzle and squeeze the lever in the middle," she whispered to Gen.

Gen trembled, "I—I can't—"

"You have to."

"One of you is not identifiable. Step out so that you may be properly identified." The warbot moved toward the girls.

"Fire," Eva said.

"I can't!" Gen fell to her knees.

"Voice recognition is affirmative. Eva Nine of Sanctuary five-seven-three, your location has been confirmed." The warbot closed in. "Notifying the Prime Master. Prepare for immobilization." The flaps on its ammo canisters opened, revealing a cluster of SHOCdarts.

"Fire, you short-out! FIRE!" Eva screamed.

Gen squeezed the trigger and was thrown backward into the wall by the boomrod's kickback. Her shot clipped the top of the warbot's head. It staggered backward several steps and stumbled over the remains of a smoldering building.

"Sorry," Eva said. "I forgot to mention the kick when you shoot."

"Thanks. And, for the record, I am not a short-out!" Gen shouted.

In the alley beyond, another warbot appeared.

"We've got to get out of here!" Eva yanked on the lever to the hatch. "Get up and keep firing at them!" She climbed up onto the duct and pushed on the lever with her entire body weight.

As Gen scrambled to her feet, she fired again. This time she remained standing, but missed and hit the building. Flaming rubble cascaded down onto the warbot, but still it continued toward them.

"It's not stopping. It's not stopping!" Gen screamed.

Eva grunted as she strained against the lever with everything she had. SHOCdarts peppered the ducts and ricocheted off the wall next to her.

Gen yelled as she fired once more. The shot connected with the warbot, and it went down, but the first one was now stepping over it. Another volley of darts flew at the girls.

Gen cowered behind the duct. Eva screamed in pain as a SHOCdart pierced her arm. Another dart entered her thigh. "Fire before it fries me!" Eva shouted. She pushed through the agony and continued struggling with the door. At last the lever screeched as it turned and the door creaked open.

Gen fired the boomrod again. The sonic blast hit the housing units next to the warbot, and the entire building collapsed onto it. On hands and knees Eva crawled into the hidden passage, with Gen close behind her.

"Shut the door," said Eva, panting. "And turn the latch until it locks."

Gen did as she was told.

Eva winced as she pulled the pencil-length dart from her upper arm. "We are safe now." She yanked the other from her thigh. "Take off your skirt."

"My skirt?" Gen unfastened her frilly underskirt.

"Yes. I need it to wrap my wounds." Eva swallowed down the throbbing ache where the SHOCdarts had punctured her. "Use this to rip it into strips." She handed Gen a bloody dart.

Using the sharp pointed SHOCdart, Gen ripped a hole in the skirt. She grabbed the hem and tore off a long strip of fabric. She wrapped the strip tightly around Eva's arm and tied it.

"I've never seen blood—real blood—before today," said Gen.

Eva snorted in response. She reached up and wiped her hand on Gen's forehead. Eva showed her scarlet fingertips. "That's your blood. You must have gotten nicked by a dart."

Gen put a trembling finger to her blemish. She rubbed the red droplets between her fingertips. "I'm bleeding. Will I have a scar?"

Eva shrugged.

"Do you think Hailey will think it's rocket?"

Eva rolled her eyes and ignored the comment. Using the remainder of the skirt, she bound the wound in her thigh and staggered to her feet. "Come on. Let's get out of here."

She led Gen through the dark passage past pipes and grates. Unlike the first time, when she had been here with her sister, the steam and humidity had been replaced with a dank chill. The girls made their way to the end of the passage.

"Where are we?" Gen asked in the gloom.

"If my guess is right, we are somewhere near the gate that leads in and out of the city," replied Eva. She felt the distinct seam of a hatch set in the wall in front of them. "Do you have a light?"

Gen activated the central eye of the Omnipod embedded in the palm of her hand. Eva smiled when she read the sign on the closed access hatch.

# EASTERN SUBFERRY STATION
## MAINTENANCE PERSONNEL ONLY

# CHAPTER 22: REGENERATION

Eva trudged up the steep incline of the subferry tracks. She remained silent as the full impact of the events she'd just witnessed began to sink in. For a while the only sounds were the girls' footsteps and Gen's sniffling.

"My clothes are soaked from the rain," Gen finally said aloud, walking a few steps behind Eva. "They smell different . . . like dirt."

"The rain smells of the earth," Eva replied. "I love that smell."

"Is everything dirty outside?" asked Gen. "Like the Toilers?"

"Yeah," answered Eva. "But you get used to it."

"Will my quotacard work out here?" Gen asked.

Eva shook her head. How could she explain the real world to Gen?

"What will I do?" asked Gen. There was panic in her voice.

Eva placed Gen's hand in hers. "Your life is not over. It is just now beginning."

Gen said nothing further. Eva continued leading the way up the tunnel. The girls didn't speak again for the rest of the hike. Finally they arrived at the subferry docks at the peak of the tunnel.

"Shine your light over here." Eva skirted between the park subferries. "The exit is just past this docking station."

The girls crossed the abandoned station platform and came to the entrance. A pale glow of moonlight shone in from the outside.

Eva gasped. "The outer gates. They've been

destroyed." She clambered over the rubble and peered through the opening of the wrecked city gates. The barren wasteland that surrounded New Attica was still. A full moon looked down between the Rings of Orbona. "There doesn't seem to be anyone here. Can you call Hailey and tell him to pick us up?"

Gen wiped away her mascara and ran her hands through her hair before contacting Hailey.

"Hey, you made it!" Hailey's holographic head floated in Gen's palm.

Eva smiled. "Yeah, we are at the outer eastern gate where you brought—"

Gen interrupted. "You have to save me! Everything is gone."

"How many of you are there? Three?"

"Two," Eva said in a low voice.

"What about Cadmus?" Hailey asked. "I thought—"

"Just two of us," said Eva.

"Stay put. I found an emergency shuttle on the warship. I'll be there in a nano," replied Hailey. "Oh, and, Eva? I found a little surprise too, just for you." Hailey cracked a grin right before he signed off.

The hovering shuttle came to a stop just outside the city's outer gates. Through the bulbous canopy

Eva could see Hailey waving. With a hiss the side door opened and unfolded to the ground, becoming an entry ramp. Eva and Gen scrambled from their hiding place into the cramped cabin. Hunched over in the backseat was a familiar smiling face.

"Huxley! You're alive!" Eva jumped into his lap and hugged the gawky alien.

"Eva Nine, my little bayrie." Huxley patted her head. "You thought I was dead? I told you ol' Huxie's gotten out of worse scrapes."

"Let's get going," said Hailey. "The skies are clear of warships for now, but I don't know for how long."

Cautiously, Gen took the seat across from Huxley and scooted as far away as possible.

"Your arm?" Eva saw a bound stump where one of Huxley's arms should have been.

"Lost that and a leg in the explosion," Huxley grimaced. "They both will take *forever* to grow back."

"Grow back? Will they really?" Eva peered at his wounds.

"I'm a Mirthian, aren't I?" Huxley responded in his usual cheery tone.

"Strap in," Hailey announced from the cockpit. "This little thing has some kick." He pushed the throttle forward, and the shuttle shot off. With ease he navigated the speeding craft down into the depths of the canyon ravines. "I'm gonna take a longer route just to make sure we aren't spotted. I don't want to reveal the location of our camp."

"Smart move, hero," Huxley said. "So who's this little one?" He looked over at Gen. "A friend of yours?"

"Yes," Eva said with some hesitancy. "Huxley, this is Gen. Gen, this is Huxley. Hux and I met in . . . Attican Hall," she said to Gen.

"You mean we met in the lockup of Attican Hall," Huxley added with a bitter laugh. "What a pair of pretty bayries you two make! One of you is dressed mysteriously, as dark as the night. And the other . . ." He looked at Eva's hair. "You're now as white as a star, Eva Nine. You've changed color like an arboreal loriped. Is that normal for your kind?"

"No." Eva glanced at Gen and tucked her hair back behind her ears. "Not usually."

"Well, it suits you," Huxley replied with a smile. He addressed Gen, "Sorry to hear about your grand city. At least you made it out in one piece— not like me."

Gen stared blankly at Huxley.

"Oh, she doesn't understand you, Huxley. She doesn't have a vocal transcoder," Eva said.

"I think Vanpa has a few back at camp," said Hailey.

Eva translated Huxley's words. Gen crossed her arms and retracted farther in her seat. Her body seemed to become smaller, yet her eyes became wider.

Huxley looked at Eva. "This one's not a talker, eh? Not like you and I?"

"She's had a rough day. She lost her father," Eva whispered back. She decided it best to keep Gen's family a secret for the time being. "She's never been outside the city, nor seen anyone from another planet."

"Wow. That is a lot for one little bayrie to handle. I'd need a bottle of ol' usquebaugh to work through all that," Huxley said with a wink.

"I'm so glad to see you here. How did Hailey find you?" Eva squeezed Huxley's large hand.

"I found him locked up on the warship," Hailey said.

"Wait. What?" Eva gave a puzzled look. "How'd you get on there?"

"Well, right after I took off on that Dorcean glider, I zipped right between those tracker missiles, remember? Of course I lead 'em right smack into that mother ship, and WHAM! The whole thing blows!" Huxley's voice rose with excitement, causing Gen to jump in her seat. "But wouldn't you know, the glider and me get caught in the explosion. I'm tumbling head over heels, and before I know it, the other ship harpoons the glider right out of the sky—and me with it."

"Wow."

"Crazy, right?" said Hailey.

"Well then, what else could I do but be taken? After all, I was banged up pretty bad. So they bring me on board and patch me up, but here's the crazy thing: robots—the entire ship was manned by nothing more than robots! Can you believe it? There was not a single living soul on that floating hunk of metal. No wonder their actions were carried out remorselessly."

At Huxley's words Eva glanced over at Gen. Her eyes, unblinking, stared out the window at the barren landscape.

"I talk to a projection of the frilly guy for a bit, Marzug I think he was called. He's interrogating me about what I know and don't know about the invasion. He was especially intrigued with you, Eva, and where you might be headed—but I didn't tell him anything. I don't think he believed me. At one point I heard him talking to that creepy-looking 'Prime Adviser.'"

"Loroc?" Eva asked.

"No, no, that isn't Loroc. I've seen images of him. Loroc looks like little Zin; round and smiley, not creepy with all those eyes and arms." Huxley wriggled his fingers for effect.

"That *is* Loroc," said Eva. "Something happened to him, and now he's become corrupt, which has caused him to devour . . . his . . . sisters."

"Really?" Huxley grimaced.

"He masterminded the whole invasion on Lacus and Solas."

"What! He's a royal counselor," Huxley said, aghast.

"And what's more, he duped Cadmus," added Hailey. "This invasion of New Attica that just happened was controlled by Loroc. He used Cadmus's army to take out his own city."

"The queenie's counselor turned on her? I can't believe it." Huxley shook his head.

"Believe it," Eva said.

Gen adjusted in her seat. She kept her eyes out the window at the landscape zooming by. It was clear she couldn't take much more.

Huxley let out a slow sad sigh. "This is not good. The Arsians are a mysterious and powerful race. Now I am officially worried."

"Me too," added Eva.

The mass of refugees at the Toiler's camp numbered over a thousand. Hailey instructed Eva to open the shuttle door and wave people away so that he could bring the craft inside the cover of his cavernous hangar. As Eva debarked, the other two Gens came rushing up.

"Where is she? Is she all right?" one of them asked.

"She's here," Eva replied. "And unharmed." Eva helped Gen out of the shuttle.

"Beeboo, you're okay!" The girls huddled together. "I'm so glad you're here!" Gen Pryde hugged them but remained silent.

"What's wrong?" the second Gen asked.

"New Attica . . . Everything . . . was a lie. I don't want anything to do with it." Gen dropped Cadmus's Omnipod on the ground.

Eva knelt down and picked it up. "Hold on. Your father asked that you keep this."

Gen shook her head.

Eva held out the Omnipod to Gen. "Hey, I don't

agree with everything your father did. He made some big mistakes. But he also did some great things. We wouldn't even be here if it weren't for him."

Gen stood, silent.

"My Muthr and I didn't always see eye to eye, but what she did for me—what your father just did for you—that shows how much he loved you. Please keep this. He wanted you to have it."

One of the Gens put an arm around Gen as they led her away. "Come on, Beeboo. We'll take good care of you."

Gen looked back before disappearing into the crowd with her friends. It was hard for Eva to discern the expression on her face.

"Well, that's gratitude for you," Hailey said as he hopped off the shuttle's ramp. "Aren't you glad you went back just to save her?"

"Easy, hero," Huxley said as he ducked down to exit the cabin. "Not everyone is as tough as Eva here." As Huxley rose to his full height, nearby bystanders gasped and backed away. Some took holo-photos with the Omnipods implanted in their hands.

Eva placed her hand in Huxley's. "These people have grown up only around other humans. To them you are a creature from fairy tales."

"The stuff of legends and lore, eh?" Huxley

smiled. "About time I was treated proper."

From the gathering someone yelled, "What's that thing doing here? Aren't their kind the cause of all this?"

"Yes! The aliens are the ones trying to take our planet!" shouted another.

"Who is going to stop them? When do we go to our new home?" More rants erupted from the throng.

"Where is Father Pryde?"

"Time to leave," said Hailey.

"Not so fast." Van Turner hobbled up and put a hand on his grandson's shoulder.

Hailey rolled his eyes. "We rescued them. Now let 'em have a taste of their own medicine. Let 'em try to live off the land like we've been doing for decades."

"It's not these people who shunned us, boy. It was their silly nincompoop of a leader. Where is he, Eva? I need to tell him a thing or two."

"He didn't make it," said Eva.

Van Turner shook his head. "You don't say? Hmmm. . . . I didn't see that coming."

"So let them start a new city—New Attica II— and we'll get out of here," said Hailey.

"We can't," said Eva. "They can't function out here. They'll die."

"Some will. Some won't," Van Turner said, pondering. The crowd began to gather in a knot around the shuttle. "Only the most hardy will make it. Unless we help them."

"Agreed," said Eva.

"Hero," Huxley said to Hailey, "you need to listen to Eva and your grandfather."

Hailey threw up his arms. "Aw, come on! Seriously, Hux? You're gonna side with them? After what those people did to you back in New Attica?"

"I'm an optimist. What can I say?" said Huxley. "You should try it sometime."

"If I'd given you 'a taste of your own medicine,' where would you be right now?" asked Eva. "Dead in a lab of Attican Hall or dead in the wreck of the *Bijou*?"

Hailey sighed and folded his arms.

"They're scared little newbies. Their entire reality has been obliterated. Kaput. On top of that, everything they've known is false," said Van Turner. "If anyone knows how that feels, it's us. *All of us*. Now their life is just like ours. They can't go back—just like we can't go back."

"Just like the others who left their home planets can't go back. We are in this together," said Eva.

"So what are we supposed to do?" said Hailey.

"Do what a retriever does," said Eva. She placed both hands upon his shoulders. "Deliver them someplace safe."

"She's right," Van Turner said. "These people didn't put us here. Cadmus did. What did his close-minded thinking get him?" He dragged his finger across his neck, executioner-style. The old man hobbled out in front of the shuttle. He held his hands up for silence. The din of the crowd subsided.

"My name is Van Turner, but you all can call me Vanpa. Now, I know you are probably scared and confused about what happened today. I am here to tell you that the people who rescued you, the 'Toilers' as you called us, hold no ill will toward you for our poor treatment. The person guilty of ostracizing us was your leader, Cadmus Pryde." This statement caused a wave of murmuring throughout the gathered crowd.

Van Turner continued, "Cadmus ruled with the best of intentions, but he was afraid of what lay beyond the walls of your city. But that is the very place where you will find yourselves living from here on in."

"What about New Attica? What about Cadmus?" one of the citizens near Vanpa cried out.

Eva stepped out of the crowd, walked up to Van

Turner, and placed her arm around his shoulder.

The old man continued, "Your city is destroyed and Cadmus is dead. It is time to start thinking and caring for yourselves now."

The shock from the crowd was palpable to Eva. She could see it on the faces in the crowd as they heard the news.

"Now, there are others who live out here who know exactly what you are going through," said Van Turner. "They are travelers who have come from other planets, and they have helped heal Earth so that it is habitable once more."

Words of dissension rumbled through the gathering.

"These visitors are peaceful," said Eva. "They wish humans no harm, but Cadmus's fleet was used against them, too. So now they also have reason to fear us."

"Then why would they help us?" a bystander shouted, pointing at Huxley.

"Because we know what it's like to have your home and family taken from you," said Huxley. "We know what it's like to leave memories of everything you ever loved behind and start all over."

Eva translated Huxley's words for the audience.

"Why should we believe it?" another bystander asked. The question was followed by a wave of similar sentiment.

"You don't have to believe us!" Hailey joined the others. "And you didn't have to believe me today when I asked you to come on board this ship so I could carry you away from the danger. Now you are free to make whatever decision you want. Come with us or stay here and take your chances."

"Just remember," said Eva, gesturing to Van Turner's friends, "these people, the Toilers, risked their lives today so that you could still have yours." She grasped Van Turner's hand tight. Along with Huxley they walked up the ramp of Hailey's warship.

One by one the crowd lined up and boarded the ship with them. Hailey climbed into the shuttle and navigated it over the crowd and into the loading bay.

Van Turner stroked his beard in thought as he watched the mass of people file on board. "They're gonna need a leader."

"What they need is an elder, one who teaches from experience and wisdom," said Huxley.

"One who is easy to talk to and always tells the truth," continued Eva.

"Fine! I'll do it!" Van Turner said with a yellow grin. "For now at least, until they find someone better suited for the job."

Hailey jogged over to them. "The shuttle has been loaded up and all of our provisions are secured. I'm gonna check the radar to see if the skies are clear and prep this baby for flight," he said. "Someone come let me know when everyone has boarded."

"Good! The sooner we leave, the better our chances of escape," Van Turner said.

"Where are we going, hero?" Huxley asked.

Hailey looked at Eva for an answer. "Solas and Lacus are under Loroc's control. The ruins?" he asked.

"No. Not there," Eva said. "We are so close to ending the battle. I think it's time we go to see the wisest friend I have."

Huxley feigned shock. "What! You're not standing right next to him?"

Eva giggled. "You're the *best-looking* friend I have."

"That is true." Huxley beamed.

Even Hailey chuckled. "So we're going to see Rovender, huh?"

Eva smiled. "Yes. Let's head to Faunas."

Huxley followed Hailey to the cockpit. "Let me help you. I know the way."

The last of the refugees walked onto the ship, leaving the Toiler camp completely abandoned.

"Well done, Eva Nine," Van Turner said. He placed his arm around her shoulders. "With you around, there may be hope for us reboots yet."

Eva smiled and helped Van Turner up the ramp, and it closed behind them.

# CHAPTER 23: FAUNAS

**W**hile Huxley navigated, Hailey piloted the ship through the night, and they arrived at Faunas a few hours before sunrise. Hailey put down in a large grassy field outside the Cærulean's village.

Eva and Huxley tacked up the munt-runners and led them down the ramp of the ship to where Hailey and Van Turner waited.

"I think these guys are happy to be on solid ground again," said Eva as she climbed up onto Bix's saddle.

"To be honest, I am amazed they both flew so well." Huxley yanked a handful of grass from the ground and fed it to them. "These old munties can be pretty skittish."

"It was my smooth flying." Hailey grinned and mounted Bax. "Come on, Vanpa. I'll help you up."

Van Turner waved him off. "You go. I'm gonna stay here."

"Why?"

"The people need me." Van Turner grinned.

"They'll be okay," said Hailey.

"I don't think so, boy. They need a Vanpa to take good care of 'em." He pulled out his old banged-up Omnipod. "Today we start my first class—Surviving Beyond the Walls of New Attica."

"You sure nothing will bother them out here? No eaters or spitters or slicers?" Hailey asked Eva.

Eva smiled. "I don't sense anything beyond a few turnfins and a couple of wandering trees."

"But don't explore too far from the ship," said Huxley.

"We won't. Now go on. Tell Rovender I wanna share another drink with him soon." Van Turner patted Bix as he passed in front of him.

"Will do," Eva said as she waved back.

Huxley led the munt-runners across the field. They traveled toward Faunas through the predawn forest, their tired silence broken by tribal rhythms and the melodies of woodwind instruments.

"Music? This early?" said Huxley.

"These guys know how to start the day," said Hailey.

Still holding the munt-runner's reins with his sole hand, Huxley cocked his head to listen. "If I know anything about Cæruleans, I know they don't make noise like this. It sounds like Halcyonus music."

"The refugees from Lacus are staying with them," Eva said from her seat on Bix.

"Maybe it was a good idea that we left everyone back at the ship," said Hailey.

"I agree," said Huxley. "You're sure their leader likes humans, Eva? An angry blue is not one to mess with. An angry village filled with them is worse."

"We're fine," said Eva. "Antiquus and Soth know me. Besides, Rovee will take care of everything."

As they reached a wooden footbridge leading into the village, there was a piercing call from high above. Eva looked up to see the silhouette of a figure pointing at them from the rooftop of a gigantic round hut. The music stopped.

"That would be the warning call," said Huxley. "You best let me do the talking." He stepped onto the footbridge. A pack of Cæruleans jumped from the surrounding brush, each holding a boomrod.

"Who's there?" one of them barked. More Cæruleans arrived holding weapons.

"Hello, blues. We did not mean to disturb your revelry. We are here to see . . ."

"Rovender Kitt," Eva said.

"Eva the Nine? Is that you?" One of the Cæruleans moved closer to the lantern hanging from Bix's saddle. Eva recognized the rugged face.

"Yes, Galell . . . and these are my friends." Eva hopped down from her saddle and raised her palm in greeting. Immediately she felt a recognizable presence rushing toward her.

Otto, the giant water bear, burst through the bushes hooting loudly.

"Eva!" Rovender Kitt hopped down from Otto's back and ran toward her.

Eva held out her arms and squealed with joy. "Rovee!"

Rovender dropped his walking stick and embraced her in his thick arms. "Rings above, you are all right! I have been ill with worry."

Eva hugged her friend tight and buried her face in his jacket. "I am so happy to see you." Eva felt a nudge at her back, followed by a familiar growling purr. A large dry tongue licked her head.

*Little one. You are safe.*

"Otto!" Eva threw her thin arms around the neck of the giant water bear. She kissed him on the beak.

*I wait. For you. I. Missed you.*

"I missed you, too." She scratched behind his floppy ears. "I missed you both so badly." She hugged Rovender one more time.

"I searched for you in Lacus." He stroked her white hair. "Though I could not find you, I knew that you were safe, otherwise Otto would have gone after you. So he has been waiting here, sick with worry, like me."

"I am okay, Rovee. It's good to be with you both again."

"You too." Rovender looked over at Hailey,

still seated on Bax. "Hailey Turner, I figured your piloting skills would keep you among the living."

Hailey hopped down. Grinning, he shook the Cærulean's hand. "It is good to see you again."

"You guys are having a party and you didn't invite me?" Huxley remained next to Bix and Bax, having some difficulty holding both reins.

"Huxley? Am I dreaming?" Rovender wiped away tears of joy from his eyes. "What bright lights arrive after such dark days. All of Faunas knows of our adventures. They will be happy to see you and hear your news."

"There is much of it, my friend." Huxley gave Rovender a warm embrace.

"We have a ship full of people camped out beyond your village," said Hailey.

"That was you?" Galell asked. "Our lookout heard a ship fly by. At first we feared the worst. But with the battle now over we assumed it was simply returning to the hu-man city."

Rovender beamed. "The elders will be happy to know it is a ship of friends that has arrived instead, to join in the celebration."

At this statement Galell and the other Cæruleans exchanged skeptical glances.

"Wait—the battle is over?" Huxley asked.

"Why, yes," Rovender said. "We just received word that Ojo is triumphant and that Cadmus has retreated from Solas and Lacus."

Huxley and Hailey looked at Eva to answer.

"There is more to it than that," Eva said. "It turns out that the Prime Adviser is Loroc after all. He is controlling everything, including the invasion that happened on Lacus and Solas."

Galell scoffed. The others in his party grumbled.

"She is telling the truth." Huxley's tone was defensive. "Your victory celebration may be premature."

A look of concern came over Rovender's face. "How do you know this, Eva?"

"Loroc told me at Lacus when I tried to warn Arius."

"And why wouldn't we think that this is not more manipulation from Cadmus?" asked Rovender.

"Cadmus Pryde is dead," said Eva.

Rovender blinked in astonishment. "Dead?"

"New Attica is gone," said Hailey.

"Burned to the ground by Cadmus's own devices," added Huxley.

Galell and the others whispered among themselves.

"I want to hear everything, but so too will the elders," said Rovender. "Galell, go ahead and alert them. Let us meet immediately so that you will have to recount your news only once."

Rovender led Eva and her friends into Faunas. Just as Eva remembered, the huts resembled gigantic woven urns decorated with ornate pictographs. Each hut towered above nearby treetops to meet the golden rays of the rising sun. On the ground below, under glowing lanterns hanging from the belly of each hut, gathered both Cæruleans and Halcyonus. Though smaller in stature than Rovender's clan, the Halcyonus were similar in shape but adorned in brightly colored garb. Eva noticed several other species she had never met before. The gathering parted for Rovender, but the crowd whispered and pointed as they passed by.

"Now, this is living." Huxley smiled at the villagers. "Hey, blue, any chance we can get some of that food for this meeting? I'm trying to grow some new appendages here."

"I will make sure there is breakfast brought to you all," said Rovender in a low voice. He ushered his friends around the base of a large hut toward a small, squat structure tucked behind all the others. The wooden stairs creaked as everyone filed inside.

As before, the council of elders was seated in a circle at the center of the round room. Each Cærulean elder was tethered to the wall by a thick fibrous cord. But now there were Halcyonus tribe leaders seated between the elders. Crammed in the remaining space of the room, members of Faunas and Lacus stood and watched as Eva and her friends entered. Even Hostia and Fiscian Haveport were present. Eva waved, but her Halcyonus friends did not return the greeting.

"Come in and sit," said Antiquus, the aged leader of the Cæruleans. He sat on a hoverdisc with a curved ear horn in hand. Next to him was Soth, the decorated shaman, who smiled when she saw Eva. Behind them sat the wooden perch for the treowe, the truth bird. The tiny animal sang as the group entered. Eva could now hear the bird's tinkly voice within its trills:

*Hello! Sit! The day is new! Hello! Sit!*

"Eva Nine." Antiquus reached out and grasped her hand. "What a reward for these eyes to see you here in our village at the start of the day." His large bushy eyebrows rose as he watched everyone enter. "You have brought others with you, including a Mirthian."

"Name's Huxley. Huxley the Brave," Huxley said,

holding up his palm in greeting. "Royal Beamguide Scout for Her Majesty, Queen Ojo."

"And this is my friend, Hailey Turner," said Eva, palm raised. She gestured at Hailey, and he mimicked the greeting.

Antiquus kept his gaze on Hailey. "Hailey Turner, are you the one also responsible for helping our brother, Nadeau, escape from the hu-man city?"

"I am—that is, we all are, sir," answered Hailey in a sheepish tone. He yanked his flight cap off and wrung it in his hands.

Eva could see that the pilot seemed oddly reserved in this situation . . . perhaps even a bit humble. Eva smiled at this.

Antiquus spread open his arms. "Then on behalf of our entire village, I thank you all for risking your lives—"

"And limbs!" Huxley interjected, waving his arm stump.

"And limbs," Antiquus continued with a slight grin, "to return our brother back home. We accept this as an act of goodwill among our species and hold no discord toward you as individuals. Please sit with us over a meal and share what news you have."

## CHAPTER 24: ELDERS

# And so Eva

and her friends sat with Antiquus and the council of elders. Over a fine breakfast of fresh fruit and juices, Eva told them everything she knew.

When she was finished, Antiquus regarded her for several minutes in silence. Eva wondered if he was contemplating having Soth use the truth-bird on her. A large hand rubbed her shoulder, and she turned to see Rovender offer a reassuring smile.

Antiquus finally spoke, "Eva, when you came here

last, you and my son warned of a pending invasion by Cadmus. You expressed your worry for the safety of Arius and the Halcyonus living in Lacus."

"Yes," said Eva. She glanced over at Hostia in hopes that this statement from Antiquus would clear all doubt toward her, but Hostia averted her eyes away from Eva.

"You also presented us with a mystery: Who was this 'Prime Adviser' who was working with the hu-man leader? This is a mystery now solved. You have come to the conclusion that it is the Arsian known as Loroc."

"Right. He mutates after he . . . eats his siblings and then somehow absorbs their powers, which is why I could not identify him before." Eva's words sent murmurs of discontent through the council and assembly.

Antiquus quieted everyone with a wave of his hand. "Now you believe that Loroc deceived Cadmus and gained control of his war machines. Once accomplished, Loroc then destroyed their maker and the hu-man city, correct?"

Eva nodded. "And if Zin cannot stop him, I think Loroc will kill Zin and Queen Ojo." Eva waited for an eruption of upset voices from the council, but they remained silent.

"And then?" Antiquus asked.

Eva looked around at all the gathered faces: the Cæruleans, the Halcyonus, and her friends. Did they too feel the same mix of anxiety and helplessness that she did? "I think Loroc wants to rule over all of Orbona. He told me he would 'be king' . . . like King Ojo."

Antiquus rubbed his dewlap in thought.

Soth spoke up. "Eva, the glyph that Arius gave you, may I see it?"

Eva rolled up her sleeve and showed her forearm.

Soth put her hand to her mouth in shock. "The glyph is gone! Arius has passed onto her next journey. May her spirit find serenity."

The council held up their palms and spoke in unison, "Spirit find serenity."

"And so Loroc's surviving sibling, Zin, seeks to unravel why his brother has done what he has done?" asked Antiquus.

"Yes," replied Eva.

Antiquus pulled a small translucent cube from his robes and held it flat in his palm. He gestured for a lantern, which Soth lit and handed to him. Antiquus placed the cube on top of the lantern. The light filled the cube and projected alien writing onto the ceiling, walls, and faces of all those in the hut. Antiquus pointed to the writing. "Eva, the reason I asked you these questions is that yesterday we received official word here that the hu-man's invasion of Solas had failed. Their kind have been defeated and would bother us no longer."

"That's an understatement," Hailey said with a snort.

Antiquus ignored this comment. "See here, Eva. It reads that tomorrow representatives from every known village will attend a Victory Feast—a mandatory audience with Her Majesty, Queen Ojo. Her adviser shall explain to us the details of the invasion, why it failed, and Her Majesty's plans to protect us from further attacks. Then the queen shall present her plans for rebuilding the city and Lacus." He removed the cube from the lantern, extinguishing the projection. "In light of your news, you can see that I am torn as to what actions are best."

"But that is not what happened," Eva said. "I don't think that message is telling the whole truth."

"If I may." A Halcyonus elder sitting next to Antiquus spoke in concise diction. "Is it not interesting to hear that the hu-mans have failed to conquer our cities and so now blame another for all their actions?"

"We aren't blaming another," Hailey retorted. "We are simply stating the facts that we've uncovered."

The Halcyonus frowned. "The fact that your leader planned an invasion of our peaceful village? Or that Loroc learned of it and neutralized him before all was devastated?"

"Eva, your sister herself said that Cadmus had been preparing his people for just such an invasion," said Soth.

"She did," said Eva.

"But his people are ignorant," said Hailey. "They didn't know what was really going on or what Cadmus was preparing to do."

"And so their ignorance excuses them?" There was a fire in the Halcyonus leader's orange eyes. "Their ignorance allows them to carry on their lives guilt-free of the destruction their chosen leader has caused? Or the lives he has taken?"

"Lives have been lost on the human side as well." Eva tried to dispel the vision of the girl lying in the street, covered in ash.

"Their city is obliterated," said Huxley.

"By their own machines, correct, hu-man? Perhaps now they will learn that venturing down the road to dominance over many only leaves oneself unprotected back at home," the Halcyonus leader said, and the other Halcyonus shouted out in agreement. Several Cærulean elders chimed in.

Eva could see anger and frustration reddening Hailey's face. Her gaze met with his, and he gave her an *I told you so* look.

"Why not just bring the truth-bird?" Eva spoke out, hushing the din of the room. "Bring the bird to your meeting with Ojo and have Loroc tell you the truth."

Antiquus shook his head. Soth replied, "The bird will not work on an Arsian, Eva. Their kind are far too powerful to succumb to a treowe's effects."

*I think you would work*, Eva thought to the bird. *Loroc needs to confess his actions.*

"Loroc needs to confess his actions," the bird sang, but no one seemed to pay it any mind. It continued on chirping. *I sing the purest of songs*, Eva heard within its chirps.

Antiquus hushed the group once more. "Eva, I know that you and your friends truly have good intentions," he said. "But let me be clear when I tell you all that the majority among those of Solas and Lacus will not be as understanding toward your kind based on the actions they have witnessed."

"What are we supposed to do, then?" Eva asked. "Where will we go?"

"Well, we're not going to the queenie's soirée, I can tell you that," said Huxley.

"Father." Rovender spoke. "What advice do you suggest for Eva and her people?"

"Find a new location to start your village, away from all this. Let time heal these wounds that are so very raw at this moment," said Antiquus.

"Run away and hide. That's just great." Hailey threw down his food and stood, clearly disgusted. "She risked her life to stop a battle that will ultimately enslave all of you, and your advice to her is 'run away'?"

"To keep your tribe safe? Yes," said Antiquus.

"I've heard enough. Eva, let's go," said Hailey.

"This is not the answer, Father," Rovender said. "We have but a moment right here and right now to clear away what has been done and start anew."

"As much as I wish for that, I am not sure that the moment is now," replied Antiquus. "Let us break, go outside for some fresh air, and celebrate another day. Perhaps in the sunlight we shall discover something we have yet to see."

Heated conversations broke out as everyone shuffled out of the hut.

Eva trailed behind Rovender at the back of the crowd. A crooked staff dropped in her path, blocking her exit. She looked up to see Antiquus watching her. "I'd like to have a word alone if you do not mind," he said.

Eva looked to Rovender. He nodded and exited the hut.

"Of course," Eva said.

"Sit." The Cærulean leader patted a woven mat lying on the floor next to him. Behind him the truth-bird chirruped from its perch. The nearly empty room appeared much larger with just the two of them left alone. "Eva," said Antiquus, "I'd like you to tell me what you think the word 'truth' means."

"'Truth'?" Eva repeated. "It's the facts. It's reality."

"Mmm." Antiquus nodded his head in agreement. He tapped the side of his hoverdisc with his cane. "Would you say that the truth is that I can no longer use my legs?"

Eva studied the floating disc that held Antiquus. His legs were folded underneath his simple drab robes. "I . . . guess. I've never seen you walk."

"Correct. You have not. Even if I used the treowe on you, you'd state what you view as the truth. However, the fact is, I can walk." Antiquus stepped off the disc and hobbled around Eva. "On good days I do not even need my cane to aid me." He handed his cane to her. "I choose to use the disc because my old knees find it difficult to hold me for great lengths of time. Soth tells me to rest them as much as possible."

"Oh," said Eva, and she helped him back onto the disc.

"So you see, truth is how we perceive facts. For those in my village, I can no longer walk. They have arrived at this conclusion because they have not seen me on my feet for a very long time. There have even been times where the pain was so intense that I myself doubted I would ever walk again. Truths can change."

Eva thought about how the facts had changed for her in the short amount of time since she had been out of her Sanctuary. Some facts, like Cadmus's true motivations, had changed so many times that she became more confused the more she thought about him. "But what about truths in science? I was taught laws of physics in my Sanctuary. Those aren't just assumptions."

The elder nodded. "Those are the greatest of truths. You do speak wise for someone so young."

The truth-bird sang from its perch.

*I sing the prettiest song. I sing the purest song.*

"What about the bird?" Eva asked.

"The treowe?" Antiquus wore a sly grin. "Though this variety is more effective than those that were brought from our planet, the treowe's true magic is in the dust it releases from its feathers. For many who inhale it this dust causes them to enter a relaxed, trancelike state. Once in that state, most are willing to speak freely of what they believe is the truth. The bird's body somehow becomes the conduit to do so."

*You little trickster,* Eva thought to the bird.

"You little trickster," the bird repeated from its perch. It began to preen its iridescent feathers.

Eva watched the truth-bird, fascinated.

"They speak out like that sometimes," said Antiquus. "Singing the songs of old voices. Pay no attention to it."

"So without this bird, who do I believe is being truthful?" she asked.

"Now you are thinking." The old Cærulean playfully tapped Eva's forehead with his finger. "Unless someone is actively deceiving you— lying—most will speak their truth."

"But wait. If that is the case, why did you use the truth-bird on me? I told you that I'd tell the truth."

"You did. Please understand, Eva, I had no

experience in dealing with your kind. I'd only heard stories, and of course, you were highly suspect because of Nadeau's condition. I arrived at a conclusion—one that was wrong. My assumptions toward you changed, as it did for many who were present that night."

Eva hadn't given much thought to how others viewed her and her actions. Her mind was constantly occupied with how she viewed everyone else.

"Most will tell you what they believe to be fact because it is much harder to conceal it. It takes effort to suppress the truth. It usually eats you up from the inside out if you try to contain it in silence. In the end you have to decide what truth resides best within you . . . even if your point of view does not agree with others."

"Hailey doesn't always agree with my point of view, that's for sure."

Antiquus chuckled. "He is young and brash, like Galell. Give him time."

"Rovee talks the same way you do. Now I know where he gets it," Eva said.

Antiquus smiled. "Yet I've learned much from you, Eva. When you returned my son to me and he spoke the truth—*his* truth, from *his* point of view— it was then that I understood that we are all seeking the same thing, but we are not all occupying the exact same space or the exact same life. We are each unique. We each bring slightly different viewpoints to the circle based on where we stand in the world." Antiquus pointed to the mats arranged in a circle on the floor. "Even Loroc, from his place of corruption, somehow believes he is seeking answers despite the effect his actions may have."

"You're saying because he believes he is true, then he is not wrong?" asked Eva.

"In his mind? Yes." Antiquus sat with his cane in his lap. "Have you not felt the same way? Have you not caused anger and pain in others? Even when it was furthest from your mind?"

Eva thought of arguments with Muthr. She thought of fighting with Eva Eight. Then there was the horned beast in the forest and its abandoned cubs that Eva could have saved. But that was different, wasn't it? "Loroc has caused pain and death to so many." Eva put her head in her hands. "Even to his own family."

"From where you stand you speak a truth. But there are others who would disagree."

"Ojo?" Eva looked up at him.

"Possibly. The burden of leadership is that sometimes difficult choices must be made for the greater good of all involved and not just for oneself. It is a matter of 'we' and not 'I.'" Antiquus leaned in close. "I know this is much for you to hear and ponder, Eva. But I tell you this for the simple reason that I observed firsthand today what my son has told me repeatedly: *you* are the leader of your friends. They believe in you and your words. *You* speak *their* truth."

"But I don't want that responsibility. All I wanted was a . . ." It dawned on Eva. The picture—the characters all joined arm in arm—the WondLa. "A family." Tears welled in Eva's eyes. "Hailey, Huxley, Vanpa, Otto, and Rovee. They are my family."

"They are indeed, Eva Nine. Had you not seen it?" Antiquus smiled. "A more unusual family I have never known, but you all are bound together, including my son. And that makes me happy."

"So what do I do?" Eva held out her finger. The truth-bird fluttered over to her and landed. It chirped as she stroked its head with her fingertip.

"I cannot tell you. But I can recommend this: be with your family." Antiquus floated toward the door of the hut. "During these confusing times, talking with our loved ones can sometimes make clear a path to our own truth."

## CHAPTER 25: MESSAGES

**W**ell, we're outta here," Hailey said to Eva as she approached him and Huxley huddled behind the elders' council hut. "I told you we should have just let the leaders sort this out."

"Should I remind you that Vanpa is also the leader for the entire human race?" Eva asked.

"Well, I'll go report to 'our leader' that I think it is best that we move on," said Hailey. "I got the message loud and clear that we are not wanted here."

Eva let out a heavy sigh. "This did not turn out the way I had hoped."

"Nothing ever does." Huxley patted Eva on the back. "But at least we tried."

Hailey flexed his hands into fists. "I wish we could just barge into that meeting and blast Loroc with SHOCdarts. That would short him out for good."

"As much as I agree with that action, that would not be a good idea, hero," Huxley said. "Destroying Loroc in front of everyone would only reinforce the idea that humans are enemies of us all."

"But at least then we'd know he was no longer a problem," Hailey said, and snorted.

"Huxley, can't you just go and talk to Queen Ojo?" asked Eva. "After all, you are one of her royal scouts."

He smiled down at Eva. "I love that you think so highly of ol' Huxie, little bayrie. But the truth is, I'm just a surveyor. A mapmaker. Nothing more. I'm certainly no diplomat who can chat about planetary peace with the queenie."

"I think that's it for ideas," Hailey said. "I'm sure Vanpa is anxious to find out what happened here and figure out our next steps."

"We best saddle up and head out," added Huxley. "Wanna walk us back, bayrie?"

Rovender appeared from around the hut. "There you are, Eva. I've just received a message from Zin for you."

Eva smiled smugly at Hailey. "I knew he'd do it! What's the message?"

Rovender answered in a low whisper, "It has arrived via messenger, and a most intriguing messenger at that." He looked around as if to see if anyone was watching them. "Nobody else in the village is to know, so let us keep this among ourselves."

Otto shuffled up from the woods behind the village and poked his head out of the brush.

*I take you. Little one.*

"Go on," said Hailey. "Hux and I will get back to the ship. We won't take off until we hear from you, okay?"

"Okay," Eva said.

"A good idea." Rovender nodded. "I would suggest departing immediately after." He turned to go, and Eva followed.

Hailey grabbed Eva by the wrist. "Be careful, all right?"

She smiled. "You too."

"She's in good hands." Huxley grabbed the reins of the munt-runners. "Blue will take good care of her, right?"

"Of course." Rovender climbed up onto Otto's head. He held his hand out to help Eva up. "Come. Our messenger is waiting."

"Who is this messenger?" Eva asked.

"I will tell you on the way. Come on." Rovender gestured for her to hurry.

"Is Zin okay? Did he speak to Loroc?"

Rovender let out a frustrated sigh. "Eva Nine, do you trust me?"

"Of course, Rovee—"

"Then let's go."

Eva scuttled up onto Otto's plated back and sat next to Rovender. On his six large legs, Otto slowly turned and traveled through the wooded area.

"I'll see you guys in a bit." Eva looked back through the clearing to wave to her friends, but they were gone. "Rovee, where are we going?"

"I've risked us being spotted by curious eyes as it is." Rovender glanced over his shoulder. "Hopefully our friends departing the village will create enough of a diversion to allow us to slip away unnoticed."

They traveled deeper into the wood for some time without speaking. Eva thought out to Otto, *Are we safe?*

*Safe. I protect. You.*

*And I will protect you.* Eva patted the soft patches of moss that grew over Otto's pebbly carapace.

Rovender exhaled, and his shoulders slumped.

"I think we are far enough away for me to speak freely at last."

"What on Orbona is going on?" Eva turned to him. "You were acting so weird back there."

"The Halcyonus are traumatized by all that has happened. They are a very peaceful race, so this blatant aggression against them has angered their leaders and many of our council elders as well," explained Rovender.

"Rovee, the only reason we came here was to talk to you—not the elders. I like your father and all, he's really wise, but you know more about the humans and everything that's happened."

"I appreciate that." Rovender's voice rose in frustration. "But you have to remember, the Halcyonus believe that the hu-mans became aware of Lacus only from *me* bringing *you* there. Hostia and her family feel responsible and ashamed for what has happened."

"That's ridiculous!"

"Shhh. Keep quiet," whispered Rovender. "You are upset, as am I. But together we can sort this out."

"You just need to be the leader of your tribe that I know you can be," Eva said. "You are also wise. You are experienced. You see the bigger picture."

Rovender gazed at her with indigo eyes. "I worry that you see a harmonious ending to this that no one else is capable of envisioning."

Eva contemplated his words. "I think that Cadmus and Ojo wanted the same thing: to watch over and take care of their people, but as if their subjects were children. I don't think that a ruler . . . a leader . . . should ever do that. Loroc would eat his subjects and anyone who tries to stop him."

Rovender took a deep breath. "Despite who you are about to meet, I believe Queen Ojo may have come to her senses."

"What do you mean? Who is this mysterious messenger?"

"A Dorcean."

Eva's eyes went wide. "A . . . Dorcean! Here? Why are you taking me to him?"

Rovender put a reassuring hand on Eva's shoulder. "Remember what I said about actions versus words."

Eva shrugged his hand off. "I remember what actions Besteel did."

"Well, like all hu-mans, not all Dorceans are evil. Think of Loroc and Zin."

Eva crossed her arms. "Even when we were looking for Zin, there was a Dorcean hunting for me. Rovee, you know I don't trust them."

"Dat would have been me, Eva Nine," a gravelly voice said.

*No! No! No!* Otto growled.

In the clearing ahead was a parked Dorcean glider. Leaning against it was Besteel's brother, Redimus, polishing the muzzle of his boomrod.

"Otto, halt!" Eva climbed and stood on his armored back. "Don't go a step farther!"

Otto did as he was told. However, Eva could feel him fighting the urge to pounce on the Dorcean and rip him apart with his claws.

"Rovee! How could you?" Eva spoke through clenched teeth.

"Calm down." Rovender spoke softly. "It is not what you think."

"It's not what *you* think!" She pointed at Redimus. "This guy is after Zin. He works for Loroc!"

Redimus shrugged and continued polishing his weapon. "And who told you dat? De truztworthy Caruncle?" He laughed to himself. He sounded just like Besteel.

"So now you're after me?" Eva considered calling an army of wandering trees to trample Redimus. But for the moment she felt safe enough with Rovender and Otto at her side.

"I waz looking for Zin." Redimus holstered the boomrod and placed it on the wing of the glider. "But I waz *not* searching for him under orderz of any Arzian, including de mighty Loroc. And eet iz alzo true dat I am now here looking for you, Eva Nine."

"So you can kill me and finish the job that your brother couldn't?" spat Eva.

Otto grumbled in agreement.

Redimus picked at something caught in his pointed teeth. "Wrong again."

"Eva, you need to know the truth," said Rovender. "Dorceans are honorable. They do not believe in vengeance for another's actions."

Eva put her hands on her hips. "Your father just got through telling me there are no 'real truths.'"

Redimus chuckled. "Cærulean nonzense." He leaned against the glider. "My brozeel iz dead. He waz as recklazz as he was stubborn. I am none of deez things. But I have made my share of miztakes, which I carry wiz me every day." Redimus turned his head toward Eva. In the daylight she could see deep scars raked across the side of his face. A mechanized eye patch with a bright light set in it covered one eye. "I saw you and de boy pilot de night I encountered Caruncle. I tried to zeek an audience wiz you then, to inform you of hiz eel-begotten allianze wiz Loroc, but he waz onto me."

"Did you figure out where Zin went?" asked Eva.

"Az you know, I did not need to. He returned to tend to heez 'family matterz' in Zolas," Redimus said. "Which bringz us to why I am here."

Eva remained on top of Otto. She tensed, worried about Zin.

"Zince we are speaking of truz. I have two truz for you." Redimus held up a pair of sickle-shaped talons. "One, your stolen warzhip has not gone unnoticed; you were tracked leaving New Attica. Loroc's forcez will find you here. When dey do, eet will not end well for you or your friendz."

Eva's pulse quickened. "A warbot did identify me back in New Attica."

"Which brings me to my zecond truz: Queen Ojo would like to speak wiz you *before* de Victory Feez. Loroc does not know that I am to ezcort you to zee Her Majesty first."

"Why?"

Redimus smirked. "You are afraid. I can hear your zingle heart raze. My brozeel would be flattered dat you steel fear Dorceanz—but I am not. I am, however, honor-bound to deliver you zafe to Her Majesty. What she wishez to zee you for I am not privy to, but she commanded me to give you dis."

Redimus reached into his satchel. He unwrapped a small familiar object and placed it on the glider's wing.

"A beamguide?" Eva remembered using one of the holographic maps before. "Zin already gave me one of those."

"Though it was confiscated," Rovender muttered.

"Dis one is zpecial." Redimus pointed to the small cube. "Very zpecial. I zuspect Zin has created eet just for you, Eva Nine."

*Why would I need another beamguide?* Eva thought. She looked to Rovender. "Well?"

"This is an intriguing turn of events." Rovender scratched his whiskers. "I think it best that you go, Eva."

"Will you come with me?" she asked.

"I can attend the meeting of the leaders as my father's aide. We can rendezvous after."

Eva picked at her fingernails. "The last time I met with Ojo, she wanted me stuffed and mounted for her museum."

Rovender asked, "When you and Zin parted ways, how was it left?"

"He was going to speak with Ojo, then his brother." Eva studied Redimus. He was grooming his hairy hide, and giving the impression that he was not listening to the conversation. The beamguide remained on the wing of the glider.

"Well, you know he's spoken with the queen," replied Rovender. "Otherwise Redimus would not be here."

"But is it all just one elaborate trap?" Eva asked. "If Loroc wants me dead and can't find me, then all he needs to do is lure me to him. It's just like the floatazoans grounding the turnfins—"

"For a hungry sand-sniper," Rovender finished her sentence. "But if Loroc knew your whereabouts, he would not just send a single Dorcean. Faunas would now look like Lacus after he hunted Arius down."

"Why does this have to be so confusing?" Eva sighed, sat down, and closed her eyes. She let her mind receive the frequency of the entire forest. Life seemed to move in its natural ebb and flow. There were no foreign machines here marching about searching for her.

A cool breeze brushed Eva's face, and she heard the mournful call of an air-whale far in the distance. She thought about the air-whale skeleton she and Rovender had explored, its bones like bleached branches of a great fallen tree. She thought of the wandering trees, the weeping bird-catchers, and the giant sundews digging their roots down into the earth and staking their claim in the forest. She thought of the hairy horned beast dying in the sticky clutches of the sundew and the hungry cubs it had left behind. She thought of the moss used to heal Hailey's wound just as it had Rovender's.

And that reminded her of so long ago—the moss that carpeted the forest floor during her holographic exercises back at her Sanctuary. The snakebite that would have killed her had it all been real. *How does such an insignificant thing survive in a big world? What is its purpose?* she had wondered. *What is my purpose? To find WondLa?*

That deep resonant hum entered Eva's mind again. It filled her senses and vibrated her to the core. In doing so it overpowered all other frequencies from the forest. Eva opened her dilated green eyes and focused them on Redimus.

He pointed to her with a sharpened claw. "I can zense power emanating from you. I have not zensed anything like dis from another before."

"She is, indeed, unlike any that you have ever met before," said Rovender.

"Then perhaps I understand how my brozeel failed. I am glad you are not my adverzary for the time being."

Eva let out the tiniest exhale of relief.

"I admit I did not underztand why I was zent on dis errand to fetch a young human girl. Now I zee why de queen would zeek you out," said Redimus.

Eva rose to her feet. "So let's go hear what she has to say."

# They dropped

off Rovender so that he could prepare for the trip. It was late afternoon by the time Otto returned Eva to Hailey's warship. She found him with Huxley, sitting around a small campfire outside at the foot of the loading ramp. Van Turner was handing out Sustibars to a gathering of refugees while Huxley prepared a kettle of seabrine tea over the fire. Eva relayed the plans concerning Queen Ojo.

"You know what this tea needs?" Huxley stirred the steaming pot. "A dash of pinquat powder. When this Dorcean sneaks you into the palace, perhaps you can borrow some for me? It's a red spice . . . though sometimes it is yellow . . . but I

haven't seen the yellow pinquat powder in a long time. You know what? Just ask the queenie."

"I'll see what I can do," said Eva with a smile.

"Well, that's the last of the bars for today." Van Turner joined the group.

"How are we looking?" Hailey asked.

"We've got plenty of food for a few more weeks, but after that it's gonna get . . . interesting."

"We'll teach 'em how to live off the land." Huxley wrapped a rag around the pot's handle and poured four cups of tea.

Eva turned to Van Turner. "We *need* to figure out what to do with these survivors from New Attica. According to Redimus, Loroc is looking for them."

"The humans?" Van Turner asked.

"Or the ship?" asked Hailey.

"Well, he did say that they knew that the ship had been stolen," said Eva.

"So he may not know of the survivors," said Van Turner.

"He will soon, though, if that Halcyonus leader has anything to do with it," grumbled Hailey.

"So if he's looking for the ship, let's give him what he wants," said Eva.

"What do you mean?" Hailey sniffed his tea, then took a tentative sip.

"Hold on before you drink it," said Huxley. He set down the kettle. "I have to add the sweet stuff or else it's completely toxic." He winked at Eva.

She rolled her eyes at his joke.

Huxley unwrapped a small gooey brown bar. With Hailey's pocket laser-cutter he lobbed off several small pieces. "There. Put a lump of that into each of your cups and give it a moment to melt."

Eva continued. "If Loroc is looking for a stolen warship, then let's let him find it. Then you can lead him on a wild goose chase."

Hailey stirred the sticky glob at the bottom of his cup. "That sounds risky."

"But it could draw Loroc's attention away from the queen," said Eva.

"Ah, so he'll think Eva is on that ship trying to stir up trouble." Huxley took a sip.

"What about the survivors?" Van Turner stirred his tea with his finger.

"The ship would be empty—it would be just Hailey piloting," said Eva.

"And his navigator!" Huxley said with a grin.

"*And* your navigator," Eva repeated with a smile. "We'll find a place to hide the survivors so they are safe for the time being. Vanpa will continue to look over them."

"The *entire fleet* will probably be at Solas," said Hailey. "We won't last five nanos against their firepower."

"I don't know about that." Huxley burped. "I can't imagine ol' Loroc would order an 'open fire' while there is an assembly of every leader in Orbona. Not only would it be dangerous, but it would not look good for him or queenie in reassuring everyone that the battle is over and everyone is at peace."

"Besides, if anyone can outmaneuver a robot-piloted fleet, it's you," Eva said.

"Especially if your ship is empty." Van Turner sat back, pondering it all. "It is dangerous, Eva. And it is the only ship we've got. Hailey, could it be done remotely?"

"Without me on it?" Hailey said. "Maybe. But you know I'm better flying when I'm actually on board. With Huxley's knowledge of the terrain, I think the two of us could handle them." He finally took a sip of his tea.

Hailey scowled as he swallowed, gagged as if poisoned, and then smiled and belched. Everybody laughed. He slurped down more tea. "So my job is to keep Loroc's eyes on me while you meet with the queen and Zin. Then what?"

Huxley's jovial voice turned grim. "I'd say,

between the royal guardsmen and the pillar guards, Loroc will be dealt with. But we can swoop in and get you out if it gets hairy, Eva."

"Yeah, just call us." Hailey turned his cup upside down to get the last drop.

"I can use this to stay in touch." Eva pulled out Cadmus's Omnipod.

"Good idea," Van Turner said. "Now where do we hide a thousand-plus refugees?"

Everyone took a sip of tea, except for Hailey who had finished his.

"If we could put 'em in a safe place, but also use this opportunity to let 'em poke around a little and open their eyes to their new way of life, then that would be good," said Van Turner, thinking aloud.

"Then stay at the ancient ruins." Eva swirled her hot tea over the brown lump at the bottom of her cup. "Let them see what I have seen. Let them understand what could happen."

"And if Loroc's forces find us?" Van Turner asked.

"There is an entity at the ruins who will protect you. A lone pillar guard who would stop any warbots that might land." Eva grabbed the liquid light pen from her poncho. She plucked up the rag wrapped around the teapot's handle and drew a picture of the pillar guard on it. Next to the guard she drew herself. She handed the rag to Van Turner. "Show the guard this, and he'll know you're with me."

"That's it? Really?" Van Turner looked at the drawing on the rag.

"Really," said Hailey. "*Trust* her."

Eva smiled at him.

Huxley extinguished the campfire. "And as long as you remain in the ruins and don't venture out into the desert, you should be fine for a couple of days."

"I think we have plenty of hydration tablets for that," said Hailey.

"Goody! Time for class number two: How to Make Water." Van Turner rubbed his hands together. "I'm gonna go tell them, and we'll load up for takeoff."

"So soon?" Eva was enjoying the moment.

"The sooner the better." Hailey tipped the teapot for more tea, but it was empty. "Unloading everybody and settling them at the ruins is going to take some time."

While she finished her tea, Eva walked over to Otto and patted his head. She whispered into his ear, "I want you to stay here and watch over the Cæruleans and Halcyonus, okay? They need someone to protect them."

The water bear looked up and hooted while munching on the corrugated leaves of giant lichen.

*I watch. You. My herd.*

*I'll be okay,* Eva thought to Otto. *And I shall see you soon.* She nuzzled Otto on the nose and returned to her friends.

Van Turner was stroking Bix's fine coat. "You don't mind if we take them with us, do you?"

Eva scratched Bax around his horns, causing him to nicker with delight. "Of course not. They love Sustibars, though, so keep those in a secure place."

"Class number three: Munty-runner Riding and Care," Van Turner said with a grin. He hugged Eva. "Good luck, reboot."

"You, too." Eva squeezed him tight.

Huxley mussed Eva's white hair. "I'll see you soon, right?"

"Do you think they'll write songs about our bravery?" Eva asked.

Huxley chuckled at her joke. "Don't change, little bayrie," he said with a wink. He helped Van Turner lead Bix and Bax up the ramp and into the ship.

Eva gulped down the last of her tea. She handed her cup to Hailey, but he grabbed her hand before she could withdraw it.

"What?" Eva looked down at the pilot's dirty fingers. Her gaze rose up and met his.

"Eva." His voice was just above a whisper. "You know that I always wanted to be a retriever, just like my dad?"

"I think your father would be proud of what you've done."

He shook his head. "Just—let me finish. There's a motto the retrievers used to have. I memorized it when I was a little kid: 'Wherever you may roam, we'll safely bring you home.'"

Eva smiled. "That's a good motto."

"But none of us has a home anymore." Hailey swallowed. "Where am I going to bring you?"

Eva glanced down at her pale fingers in both his hands. "I think home can be more than a single place. I think it is wherever you find those that you love. A family." She gazed into his hazel eyes.

Hailey broke the gaze and looked down at his feet.

Behind them the Cærulean shuttle set down in a clearing and the ramp opened. At the entrance stood Rovender.

"I have to go," said Eva.

Hailey looked back up at her. "I will bring you home, Eva Nine, I swear."

"You better." She smiled. "Or I will hunt you down like a sand-sniper."

He gave a lopsided grin. "At least I don't smell like one."

Eva stood on her tiptoes, kissed him quickly on the cheek, and dashed off to join Rovender on the shuttle. As the shuttle began to ascend, she watched Hailey give a final wave from the ground below and walk up the ramp of his warship.

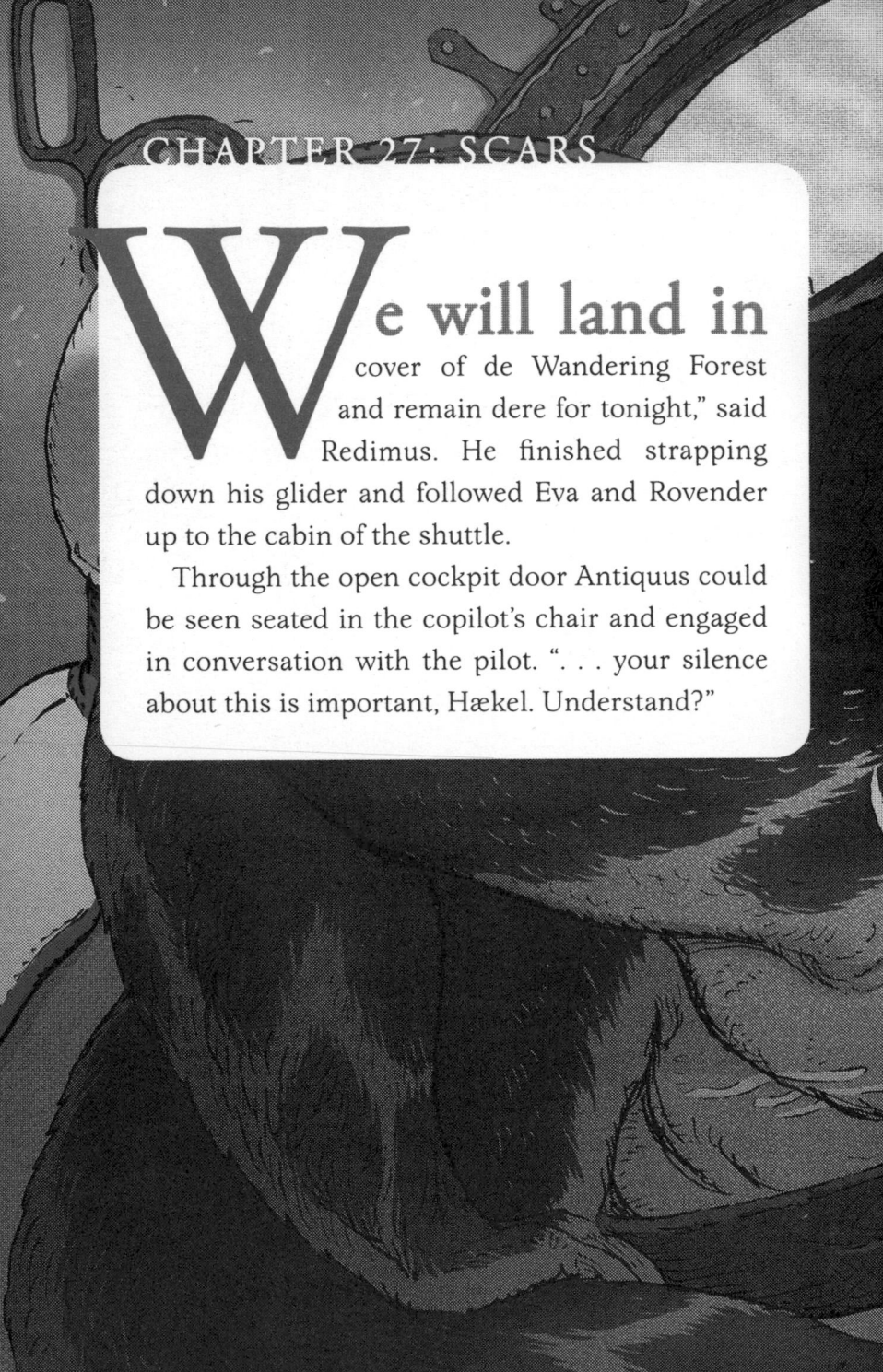

# CHAPTER 27: SCARS

We will land in cover of de Wandering Forest and remain dere for tonight," said Redimus. He finished strapping down his glider and followed Eva and Rovender up to the cabin of the shuttle.

Through the open cockpit door Antiquus could be seen seated in the copilot's chair and engaged in conversation with the pilot. ". . . your silence about this is important, Hækel. Understand?"

"Understood," Hækel replied, and gave a little wave to Eva. "We all set, Rovender?"

"All set." Rovender sat down and strapped in. Eva did the same.

Flopping down opposite them, Redimus's large frame sprawled out over several passenger seats. "Eva Nine, tomorrow morning, before de feaz, I will take you to zee de queen."

"That should be when the first tribal leaders shall be arriving," Antiquus said from the copilot's seat.

"So it will simply seem like we are also arriving for the meeting," said Rovender.

Redimus yawned and nodded.

"What about the Halcyonus leader staying at your village, Rovee?" Eva asked.

"She's not a fan of flying," Hækel said.

"She and her aide leave today on our prized munt-runners. Galell is guiding them," Antiquus said.

"If the weather is good, they should arrive midafternoon, just before the feast starts," added Hækel.

"Redimus, how do you plan to sneak Eva in to see the queen?" Rovender asked.

"I have eet under control." Redimus grinned,

showing the edge of his sharpened beak. "Onze we arrive in Zolas, I wheel tell your shuttle pilot what to do."

Eva and Rovender exchanged concerned glances. This did not go unnoticed by Redimus.

"What?" he asked.

"That part of the plan seems a little vague," said Eva.

"Do not fret, Eva Nine. As I have zaid, eet iz under control," said Redimus. "I will tell you when de time arrivez."

Eva crossed her arms and gave Redimus a look.

"Do I frighten you, Eva Nine?" asked Redimus.

"It is a little much to ask, Redimus. After all, the last Dorcean—the only Dorcean—that Eva encountered was Besteel," said Rovender.

"I know dat you crozzed pazz wiz my brozeel and he left a bad imprezzion . . . as he waz known to do. If I may, I would like to share a ztory about Bezteel and myzelf. Perhapz eet will offer zome fragment of understanding. Yez?"

Rovender looked at Eva. She scooted close to him. "Okay," she mumbled.

"Our zire raised us in de forest, north of Lake Concorz. De woodz dere are wild and untamed, full of beasts unlike any you wheel ever zee. My zire waz an exzellent huntsman and able to live off de land and eat any-zing he came acrozz. Do either of you have ziblings?"

"I do not," said Rovender. "But she has an older sister."

Redimus leaned back in his seat. "Zo, Eva Nine, you underztand then dat your zibling, even if born of de zame litter and raised by de same zire, iz not identical to you?"

Eva reluctantly nodded in agreement.

Redimus continued. "At a young age Bezteel proved to be an exzellent huntzman, just like our zire. A good tracker, stealthy, quick, and eager to kill."

"Yes, yes, we know the Dorcean values," said Antiquus, listening from his seat.

"Yez. But you do not know *me*." Redimus gazed at Eva with his good eye. "My zire favorz Bezteel." He began counting things off on his clawed fingers. "I am an exzellent tracker. I am quite stealthy. But de killing . . . I lack de zeal for eet."

"Really?" Rovender leaned in toward Redimus, his curiosity piqued.

"Yez. Keeling to zatisfy your hunger is just. But to zlay for sport or trophy? Dis I cannot do." Redimus looked down at his taloned hands. "One time we had znared a horned martick dat had been poaching our ztore of food during de night. Vizious creaturez, dey are. My zire demanded dat I be de one to crush iz skull. I hezitated. Eet attacked." He pointed to the scars on his face. "I think I pauzed because I knew de martick did what eet needed to zurvive. But dat split zecond cozz me an eye— and my zire. He wanted me to carry de scars of my miztake as a reminder. Later he told me from heez deathbed, 'You are embarrazzment to our heritage, our way of life, and our kind.' And zo, before my father pazzed, I left heem, Bezteel, and de forest. I travel to Zolas."

Eva stayed close to Rovender, wondering if a horned martick was the beast she'd encountered in the forest. As she listened, she could hear both the sadness and the pain in Redimus's voice.

"What did you do in Solas?" Rovender pulled out a bag of dried berries and seeds. He offered some to Redimus, but the Dorcean declined.

"I joined de Royal Beamguide crew for a bit," he said.

"Like Huxley?" Eva asked.

"I am nuzzing like dat one. But yez, although I azked for a different ezpedition team. We mapped north of Zolas, whereas hiz team went west. Of courze, he choze de wrong team and de humanz capture heem."

"And Besteel?" Rovender asked.

Redimus reached into his own satchel and pulled out an elongate fruit with spikes running in rows down its length. He began to peel it. "Becauze I knew de area zo well, I led de beamguide crew through de northern forezz. Dere, we came across Bezteel. I had not zeen him zince our zire pazzed on. Dezpite our different lives, he is de only family I have. Zo I azked him to visit me zometime in de city." Redimus adjusted his weight in his seat, as if uncomfortable. "One day he came, and I showed him around. We ate and drank until our ztomachz and cropz were full. While at de tavern we maybe had too much Nuccan usquebaugh."

Rovender shook his head. "Usquebaugh. Yes, I know what you mean."

"Zo my brozeel got belligerent and he became boastful. He zaid to me, 'I can hunt down and nab *any* prey. But you never could. Zire was ashamed of you.'" Redimus let out a heavy sigh. He wrapped up the fruit and put it back in his satchel, uneaten.

"The relationship with your father must have been difficult," Antiquus spoke softly. "It hurts me to hear how you were treated."

"Yez. My only family . . . I thought dey hated me."

Rovender and his father looked at one another.

Anger surfaced in Redimus's tone. "Zo I told Bezteel, 'I can do de thingz that you can do; I juzz chooze not to.'"

During her brief time spent with her sister, there had been frustrating moments when Eva Eight had not always seen things Eva's way. She remembered arguing with Eight, abandoning her . . . even kicking and hitting her.

"Zo Bezteel, he zaid, 'Prove eet.'" Redimus wrung his many hands together. He kept his eyes fixed on the floor of the shuttle. "I took heez boomrod and went to de Royal Menagerie."

"No!" Rovender put his hand to his mouth in shock.

"That was you?" Antiquus's eyes were wide.

"Yez." Redimus did not raise his head.

A wave of nervousness came over Eva as she anticipated his answer. "Wait, what did you do?"

Redimus looked Eva in the eyes. "I zlaughtered every animal in de queen'z menagerie."

Eva recoiled into Rovender. He put a reassuring arm around her and held her close to him.

"Eet waz wrong. I know," said Redimus. "But I killed dem to show my brozeel. I killed dem to show my zire. But in showing Bezteel that I choze not to be de monzter that he waz, I became zomething worzz." Redimus put his head in his hands.

"And you were captured immediately. I have heard this part," said Antiquus.

"Yez. Both of uz were caught, and I waz imprizoned. Bezteel begged for my freedom. He told de queen dat he waz de one rezponzible, and for her to jail heem inztead of me. But Ojo would not have eet. She knew de truth." Redimus took a deep breath as if releasing the haunting memory from his body. "She challenged Bezteel to capture one zingle specimen of every creature known to Zin. If he accomplished thiz, then she would zet me free."

"And so off he went." Rovender leaned back in his seat.

"On a fool's errand," said Antiquus.

"Becauze of me," said Redimus.

Eva kept her arms folded and said nothing. Unlike her, Redimus had endured a terrible upbringing. But did that excuse him or Besteel for what they had done?

Redimus gazed back up at Eva. "My brozeel could hunt down and capture any-zing. Exzept you. Eet is he dat should have feared you, Eva Nine, not de other way around."

"He was relentless," Rovender said. "And he did . . . much damage."

"My home, my life, and my Muthr—all were taken away by him." The scorn in Eva's voice made the words stick in her mouth.

"I know dere is nozing I can zay that wheel bring dose things back," Redimus said, his voice but a whisper. "I azzept dat I am juzt az much to blame for what haz tranzpired. Unlike Bezteel, who haz left dis world, I muzz continue on carrying de burden of my pazz actions. Know dat, if you know forgivenezz, my burden wheel become dat much more lighter."

Eva stood and walked toward the cockpit to sit with Antiquus and Hækel. As she passed Redimus, she found no words of comfort. She doubted that she ever would.

That night Hækel landed the shuttle in the forest just outside Lacus at the southern edge of Lake Concors. The group sat around a small campfire and enjoyed a meal of blackened spiderfish followed by fresh voxfruit for dessert. Redimus chose to eat alone, close to the ship.

"What are you doing there, Eva?" Rovender picked his teeth with a spiderfish bone.

"This is Cadmus's Omnipod." Eva scrolled

through the many virtual menus. "I am searching to see if I can find anything of use for tomorrow's meeting with Ojo."

"You won't need that device to impress the queen," Antiquus said. "I think it's what *you know* that intrigues both Zin and Her Royal Majesty."

"I hope you're right. But just in case . . ." Eva continued searching through the files.

With some effort Antiquus rose from his seat near the fire to climb onto his hoverdisc. "I am going to retire for the evening. Hækel, if you don't mind, I suggest we all sleep on the ship."

"Certainly," Hækel replied.

"I agree, Father." Rovender helped him onto his hoverdisc. "Though I do not think we will be bothered. Redimus told me he would keep watch throughout the night." He pointed to the Dorcean, standing guard near the shuttle. "Hækel, do you need help setting up the sleep-mats and blankets?"

"Sure," said Hækel.

"I shall be back, Eva." Rovender followed the pilot onto the ship.

"Okay." Eva kept to her task.

"I hope you find what you are searching for, Eva," Antiquus said.

"Me too. Good night." Eva gave him a hug. "I'll be in soon."

As Antiquus boarded the ship, he passed Redimus. The Dorcean's burly frame filled the shuttle's portal, and yet he seemed so little with his head hung low, almost like a lost child. Eva watched him sling his boomrod over his shoulder and take a seat under the nose of the ship.

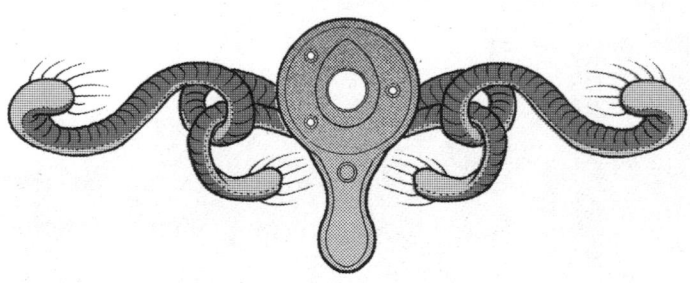

# CHAPTER 28: PREDICTION

The gilded light of the morning sun raked across the burned-out buildings that lined the streets of the city, Solas. Eva looked out the shuttle's cockpit windshield as the ship soared over the devastation. *Now it looks just like New Attica*, she thought.

"Cadmus's fleet?" said Rovender, standing next to her. "I wonder where it is?"

"The warbots are gone too." Eva scanned the rubble-strewn avenues for the menacing machines.

"Orbona's seven rings! Is that what I think it is?" Hækel pointed to the street below. Variously shaped bodies were lying supine in rows on the ground.

Once Eva realized what they were, she could see that the rows went on and on, stretching down entire blocks.

"That is a lot of casualties," said Rovender.

"It's like the hidden plague all over again," added Hækel.

"Except there is nothing hidden about what caused these deaths," said Antiquus. "Which is why they have been put here, on display."

Eva's eyes locked with Rovender's for a beat.

Rovender looked at Redimus and said, "Promise me that no harm will come to her, Redimus, or so help me . . ."

"I promize." Redimus pulled the beamguide from his satchel and held it in his talons. "Thiz beamguide holdz de location of all known human underground domicilez az dizcovered by de Royal Beamguide crew. Dere are many more beyond our immediate area."

"Sanctuaries?" Eva asked.

"If dat iz what you call dem." He placed the beamguide in her hands. "Now tell me dis: Would Ojo releaze dis information to you if she thought eet would rezult in her undoing?"

Eva passed the beamguide to Rovender. "Keep this safe." She swallowed down the nervousness that shivered inside her. "Let's get this over with."

Redimus turned to Hækel. "Take de ship to de palace and zircle de tower once."

"Once?" Hækel asked.

"Yez. Be inconspicuouz, az if you were azzezzing de damage."

"Understood. We will be there in just a couple of minutes."

"Let uz go, den." Redimus scrambled out of the cabin. In the loading area he quickly unstrapped his glider and unfolded its wings.

"Almost there," Hækel called out from the cockpit.

"Speak your truth. That's all you can do, right?" Antiquus squeezed Eva's hand.

Eva nodded.

"Ruzender, open de loading ramp." Redimus started the engine of the glider. "Eva Nine, geet on and be quick!" He tossed her a pair of flying goggles.

Rovender gave Eva a hug. "If you don't want to go, you don't have to."

"I know." Eva hugged him tight. "But if there is a chance to change this, I have to try."

"Very well. Please be careful." Rovender kissed the top of her head.

"I will." Eva climbed onto the back saddle of the glider. She donned her goggles and grasped the passenger handgrips mounted on either side of her seat. At this proximity to the Dorcean, Eva smelled his earthy musky scent. It was a scent similar to that of the horned beast that had stalked her in the forest.

"I will return her zafely home after de meeting." Redimus pulled a large flight cap with goggles over his face. With his eye patch now covered, he looked just like Besteel.

"I'll see you back at the village." Rovender waved. He opened the loading ramp.

The glider dropped out of the shuttle toward the tall spire of the palace. Near the spire's pointed peak was an alcove carved into the wall.

"It's so windy," shouted Eva. "Can you land?" The tattered pennants that hung from the palace spire flapped in the gusts as if they would break free from the cable that tethered them.

With ease Redimus wove the glider through the pennants. "Do not be afraid," he said over his shoulder, "but do not look down." A strong gust buffeted the glider's wings, but Redimus's reflexes were quick. He compensated for the wind and brought the craft level again.

Despite the warning, Eva glanced to the ground far below. Though they were almost to the alcove, their height made her feel dizzy. She clutched the handgrips tight.

The glider swooped down and landed on a wide balcony. Redimus shut off the engine and dismounted. "Let uz hurry, Eva Nine. You cannot be zpotted."

Eva climbed off the seat and looked out over the grand balcony. The city's battered skyline was laid out before her. *This must have been a majestic view,* she thought, *before the battle.* At the foot of the palace she saw the Cærulean shuttle land next to other ships already docked along the waterfront. "Good luck, Rovee," she whispered before joining Redimus at the balcony doors.

Redimus pushed open one of the tall double doors and led Eva down a curved staircase into an ornate bedchamber. The opulent room was gigantic by human standards. Exquisite ornate patterns decorated every centimeter of the walls, which led up to an intricate mural that covered the entire ceiling.

At the center of the room hung a chandelier larger than the glider that Eva had just flown in on. Radiating from the finial that held the chandelier was a series of long thin metal rods, each ending in a colorfully painted sphere. It brought to mind holograms of old orreries that Eva had studied in her history programs. But this orrery represented no solar system that she was familiar with.

A towering curtain-framed bed sat opposite the balcony staircase, draped in the finest fabrics ever seen. As Eva walked closer to the bed, she realized the pattern on the fabric seemed to ebb and flow like ripples on water. In fact, the decorative wallpaper appeared to be doing the same thing. Along with the spinning orrery in the light of the chandelier, the entire room seemed to be alive. And singing.

Eva's attention shifted to a large perch sculpted in the shape of an ancient tree. The dark patina of the metallic perch contrasted with the brilliantly colored tiny birds that sat upon it. Eva recognized the birds and their song.

*I sing the prettiest song. I sing the purest song.*

"These are all—" Eva started.

"Treowes," a succinct yet throaty voice answered. Standing in a curtained doorway was Queen Ojo. As before, she was draped in many layers of heavy embroidered robes over her tall frame. Several long pendants swung under the thick frilled collar wrapped around her long neck, while a large vocal transcoder hovered over her, following the queen's every move. Iridescent eyes, made brighter by the dark face paint that lined them, watched Eva closely as the queen glided into the room. Behind her followed two royal guardsmen and another extravagantly attired creature, which Eva assumed to be a courtier to the queen. "Treowes captured from the forests beyond and gifted to me by many of the representatives who shall be joining us for our victory feast—a token that we shall always speak the truth," Ojo said, observing the birds. Next to her towering figure the treowes looked like a collection of insects.

"Your majezty." Redimus approached the queen and kissed one of the pendants hanging from her neck. "I have done az you have commanded."

"You have indeed. Very good, Dorcean," said Queen Ojo. "Wait on the balcony until you are summoned." She turned to her attendants. "You may leave me for the time being." The attendants bowed and shuffled out of the bedchamber.

"Where's Zin?" Eva craned her neck, hoping to see him float out from behind the queen. He did not, causing a twinge of unease in Eva.

"He'll be along." Ojo walked to the doorway where her attendants had exited. She closed the door and locked it. "He is speaking with his brother."

Eva's pulse quickened. "We are meeting without him?" She glanced around the room, looking for another exit.

Ojo watched Eva and folded her fingers on all four hands. "I have much to do on this day. But Zin insisted that I hear you out as soon as possible."

Eva inched close to the balcony stairs.

Ojo walked toward her. "I find myself at a difficult crossroads. Zin has told me many things since his return to our city. Many things that I was not pleased to hear in the slightest."

Eva took another step toward the balcony. "But I am here to help."

Ojo made a gurgling sound. It was hard for Eva to discern if it was a choke, a groan, or a laugh. "Help? I think your species deserves to strike this word from their vocabulary."

Eva dashed up the stairs and pushed open the large balcony door. The gusty winds from outside nearly blew her back down the stairs. "I knew this was a trap! Get me out of here," she shouted, and hopped onto the glider. "You promised Rovee! Do it!"

"Eva Nine, what?" Redimus ran to Eva.

"SILENCE!" Ojo shouted. "Redimus! Fetch her and bring her in off the balcony."

Redimus looked at Eva sitting on the glider seat.

"Redimus, you dare risk my wrath again?" asked Ojo.

He plucked Eva off the glider. "I am zorry," he whispered to her. "I had no idea."

"Put her there." Ojo pointed to a large tufted stool trimmed in gold tassels. Redimus did as he was told. "Now return to your post and keep an eye on the doors," commanded the queen.

Eva watched Redimus slink up the stairs and back out onto the balcony, closing the door behind him.

Ojo gazed down at Eva. It seemed as if she were examining Eva like a Beeboo doll. The queen then recited,

> *"A nymph, born of the earth, forged by machine,*

*Will herald your end.*
*The Change of all Changes.*
*The death. The rebirth.*

*Darkness shall shroud the sun, the land,*
*    and its people.*
*No living being—neither here nor there—*
*Shall find light to dispel the shadow*
*Whose caster is at your doorstep.*

*A beacon will arrive from the ends of the*
*    earth,*
*To light the way through hate, through*
*    fear, through war.*
*The feast shall come to an end,*
*But in the end, all one is left with is the*
*    truth."*

Ojo finished, closed her eyes, and let out a heavy sigh.

"Arius," Eva said. "Those are the words of Arius."

"They were told to me many years ago when I was but a child." Ojo pointed to a painting on the wall.

Eva recognized it to be a portrait of the queen, much younger but still decorated in ornate attire.

Eva felt sadness from the child in the painting. It was apparent in the young queen's eyes. This sadness had grown to overtake the older Ojo that now stood before Eva.

"Arius told me this only once. I have spent much of my life recording bits of it as it returned to me in dream and memory," said Ojo.

"Like a long-lost song," said Eva.

"Unlike with a song, I have come to dread these words. For many years I pondered the hidden meanings of her prediction. Zin told me I was foolish for doing so, but I felt that somehow Arius's words were meant to harm me."

"No. They were meant to help you and to guide me," said Eva. "I mean, at least that's what I think."

"When you arrived in my museum, captured by Besteel, I wondered who you were and what role you would play—if any. Zin informed me you were of the species responsible for all of the ancient machinery he'd excavated from the ruins."

"'A nymph, forged by machines.' I remember. Arius used that same phrase in my prediction."

"Yet another reason why you, and your kind, are likely what will 'herald' my end. Do you not agree?" Queen Ojo crossed her arms.

"Herald? Me? I'm not that. I am not responsible

for what Cadmus did here," Eva said. "*I* tried to stop him at Lacus. When I first met you, I was still looking for my family. You ordered that creepy taxidermist to freeze me alive. Remember?"

"If Arius had told you that I was to bring about your demise, would you not have done the same to me?" Ojo asked in a haughty tone.

Eva thought about Besteel and the sand-snipers she had called . . . and Caruncle and the knifejacks . . . even the horned beast in the forest. Had she not done the exact same thing as Ojo? She did not want to dwell on these thoughts. She just needed to convince the queen that they were on the same side. "Loroc predicted your demise," said Eva.

"So Zin informs me. Zin further explained his theory that it is not his brother who is my 'beacon' of light, but it is in fact you, Eva Nine." Queen Ojo moved closer. She was at least three times Eva's height. "What do you have to say about that? How is it that you can cast a spell on Zin to alter his thinking?"

"Just like your treowes, I told him what I know to be the truth."

"I see. Well, while you and Zin were talking, my city and subjects were under attack, as were the peaceful residents of Lacus. Since I had been under the impression that we were the only civilized inhabitants on this planet, we had never seen a need for defense against such attacks—and so we could not defend ourselves against your aggression."

"But—" Eva started.

"Loroc arrived just in time to help turn the tide in our favor. He explained that he had taken on, or absorbed, his sister Darius's pain. In doing so he also gained her ability to see into the past. It was in this way that he sought out Cadmus's weakness so that he could exploit it." Ojo put all four hands on her hips. "And he has delivered what he promised: swift victory over the humans."

"Do you know how he accomplished that?" asked Eva.

"He became familiar with their machines of destruction and seized control of them for our gain," Ojo said.

"No. He tricked Cadmus into believing that if the humans invaded Solas, Cadmus would win."

Ojo made that noise again. It was a chuckle. "Is this the tale that you told Zin?"

"No. New Attica wasn't destroyed then! Cadmus was still alive," Eva said. "I went there and tried to talk sense into him. It was then that Loroc betrayed Cadmus and invaded the human city."

"Why would any Arsian do such a thing?"

"I think there is something wrong with Loroc. Don't you see? He didn't just 'absorb' Darius's powers. He *ate* her. Just like he did to Arius and just like he'll do to Zin if we don't help." Eva's frustration gave way to pleading. "You have to stop him now before it's too late."

"Too late for whom? You and your kind?" Ojo mused. "You had your chance. Your time. Now it is *our* time. Did you not see how many of my subjects were lost to this invasion? I could not allow this conflict to continue."

"If that's the case, why did you give me the beamguide with the location of all the human Sanctuaries?" asked Eva.

"Zin felt that you could rally your kind and we could see to some sort of truce between your people and my subjects."

"They won't be *your* subjects anymore." Eva pulled out Cadmus's Omnipod. "Everyone will be under Loroc's control. You and I will be dead."

"I have had enough! I don't know why I allowed Zin's counsel in the first place. You have infected his judgment with words. You may believe these words to be true, but my judgment is final!" Ojo's voice rose in anger.

"Omnipod, please locate any recorded interactions with Cadmus and his Prime Adviser. The keyword I am looking for is 'victory,'" Eva said into the device.

"Retrieving all such recordings," said the Omnipod. "There are several hundred recorded conversations."

"Play back the first one please, in three-hundred-sixty-degree mode," said Eva. She glanced up at Ojo. The queen was bent over watching closely. Eva had her attention.

A fully rendered hologram of Cadmus appeared. Ojo reached out to touch him, but her hand passed right through the projection.

"What is this? More trickery?" she asked.

"Not trickery—technology," Eva replied. She looked down at the date on the Omnipod. "It is a recording from a long time ago."

Cadmus was in the Chamber of Historic Thought sitting in an antique armchair and stroking his long beard. A holographic Loroc floated over to him.

"It appears so real," said Ojo. "I can see the fibers of Loroc's cape."

"Does he look different?" Eva paused the recording.

"Yes." Ojo's head turned as she examined him. "His appearance is different here from when he left, and yet different still from when he returned. His eyes, they number four instead of two."

"That means he'd already found his sister, Darius, when this was recorded." Eva's tone was grim. She continued the recording.

"Well, what did you think of that?" the holographic Cadmus asked.

"It is impressive how you are able to confer with your long-deceased leaders of the past, both in art and invention," Loroc replied. "And yet I see that there is much disagreement and strife among your own."

Cadmus murmured in agreement. "Sadly, our history is one rife with aggression and anguish. That is not the case with my people currently living here in this city. They are peaceful."

"And yet confined," Loroc observed.

"Yes," replied Cadmus. "Our plan was to resurface to a planet that had healed itself. Obviously that is not the case and our resources here are greatly depleted."

Loroc was quiet for a bit as he floated around the room.

"Your kind . . . they were here but not extinct?" Ojo asked.

"We were dormant in laboratories underground," said Eva. "There is no way Zin would have known when he saw the reports from your father."

Ojo returned her attention to the hologram. Loroc was explaining the Vitae Virus generator to Cadmus and comparing the technology used to Cadmus's own. ". . . if you were to divert all your resources to the manufacturing of machines for invasion, I could advise you on ways to take the primary city. The one I told you of that sits on a large body of vitally rich water, near the great forest."

"What do you mean by 'take'?" Cadmus stopped stroking his beard.

Loroc turned to face Cadmus. "Let me help, and I will show you. I know the way they operate. I know their strengths and weaknesses."

"Oh no," Queen Ojo gasped.

"I just want to understand them," Cadmus replied. "Perhaps they can teach us?"

"They will not." Loroc's tone was chilling. "The return of your kind is but a nuisance that will be dealt with accordingly. Your species was not part of their plan here."

"Is there no other way?" There was alarm in Cadmus's voice.

"There is not." Loroc's grin grew bigger. "Create a fleet of machines for war, and we shall conquer the young queen before she learns of your existence. Strike before she can act, and her city shall become yours."

Cadmus stood and pondered this proposition. "I have worked so hard to end all violence within our population. There is no need for it. However, the unforeseeable and extraordinary circumstances in which we find ourselves seem to leave me little choice. Can you promise a swift takeover with minimal casualties?"

"Of course," Loroc hissed. "Put me in charge, and you will have your victory, Cadmus Pryde."

# CHAPTER 29: DISINTEGRATION

**Q**ueen Ojo sat down on a stool opposite Eva. Remaining quiet, the queen gazed out a high arched window to the vista outside. The ruins that made up her once great city now smoldered in the hazy light. "I have memories of my home world from when I was very young," she said, her eyes still transfixed on the view beyond.

Eva sat cross-legged on her stool and listened.

"As far back as I can remember, there were falling stars in our sky. Day or twi-night, you would see the fiery streaks crisscross over the horizon. I used to think they were so beautiful. My father told me that the falling stars were actually pieces of our smaller sun, Safir, which was slowly disintegrating. It was breaking apart and entering our atmosphere. Eventually the sun's death would consume our entire planet in fire. Zin concurred that this event was inevitable but believed that it would not happen in Father's lifetime, or mine . . . but it did. It happened faster than anyone could have predicted, even Arius." The queen's voice was heavy with recollection.

"So my father ordered the construction of a great starship, the largest ever conceived. His plan was to take as many people as he could and leave our dying planet to find a new home, far from danger. Many said his plan would not work and they stayed behind. It is believed that they have all perished, as has my old home." Ojo looked down at the pendants hanging from her neck. "I scooped this soil up with my bare hands the day before we left," she said, pointing to the rust-colored dirt in the glass vial.

"Soth had a similar vial," said Eva.

"Many elders do. It is so we might remember. When there is disagreement among one another or life on Orbona seems difficult, we can look at what we left behind and be reminded that it all can be taken away. Erased. No machine can stop it. No entity can protect from it." Ojo seemed less like a regal queen in a majestic palace and more like a prisoner held captive by the weight of knowledge.

"Your story sounds similar to what happened here with the human race."

"This planet was dormant, ready to be reawakened," Ojo said. "Despite how many planets there are in the known universe, do you know how difficult it was to find a viable habitat for my subjects? One that wasn't already inhabited by another species, one that was durable enough to become reestablished?" Ojo rose from her seat, reached up, and tapped one of the model planets on the orrery. Slowly the planets circled around the brightly lit chandelier. "Life here was like a second chance for us. A gift."

"A gift given that none may own," Eva said.

"Precisely." Ojo's eyes now focused on Eva. "A gift that is meant to be shared, to be respected and nurtured." Four hands lightly touched Eva's face for a moment.

Eva stood. "By all of us."

"Yes. By all." Ojo pulled a device from her robes.

A chirpy voice on the device spoke out, "Yes, Your Majesty?"

"Get the captain of the guard to my quarters here immediately," Ojo commanded.

"Yes, Your Majesty."

"And locate Zin and escort him back here. But be quiet about it," she added.

"Right away, Your Majesty."

"Where are my royal guardsmen now?" asked Ojo.

"Welcoming our guests, Your Majesty."

"Of course. The guests are arriving." Ojo paused in thought.

"Shall I order them to leave?" asked the voice.

"No," said Ojo. "Leave them there for the time being. I want our guests to feel safe while they are here. I'll discuss what is best with the captain."

"As you wish, Your Majesty."

Ojo put away the device and walked up the stairs to the balcony doors. "Redimus, you may enter," she said through the cracked door.

The Dorcean slipped into the room. "Your Majezty?" he asked. His good eye moved back and forth between Queen Ojo and Eva as if he were searching for a clue to the outcome of their discussion.

"Redimus, I need you to protect Eva Nine at all costs. As far as I am concerned, she is the representative of the human population," said Ojo.

"That's not me. We have Van—" started Eva.

The queen cut her off. "See to it that she is hidden in a safe place until Loroc is dealt with."

Redimus bowed. "Yez, Your Majesty. I shall return her to Faunaz."

"I will send word once Loroc has been apprehended." Ojo tapped a wall, causing the ornate wallpaper to ripple and evaporate. Behind it was a wardrobe of exquisite finery. "Then my counsel and I will arrange a meeting between you and the various leaders."

"Can I let Rovee know I'm okay? He is here with his father, Antiquus, representing their village of Faunas," said Eva.

"I would rather you didn't. It would be wise to wait until Loroc has been dealt with and the representatives have been apprised of these recent developments," Ojo said.

"But he is like my father. He looks out for me and cares for me. I don't want him to worry," Eva said. Redimus helped her off the stool to the tiled floor.

"A Cærulean who cares for you?" Ojo pondered this for a moment. "I am sorry, but I cannot allow it. If you were discovered down there, it would be calamitous to us all, especially your Cærulean surrogate. Understood?"

"Underztood," answered Redimus.

There was a chime at the bedchamber door.

"The captain of my guard is here. Let me brief him on what is about to transpire," Ojo said. "You best be off before you are discovered."

"Thank you," said Eva.

"Thank you." Queen Ojo gave a nod. "We shall meet again. I shall inform Zin he was right after all."

Eva was bent over the rail of the balcony, watching the procession of leaders enter the palace far below. "How do we get down to the banquet hall?"

"Zorry, Eva Nine." Redimus hopped onto the glider and started the engine. "We are not going to de banquet hall."

"Redimus, I *have* to see Rovender. I need to let him know how the meeting went with Queen Ojo. I know he'll be worried if he doesn't hear from me.

Give me five minutes. After that you can take me back to Faunas."

Redimus shook his head and sucked his teeth. "I cannot do dis. I gave my word to da queen." He handed her the flight goggles.

"She asked that you *protect* me at all costs and make sure I was hidden and safe." Eva put her hands on her hips. "She didn't ask you to *take* me back to Faunas."

"But Ruzender—"

"Made you promise no harm would come to me." Eva put on her goggles and slid onto the backseat of the glider. "So get me into the banquet hall, keep me hidden, and make sure no harm comes to me."

"You are az zlippery az a zpiderfish, Eva Nine." Redimus grumbled and pulled his helmet over his head.

Redimus led Eva down a great hallway that was lavishly decorated with objects that clearly showed fine—yet otherworldly—craftsmanship. Giant urns filled with exotic plants were placed at intervals down the length of the hall. As they walked along, Eva became dizzy gaping up at the animated murals that covered the arched ceiling. Many images depicted a turbulent sky with fire raining down to the land below. Others displayed celestial maps of constellations that Eva did not recognize from her own night sky. *It's just like the paintings in Attican Hall,* she thought. *It's the history of their world.*

"Stay cloze," Redimus whispered. "Do not draw attention."

"Got it." Eva tucked her hair under the hood of her poncho.

"I do not know how I let you talk me into doing dis. If de queen were to find out, I would be incarzerated all over again," he muttered under his breath, and glanced nervously over his shoulder.

"She won't see you, or me," Eva whispered back.

"Five minutez. Find Ruzender and tell him what you need to tell him. Then get out." Redimus checked the controls on his boomrod.

Eva pulled out Cadmus's Omnipod. "I'm going to let Hailey know not to come."

Redimus nodded. "I think the queen has dis situation under control. As long as she doesn't zee me, we are good."

They reached the end of the hallway and came to a grandiose doorway flanked by two pillar guards. Extending from the entrance inward was a long flower-covered walkway with royal guards lined up on either side. At the head of this walkway stood a tall, decorated individual, along with Queen Ojo's courtier. Redimus and Eva hung at the back of the line as various representatives and leaders filed into the royal banquet hall.

"Did you know that those pillar guards were constructed by ancients?" Eva gazed up at the giants standing stoically on either side of the banquet hall doors. "Even though they are controlled by a remote, they actually do have minds of their own. They're not just automatons."

Redimus looked up at them. He continued with his mumbling. "I have a mind of my own too. I make my own decizions—good or bad."

"What's that?" Eva asked. "It's hard to hear you with my hood pulled up."

He waved her question off. "Nuzzing. Don't worry."

After the representatives had entered, Redimus approached both the tall individual and the courtier and spoke with them in a hushed tone. Several times he pointed to Eva. Finally the tall individual nodded, and the courtier moved to the side, allowing Eva to pass.

Redimus approached Eva. "No weaponz are allowed inzide, zo I wheel wait out here for you.

Ojo haz not yet arrived, but Ruzender and hiz zire are checked in, zo go find him and hurry back. Be quick."

"Okay," Eva whispered. She stepped gingerly past the guards and slipped through the open doors into the banquet hall.

The domed roof of the hall was a gigantic skylight that stretched up for many stories. The skylight offered a vast view of the southern districts of Solas, as well as Lake Concors. Eva could make out the towers of Lacus far in the distance. Even though the vista outside was tarnished with smoking rubble and burned-out buildings, the sheer size of the opulent room took Eva's breath away.

Everywhere Eva looked there were Orbonians of all different shapes and sizes. Some she recognized—like the Halcyonus, Mirthians, and Dorceans. Others were completely new to her. Most appeared wizened and elderly. She wondered, *Do they all live in Solas, or are there villages I have yet to explore?* The crowd of representatives was gathered near the various food stations placed around the perimeter of the room. Next to a giant urn, studying an impressive mural that stretched around the entire hall, stood a familiar blue figure.

"Rovee," Eva whispered as she neared her friend. "Rovee, it's me."

Rovender turned his attention from the mural. "Eva!"

"Shhh!" Eva placed her hand in his and whispered. "I'm not supposed to be here."

"I'd say," he whispered back, and glanced around the room surreptitiously. His father was near a food station in deep discussions with Cærulean leaders from other tribes. "How did your meeting go with the queen?"

"She now understands what happened and no longer blames the humans." Eva's heart raced as the enormity of what she'd accomplished sank in.

Rovender straightened, his indigo eyes went wide with astonishment. "Is this true?"

Eva nodded.

He hugged her tight. "I'm so proud of you."

"Thanks," Eva spoke into his ear. "But I need to leave. Redimus is going to take me back to Faunas until the queen is finished dealing with Loroc."

"I think that would be best. I've overheard discussions with the other leaders. As with our council back home it will to take some explaining to realign their attitudes." Rovender led Eva back to the entrance of the hall. "Hækel is downstairs at the shuttle, so let me escort you out of here."

"Can you come with me?"

"As much as I want to, I believe it would be best if I stayed. I want to witness these discussions firsthand," said Rovender. He and Eva were almost to the door. "Perhaps I may even be called upon to verify the queen's story."

Both doors of the hall swung open, and the royal guardsmen filed in. They lined up to form an entry with boomrods held at attention.

"Oh no. Is it Queen Ojo?" Eva asked. "She'll be upset with me."

"Sheesa," Rovender hissed, and turned Eva away from the door. He pulled her hood down over her head to further conceal her face. "It's Loroc!"

The Arsian had grown since Eva's last encounter and looked immense under the long extravagant robes that adorned his body. His three rings of arms waved about and a triple pair of eyes scanned the room as he floated in. All the leaders stopped and turned. Eva could see confusion and uncertainty on their faces.

"Greetings, Orbonian leaders. Orbona and I greet you." Loroc's voice echoed as if three voices spoke slightly out of unison. "Many of you may know me. I am the Ojo family's Prime Adviser. I have returned to advise and serve Solas. I am the one responsible for defeating the humans and liberating our many varied and celebrated races. You are all liberated because I am Loroc."

Cheers erupted from the crowd. Those who had drinks in hand toasted to victory.

"Let me get you out while he is occupied," Rovender whispered, and ushered Eva to the door.

"Shhh! Don't!" Eva countered. She pointed to the royal guards standing in the doorway. "If we try to leave now, he'll see us for sure."

"You are right," Rovender growled, frustrated. They shuffled to the back of the crowd. There they met up with Antiquus seated on his hoverdisc. Rovender leaned over and whispered into his father's ear.

Antiquus's eyebrows rose in surprise, and he looked over at Eva. Smiling, he hovered near her and squeezed her hand tight. "I am proud of you," he said. "Don't worry. Loroc shall be dealt with. And we'll get you out of here." Eva gave a weak smile. She wanted to bask in this moment of achievement, but Loroc's presence was unsettling. She watched as he floated about the hall.

He gestured out the large window. "As you know, we suffered a full-scale invasion here in Solas. An invasion we fully won. But these battles take quite a toll—on lives, homes, and loyalty. To ensure our freedom, sacrifices had to be made—sacrifices that my family and I were willing to make. But you all must know that these sacrifices went on long before this battle. They went on long before many of you were even present." He bowed his head. "To be honest, my sisters—Darius and Arius—and I did not want to make this journey here to Orbona."

This statement caused a ripple of murmurs through the crowd.

"Do not take it as a strike against you, my good subjects. You see, my sisters and I longed to return to our home planet just prior to King Ojo's Great Migration. We had shared all the wisdom of the past and all the knowledge that we had with your good king. We foretold of a successful voyage and provided him with the fortitude to complete his incredible starship. But for one of us this gift of our combined power was not enough. One of us was insistent that we journey here, far from our own home, to accompany the Ojo family and your ancestors. We arrived at this forsaken place, Orbona, where my poor sister Darius grew mad with constant nightmares from this planet's violent history. A place where my other visionary sister would become but a simple fortune-teller, spitting forth predictions in exchange for a meal." Loroc lowered his head in shame. "Their pain was my pain, and I did what I had to in order to ease it. It is an ancient Arsian ritual to consume another. I did this so that the burden of life, the pain, and the anguish could be lifted away from the body so that their spirits could rest at ease. Spirits find serenity."

"Spirits find serenity," the gathering repeated.

The doors opened wide, and the guardsmen moved to the side.

"Now." Rovender pushed Eva. They scooted through the crowd, close to the open door.

"And who was the one who insisted we come here? Who was the one who cared not if his siblings were in pain as long as he accomplished his own goals? Why, it is the very one who fled this great city when the attack began. Behold my traitorous brother, Zin!" Loroc pointed to the doorway.

Eva recognized the tall glass cylindrical cell that floated in. It was exactly like the one she'd been confined in at the taxidermist's lab. The runty taxidermist shuffled behind the cell, holding one of the many remotes that were kept holstered in a belt around his waist. Once the specimen cell reached the center of the hall, the taxidermist aimed the remote at it and pressed a button, causing the condensation on the cell walls to evaporate. Inside Zin zipped about banging on the glass. His slit eyes were wide with fear, and he'd been stripped of all attire.

Loroc floated around his prisoner with his many arms folded behind his back, a satisfied look on his mutated face. "Not only did my brother leave you during your darkest hours, but he knew the danger of the humans. He'd collected their refuse and displayed it in your museum as artifacts from a long-lost civilization."

Eva went to speak, but Rovender placed his large hand over her mouth. "This is neither the time nor the place, Eva. You must leave, for I fear what is about to transpire."

Eva pushed his hand away, and tears pricked her eyes as she watched Zin, helpless in the cell. There were no captive sand-snipers Eva could call to save him.

"As if this were not enough, he also conferred with the humans, especially their most dangerous spy, Eva Nine. He invited her into *our* city and then spoke with her—during the time when we were being invaded!" Loroc shot several accusatory fingers at Zin. Shouts came out from the crowd. One representative threw a bottle at Zin's cell, and it smashed against the thick glass wall.

"I must consume Zin so that his weakness for the humans will be eliminated. Under my control he will no longer be a threat to us all." Loroc smiled at the taxidermist. The taxidermist responded by hitting another button on the remote. A thin rod rose up from the bottom of Zin's cell.

"Rovee," Eva nearly shouted, but once again Rovender clamped his hand over her mouth. She struggled and pulled his hand away. "He's going to paralyze him!" Eva made a move to stop the taxidermist, but Rovender held her tight.

"If you interfere now, he will do the same to you," Rovender hissed.

Tears burned Eva's eyes as she watched the mist from the rod fill Zin's cell. His floating body fell to the bottom with a sickening thud. With her abilities Eva reached out to every living creature in Solas to swoop in and attack Loroc, but the animals and plants had abandoned the city, leaving Eva helpless.

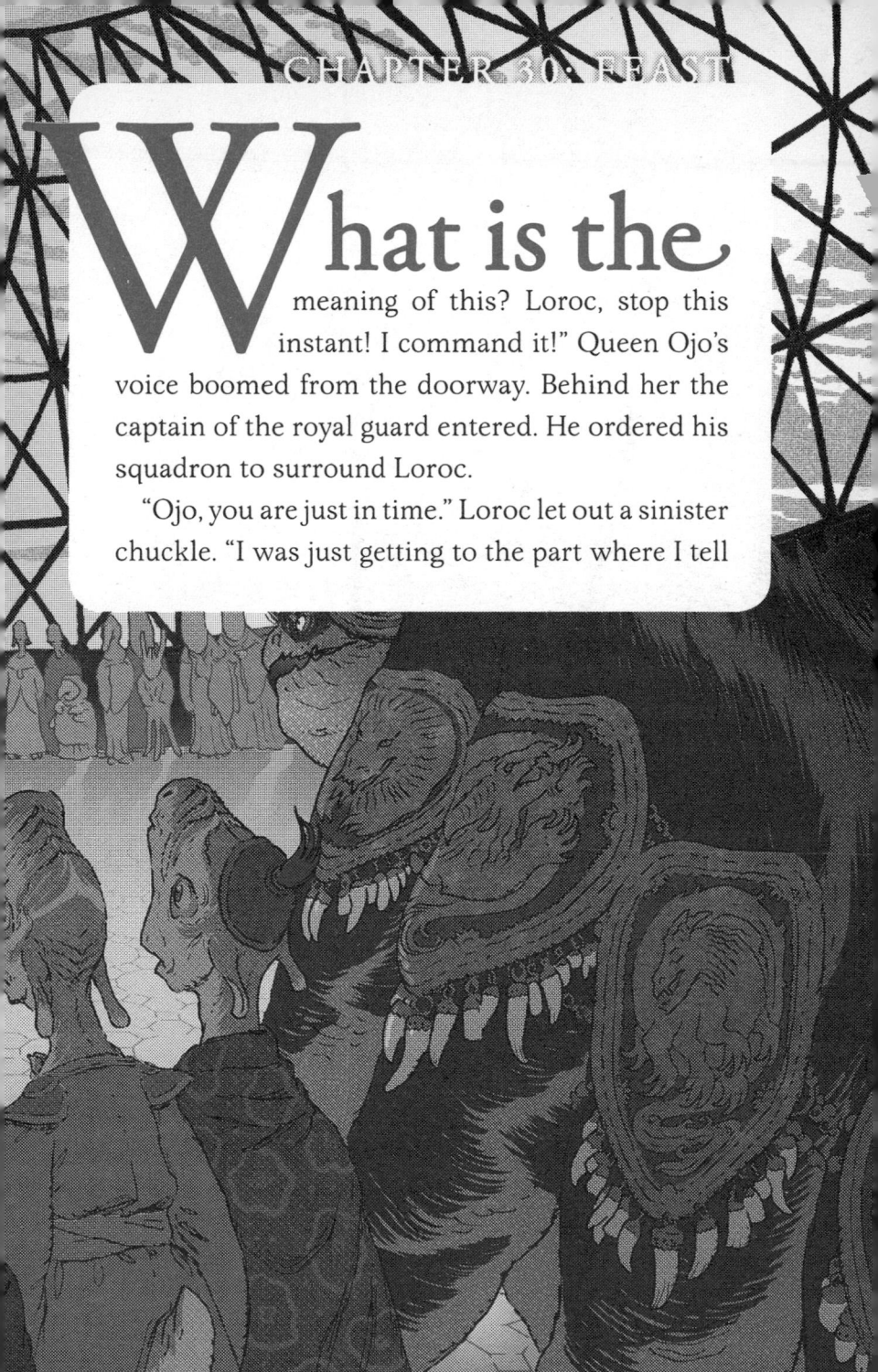

# What is the

meaning of this? Loroc, stop this instant! I command it!" Queen Ojo's voice boomed from the doorway. Behind her the captain of the royal guard entered. He ordered his squadron to surround Loroc.

"Ojo, you are just in time." Loroc let out a sinister chuckle. "I was just getting to the part where I tell everyone how utterly useless you were during this battle . . . and how sympathetic you've became to the human's effort."

"You know nothing of my affairs!"

"Is that so? Was it not you who allowed Zin to display all these 'wonderful' human artifacts in your museum?" Loroc moved closer to the queen.

"I have heard enough! Guards, ready your weapons." Two dozen royal guardsmen charged their boomrods and aimed them at Loroc.

One pair of Loroc's eyes began to glow, and he began to chant in a voice Eva did not recognize.

*"It is the queen child.*
*The one who did not want her crown,*
*But the one who inherited it nonetheless.*
*She is but a child who is weary of ruling,*
*Weary of trying, weary of the royal life."*

"That was long ago. It will not work." Ojo waved away Loroc's words in a dismissive manner. "Surrender now, or I shall be forced to execute you, here and now."

The next pair of Loroc's eyes began to glow. Once more he chanted, this time in a tone similar to Arius's voice,

*"The queen shall not serve my demise,*
*But her hive's demise, I shall serve."*

One of Loroc's arms shot out and wrapped tight around Queen Ojo's throat. She struggled but could not loosen the constriction. Another arm snaked through her robes as if searching for something.

"Guards, drop your weapons or the next breath will be her last," Loroc yelled. He plucked the pillar guard's remote from Ojo's robes. "Do it!"

Queen Ojo gasped for air as Loroc lifted her up off the floor.

The Mirthian representative rushed toward Loroc, shouting, "Stop! Not our queen!"

Loroc lashed out and struck the Mirthian. The force of the blow sent him back into the wall, where he slid to the floor, unconscious. Several other leaders ran to his aid.

Queen Ojo tried to speak but could not. She struggled against Loroc's strong grasp.

Rovender, Antiquus, and Eva inched toward the banquet hall doors with a small group of representatives. In the hallway beyond, Redimus recognized Eva and rushed toward the doorway. The pillar guards on either side of the door blocked his path. One of them swatted Redimus to the side. With claws extended the guards slammed the doors of the hall shut, trapping everyone within.

"Don't try to run," Loroc said, brandishing the pillar guard remote. "You have yet to witness what will no doubt become a historical moment in Orbonian history."

Rovender led Eva through the crowd to the large urn in the back of the room. "Get behind here," he whispered. "And stay hidden."

"But—"

"Eva." Rovender looked directly at her. "Whatever happens, do not come out. Promise me?"

Eva nodded.

"I'll be close by. And I'll try to think of some way to get us out of here." Rovender took his post in front of the urn. Antiquus stayed next to him.

The captain of the royal guard spoke. "If we surrender our weapons, you will not harm our queen?"

"No harm to her, I promise. But hurry with your decision." Loroc tightened his grip. "Your beloved queen is running out of time."

The captain threw his boomrod to the ground. His entire squad followed suit.

"No!" Eva stifled her scream.

"As I said, I won't hurt her." As quick as a flash Loroc grabbed all twenty-four charged boomrods with his many arms. "But I will eliminate you." He fired the boomrods out in every direction. The squad of royal guardsmen fell to the ground. Some were blown across the hall. The crowd huddled to the far end of the room, near Eva's hiding spot.

An angry Dorcean tribe leader picked up an entire food station and hurled it at Loroc. Along with a band of other representatives, he rushed Loroc in an attempt to snatch a weapon. Loroc fired a boomrod directly at the Dorcean leader. The shot blasted the leader into the far wall and the band of attackers dispersed.

The bloodied Dorcean leader pulled himself up. He climbed onto a table and shouted to the crowd, "There are more of uz than heem. We can take him down! Who iz with me?"

Loroc fired another boomrod into the skylight, causing a large portion of it to collapse. The thick glass shattered on the floor just behind him. "Back down, Dorcean!" He held the muzzle of the boomrod to Ojo's head.

The representatives retreated to the back of the hall, far from Loroc.

With his eyes fixed on the struggling queen,

Loroc spoke. "I still have a meal to enjoy. My victory feast. Taxidermist, let's start with my appetizer."

The runty creature cowered behind Zin's cell and did not move.

"Well?" Loroc aimed a boomrod at the taxidermist.

"I–I . . . ," the taxidermist stuttered.

"Bring the remote here, and I shall do it myself," Loroc hissed.

Trembling, the taxidermist approached Loroc and held out the remote. Loroc seized him by the neck with one arm and plucked the remote out of his hand with another. He hurled the taxidermist across the hall. The runt landed in a heap next to

the large urn that Eva was hiding behind. Huffing, the taxidermist struggled to roll over and get up.

Eva and Rovender locked eyes. Unmoving, Rovender mouthed, "Don't move."

Perched on his hoverdisc, Antiquus floated over to the taxidermist and helped him. "You should be ashamed of your actions. Zin was a fine curator for the museum."

The taxidermist squirmed away from Antiquus. "You don't know anything, old Cærulean." He sniffed the air and scuttled toward the urn.

Eva held her breath.

Rovender moved to intercept the taxidermist, but Antiquus reached him first. His voice was severe. "What I know is that you have succumbed to the wrong power. So you best huddle under his shadow, where you are safe . . . for now."

The taxidermist stopped and looked up to see the glaring faces of the other Cærulean leaders surrounding him. He quickly wriggled past them, back to his master.

Eva exhaled a small sigh of relief.

"That was too close," Rovender whispered to her.

"And now, Your Majesty . . ." Loroc's booming voice called their attention once more. He aimed the taxidermist's remote at the cell, and the transparent walls became gelatin-like. Loroc reached into the cell and pulled out Zin's paralyzed body. "The feast begins." He opened his mouth wide. There was a rending sound as ligaments in Loroc's jaw stretched, bringing to mind the holograms Eva had seen of snakes preparing to eat a bird's egg whole. Slowly and steadily he devoured Zin right in front of Queen Ojo.

Eva buried her head in her hands to muffle her sobs. Over her own weeping, she could hear gasps of horror erupt from the crowd. Sickened, Eva peered one last time from behind the urn and watched Zin disappear down Loroc's maw.

Loroc's mass trembled and enlarged as he absorbed his brother's body. His stubby tubular arms stretched into tapering tentacles. A fourth pair of slit eyes appeared on his face. The eyes opened, and he spoke. His voice now resonated as a chorus of four. "I can see all pasts; I foretell all futures. I am strength, all-knowing, and all-powerful. I, the Prime Master, am complete at last!" He tossed Queen Ojo into Zin's abandoned cell. Using the remote, he solidified the walls. Ojo pounded on the glass and yelled, but to no avail.

Loroc's giant form spun to face the gathered

representatives. "The citizens of Orbona will soon have no need for you. But I still do." He floated over and lifted up the fallen Mirthian leader. Once more Loroc opened his mouth wide and began to consume the unconscious leader.

The crowd huddled together in the back of the hall, near the urn that Eva hid behind. One of the representatives shrieked and pointed to the Mirthian, who had regained consciousness just in time to disappear down Loroc's gullet.

Loroc's body rippled from consuming his prey. "Once I ingest each and every one of you, I will contain all your collected knowledge and wisdom. We shall become one. I will be the perfect ruler for this world. Queen Ojo will become the key attraction of a new exhibit in *my* royal museum: Bygone Relics Who Lacked True Power. The future generations shall wonder how it is that any of you survived this long." He was moving to snatch up his next victim when the taxidermist approached. The runty creature whispered and pointed at the urn in the back of the hall. Loroc smiled and floated to the center of the room.

"This does not look good, Eva," Rovender whispered to her. "I am going to create a diversion, and you try to make a run for it."

"That will not work." Antiquus's voice was calm. "Wait and see what transpires."

Eva's heart was pounding as she scanned the room for a way out. The banquet hall doors were shut, with two pillar guards just on the other side, and the shattered hole in the skylight was too high up to reach.

"Failed leaders, I am told that my brother may not be the only traitor among us." Loroc glanced over in Eva's direction. She shrank back behind the urn. "Today you will each leave this life so that you may join me as one glorious entity, to rule over all. In doing so the residents of your respective communities will go on living in bliss with the knowledge that I am watching over them." Loroc's face darkened. "However, should I learn you are harboring humans, then I shall eradicate your tribe, leaving nothing behind. I am told that one of you reeks of the human species, so I give you all this one opportunity to confess your crime. If you do so, I will consider sparing your village."

Not a word was spoken as Loroc drifted around the room inspecting each representative. As he made his way toward Eva, still in her hiding place, Rovender went to step out. But a wooden cane stopped him.

"You watch what he does and then you find a way out of here, Son. Take good care of my granddaughter," Antiquus whispered. Before Rovender could say a word, the Cærulean elder floated out to the center of the room.

*No!* Eva wriggled out of her hiding spot and slipped next to Rovender. She waited for him to push her back behind the vase, but he made no move to do so. Even with her hood concealing her face, Eva could see Rovender breathing fast, just like she was, in fear and anticipation. She slid her small hand into his.

"Well, I confess, I am a bit surprised by this." Loroc hovered close to Antiquus.

"You should not be," Antiquus replied. "As you have expressed to everyone present, you are all-seeing. Your powers of cognizance should already know the answer to the question you have posed. You should have known that the one who interacted with the hu-mans was me . . . and it was you."

A hushed murmur moved among the huddled representatives.

Loroc chuckled. "Your talk will get you only so far, old one. My experience with the humans gained me the knowledge to defeat them and save this city . . . and your peasant village."

"Perhaps that is part of the truth, Loroc. Or perhaps there is more. Maybe you should tell us your whole truth. What is it that you are concealing? What would possess you to destroy your family?"

"Like you, they were weak where I am strong," Loroc replied.

"If your own family is of no value to you, why should we believe that the citizens of Orbona will be? Can you tell us that?"

"I have told you enough! Now you tell me where the humans are hiding. Tell me willingly, or I will extract it from you." His tentacles slithered around Antiquus, curling over his hoverdisc.

"If that is what you must do. Regardless, I shall walk on through the memories of those still with us long after you consume me."

"You are not worthy of my consuming. The only one who shall be remembered here is Loroc, the Prime Master." He wrapped his tentacles more tightly around Antiquus, lifting him from his seat.

"NO!" Rovender cried. But it was too late.

The tentacles coiled over Antiquus's arms and into his mouth, constricting him. A pair of Loroc's eyes began to glow, and he recited in Darius's voice:

*"Tradition is upheld in our forest home.*
*My son lost, he left, he returned*
*With a human girl, a child of his own.*
*She came to stay, they came to speak*
*In Faunas."*

"Eva Nine and the humans are there," Loroc hissed. He hurled Antiquus down to the tiled floor. The elder's lifeless body lay unmoving. "Fetch my Omnipod, runt," Loroc said to the taxidermist. "Today we obliterate Faunas from all beamguides."

"No. Don't do this," Rovender pleaded, and rushed to his father's side.

"Back down, Cærulean, or you'll be next!" Loroc barked.

Rovender moved to stop him, but Eva stepped out into the open. Her hood was still pulled over her head, concealing her identity.

"What's this? We have another confession? Good," said Loroc. "You all see that I am not one to issue false threats." He pointed at Eva. "What village are you from? Show yourself."

All the representatives turned to look at Eva. Queen Ojo watched from her cell.

"Don't do this," Rovender said.

"I am speaking to you." Loroc was already losing his patience. "Answer, or I will smite your village."

"You already have." Eva pulled her hood down. Her long white hair spilled out over her shoulders. With her ears now uncovered, she heard a distinct whine from outside.

The gathering cried out and withdrew from Eva as she walked toward Loroc. His many eyes blinked in surprise for a second. Then a fire ignited within them. "Eva Nine. Today's victory just became all the more grand. I no longer have to hunt you down and exterminate you."

"You may not have to," Eva glanced up. "But then again, the day is not over yet."

The whining grew louder as Redimus zoomed in on his glider. He rocketed through the hole in the skylight into the banquet hall. He swooped down toward Eva. Rovender seized Eva by the waist and hoisted her onto the glider. "Go! Get her out of here!" he shouted to Redimus. The glider shot up and circled out of Loroc's reach.

"Kill them!" Loroc aimed the pillar guard remote at them. The guards burst through the doors and swiped at the glider. Redimus dodged their blows with ease and headed back toward the hole in the skylight.

"No," Eva shouted. "We have to get Rovender!"

"We cannot," Redimus cried over his shoulder. "It iz too dangerouz."

"It isn't! Give me the boomrod! I can cover us," Eva cried.

"I am zorry, Eva Nine." Redimus flew at full speed toward the hole. "I promized him I would protect you, no matter what."

"NO!" Eva looked back down to the crowd below. She caught a glimpse of Rovender before the glider escaped. He was smiling and mouthing the word . . .

"Good-bye."

I hate you! I HATE YOU!" Eva punched Redimus's hairy back as they soared over the desolation of Solas. "How could you leave them all behind to die?"

"I have fulfilled my promize." He kept a steady course south and west along the shore of Lake Concors, toward Lacus. Behind them a thunderous sound reverberated over the city.

Eva looked over her shoulder back toward Solas. On the horizon the sky was filled with warships heading in their direction.

"He really wantz you dead. Hold on tight," Redimus said.

Eva felt her stomach plunge as the glider dropped down in altitude, close to the shoreline.

The engine screamed as it accelerated at top speed, zooming toward Lacus.

"These aren't for us. They're heading to Faunas!" Eva yelled over the sound of the warship's engines. "We have to do something." She suddenly remembered her plan and activated the Omnipod. "Hailey! Hailey, it's me, Eva."

Hailey's head appeared over the Omnipod's central eye. "Hey, how did the talk go with—"

"Never mind! Please get to Faunas as fast as you can. Loroc has ordered an attack because he thinks the humans are there. Please hurry!"

"We're—" Hailey started, but Eva never heard the rest. The spray of SHOCdarts that erupted from the warship peppered the wings of the glider, sending it spiraling out of control. Eva was thrown from her seat and disappeared with a splash under the gray waves of Lake Concors.

Eva Nine was dying. The tiny lights of Cadmus Pryde's Omnipod, still strapped around her wrist, blinked in time with the beat of her heart. She lay on the sandy shore as waves lapped at her feet. Slowly she lifted her head and opened her glassy eyes. Round stones, polished from eons of tumbling in the surf, covered the shore. Eva's eyes focused on a nearby stone. Its smooth texture and swirl of earthen colors reminded her of the model planets she had seen on the orrery in Ojo's bed-chamber. *So many little worlds within one world.* She sensed a familiar presence and then felt a gentle nudge. Eva rolled over.

*I protect. You.*

"Otto." Tears streamed out of Eva's eyes. "What are you doing here?"

*I follow. You. I protect. You.*

"I don't know if anyone can protect me," Eva said.

*Do not. Hurt.*

From behind Otto several more water bears joined him. Eva recognized one of them as the grizzled leader of the herd. Above, the squadron of warships rumbled west across the sky.

"It's over, Otto." Eva sat up. "I couldn't save Zin. He couldn't stop Loroc. I . . . failed." A shivery chill overtook Eva. It was as if her body could no longer hold warmth within it.

*You. One of us. Herd.* Otto nudged Eva with his large head.

"Thank you." Eva stood on uneasy legs. "But you must go away from me. Anybody who gets too close to me dies."

*You. Are. Forest.*

"I'm not the forest. I drank the water, and I can speak to you all, but I'm not one of you. I'm . . . just a girl. A girl who wanted a home and a family." Her mind tried to block out the image of Rovender. "This battle is not the forest's to fight. You must go and hide. Maybe Antiquus was right after all." The thought of Rovender's departed father caused Eva's body to shake uncontrollably.

*You must. Listen. You must. Sing.*

"No. I have to save Rovee." Eva stumbled and fell back onto the sand. "But I don't know how." She held in the sobs that tried to overtake her.

Otto gently lifted Eva up with his beak and sat her upright on the shore. He then raised his head and called out. One by one the other water bears did the same. Soon the entire herd was singing. In the forest Eva could hear other water bears joining in.

*You must. Listen. You must. Sing.*

Eva closed her eyes and allowed the frequency of the forest to speak to her. She could feel the connectivity of each member of the herd. She could even sense the other water bears far beyond, on the other side of the lake. The familiar low hum began, quickly diminishing any other sounds. Eva opened her eyes and stood. "I can't do this, Otto. Every time I try, I hear this loud noise that drowns out everything."

*That is. The song.*

"I can't hear any singing. All I sense is—"

*Listen. Little one. Sing.*

Eva sat down on the shore and closed her eyes one more time. Immediately the hum filled her mind and overcame all senses. Somehow, in the frequency, she could discern Otto's gentle warble.

*Listen. To me.*

Eva concentrated and listened. As before, she could hear that the hum was a chorus, composed of many sounds. She concentrated on each sound and realized they were voices—countless voices speaking out at the same time.

*Listen. To others.*

Otto's voice was similar to others she heard— voices of his herd and other water bears. Then she recognized the cry of the turnfins. Next she picked out the creak of the wandering trees, followed by the chittering of knifejacks, the song of the air-whales, the clicking of sand-snipers, the swish of the spiderfish. Eva heard the voice of moss as it crept over rock, plankton as it wriggled through the sea, and insects as they buzzed through the sky. Then she heard the voice of the rocks themselves, the water . . . the air. Within those voices she heard yet another voice, both ancient and powerful. It called Eva's spirit down through soil, stone, and ore.

As she descended, distant voices of her past echoed through her mind.

*"How does such an insignificant plant survive in a big world?"*

*"Earth is entering a state of planetary hibernation."*

*"The forest is alive. Here it has protected one of its own."*

The memories evaporated as Eva focused all attention on the ancient voice—the overwhelming hum.

The voice of Orbona.

Eva opened her eyes and heard, with clarity, the song the water bears sang. It was in harmony with everything surrounding them, just like the song of the mouls.

*You are our herd.*

*You are their flock.*

*You are his family.*

*You are the forest.*

*You are the earth.*

*We are one.*

Eva's mind was clearer now than ever before. Like a tree, she could feel the vitality of the sunlight coursing through her body. She inhaled the cool mineral air off the lake. As they had done before, these elements soothed her aching heart. Eva opened her bright green eyes and looked at the gathered herd. "We are one, Otto," said Eva, stroking his warm knobby hide. "Together. Safe. Strong."

He nuzzled her and purred. *We will help you. That is what a herd does.*

"Thank you. Thank you all."

Otto let out a long loud hoot of joy. It was answered by a pod of air-whales drifting over the lake. The herd closed in around Eva.

"We shall become one." She repeated Loroc's words. "Loroc sees it all the wrong way. He wants to devour everyone and everything that opposes him. All inhabitants of Orbona will be consumed under his rule. I have to stop him."

*You can stop him. We will help you.*

A groan drew Eva's attention from Otto. Down the shore several water bears were snapping at a large dark figure sprawled out on the sand—a Dorcean.

"Please don't hurt him," Eva said to the water bears, and jogged over to Redimus. "He will not harm our herd." She bent over to inspect him.

"Eva Nine," Redimus wheezed. "You are zafe. Dat

is good." He coughed. Violet blood ran from his nostrils and the corner of his jagged mouth.

"Are you okay? Can you stand?"

With great effort Redimus rolled onto his side and tried to lift himself up. His legs shook and flopped back down. A layer of white sand covered his matted hide.

Eva knelt close. "Redimus. I have to go back to Solas. I have to stop Loroc."

"You are de most determined creature I have ever met," he said, panting.

"We don't have a lot of time. I'm going to ask some of my friends from the forest to help, but we could really use you. Can you do it?"

Redimus winced as he sat up. "Friendz? Your forest friendz? I know where some of your friendz are. And eet iz clozer than de Wandering Forest." He reached out a clawed hand. "Help me up. I'll take you dere."

Eva scooted under his burly arm. With Otto's help she got the Dorcean back on his feet. Redimus pointed out over the lake toward Solas. "If you can, get uz back dere and wheel find your friendz."

Eva gazed out at the city. "What animals could be in Solas? They've all fled."

"Not all."

"The menagerie?" asked Eva.

"Yez, de menagerie."

"Otto, can you carry us across the lake?" Eva scratched the barbels on his chin.

*Yes. We will join you.* Otto thrust his head under Redimus and scooped him up onto his back. Eva climbed up next to him, and the water bear waded into the water.

"Eva Nine, your water bear friendz . . . dey may be eager, but dey are alzo slow. I thought you zaid we need to hurry?"

Otto uncurled his fan-shaped tail from under his belly. With a quick thrust he lurched forward at such a speed that Redimus nearly rolled off his back. The rest of the herd followed. All around, flocks of turnfins called out as they rode on the wind currents above.

Redimus gripped Otto's thick scutes. "I never knew dey could move zo fast."

Eva gave him a wide grin. "Wait until you see them leap."

As they drew close to the city, it was clear that not all the warships had been dispatched to Faunas.

"I zee three of dem, hovering near de palace," said Redimus. "Loroc iz zertainly not taking any chances with you."

Eva squinted her eyes and stared at the waterfront. There was movement between the buildings, but it was hard to tell exactly what it was from this distance. Overhead she heard the call of air-whales.

"They are moving." Redimus pointed at one of the warships drifting out toward the lake. "I think we have been spotted."

Eva closed her eyes and focused on the entire pod of air-whales. *Friends, I need you to fly over us as we enter the city so that no harm may come to my herd. Will you do this?*

The air-whales sang out and floated toward Eva. *Together. Safe. Strong.* Their large shadows fell over the entire herd.

"What is dis, Eva Nine?" Redimus gazed up at the gigantic creatures.

"The warships have an anti-collision warning in their navigational programming." She looked up. The air-whales were in a tight, wedge-shaped formation. It was perfect. "The ships will automatically avoid flying into anything larger than them that comes too close—like a pod of air-whales."

The warship's engines roared as it accelerated toward them.

*Don't move,* Eva told the pod. *The flying machine will turn away from you if you stay on course.*

*Together. Safe. Strong.* As the pod approached the city, the warship veered away. It rumbled out over the lake to circle back. The remaining two warships barreled toward Eva. But they, too, turned away from the pod. The warships continued to circle wide around Otto's herd but were unable to get within firing range because of the pod of air-whales.

"Dere are de humanz machinez waiting for uz," Redimus said. On the high seawall that surrounded the city stood a line of warbots. All weapons were aimed at Eva.

She closed her eyes again. *My herd. Do not be afraid. These machines will attack, but they cannot penetrate your tough armor. Aim for their heads, and they will fall.*

The herd crawled out of the water onto the shores of Solas. Eva and Redimus slid down from Otto's back onto the sandy beach. They stood in line along with the herd facing the army of warbots while the air-whales circled overhead.

A warbot's red laser flickered over Eva. "Physical identification of the human traitor known as Eva Nine is affirmative. You are to come with us immediately. Any deviation from our instructions will result in immobilization."

"My herd," Eva said. "Please help me."

Snapping their fantails onto the sandy ground, the entire herd leaped up with astonishing speed. At this the warbots released a volley of SHOCdarts. At the apex of their jump, the water bears curled themselves into armored cannonballs. They rained down on top of the warbots, crushing most of the army in a single wave. The remaining warbots fired at the water bears, but their darts harmlessly ricocheted off the thick armored carapaces. The water bears struck the legs of the warbots with their tails, toppling them.

"Behind me, now!" Redimus yelled, and jumped in front of Eva as a warbot stormed through the melee toward them.

"Prepare for—"

The warbot did not finish its sentence. A water bear crashed down upon the machine, crushing its metallic body.

"Otto!" Eva crawled out from behind Redimus. Her companion crawled from the wrecked warbot with a visible limp. "Oh no! You're hurt."

*I will live.*

Eva dropped to her hands and knees and crawled

under Otto's giant frame. Blood trickled from the joint where his front leg met his underside. Eva touched the wound, and he flinched. "It looks like you might have been stabbed by a piece of metal from the warbot."

"There iz enough poking partz, thaz for zure." Redimus examined the sparking remains of the warbot.

*Move, little one,* the leader of the herd said.

Eva did as she was told. The leader nudged at Otto with his head until he flipped Otto onto his side. A stream of emerald blood ran across Otto's chest.

"Wait, what are you doing?" Panic rose in Eva's voice.

*Do not fret,* the leader of the herd said. He began licking Otto's wound.

*He will heal me,* Otto said.

With the last of the warbots destroyed, the herd shuffled back to the shore. As with Otto, they tended to their wounded and moved them to the center of a tightly formed circle.

*You must go on, little one,* Otto said. *Rescue your father.*

"Okay. You be careful." Eva kissed Otto's beak. She could feel the exhaustion in him and in many of the water bears, after they had exerted such energy.

"Let dem rezz here. No one will bother dem," said Redimus.

Eva and Redimus scrambled up the beach to the waterfront. She looked back one more time at the herd—her herd. "Thank you," she called out to Otto. The herd began to sing aloud, filling Eva's heart with a flicker of hope. "Okay, Redimus. Show me where the menagerie is."

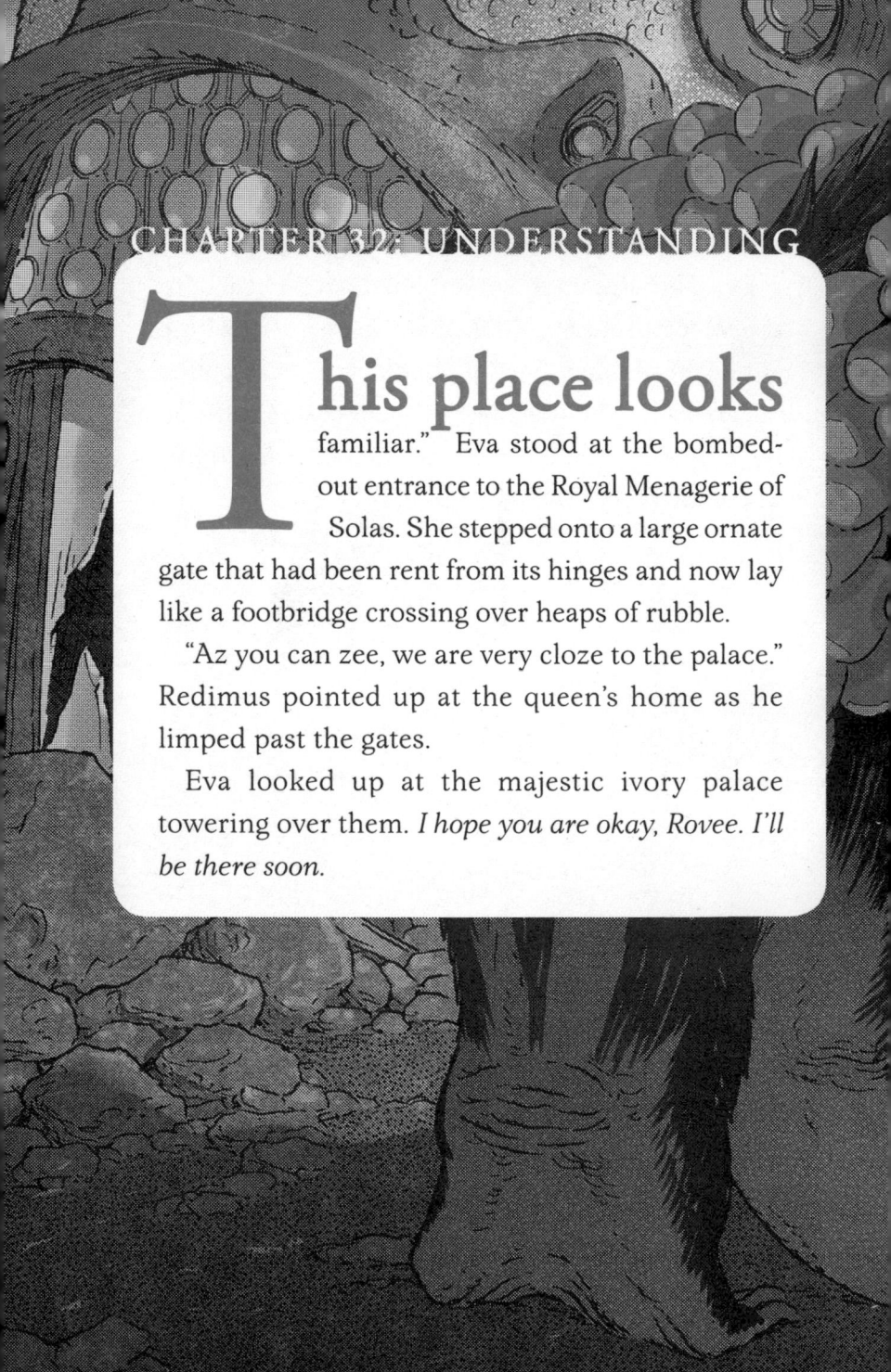

# This place looks

familiar." Eva stood at the bombed-out entrance to the Royal Menagerie of Solas. She stepped onto a large ornate gate that had been rent from its hinges and now lay like a footbridge crossing over heaps of rubble.

"Az you can zee, we are very cloze to the palace." Redimus pointed up at the queen's home as he limped past the gates.

Eva looked up at the majestic ivory palace towering over them. *I hope you are okay, Rovee. I'll be there soon.*

Redimus pointed. "Dat way is de royal gardens, and beyond iz de museum."

Eva hopped off the gate. "That's how I know this. We must have gone past it when Muthr and I were escaping from . . ."

Redimus looked over to see if Eva would finish her thought. "From my brozeel?"

"No. From Ojo," said Eva.

"Sometimez thingz are not always az dey first appear, eh?"

Eva nodded and began down the walking path that circled the menagerie. Ornate enclosures lined the outside of the walkway, while a large round pavilion sat at the center. "I'm not sensing anything alive here, except some turnfins roosting in the central pavilion." Eva sighed. "We've got to hurry. Redimus, you go that way. I'll go the other way, and I'll meet you on the other side. Give a shout if you find anything."

"Wheel do." Redimus hobbled off.

Eva searched through the ruined park, but found only empty open cages and a fallen warbot.

She rounded the scorched trunk of a wandering tree to discover a young water bear, half-buried under its collapsed enclosure.

Eva placed a hand on its plated sides. It was cold to the touch. "I am sorry, little one."

"Eva Nine, come quick!" Redimus called.

Eva scrambled across the menagerie to Redimus. As she drew near him, she sensed the slightest bit of life from another large and familiar creature. An adult sand-sniper lay coiled on the floor of its enclosure. Its bioluminescent organs were dimmed and its color faded.

"Eet is alive." Redimus peered through the glass membrane that contained it. "I zaw eet move."

"Barely." Eva knelt down to get a better look. "I'm sensing more than just this one, though. I sense . . . eggs."

"Probably bezz to leave it be. Even with your zpecial powerz, dey are not to be trifled with."

"Can we break the glass?" With both hands Eva picked up a large chunk of rubble and stepped back from the enclosure.

"Wait!" Redimus gasped. "De air-whalez, de water bearz, dey are peazeful creaturez, Eva Nine. Dis is not like dat—especially when protecting itz young."

"We are running out of time." She flung the rock at the glass.

On impact the sand-sniper snapped to life and reared up to her full height. Like other individuals that Eva had encountered, this one looked like a gigantic praying mantis. She raised both spiked graspers in a threat display and flexed them. The thick glass of the enclosure was cracked but not broken.

"Dat iz one beeg zniper. I don't know how Bezteel nabbed dis." Redimus's mouth was agape as he looked up at it. He caught himself as Eva walked up. "Oh, zorry."

Eva ignored the comment. "It is big. I don't know how I couldn't sense it." She peered around the sniper's pen. It probably hadn't eaten for days.

"Dey can become dormant in dere borrows during de dry zeason."

"It's like she was going into hibernation. That would explain it." Eva watched the sniper through the glass. "You are a mother with eggs, aren't you?"

The sand-sniper's bowl-shaped eyes moved independently of each other. Her long corded antennae quivered while her clawed mouthparts clicked in cadence.

"What iz eet zaying?" asked Redimus.

"Nothing," Eva replied. "She's just clicking with her mouth." Eva moved near the enclosure. The sniper extended her paddle-shaped antennae and flashed her bioluminescent lights. *Go away. Go away. Go away.*

"We will not hurt you." Eva placed her palm on

the fractured glass. "Are your eggs still good?"

The lights flashed in a new pattern. *I will strike.
I am strong. I will strike. I am strong.*

Eva closed her eyes. With her ability she focused
on the frequency of the sand-sniper. "You and I are
alike. We are both of this earth," she whispered.

*You are the soil. You grow to a hunter. Then you
become prey,* said the sniper. *Then you become soil.*

"I have been trapped in this place too. Captured."

*I will strike you and kill you and eat you alive.*

"You need to eat because you have to protect
your nymphs."

*My strength and my might and my cunning will
prevail.*

"Not in this cage. You will die in here, as will
your offspring."

The sniper did not reply.

"I can set you free. But I need your help in return."

*You will trick me and kill me and eat me alive.*

"I would do none of these things. But time is of
the essence."

*What of me? What of my nymphs? What of our
freedom?*

"The Dorcean will see that your eggs are hidden
someplace safe. Tell me where you want them to
go, and I will instruct him."

*To the sand. To the desert. To the edge of this land.*

"That we can do. You will have to come with me. I need your protection."

*He will trick. He will slaughter. He will eat my young.*

"Not this Dorcean. His promise is his bond."

Eva opened her eyes. The sand-sniper raised herself higher still to reveal a cluster of eggs held tight by the secondary legs under her segmented abdomen.

"Well?" Redimus asked.

Eva lifted up the large rock and hurled it at the glass again. The entire front of the enclosure shattered down in great shards.

The gigantic sniper crawled from her enclosure, clicking loudly.

"Dey are a whole lot bigger when dey are aboveground." Redimus backed away from the sniper. "I hope you know what you are doing, Eva Nine."

"He will carry your eggs." Eva pointed to Redimus. "And he will protect them."

The sniper's lights flashed. *Eat. Eat. Eat.* She shot off across the grounds of the menagerie.

"Sheesa!" said Eva, and she gave chase. Redimus followed.

They found the sniper at the water bear's pen. She had yanked the carcass from the rubble and was now devouring it.

"I'm glad Otto is not here. I wouldn't want him to see this." Eva turned away.

"Eet has died, Eva Nine. She needz to live. Zo it goez." Redimus shrugged. "Truzz me, your water bear herd understands thiz."

The sniper finished consuming her meal and crawled back. Circling Eva and Redimus once, she released her clutch of eggs and carefully laid them on the walkway.

"Take these to the southern edge of the pollen fields and bury them." Eva watched Redimus lift the mass of eggs and drape them over his wide shoulders. They looked like a gigantic cluster of orange grapes. Inside each egg, bubble-eyed nymphs wriggled about.

"Are you zure about dis? Dese are a lot of eggz. Doez thiz world need dis many zand-sniperz?"

"Just promise you'll do this."

"Eef dis helpz rectify my pazt actionz wiz you . . ."

With her fingers Eva gestured, *Just a little bit.*

"Very well. I promize." Redimus gave a nod. "Good luck."

"Thank you," said Eva. She watched him limp

down the rubble-strewn alley. The Dorcean looked back at her one last time before turning the corner and disappearing.

The air-whales called from their circling overhead. They had remained near the palace, thus preventing the warships from entering the airspace. *Just a little longer, my friends,* Eva said to them.

The sand-sniper watched both the whales and Eva with independent rotating eyes. Eva pointed to the shattered domed skylight in the palace where the royal banquet hall was located. "See that opening? I need you to meet me there. Can you crawl up to it?"

*I can crawl. I am strong.*

Eva approached the sniper. Spikes, some as long as half a meter, projected from the graspers. Tentatively and carefully Eva stroked one of the spikes. "If you help me, I promise your freedom."

The sand-sniper touched the top of Eva's head with one antenna.

*I do not do because you ask. I do because you met my hive. You met my queen.*

"I did?" Eva wondered about the snipers out by the ancient ruins.

*Since she did not consume you, I will not consume you.*

"I understand," said Eva, and backed away from the spike graspers. "At least you're honest." She peered up at Queen Ojo's tower high overhead. "I have to go now. I need to make a stop before we rendezvous. Wait for my call, and I will meet you inside."

*You will call. I will wait. I may die, but my nymphs will live.* The sniper clicked loudly and crawled toward the palace.

Eva ran across the grounds of the menagerie into the round pavilion where she had sensed the turnfins. For the most part the ornate structure had remained undamaged, despite the destruction that surrounded it. The circular skylight was missing, allowing a lone beam of sunlight to shine down into the room. The many cages that had once held birds of every sort were now empty and abandoned. Perched on a circular bench in the center of the pavilion was a clacking gaggle of turnfins and other birds. Eva held her arms out. "I wish I could fly."

As they had done once before, the turnfins flapped their wings and landed on Eva. In unison they lifted her up off the ground. They flew through the open skylight of the pavilion and up to the alcove of Queen Ojo's quarters.

This is it." Eva pointed to her destination. The turn-fins released her, and she landed on her feet on the balcony.

"Wait for me, my flock." She pushed open the doors to the queen's bedchambers. Eva stood at the top of the stairs, her eyes roving around the empty room. "I need your help. Will you come?"

Like a burst of color the captive flock of treowes flew up from their perches and circled around Eva.

*We sing the prettiest song. We sing the purest song.*

*I need you to sing one special song for me,* Eva thought to them.

"One special song for me," they repeated aloud in unison.

"Thank you, my beautiful friends. Let us go." Eva walked back out onto the balcony and climbed up onto the ledge. To the west she saw the sun hanging low in the cloudy sky. Around her the growing flock of birds competed against the gusty wind to stay close. *We fly with you,* they sang. *We fly for you.*

Eva looked down at the skylight roof to the royal banquet hall. It was countless stories below. *I ran and ran from Loroc and now I run to him,* she thought. *Was this my fate after all?* She removed her tattered poncho and let it drift from her hands. It danced away in the wind. *My ending has yet to arrive.* Eva ran her fingers over Rovender's cord, still wrapped around her waist. "Rovee, you are my WondLa," she whispered.

Eva leaped off the balcony. The flock of birds caught her in midair, and together they dove straight toward the hole in the domed skylight below.


Eva alighted on the tile floor of the banquet hall, carried by the combined flock of turnfins and treowes. *Where is Loroc? Where are the leaders? Where is Rovee?*

Cylindrical specimen cells from the taxidermist's

lab now lined the perimeter of the room. Eva suspected that each cell contained a representative of the various Orbonian tribes. The snouted head of the taxidermist poked out from behind one of the cells. Through thick-lensed goggles his beady eyes scanned the hall and he pulled a remote out from a pouch on his utility belt.

"You!" he said in his nasal tone. "You came back? Perhaps you are not as smart as the Prime Master believes."

"I've outsmarted you both before. I'm sure I can do it again." Eva walked between the cells. Though the cell walls were coated in condensation, she could see movement. The prisoners inside were still alive.

"Don't bet on it. Master is much more powerful than the queen and now is as clever as his brother was." The taxidermist stayed put but kept his goggled eyes on Eva.

"He can't be that smart if he has you working for him," said Eva.

"I can't wait to capture you, little dirt-burrower," the taxidermist said with a sneer. "Once you're paralyzed, I am going to enjoy watching your skin dissolve and seeing what it is that makes you so self-assured."

"I have to admit that Loroc did find one thing in you." Eva kept moving through the rows of cells. "It takes a certain deplorable individual to betray someone like Zin."

"Don't be so quick to judge. You betrayed him too."

Eva stopped. "That is not true."

The taxidermist snickered.

"But that doesn't matter now," Eva continued. "Zin and I came to understand and respect each other. A trait you obviously do not have."

The taxidermist clucked in condescension. "You don't get it. It's all about survival, dirt-burrower. You must—"

"Do what you have to in order to survive?" Eva finished his sentence.

"Exactly," the taxidermist said.

"I wonder, how will you survive, then, after this journey ends for you?" Eva kept walking around the cells. "Without your remotes and chemicals, you will be at a severe disadvantage."

"What gibberish are you talking with 'this journey'?" the taxidermist asked.

"Oh, I may not be the one who will end your life. In fact, I have no desire to do so. But your list of enemies is long. It grows every time you kill another specimen."

"These specimens don't care," the taxidermist said with a snort. "They're just animals."

"Every specimen has a family—a family that loves them and mourns the end of their life. Eventually your end will come," said Eva.

"As will yours, dirt-burrower." The taxidermist gnashed his pointed teeth.

"It will," Eva responded. "But I am at peace with the denizens of Orbona. The spirits of the deceased will welcome me on my next journey. How will they receive you?" Eva stepped out in front of the row of cells. Without so much as a chirp or squawk, the turnfins, treowes, and other birds fluttered in from outside and alighted on the cupolaed tops of the cells. There were more birds now present than before, as if a call for aid had gone out. Indeed one had, for Eva had been silently calling the birds with her abilities the entire time. All eyes of the flock were fixed on the taxidermist.

"You . . . you're tricking me!" the taxidermist squealed. He looked up at all the birds watching him. "This is some trick! I know it!"

"Is it?" Eva walked right up to the runty creature and knelt down in front of him. "Look within yourself. Count the souls you've paralyzed and embalmed. Not for food. Not for sustenance or shelter. I'm not even sure you did it for knowledge or understanding. And now you plan to do the same to the leaders of your very own city?"

"That is correct. Every representative." Loroc's monstrous tentacled mass slid into the banquet hall, bringing to mind holograms Eva had seen of an octopus crawling across the ocean floor. Behind him the two towering pillar guards lumbered into the room. "I put them all here for the time being so I could personally oversee the battle at Faunas and your own termination. I should have known your audacious behavior would bring you right back to me."

"Yes, you should have known, Prime Master." Eva felt the sand-sniper's presence nearby. *I have to do this at just the right time*, she thought.

"He is THE Prime Master, the ultimate ruler, as you'll soon see." The taxidermist scurried behind Loroc.

Eva faced them both. "We'll see if your leader will protect you on your next journey, taxidermist," she said. "If you ask me, anyone who turns on his own family is not one to be trusted."

"No one asked you." Loroc aimed the pillar guard remote at her. "Get her," he said in his chorus of voices. The guards stormed toward Eva.

Eva slipped quickly away from the pair of behemoths toward the hole in the skylight of the hall. One of the guards lashed out with a clawed arm to strike her. It missed and smashed one of the taxidermist's cells. The limp body of the Halcyonus leader fell out and onto the floor. Eva paused and glanced back, wondering if the leader was alive or dead. In a split second she looked up to see the hand of the other pillar guard coming at her. She leaped out of the way, but its sickle claw came down on her foot. Eva howled in pain and curled up behind a cell. "I need your help now," she whispered.

From outside, the mother sand-sniper crawled in through the hole in the skylight. Her immense length moved surprisingly fast by means of numerous legs. Both pillar guards backed away from the sniper, which was as long as they were tall.

"What is this thing doing in here?" Loroc ordered the pillar guards, "Kill it!"

The sniper coiled around Eva, knocking cells aside in the process.

"I can't stand." Eva spoke to the sniper. "I've hurt my ankle."

*Trust me. Trust me. Trust me*, the sniper said to Eva.

"I trust you," said Eva.

*Look through my eyes.*

"See what I see," Eva replied.

*Do as I do.* They spoke in unison.

The sand-sniper reared up and rose to her full height. In her secondary legs that had once held its clutch of eggs close, she now held Eva. Eva saw through the sniper's eyes—the heat signature of the prisoners in the cells, the birds flying around the room, the electric circulation of the pillar guards. She saw Loroc as a gigantic dark entity with layers of light twinkling inside him, like nesting dolls.

Loroc gasped. "How? How is that possible?"

The Eva-sniper swiped the legs of one of the pillar guards. It toppled over, nearly taking the second guard down with it. Many of the floating prison cells collided in the guard's wake.

"Kill them!" Loroc pointed the pillar guard remote at the Eva-sniper.

Eva spoke to the mother sniper. "We don't want to kill the guards. They are under his control. We just need to get them out of here."

*We will cripple but not kill. We will cripple but not eat.*

The Eva-sniper shot around and rose up behind

the guard who was still standing. At lightning speed it snapped its graspers at the guard's back, striking him like a hammer. The blow sent the guard crashing down toward Loroc, who barely averted the collision. The first pillar guard stood and wrapped its hooked arms around the Eva-sniper's segmented body. But the Eva-sniper doubled over, slid right through the guard's tight grasp, and crawled under its legs. She seized the guard around the waist and flung it backward. The pillar guard crashed through the doorway and landed in the hallway beyond.

"Sheesa! I can't believe how strong and fast you are," Eva said. It was then that the second pillar guard struck the sand-sniper on her back, knocking Eva free from its grasp. Eva crawled under the cells, now collected at one end of the room. Like an enormous dark octopus, Loroc slithered past the sand-sniper and rushed toward Eva.

Holding on to a nearby cell for support, Eva scrabbled up to her feet and called the birds. Above, a riot of turnfins and other birds swooped down onto Loroc.

"Not this time, little nymph." He swatted the flock away. "These birds won't save you!"

On one foot Eva hopped out in front of the specimen cells. A turnfin landed on her shoulder. In its beak it held the pillar guard remote that it had swiped from Loroc during the fray. The turnfin dropped the remote into Eva's hands. She aimed the remote at Loroc. "Guards, destroy him."

Both pillar guards left the mother sniper and charged, attacking at once. Loroc wrapped tentacles around their clawed hands and grappled with them to keep them immobilized.

Eva gave the remote to the turnfin, and it flew off with it in its beak. She hopped around the room, making her way past the clash of Loroc and the giant guards, and came to the sand-sniper lying coiled on the floor. Eva ran her hands over the spiked carapace and realized the sniper had been stunned from the blow of the pillar guard. A nearby movement caught Eva's eye. The taxidermist was worming his way past the melee toward the opened doorway of the banquet hall.

Ignoring the fiery pain of her twisted ankle, Eva bolted to intercept him. She arrived at the battered doorway, blocking his escape.

"Give me that." She pointed to the cell remote in the taxidermist's hand.

"Forget it, dirt-burrower. I'd rather—"

As fast as the knifejack, Eva punched the taxidermist in the snout, sending the goggles flying from his head. The runt howled in pain and fell onto his back. Eva straddled him and continued to pummel his face. Every bit of anger, pain, and fear that he had caused her and her friends fueled blow after blow. Breathing hard, she paused and looked at her shaking hands, now covered in his ochre-colored blood. She yanked the remote out of his belt and left him lying on the tiled floor.

Eva crouched down and glanced at the buttons on the remote while the battle raged on between Loroc and the guards. There was a gruesome rending sound as Loroc ripped the arms from one of the guards. Loroc spun around and threw the giant arms at Eva. She ducked away from the enormous projectiles and hid behind a cell. The arms crashed through the doorway and landed out in the hall, where they wriggled about, mindless. Nearby, on the floor, the taxidermist crawled about, blindly searching for his goggles. Back in the banquet hall the amputee guard fell to the floor like a dead tree falling in the forest.

Eva blocked out the sadness that she felt for the felled guard. "I'm running out of time. What button do I press?" She aimed the remote at the nearest cell. Wincing, she pressed a button with a round circle printed on it. The condensation that normally coated the glass walls of all the cells evaporated. Inside a nearby cell was Queen Ojo. The queen placed a hand on the cell wall. Excited, Eva pressed another button, causing the paralyzation rod to rise up inside everyone's cell. "Oh no." Eva gulped.

"Very good!" Loroc wrapped his tentacles tight around the legs of the second pillar guard and pulled. In a shower of sparks and plasma the guard was torn in half vertically by Loroc's incredible strength. He dropped both pieces to the floor and came down upon Eva, seizing her with a tentacle. "Now let me finish what you've so kindly started for me." He reached for the taxidermist's remote. The sand-sniper struck the tentacle that held Eva, severing it in one stroke. Loroc roared in fury.

Eva fell to the ground and threw the remote across the banquet hall, away from Loroc. A turnfin scooped it up and carried it away. Eva looked up to see Loroc face off with the sand-sniper. The two circled the hall, sizing each other up. Even though the mother sniper was much larger, Eva knew that Loroc would kill her. It was obvious he was just too strong.

"Stand down." Eva slowly rose to her feet. The

piercing agony of her ankle gave way to a numb throbbing pain. She could feel her foot swelling up in her sneakboot. The sand-sniper rotated one of its eyes back to Eva while keeping the other on Loroc. "You've done enough," Eva said. "This is my fight. Go be with your nymphs."

In a flash the sniper shot through the doorway of the banquet hall. She paused, looking down at the taxidermist who was still crawling about on the floor. The sniper seized him with her graspers and bolted down the hallway and out of the palace.

Before Eva could turn back to face Loroc, more tentacles wrapped around her, pinning her arms to her body.

"How ridiculously noble you are, sending your pet monster away so that you may fight your own fight." Loroc floated into the center of the banquet hall. Inside all of the cells the leaders watched helplessly. "I don't know what all your gallantry is about, nymph," Loroc said. "I told you before that I do not fall by your hand."

"And Arius told me that you had a family that once loved you," Eva replied. "Don't you realize the pain you've caused them?"

"Their pain is gone. My path is chosen. It is a path of no remorse. It is my destiny, my fate."

Eva could feel anxiety worming within her as Loroc's grip tightened.

He continued speaking. "You are working against fate. A fate that holds your eventual demise."

"My end will come in time," Eva said, "as will yours."

"Oh, I don't know about that. I shall live forever. Immortal."

"You are lying." Eva struggled against his grip, but this only caused him to constrict her body more tightly. She glanced at Antiquus's body, unmoving on the floor near the cells. She tore her eyes from the sight and pushed away the tears that tried to come. *Now I have to be strong. I have to focus.* She thought about how Antiquus had upset Loroc with just words.

"Lie? Oh, I don't lie," Loroc replied in his many voices. "The truth is far more powerful. And the truth is, you are about to join your friend Zin." He raised Eva up over his open mouth.

Eva's gaze swept across the room, looking at the scared faces of the imprisoned leaders. Scanning each cell, her eyes finally met with a familiar pair of indigo eyes. On backward-bending legs, Rovender Kitt stood in his cell. He pounded on the walls and shouted loudly, but the thick glass of the cell muffled his protests. Eva smiled at Rovender and turned back to Loroc.

Before Loroc could drop Eva into his maw, the entire flock of tiny treowes fluttered around his face, dousing him in their fine glimmering dust. While he blinked the dust away from his many eyes, the treowes zoomed in through the cloud and alighted on his tongue. "What is this?" he mumbled through a mouthful of birds.

"It is time you speak your truth," Eva said. "Zin, are you in there?"

One of the treowes perched in Loroc's mouth spoke. "I am. At last I have reunited with both my sisters."

Loroc blinked at hearing his brother's words come from his own mouth.

"Zin, I am sorry I could not save you," Eva said.

"You did save me, Eva Nine," the treowe said. "I now understand that of all the wondrous occurrences in the universe, nothing compares to the bond of a family and a home. The feeling of being wanted, appreciated, and forgiven."

"LIES!" Loroc growled. The treowes in his mouth ruffled their feathers but clung to his tongue and remained at their roost. Loroc glared at Eva with all four pairs of eyes.

"The truth-birds do not lie, and you know it," Eva said. "Arius, isn't that so?"

A second treowe spoke out. "This feast shall soon come to an end. Soon there shall be a reunion."

"A reunion of your family?" Eva asked.

The bird spoke in Arius's voice. "Yes, for even the most wicked has a family that loves them. But only if the wicked confesses their truth. Then love and compassion will bind that family."

Loroc reached toward his mouth to yank the birds out.

A third treowe spoke as Darius. "We shall journey on together now as family, but the memory of our wicked brother will be struck from our minds and hearts."

"I will miss you all," Eva said. "Your kindness and guidance will not be forgotten. Everyone present will remember your deeds for many generations to come. You shall be celebrated. You will become immortal."

"They cannot speak," Loroc roared. "They are gone!" The treowes fluttered from his mouth.

"They speak," Eva said. "Your siblings will never be gone. There is much you may consume, Loroc, but you cannot devour the memory of them."

"I will devour them over and over again if I

have to." Loroc put several of his tentacles into his mouth and began to eat. "They will be forgotten, and my great strength and power shall endure!" He shoved more tentacles into his maw.

"Thank you for re-establishing life here, Zin!" Eva spoke loudly and clearly. "Thank you, Arius, for guiding us all!"

"SILENCE!" Loroc flung Eva across the room. She was caught in the air by several turnfins and laid on the ground next to the cells.

Along with the captive representatives, Eva watched as Loroc's writhing body was drawn into his enormous mouth. Soon his whole form was wrung tight, like a wet towel being twisted at either end. As this happened, he began to glow more and more brightly.

With her hands Eva shielded her eyes from the piercing white light that now emanated out of Loroc. In its brilliant center she saw a tiny writhing shape. It appeared as the symbol of infinity before it extinguished completely.

The turnfin holding the taxidermist's remote landed on Eva's shoulders and dropped it into her hands. Eva approached Queen Ojo's cell with the remote. The queen pointed to the proper buttons, and Eva released the entire gathering of captured representatives from their confinements.

Rovender rushed up and hugged her tight. "Eva, my Eva! You are okay!"

"So are you!" She squeezed him back.

"I don't understand." Rovender looked at the colorful treowes that fluttered around the room. "How was it that the truth-birds could work on Loroc? Soth said he was too powerful."

Eva smiled. "Soth was right."

Rovender turned his head slightly and gave Eva a puzzled look. Behind him Queen Ojo approached, followed by all the representatives. The crowd huddled close to hear Eva.

"The treowes had no effect on Loroc at all," she said. "Those were my words, my truths, coming from their mouths." She looked up at Ojo and recited, "'In the end all one is left with is the truth.'"

Queen Ojo closed her eyes and bowed her head to Eva. "Much gratitude."

All the leaders of Orbona bowed their heads in unison and spoke. "Much gratitude."

Eva embraced Rovender at the center of the gathering.

"Rovender of the Kitt clan of Faunas," a Cærulean leader from another tribe spoke in a soft tone. In the leader's thick arms he held the limp body of

Antiquus. Rovender and Eva rushed to him.

"Father." Rovender brushed his hands over Antiquus's aged face, closing the older Cærulean's eyelids. He gripped his father's limp hand and held it tight.

"Your father was proud of you," the Cærulean leader spoke softly. "He told me earlier today that he was certain peace would arrive because your heart saw no difference in your love of the hu-man, Eva Nine, and your own kind."

Tears trickled from Rovender's eyes. Eva kept her arms wrapped around him.

"He said all of Orbona could learn from you." The Cærulean leader handed Antiquus's body to Rovender.

"May Antiquus's spirit walk on within all of us," said Queen Ojo.

The light of the setting sun cast a golden glow over the entire banquet hall. Outside the palace, the pod of air-whales drifted away, but their song carried out across the landscape. As it traveled, other voices joined in celebrating another day of life on planet Orbona.

## CHAPTER 34: WONDLA

Within several days' time the war-ravaged streets of Solas were transformed into streets full of festivities and celebration. The city became a place of newfound happiness and hope. Around the royal palace large colorful tents were erected, each filled with amazing and exotic foods from all corners of the world. Aliens and humans alike shared in many meals and much merriment. They shared in the memories of those gone. Around these meals, stories were recounted of the monstrous Loroc and the one girl courageous enough to save all of the inhabitants of Orbona.

Hailey and Huxley arrived from Faunas with a ship filled with humans, Halcyonus, and Cæruleans. Hailey had received Eva's message in time and had been able to thwart Loroc's warbot invasion of Faunas. They'd even enlisted the help of Eva's pillar guard.

The battle was over. Peace had arrived on Orbona.

Eva Nine stood on the shore of Lake Concors while the breeze from the water danced with her white braids. Listening to the waves lap at the shore, she gazed out at the rebuilt towers of Lacus. Everywhere, humans and aliens were working together to mend what had been broken. A new tower was even being erected right off the shore to house the new human inhabitants from New Attica.

Eva's eyes followed a flock of turnfins calling to one another as they fished over the lake in the fiery light of a setting sun. A long-lost poem drifted into her thoughts,

> "O'er the glad waters of the dark blue sea,
> Our thoughts as boundless, and our souls
>   as free.
> As far as the breeze can bear, the billows
>   foam,
> Survey our empire, and behold our home!"

Eva remembered arriving at this great lake many months ago. It seemed like years to her now. She remembered how excited she'd been to explore the Halcyonus village. She remembered the hope of finding other humans like her. She remembered Muthr.

"There you are." Hailey's sneakboots crunched on the gravelly shore of the lake. "Rovender said you might be here."

Eva smiled at Hailey, causing the sunburn on her cheeks to sting.

"Are you okay?" He bent down and grabbed a stone. "You're not at dinner."

"I'll be there soon. I was just thinking."

Hailey skimmed the stone across the water's surface. "Hard to believe it, huh? Humans and

Halcyonus living together." He grabbed a couple more stones from the shore.

"It does almost feel like a dream. I still keep waiting for someone to somehow take it all away." Eva watched Hailey skim more stones.

"Naw." He threw his last one. "People are settling down everywhere—Solas, Faunas, up north."

"That's good." Eva smiled.

Hailey clasped her hand. "Eva . . . I feel the need to continue searching for more humans. I think there may be more reboots out there."

"You're leaving?"

Hailey looked down and nodded. "Tomorrow."

Eva turned back to the water.

"Come with me," said Hailey.

Eva shook her head. "I can't. I need to be with Rovee."

"I understand." Hailey put his hands in his pockets.

They both watched the ripples on the lake dance in the orange light of the sun.

"But, you know, you may be right." Eva dug something out of her pocket. She placed a small glass cube in Hailey's palm.

He held it up to his eye. "Is this some sort of good luck charm?"

Eva laughed. "You could call it that. Tomorrow hold it up in the sunlight, and a map will project from it. A map of all the known territories that the Royal Beamguide crew has mapped."

"A beamguide." Hailey turned it over in his fingers.

"One that has been marked with every known HRP Sanctuary that the crew has come across."

"Are there more?" Hailey held it up toward the diminishing rays of the sun.

"A lot more."

"Rocket," he said in awe.

"Whatcha got there?" Van Turner crunched along the shore, followed by Huxley.

"A beamguide." Hailey presented it to his grandfather.

"Oh, good!" Huxley plucked the guide up. "We could really use one of these." His severed arm had almost completely regenerated, though it was much paler in comparison to the rest of his bluish-gray complexion.

"This one is special." Hailey looked over at Eva. "It has the locations of all the known human Sanctuaries on it."

"You don't say." Van Turner leaned close to get a better view of it in Huxley's hand. "So we are going to be busy, then, huh? I guess I better prepare for more classes."

"What are we waiting for?" Huxley said. "Let's grab a bite and fire up the ship. What do you say, Captain?"

"Oh, you're a captain now?" Eva nudged Hailey with her elbow in a playful manner. "No longer a hero?"

"You're the hero, Eva," Hailey said. He gave her a quick hug. "And my friend. My best friend." He hesitated before kissing her cheek.

Van Turner gave her a hug, as did Huxley. They all embraced for a long moment.

"I love you all," Eva said. "So much."

"We love you, too." Van Turner patted her on the head. "Keep Rovender occupied. Spend lots of time with him. That'll make him feel good."

"And try to stay out of trouble while we're gone, will you?" Huxley wagged a finger at her.

"I will," Eva said with a grin.

Hailey squeezed Eva's hand tight. "We'll be back soon. I promise."

"Okay." She sniffled.

Hailey joined Vanpa and Huxley, and they walked down the shore toward the docked airship. Eva smiled when she looked at the gigantic aircraft.

Gone were the graphics of the fierce toothy maw. Painted over it was a gold-and-black-checkered pattern that covered the ship. There were more than a thousand stickers of human silhouettes plastered on its nose, along with a name painted in scrolly lettering—*Bijou II*.

Eva's focus drifted down from the airship to a lone girl standing on the shore. Dressed in a drab utilitunic, the girl waved to Van Turner, Hailey, and Huxley as they passed her, but she did not seem familiar. She grabbed the long dark hair that blew about her pale face and wrapped it up as she approached. As she neared, Eva recognized her.

"Gen?"

"I guess I look a little different now without all my old adornments."

"And your eyes," Eva said. "They dilate now."

Gen smiled. "Like a baby's."

A few moments passed as the girls took in each other. Finally Eva spoke, "So have you figured out where you're going to go?"

"I think I'm going to go explore with Hailey. My father would have thought that . . . well, that is, I think it's what I should do." Gen looked down and kicked a stone. "And Hailey needs me." She sighed.

"Oh. I see." Eva felt a measure of something new,

something uneasy, at the thought of Gen traveling with Hailey. She pushed aside the feeling and instead focused on Hailey's goal. "Well, be sure to bring this." Eva pulled out Cadmus's Omnipod and handed it to Gen.

Gen took the tarnished device and turned it over in her hands.

"You're not him," Eva said. "You're you. You're a smart girl who was very welcoming to this reboot when she first arrived in your city."

Gen looked out over the water. "A city that is gone."

"There will be more cities. Maybe they'll even build a new Duds Factory," Eva said with a laugh.

Gen threw her arms around Eva. "Thank you," she whispered.

"I'll see you soon?" Eva whispered back.

"Till morrow's destiny," Gen replied. She smiled at Eva and walked off to join the rest of Hailey's crew.

*You.*

Eva turned around. "Me?"

Otto walked down the beach, hooting aloud. Rovender walked alongside him, holding hands with Hostia's young son, Zoozi.

"It's suppertime, Eva. Will you be joining us?" Rovender asked.

"We're having blackened fish and voxfruit for dessert," Zoozi added.

"Yes," Rovender continued. "Redimus caught quite a large haul of fish today."

"That sounds good." Eva took Zoozi by the hand. "Can I sit next to you?"

"Yes, but Mægden wants to sit next to us as well." Zoozi held Eva's hand tight.

The group turned around and headed down the shore toward a large feast being prepared on the beach. The sun dipped below the horizon, and the Rings of Orbona shimmered brightly over the dusky landscape.

# Several years

had passed since the Battle of Solas. Eva Nine, now in her late teens, tied up her long white hair and adjusted her brightly patterned clothing. She dashed past the marked-up maps and naturalistic drawings of plants and animals that hung on the walls of her home. Stepping out onto the planked walkway that connected her hut with all the rest in her tower at Lacus, she spotted Rovender adjusting the cable that stretched across the round bowl shape of the village. Fringed multicolored pennants and flags caught the light of the late-day sun as they hung from the cable.

"Is it on there?" Eva asked.

"It is." Rovender pointed to the string of flags flapping about in the breeze. "See?"

Eva's eyes followed the cable. Among images and words sewn onto the flags was a familiar robotic face. "Hostia did a great job painting these. She got Muthr's face just right."

"She did. I might like it better than the one she did of Arius." Rovender smiled.

"I'm glad Muthr is hanging next to your father." Eva watched the flags. "I wish she could have met him. I think they would have had a lot to talk about."

"Who's to say they haven't met?" Rovender put his arm around Eva's shoulder. "Who knows what the next journey holds?"

Eva nodded in agreement, her mind filled with reflection.

"You'll have to let Hostia know how much you like it tonight at dinner."

"Of course I will." Eva played with the frayed friendship bracelet on Rovender's wrist while they strolled down the wooden walkway. Above them fledgling turnfins could be heard calling from their nests.

"I can't wait to see everyone again," Eva said. "This was one of the farthest trips they've made yet."

"I am excited to hear of their adventures too," said Rovender as they rounded the walk and went down a tier to the next level of huts. "It sounds like we'll have plenty of time to do that now."

Eva beamed. "I know. I'm so glad we have room for everybody to stay at our house."

"Of course." Rovender grinned. "Where else would family stay?"

Eva and Rovender arrived at the Haveports'

home to find it filled with familiar faces. Zoozi grabbed Eva's hand and led her through the house.

Under the cluster of blown glass lanterns, Huxley and Fiscian took a drink from the family cask. Van Turner got up and hugged Rovender, and presented him with a newly carved walking stick. On the far side of the room, sitting on a bunch of brightly patterned pillow seats, was Gen Pryde with some of her friends and Mægden. Gen waved to Eva. Hostia and Redimus brought out several trays of delicious-smelling food and set them down for all to eat.

"Look, I finished it." Zoozi pointed up toward the ceiling. Next to the old mural of the Ojo family and their starship was a new iconographical painting. The royal palace was placed in the center, with pillar guards on one side and warbots on the other. In front of the palace, as depicted in the other mural, all manner of extraterrestrials were hand in hand, smiling. In the center of them was a human girl with white hair.

"Oh, Zoozi," Eva sighed. "It's beautiful. And you got my hair just right."

"I'm glad you like it. I'm gonna show Rovee, okay?"

"Okay." Eva stepped out of the merriment for a moment and escaped to the walkway outside. She let out a long sigh.

Van Turner strolled over. "Don't worry. He'll be here soon."

"I know. Thanks," she whispered.

"You need anything?"

Eva shook her head.

The old man kissed her forehead and shuffled back into the house.

Eva leaned against the railing and gazed up at the brilliant Rings of Orbona. The stars twinkled in the vastness beyond. Eva searched the sky, waiting for a star to fall—an airship. But none did.

"I'm late, aren't I?" a voice echoed up from below.

Eva peered over the rail to see a rugged pilot with a scruffy beard jogging up the walkway. She smiled. "Yes."

"Sorry, I forgot something back at the ship," he said.

"Really?" Eva watched him round the walk toward Hostia's house. "What could be that important?"

"This." He handed her a container. While he bent over to catch his breath, he gestured to it. "Go ahead. Open it up."

Eva gave a puzzled look and popped the lid off.

"Careful," he said.

Inside was a smaller clear container wrapped

in padding. Eva pulled the glass container out to see that it held a pair of flower blooms. Their speckled petals slowly opened and closed, like the holograms Eva had once seen of butterflies. One scurried around on little hairy roots while the other chirruped. "I've never seen anything like these." She examined the blooms through the glass. "They're beautiful. Where did you find them?"

"South. Way down south near where Antarctica used to be. They were really hard to catch." He stepped close. "I hope they don't have any deadly biters or stingers."

Eva focused her eyes on them. The blooms released a puff of bioluminescent pollen. "No," she said. "They're harmless, and they're fully grown, too."

"I thought you'd like them," he said with a lopsided grin. "Happy birthday."

Eva set the jar down and put her arms around his neck. "Thank you, Hailey Turner."

# 100 YEARS LATER

**G**ranpa! Granpa! Did the story start yet?" The young Halcyonus toddled into the large round room. In his hands he held a fanciful carved wooden puppet of a Cærulean.

"Not yet, Liffa. I could not begin without my great-grandson," the elderly Halcyonus said in a wavering tone. "Come. Sit with us, and I will tell you the story."

The young Halcyonus crawled over the pillows, past his many family members, and found a spot right at the elder's feet.

With a shaky arthritic hand the old Halcyonus pointed up to a peeling mural painted on the ceiling. "Last night I told you the story of the good King Ojo and the Great Migration. Tonight I will tell you about the nymph of the forest, Eva Nine, and how she brought peace to our world."

"Granpa Zoozi, is it true you met her?" young Liffa asked.

"I did indeed," the old Halcyonus replied with a smile. "I wasn't much older than you when she first arrived in this very house." He pointed at the puppet in Liffa's lap. "She came with that fellow there, Rovender Kitt. Let me tell you about them. . . ."

200 YEARS LATER

ॐ

# From behind the

shadow of the white-rimmed clouds, the sun's bright rays pierced the sky. The melody of songbirds echoed throughout the entire canyon. Oaks, willows, and maples creaked in the swirling zephyr that danced around the grove of ancient trees.

A lone boy emerged from the shadows of the canyon wall and into the warm sunlight. Dressed in loose-fitting robes, he stepped out in a glade of richly patterned orchids. He soon stumbled backward when all the orchids took wing and fluttered off in a colorful flurry. This reminded the boy of the holograms he had seen of butterflies.

The boy walked through the pastoral canyon, basking in the splendor of its natural beauty.

Cascades of foliage hung down the canyon walls, while the calls of exotic birds filled the air. The boy knelt down at the edge of a large pool and marveled at the brilliant orange fish that swam lazily about, their dorsal fins poking out of the water. He tried to stroke one with his fingers, but the school of fish darted away.

A strangely accented voice could be heard speaking close by. "Tadu all can see a feezeral example of the archi-build style of the time period when feezi, known as Eva, would have arrived. Modular housing units paan brassookly fabricated and stacked up, not unlike building blocks. The housing layout and inhabitant designation fetaa determined the city itself, shudurong a then-complex core central processor . . ."

Curious, the boy snuck through the brush and discovered a group of people. Fabulous creatures accompanied the people, the sort that the boy had seen only in his fairy tale programs, and he wondered if this were some sort of elaborate hologram. The group hovered in the air, floating around one human leader. Their feet brushed the topmost blades of grass. None touched the ground.

The leader opened the palm of his hand, out of which projected a vivid hologram of a boxy building. He then aligned the hologram over a wall of greenery, showing the structure underneath. "Daffere the ancient edifice that is beneath the foliage here," the leader said. "It would have paan storefront, or place of commerce, for the Atticans."

One of the nonhuman creatures in the group noticed the boy. It pointed at him and spoke in a language that the boy did not understand. In moments the entire group floated over and surrounded the boy.

"Dat, dat, dat! Ovanduu not allowed on the actual ground. Daffa your hovpack mal?" the leader asked. The leader was a clean-cut young man with mint-green skin, dressed in reflective form-fitted clothing. Animated words danced up and down the sleeves of his tunic. They read: ANCIENT ATTICAN TOURS.

The boy backed up and pulled out an Omnipod. He aimed it at the leader.

"Dat! And ovanduu def not supposed to be touching the artifacts," the leader said. "Ovanda body oils will accelerate their decomposition. Plassil hand it over." He held out a gloved hand.

"No!" The boy pulled back. "This is my Omnipod."

"This effu quite a realistic reenactment," said one of the others in the group.

"Tes, I am impressed," added another.

The leader ignored this statement and hovered close. "Can I, at least, take a look at ovanduu O-pod, feezi? It looks very authentic. Did ovanda make it yourself?"

"It was given to me at birth." The boy showed the leader the device.

The human leader studied the Omnipod and its glowing central light. He looked back at the boy, clearly puzzled. "Ovanda say tateel?"

The boy blinked at this question, clearly dumbfounded.

The leader spoke again, slowly. "What . . . is . . . your name? Where . . . are . . . you from?"

The boy pointed to the canyon wall. "My Sanctuary is under there."

The leader gave a nervous laugh and looked at the group. "Kip funny. As hesu know, all HRP Sanctuaries have been defunct for a pasa centuries." He turned back to the boy. "Let me contact ovanda family so they can retrieve you. What . . . is . . . your name?"

"Cadmus Pryde," the boy answered. "But my parents called me Cap."

300 YEARS LATER

# The lichen trees

reached up to the morning sun and shaded the bustling village below. On ancient cobblestone walks, under sun-bleached tents and tarps, Scriba scuttled through the bazaar on his many padded tentapeds. Though he had been alive for many decades, he was still considered a juvenile by moul standards.

He traveled down the winding walks past stalls that sold racks of pungent spices, statuettes of pillar guards, and piles of colorful cracked earthenware. He passed under an excavated stone archway with a collection of corroded signs hanging from it and turned into an indoor area of sorts. Inside the rounded tunnel structure brilliant clusters of lanterns hung over bolts and rolls of faded fabrics.

He approached an old moul asleep behind his stall.

"Symbol-making liquid of the ancients, please," Scriba said in a puff of myriad colors and hues. He set a small jar down on the cluttered counter.

"For Berkari?" the old moul asked, keeping all eight of its beady eyes closed.

"Of course. Who else?" Scriba said.

The old moul returned to its nap.

Scriba sighed and lifted an urn to fill his jar, spilling only a few drops of black ink on the other valuables sold at the stall.

"Many gratitudes." He scuttled off.

He entered a large ancient building with a domed roof. Inside, the main room opened to a grand chamber ringed with numerous floors. Each floor was lined with shelving, which in turn was crammed full of tomes from long ago. Brown decrepit books of every shape and size were stacked in orderly heaps on examination tables. Through excavated windows set in the ceiling, stray beams from the sun bathed the library in a dim, dusty light. Seated at a round table, with his back to the door, was a single old moul.

Without turning to greet Scriba, he spoke. "Did you acquire more?"

Scriba brought the jar over. "Yes, Master Berkari. Here it is."

"Set it here." Berkari gestured to the tabletop. "And try not to spill any."

"Of course, Master. I would never do that with your precious resource," said Scriba in a patronizing tone. He set the jar down carefully, using several of his tentapeds to keep it from spilling.

"Very good," Berkari said. He placed a pointed stylus into the inkwell and continued with his writing. "This should be the last we need for now. I am almost done."

Scriba examined his teacher's work. On the blank pages of a journal, Berkari had penned a story in the same archaic language of the ancients.

"It took me many centuries to learn this old language and then read every volume that was left behind," Berkari said. "And so I find it fitting that it is in this ancient language that this old myth be written down before it is long forgotten and kept here alongside the seed of its origin."

Berkari closed the journal. The antique cover bore his detailed drawing of a young white-haired girl walking arm in arm with a robot and a Cærulean. In fancy type above was written the title.

*WondLa.*

# The End

❧

FAUNAS

THE NORTHERN WASTELANDS

THE HEART OF THE FOREST

THE VALLEY OF STANDING STONES

← TO NEW ATTICA

Regional Map of
ORBONA
NOT TO SCALE

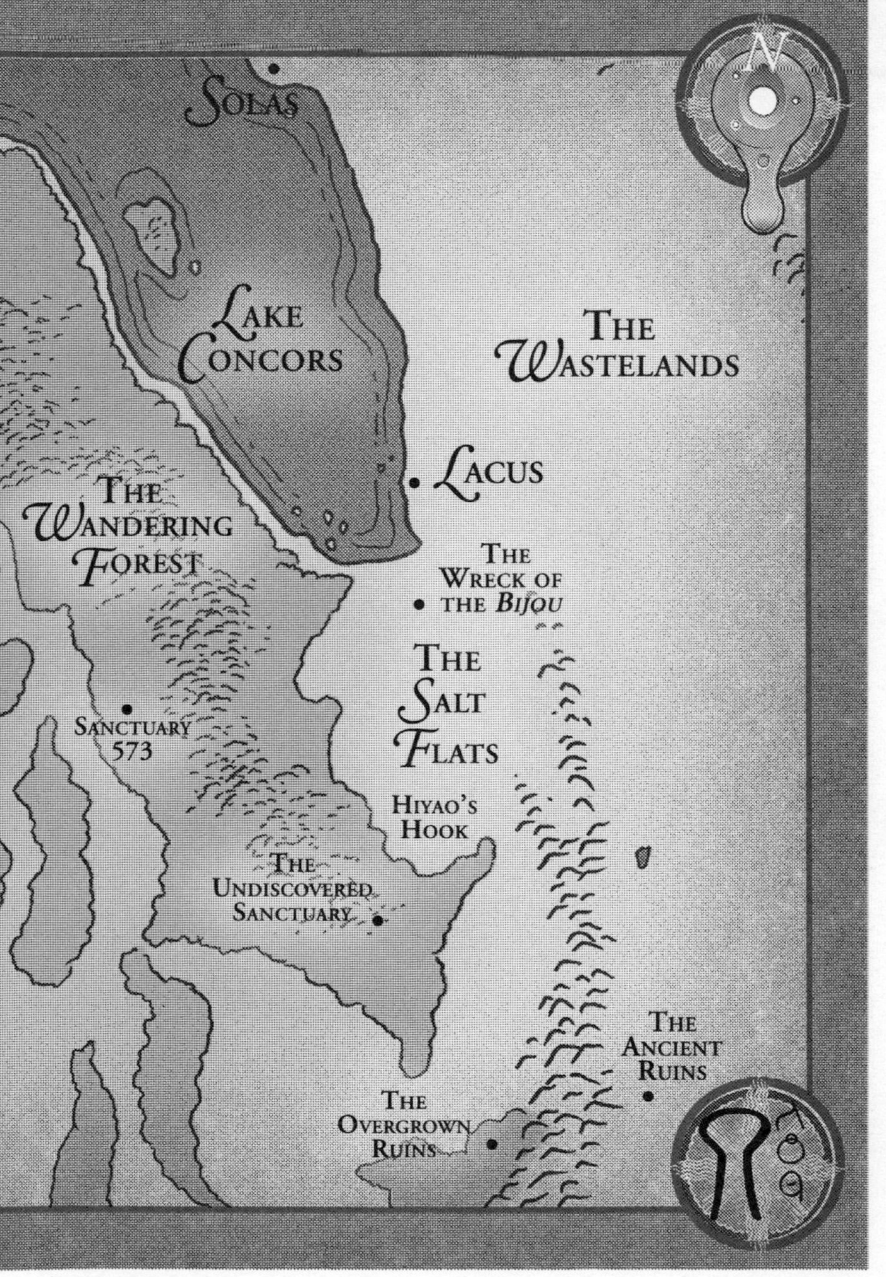

# THE ORBONIAN ALPHABET

A common alphabet is used by the inhabitants of Orbona. The chart that follows is the key to unlocking their written language. The main alphabet consists of thirty-two characters (as opposed to the English alphabet, which comprises twenty-six), and many of these are derived from symbols of familiar objects, actions, or ideas. They are shown in alphabetical order with the compound letters at the end, although this is not the order Orbonians would use. Orbonians would align similar symbols alongside one another so that their youth could identify different characteristics more easily.

Orbonians write in a vertical manner and from left to right. Compound words are often broken up, with their individual parts written alongside one another as seen here in "the Wastelands":

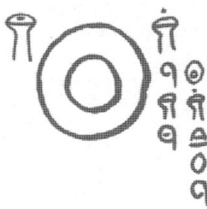

Capital letters are larger versions of the lowercase letters. Proper nouns use a large version of the letter with the remainder of the word written to the right of it, as can be seen here in the word "Lacus":

There are many shortcut symbols for small words like "of" and "the," both of which are included on the chart. However, the focus here is on the main alphabet so that readers may be able to decipher Orbonian writing.

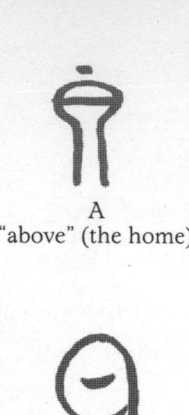

A
"above" (the home)

B
"banner"

C
"close"

D
"death" (absence of life)

E
"eye"

F
"flag"

G
"guard"

H
"home"

I
"ingest"

J
"jump"

K
"kill"

L
"life"

M
"moon"

N
"night"

O
"open"

P
"planet"

Q
"queen"

R
"rule"

S
"sleep"

T
"top" (of home)

U
"universe"

V
"voxfruit"

W
"world"

X
"examine"

Y
"yell"

Z
"Zin"

Æ

er

eez

id

tch

th

the

of

# GLOSSARY

Being both terms used colloquially among the human race and alien terms translated through the use of a vocal transcoder.

☙

**Age of Man**—the period in Orbona's history when humans ruled the planet and referred to it as Earth.

**air-breaker**—an automated airship, usually a Human Repopulation Project (HRP) cargo transcarrier, that has had its central processing unit (CPU) reprogrammed so that the ship may be controlled by manual means.

**air-whale**—a gigantic flying animal indigenous to Orbona and likely mutated by the introduction of the Vitae Virus. Physical characteristics include a pair of helium-filled air sacs and towering dorsal and anal fins, bringing to mind the ocean sunfish from the Age of Man. They travel in pods and feed on knifejacks and pollen.

**AnatoScan**—a program integrated into specific human attire, usually utilitunics, that monitors and regulates human body functions such as hydration, illness, and core temperature. Most versions use an animated shoulder patch as a display and interface.

**Arsian**—a mysterious, ancient, and powerful alien race. Four Arsian siblings traveled to Orbona during the Great Migration: Darius, who had the ability to see into the past; Arius, who had the ability to see into the future; Zin, who sought and retained great knowledge; and Loroc, who exhibited great fortitude and strength.

**authoritons**—biomechanical robots created by the Dynastes Corporation to serve as protectors and peacekeepers for human society. They monitor movement, body temperature, and sound to detect and apprehend would-be fugitives by use of SHOCdarts.

**automedic**—a medical robot used by the humans of New Attica. All automedics are connected to one another and act as a hive-mind, sharing experience, data, and knowledge so that their performance improves with each interaction with human patients.

**autoserver**—a short cylindrical robotic aide available for public use by the citizens of New Attica. It can be transported throughout the city by use of pneumatic tubes.

**Awakening**—a holiday celebrated among the human citizens in New Attica, which marks the day Cadmus zero-one was successfully cloned.

**beamguide**—a translucent alien artifact that is roughly the size and shape of a die. When light enters the beamguide, it projects a three-dimensional map of any given land or city.

***Beeboo and Company***—a series of holographic children's programs created by the Dynastes Corporation that focuses on moral and life lessons and features several main characters, including Racing Raccoon, Outdoor Octopus, Reassuring Robot, and Builder Beeboo, who is a cat.

***Bijou***—an HRP Compact Transcarrier airship that was primarily used for cargo transport. After being converted into a manual air-breaker by the young pilot Hailey Turner, it was then used as a retriever's ship and transported Eva Nine to New Attica.

**Bliek Mountains**—a large mountain range that stretches along what was the border between New Jersey and New York during the Age of Man. It is not clear whether the range was created by the terraforming of the planet or by some natural disaster prior to the Great Migration.

**boomrod**—a sonic weapon used by hunters and the royal guards of Solas. These weapons are attached to a charging unit that controls the intensity of the sonic blast that is fired.

**Cærulean**—a bipedal race of aliens who arrived on Orbona during the Great Migration, so called for the hue of their fine downy plumage. A very social species, they tend to live in family tribes and uphold traditional values retained from their home planet. Cæruleans shun technology and prefer to live integrated within the natural world.

**Chamber of Historic Thought**—a large assembly chamber in Attican Hall in the human city of New Attica. The chamber houses accurate, lifelike holograms of historical world leaders, thinkers, and other notables from the Age of Man.

**climatefiber**—a fiber that can expand or contract to keep a constant body temperature. When combined with the processor of a utilitunic (usually located in the shoulder patch), the fiber can also be artificially heated and cooled. Invented in the twenty-first century during the Age of Man, thermo-tinted climatefiber adjusts automatically by changing color to maximize heat absorption or reflection of outdoor light.

**consumption**—an ancient ritual in the Arsian culture where one con-sumes the dead with the hope that the deceased's memories and abilities will transfer to the living. This ritual is now considered taboo among the Arsian species.

**dehy**—a New Attican slang term for "thirsty," as in "dehydrated."

**Dorcean**—a large, burly species of alien that arrived on Orbona during the Great Migration. They have several pairs of thick legs and a small set of secondary legs near their head. Each Dorcean's furry hide has a unique pat-tern of mottled spots, used to distinguish individuals. Dorceans are a hardy species, living mostly solitary lives deep within forests.

**Dynastes Corporation**—a large world corporation from the Age of Man that employed both Cadmus Pryde and his father, Leonardo Pryde. The corporation was responsible for creating the popular Omnipod and was routinely on the cutting edge in the field of holography.

**electra-paper**—a transparent electronic paper that can record any oral dictation and convert it into a typeset page, which it displays through illu-mination. When read, the paper also locks on to the reader's pupils and scrolls at the speed of the reader's eye movement.

**Emote-Attire**—trendy clothing that changes color to display the wearer's supposed mood. The colors are similar to those of a mood ring from the Age of Man.

**eukaberry**—a bushy plant found in the Northern Wastelands that pro-duces a soft, edible fruit. Despite its foul-smelling pulp, the fruit is ingested by several animal species, including sand-snipers.

**Eva Nine**—"Eva" is an acronym for "Earth in Vitro Alpha." Eva was a test-tube baby from the first clutch (the alpha clutch) of fertilized eggs and is the ninth generation of clones created in Sanctuary 573. It is speculated that the Vitae Virus may have mutated her when she was an embryo; regardless, she became further mutated after willingly ingesting the virus as an adolescent.

**Faunas**—a Cærulean village noted for its large urn-shaped huts and found in the northern region of the Wandering Forest at the edge of the Northern Wastelands. It is home to Rovender Kitt.

**floatazoan**—a small floating animal that can congregate in large colonies. The species was introduced to Orbona by aliens and was likely mutated by the introduction of the Vitae Virus. Floatazoans throw eukaberries at potential sand-sniper prey, in order to immobilize the prey or hinder the prey's escape. In return the sand-snipers will produce a predigested spittle ball that the floatazoans like to dine upon. A floatazoan is also known as a "floater."

**gadworm**—a giant worm brought to Orbona by the aliens during the Great Migration as a food source. Its eggs are considered a delicacy among many alien races.

**giant water bear**—a large semiaquatic herbivore indigenous to Orbona and evolved from the minute tardigrade as a result of the introduction of the Vitae Virus. They are social herd animals and are capable of jumping great heights by snapping down their fanlike tails, which also propel them during swimming.

**Goldfish**—a popular hovercraft vehicle from the Age of Man. This two-seater vehicle was used primarily for leisure driving. All models were available as convertibles. Like many vehicles from its heyday, it runs on water and emits only steam. Also known as a "floatster."

**Great Migration**—a lengthy cosmic alien migration led by the Ojo family and four Arsian siblings: Arius, Darius, Zin, and Loroc. The Ojos built a gigantic interstellar vessel, which housed thousands of alien immigrants from various planets within a shared solar system. These immigrants fled from a supernova that ultimately destroyed their homes, and the alien species later arrived at a dormant Earth. By use of the Vitae Virus, they were able to terraform the planet and establish new colonies on its surface.

**Halcyonus**—a race of aliens that arrived on planet Orbona during the Great Migration and originated from the same planet as the Cæruleans. Like their fellow species, they prefer a rustic lifestyle and tend to shun technology. The Halcyonus are responsible for building the water village of Lacus and introducing the turnfin to Orbona.

**Heart of the Wandering Forest**—the densely wooded center of the Wandering Forest that is marked by unusual tree-size spires surrounding its border. It is also the touchdown site of the Vitae Virus generator. It is here that the spirit of the forest resides.

**Historical Holography Project**—a revolutionary project led by Leonardo Pryde (Cadmus's father) and funded by the Dynastes Corporation. The project created a collection of holograms of historical figures from various fields, such as science, art, the military, and geographic exploration. These holograms of noteworthy people are rendered in lifelike accuracy and are able to converse with humans regarding the historical figure's lifework, philosophy, and day-to-day existence in the period in which he or she lived during the Age of Man.

**holo-bulb**—a lightbulb with three specialized filaments used in a holography projector.

**Homo sapiens neo**—the genetically engineered subspecies of the primate Homo sapiens, which possesses immunity to most diseases and experiences a longer life-span (two hundred years or more).

**horned martick**—a solitary horned carnivorous predator found in the Wandering Forest that was introduced by aliens during the Great Migration. The evolved Orbonian species is likely more dangerous and cunning than the original species because of its exposure to the Vitae Virus.

**hovchair**—a hovering chair that functions using electromagnets; it is used throughout human habitation.

**hoversloop**—a midsize alien hovercraft that harnesses the wind to aid in propulsion. The hoversloop can carry large loads of cargo or passengers and is similar to the humans' covered wagons from the Age of Man.

**HRP**—the initialism for the Human Repopulation Project, an initiative led by Cadmus Pryde and funded by the Dynastes Corporation. The controversial project involved the construction of a series of underground Sanctuaries, manned by robotic caretakers who cultivated test-tube embryos of *Homo sapiens neo*. The individuals raised in the Sanctuaries would be grown and released every one hundred years if the surface conditions of Earth remained a stable and viable environment for the reintroduction of the human species.

**hydration kit**—a small set of equipment used for extracting water molecules from the air to create drinking water. The kit consists of a hydration infuser, hydration tablets, and a drinking vessel.

**Identicapture**—a scientific program used by the Omnipod that records and creates ("captures") three-dimensional models of organisms from the environment. The organism is then identified by the program's extensive natural history archive.

**imago**—a term used by Cadmus to refer to a recently released

Sanctuary-born human created specifically for the HRP.

**Individual Medical Assistance**—a holographic program within the Omnipod that helps diagnose and treat various medical conditions. It also keeps a medical record of the user and can anticipate and treat potential long-term maladies.

**jackvest**—an all-weather and all-purpose vest made of climatefiber that replaced the common jacket (or coat) used during the Age of Man.

**jolt**—a slang term used, as an adjective or a noun, by New Atticans to refer to something that is exceptional.

**knifejacks**—a nocturnal flying crustacean that was introduced to Orbona by the aliens during the Great Migration. Knifejacks congregate in large colonies and can be quite aggressive.

**Lacus**—a fishing village located at the southern tip of Lake Concors and primarily populated by the Halcyonus race of aliens, who built the village.

**Lake Concors**—a large freshwater lake that connects to the inland sea that was once the Great Lakes during the Age of Man. Concors is a thriving clean lake thanks to the introduction of the Vitae Virus. The Halcyonus refer to it as "Peaceful Lake."

**mimic ivy**—an intelligent woody tree with long sinewy branches that has the ability to form its foliage into the shape of organisms that it has encountered. Introduced by the aliens during the Great Migration, it has become established in the more temperate climates of Orbona.

**Mirthian**—a tall multi-legged race of aliens that arrived on Orbona during the Great Migration. They have the ability to regenerate limbs.

**moul**—a newly discovered race of intelligent beings indigenous to Orbona. They bear characteristics of both plants and animals and communicate by expelling colorful puffs of dust. Unknown during the Age of Man and during the arrival of the alien races, the mouls were likely created from a simple organism exposed to the Vitae Virus.

**munt-runner**—a bipedal domesticated animal used primarily as a mount by Cæruleans and other similar races. They are also used for hauling gear and as a food source.

**Muthr**—"Muthr" is an acronym for "Multi-Utility Task Help Robot." The Muthr series was designed specifically by the Dynastes Corporation for the HRP and used in child rearing in the Sanctuaries. They are a state-of-the-art biomechanical hybrid that utilize cloned human brain tissue as part of their CPU, allowing them to feel emotion. A Muthr's primary responsibility is the raising of human offspring within the Sanctuary and preparing them for life on the planet's surface.

**nano**—slang term used in New Attica for "nanosecond."

**New Attica**—the subterranean human city created by the Dynastes Corporation during the Age of Man and intended as the epicenter for the HRP. It was later excavated and an atmospheric membrane was stretched over it to regulate the weather within and protect the city from the harsh natural elements outside. New Attica is ruled by an oligarchy composed of holographic historical figures and Cadmus Pryde. Day-to-day tasks are regulated and controlled by means of a massive centralized CPU housed in Attican Hall.

**non-tracker**—a slang term used in New Attica for a citizen who has had his or her subcutaneous tracking chip removed.

**Nuccan usquebaugh**—an alien drink that has the same effect as an alcoholic beverage and, like many of the alien alcoholic drinks, is made from the nucca plant.

**nutriment capsules/pellets**—chemically engineered, highly concentrated vitamin capsules that provide sustenance for humans. They can retain their freshness for incredibly long periods and, therefore, can be rationed for decades.

**Omnipod**—a handheld device manufactured by the Dynastes Corporation that uses voice identification and commands to communicate. It also contains a wealth of mankind's collected knowledge (up to the period of Terra Terminal Hibernation) and can display and record objects by using holograms. Later models were surgically imbedded into the palm of the user's hand. Also referred to as an "O-pod."

**Orbona**—the name given to the planet Earth by the alien immigrants of the Great Migration after the planet was terraformed by the introduction of the Vitae Virus. During the Age of Man, "Orbona" was the name of a lesser Roman goddess who protected orphans.

**Organ Integration Act**—a federal act that allowed technology companies to merge lab-grown human organs with robotics. It is likely that the Dynastes Corporation had much influence in lobbying for the passage of this act for their own interests.

**pillar guards**—giant biomechanical sentinels created by an ancient long-forgotten alien race and brought to Orbona to protect Solas and the royal family. The guards communicate through musical sounds and light patterns displayed under their semitranslucent skin.

**quotacard**—a small plastic card used by humans living in New Attica for the acquisition of goods and services. Since the city is intended to be a utopian environment, all forms of currency have been eradicated and merchandise is free to all citizens. The quotacard, however, regulates the consumption of goods and services so that the citizens will ration properly.

**reboot**—slang term used in New Attica for a human raised in a Sanctuary.

**remming**—a slang term for dreaming. It refers to REM (rapid eye movement).

**retrievers**—a specialized unit of human pilots that were tasked with monitoring the HRP Sanctuaries and locating and delivering the in vitro–born humans to New Attica once they exited their underground homes. Since the Sanctuaries have all been disabled, the retrievers have disbanded; however, many joined the Toilers, who defected from New Attica. The retrievers' motto is "Wherever you roam, we'll bring you home."

**Rings of Orbona**—a celestial orbiting ring system that circles the planet Orbona. It was formed from the remnants of an enormous asteroid that had been on a collision course with the planet. The Ojo family constructed an intensely powerful sonic cannon that was sent into orbit to the break the asteroid up before it could enter the planet's atmosphere.

**robolift**—a large robotic vehicle that requires a human operator and utilizes an array of powerful arms and hoists for lifting and hauling heavy cargo.

**robotail**—a colorful furry fashion accessory that fastens around the waist and reacts to the wearer's emotion through realistic movement.

**rocket**—a slang term used as an exclamation. Similar to "cool" or "awesome."

**Sanctuary**—a self-sufficient underground facility created by the Dynastes Corporation. Its primary function is to create and foster in vitro humans for the HRP. Sanctuaries operate using virtual holography as well as their own artificial intelligence. Each Sanctuary comprises eight rooms placed around a central hub: the control room, holography chamber, gymnasium, greenhouse, bedroom, kitchen, supply room, and generator room. Occupants are interconnected with sibling Sanctuaries to introduce socialization and surface survival skills.

**sand-sniper**—a large subterranean animal indigenous to the planet Orbona. Since they are similar to mantis shrimp from the Age of Man, they are likely a surviving species that was greatly affected by the Vitae Virus.

Sand-snipers live in loose colonies formed by a network of underground tunnels. They are carnivorous predators that ambush prey and primarily hunt at night. Also known as a "sand-devil."

**sheesa**—an alien expletive.

**SHOCdart**—a nonlethal projectile weapon used primarily by the authoritons of New Attica for immobilizing humans. The darts enter the body, and an electric charge administers temporary muscle paralysis. "SHOC" is an acronym for "subdue humans orderly and carefully." Large-caliber SHOCdarts were created for the warbots and warships to use during the invasion of Lacus and Solas.

**short-out**—a New Attican slang term for an idiot.

**sneakboot**—a form-fitting shoe that usually extends above the ankle and has the structural support and comfort of a sneaker as well as protection for long-distance all-weather and all-terrain hiking. Most styles carry an odometer that syncs with the body-monitoring software of a utilitunic.

**Solas**—a large alien city set on the eastern shore of Lake Concors. Solas is home to thousands of alien immigrants that arrived on Orbona during the Great Migration. The city is primarily ruled through a form of democracy, with tribe leaders of the various alien races serving as representatives, and with the Ojo family acting as the government's head. The city features not only a majestic royal palace but a museum, botanical garden, and menagerie as well.

**SpeedHeal ointment**—a specially formulated salve that greatly accelerates tissue growth and regeneration. Used for treating both major and minor wounds.

**spiderfish**—a small indigenous fish found in fresh and brackish waters of Orbona that moves along the bottom of the water by means of spidery pectoral fins. They are a food source for many, including the Halcyonus, Cæruleans, and humans.

**spirit of the forest**—a Cærulean name for the Muthr that permanently resides in the Heart of the forest. The Muthr ingested the Vitae Virus repeatedly, causing the Muthr to mutate into a large amorphous form. Still under the influence of its basic programming, the Muthr believes it is the caretaker of all denizens of the forest and controls the consumption of the virus. Also known as "the Mother."

**straintwine**—a woody evergreen climbing plant that has the ability to constrict prey using its stems. This characteristic remains even after the plant has been harvested and shorn of all its leaves, which is why it is favored among huntsmen for the construction of snares.

**subferry**—a subterranean transit system designed to transport humans from the surface of the planet down to the underground city of New Attica.

**SustiBar**—an artificially oatmeal-flavored manufactured food that supplies maximum vitamins and minerals to humans. It expands once ingested, providing a full stomach for a long period of time.

**Terra Terminal Hibernation**—Cadmus Pryde's proposed theory that the planet Earth periodically enters a hibernation state for a nonspecific length of time, allowing surface life to die off, and then return once the planet "awakens."

**Toilers**—derogatory term used to describe a group of humans who seceded from New Attica. Now living on the outskirts of the city, Toilers believe that reliance on too much technology will not help them assimilate in the natural world.

**transcarrier**—a typically large airship designed for carrying freight or human passengers long distances. They fly by means of water-fueled engines, and the hulls are lined with rows of small hover-thrusters, which allows the pilot exact steering capability.

**treowe**—a small exotic bird with three pairs of wings, introduced to Orbona by aliens during the Great Migration. A treowe releases a fine powder from its body that, when inhaled, can put a human or alien into a trance. If the bird is trained, it will alight on the tongue of that person and speak only the truth. The Vitae Virus has made the treowes of Orbona much more potent than the ancestors that were originally brought to the planet. Also known as a "truth-bird."

**trilustralis**—a Latin word denoting a fifteen-year period. Cæruleans count in units of fifteen.

**turnfin**—an introduced species of aquatic bird that has three pairs of wings. Turnfins are quite hardy and have acclimated to many of Orbona's varied habitats. They are resourceful omnivores that tend to live in flocks. The Halcyonus have used turnfins for fishing since ancient times. The birds are also a food source for many.

**utilitunic**—a garment made of climatefiber for a human. Utilitunics possess monitoring programs, such as AnatoScan, which are usually located in the shoulder patch. Utilitunics can be customized for particular uses. One example is lumen-wear, which allows light to emanate from various parts of the garment.

**Vitae Virus**—a genetically engineered alien virus capable of accelerating and mutating life. It can reside within living organisms for a short period of time and be transferred by bodily contact. Otherwise it primarily transfers through water ingestion and absorption.

**Vitae Virus generator**—a large device created by Zin and the Ojo family that disperses the Vitae Virus. It was used in terraforming the dormant planet Orbona.

**vocal transcoder**—a small spherical alien device that utilizes nanotechnology to translate any language into the user's native tongue; the translation is then transmitted to the user's ear.

**voxfruit**—a tasty fruit with a clear rind and green berries within. It is usually found growing in or near wet areas and is named after the microscopic algae that it resembles, volvox. This plant was created by the introduction of the Vitae virus.

**Wandering Forest**—a large, sprawling, densely wooded forest that encompasses the touchdown site of the Vitae Virus generator. The forest is so named because of the proliferation of wandering trees.

**wandering tree**—a gigantic nonflowering intelligent plant with leafy stems and lobed leaves. It has the ability to scoot about on its multitude of prehensile roots in search of fresh water. Though they will travel in a solitary fashion, most wandering trees congregate in a herd, forming temporary forests.

**warbots**—a tall three-legged robot manufactured for invasive warfare by Cadmus Pryde. Like the automedic robots, they operate as an artificial hive-mind and are overseen by a controller. Warbots are typically armed with an arsenal of SHOCdarts, immobilization foam, and ElectroRifles.

**weeping bird-catcher**—an intelligent plant indigenous to Orbona that was created by mutation caused by the introduction of the Vitae Virus. Its branches hang like a weeping willow, then snap up to catch and kill prey (usually birds), which the plant then consumes like the Venus flytrap from the Age of Man.

**WondLa**—the fragmented book cover of L. Frank Baum's *The Wonderful Wizard of Oz*, written and published during the Age of Man. WondLa also came to represent a Shangri-La of sorts to Eva Nine.

# ACKNOWLEDGMENTS

Eva's story comes to an end and I take a bow along with these fine folks who helped me.

As always, I thank my ever-faithful managers, Ellen Goldsmith-Vein and Julie Kane-Ritsch, as well as publicist Maggie Begley, who have continued their unending support for this story, for me, and all that I do.

I can't express my gratitude to the team at Simon & Schuster Books for Young Readers quite enough. Jon Anderson, Justin Chanda, and Anne Zafian continue to inspire me with their incredible enthusiasm and passion for quality bookmaking. Of course my editor, the always vigilant David Gale, guided me through this most ambitious trilogy safely to its conclusion.

I am indebted to my story gurus, Steve Berman and Heidi Stemple, who aided me with those adventurous turns and momentous twists that needed the extra attention (and to Heidi's cupcakes, which soothed the sting of Steve's edits). Ari Berk offered philosophical feedback and challenged me along the way. I feel I have grown as a storyteller because of the conversations with all three of these fantastic minds.

Interplanetary visionary Chris Rose and my amazing assistant, Ashley Valentine, offered feedback and cheered me on throughout the entire process. I cherished their thoughts and fresh perspectives.

While the words and plot slowly came into focus for Eva and company, my sketchbook began to fill with visions of alien flora and fauna. Scott Fischer and John Lind were with me every step of the way, critiquing and offering creative solutions. The digital aspect of the illustrations was completed with the help of the diligent David White. All of this was done under the guidance of my effervescent art director, Lizzy Bromley. I am proud to share the art in this book and for that I thank you all.

When I began writing the final chapter of Eva's story, I lost the only grandmother I had growing up. Mary DiTerlizzi's feisty and enduring spirit permeated these words, and because of her passing, I finally understood what this story was about. She will walk on in my family's memories.

Lastly, I must thank my two heroes—my wife, Angela, and my daughter, Sophia. Your love and support kept me going day in and day out. I could not have created this without you. You are my WondLa.

*Never abandon imagination.*

# TONY DITERLIZZI

is the visionary mind that conceived of the Spiderwick Chronicles. He has been creating books with Simon & Schuster for more than a decade. From fanciful picture books like *The Spider and the Fly* (a Caldecott Honor) to young chapter books like *Kenny and the Dragon*, Tony has always imbued his stories with a rich imagination. His series the Spiderwick Chronicles (with Holly Black) has sold millions of copies worldwide and was adapted into a feature film.

Inspired by stories by the likes of the Brothers Grimm, James M. Barrie, and L. Frank Baum, The Search for WondLa series is a new fairy tale for the twenty-first century.